Cover design: Diana Elliot Graham

Original print edition: October 2022

Reprint: May 2023

Publisher: Arrobehu

ISBN: 979-8-218-12810-4

WHEN WE WERE

a novel

DIANA ELLIOT GRAHAM

ARROBEHU

To anyone who thinks they need closure,
it's not found anywhere outside of yourself.

To anyone who thinks they need control,
I promise you already have it.

Chapter One

HER

"What's a better word for cock? And please don't say 'member' again." Heads turn from all corners of the coffee shop and converge right on our table, not clearly as tucked away and remote as we thought.

"First of all, I have absolutely never said 'member,' and second, you do realize we're still in public, right?" It's a rhetorical question because we have been at this same table nearly every Sunday for the last four months as Amanda writes her seventh contemporary romance novel. While I sit here with the important task of keeping her company, offering occasional support as a human thesaurus or if we need to draw out a sex scene to test the practicality of it. Mostly, I'm just here for the company, and she tosses out the inquiries more to just involve me in the process than out of any actual necessity.

"Fine, Arden, you've never said member, but I'm not going to whisper the word cock when half the people in here have them." She shakes her head with a light laugh and looks back to her computer as she continues her original thought. "It's just that, I don't think she'd say cock when this scene is melancholy. Cock is just so aggressive, it's like *COCKK*." She says the word again, this time with additional emphasis on the harshness of the hard K. The sound that bookends the word to prove her point, in turn earning a few extra glares in our direction. Her pursed lips shift from side to side as a function of her thinking through the right phrasing, until she nods to herself in assurance and sets her hands to the keys, committing the thought to text.

"Is this the breakup scene?" I empty the rest of my mug, sipping down that end-of-cup-was-once- hot-coffee and sugar mixture. I knew her latest novel was being written with a love-triangle that resulted in an emotional breakup. Her writing pulled from different elements of her own life, but had such mass appeal, which has landed her on the bestseller list with each new release. That and she dialed up the spice.

"Yep! Breakup sex scene to be specific. It's more them accepting closure this time, but something isn't quite right yet. I need more perspective, preferably from a male point of view. And considering I can't go back to the source on this one and ask my ex..." She'd said she was most excited about this book, because it was inspired by her actual love story.

"Are you writing from a specific memory this time?" As soon as I pose the question, my mind drops me back in time to my own breakup sex scene. The only one I have.

"I always welcome more inspiration if you want to share whatever's got your mind churning." Amanda tips her chin up and replies with a wink. She's not wrong; my mind is churning with a memory I haven't thought about in years. I was nineteen. We hadn't been together that long, but it was an important relationship for me, until he ended it. We moved on, we stayed in touch, became more like acquaintances for some time, and eventually landed on the outskirts of friendship. We never dwelled on the months we spent as more than friends, never rehashed the breakup, or reminisced over our time together. Just stayed in casual communication by exchanging general updates not much deeper than what was visible on social media. Considering it was the only time in my life I've been dumped, the memory is not a hard one to recall. Even if some of what followed was.

"You know the price of admission... let's hear it." She chides in jest again, urging me for the smallest morsel of the memory my mind has latched onto.

"I was just thinking about when I was dumped." I wince as I say it, because in your thirties, who would want to think about their college breakup? "Aside from being the only time I've been broken up with, it's also my only reference for breakup sex."

Amanda interlaced her fingers and stretched them out in front of her, like she was preparing for her own writers marathon.

"Don't hold back..."

"For starters, I spoke to him recently."

"Okay, now I'm even more curious!"

"It's far from what you think. He had something at work and was curious about an alternative approach. It's just something we've done on and off for years, reaching out for perspective on different projects. It's not a big deal."

She rolls her eyes in response, clearly in disbelief. *Oh, to see through the eyes of a romance novelist.*

"No big deal," she repeats it back skeptically, "you guys just chat without any of the old feelings burning through?"

"When it was fresh, it was hard for me, but I wasn't ready to let him go. So I pretended I was fine. He was maybe the only person who ever really meant it when he said, '*We can be friends.*'"

The look on her face is bouncing between unbelievable interest and curious skepticism.

"Okay, Amanda. I'll prove it. You want a male perspective on the breakup sex scene? I'll text him and ask for his."

Bolstered by the excited look on her face and without reservation, I hit send on a text before I can think much more of it.

> **me:** A friend of mine is writing a book, and it has a big plot point around breakup sex as closure. I offered you up as a male perspective on the topic about when you ended things between us! Hope you don't mind sharing your thoughts!

I set my phone back down on the table, ready to pick up a different conversation while we waited for his eventual reply. Something I imagine will be clever, thoughtful, and insightful about remaining friends post-breakup. But it's the immediate illumination of his name that has us both snap our attention to the screen.

> **him:** Arden, what are you talking about when I ended things?

I drag my teeth across my bottom lip. Is he kidding? Trying to be avoidant? It's been years and while we have never actually talked about our breakup, surely he remembers it. If not the specifics of the fight then at least the break up sex. My throat tightens at the idea that our breakup didn't have the same impact on him. Which makes sense considering he ended it, but still. I'm suddenly feeling like the same heartbroken teenager who clung to him all those years ago. I hit send on my reply, keeping the tone light as we always have.

me: I know we're getting old, but try and remember 2008 ;)
I told her about how you dumped me when we were in
college because I thought it would be helpful for her book
him: got that part, AB
him: but I didn't dump you

We're staring at those last words. It's Amanda who finally breaks the silence, slowly closing her laptop. Forgoing her own writing in this moment exchanging it for the real life dramedy playing out in front of her.

"What are you texting back?"

"I-I'm not... I mean, I don't..." My brain is trying to catch up, but I'm not even sure what I *would* text back to that. *You're wrong. I would know. WTF?* Seriously, though. What did I just step into? Was it too bold to outright text him about our relationship, about our breakup, about our breakup sex? This was outside the bounds of our normal conversations, but I trusted him and the friendship we have built over the last 14 years. It was a friendship based on mutual respect and time.

Originally post breakup, it was a lot more cordial. Emails exchanged over summer break to start, though there were periods of time we didn't speak at all. Ultimately, we fell into a rhythm where I didn't begrudge him of the breakup and he didn't seem to resent the fact that I still clung on to him, even as my friend.

Our friendship worked now because it wasn't based on the time we spent together, which was brief. More than anything, it was based on the time away from who we were all those years ago when we were together. Even at nineteen, I had so much respect for him. His maturity went beyond his age; it was his confidence and self-respect that made him feel worthy of admiration. That didn't change over time, no matter how much we both did. He drew clear lines around who we were post breakup, and I never crossed them. Never crying to him that I missed him, except almost once, and I never made that mistake again. And because of that, he also never came back to me in a way that crossed a boundary. Recognizing there was value in our connection that wasn't worth dissolving in its entirety. No matter how it ended.

Although how it ended seems to be in question now.

Besides today's text which I shot off without too much forethought, he had texted me a few months ago looking for some advice about a potential acquisition of a small company. Our careers sometimes overlapped. He works for a big conglomerate, an evil corporation if I ever heard of one, but he'd been there for years, climbed the ladder, and seemed happy enough. If not truly happy, he was at least successful. Though I never missed an opportunity to quip about how he basically worked for a supervillain.

I've made my career as a consultant focusing on earlier stage startup companies. He would reach out when his Evil Corp. was in the market for something I might be familiar with. It has all been extremely above board, until maybe today.

I look between the phone and back to Amanda. My best friend was staring at me like she just struck romance novelist gold, her big brown eyes absolutely on fire with the possibility of what was about to play out in front of her.

"I don't really know what to text back to that. I don't even know what to *think* about that."

His initial response shocked me; his follow up paralyzed me. And now I am flooded with the doubt that bringing up our romantic relationship wasn't wise. We had never directly discussed it. We had never *indirectly* discussed it. Not until enough time had passed and we started more seriously dating other people, at which point we would casually throw out an inquiry, a litmus test to ensure our boundaries were still firmly in place. They always were.

"Looks like you don't need to worry about it now..."

With a tilt of her head, her chestnut brown hair falling forward as she does, Amanda nods toward my phone on the table, where the screen is still open to the message thread. The texts from today tell a very different story from the last exchange. Visible just above the brief back and forth from earlier, and below an inquiry about work, a simple glimpse into our casual friendship. A picture he sent me of a bright orange tabby cat sitting on a kitchen counter staring directly into the camera in dare and defiance, the message beneath it, 'World's Worst Cat 13 years running.' It was a running joke between us, he had told me when he got the cat about a year after he broke up with me, *we broke up.* When he adopted it and brought it home, he was so pleased. Little did he know, he got a broken cat. He swore the thing barked like a dog and would try to sit on his shoulder like it was a parrot out of a bad pirate novel. His world's worst cat had been a bit of humor we shared for years now as a tethered moment of friendly '*I told you so*' that I got to experience regularly as a dog-person.

Beneath that image of Bellybutton, the World's Worst Cat, and the new text revelation that we both are clearly confused by the memory of our breakup, I see what Amanda is referring to. The infamous three-dot text bubble displays as he types out his response to what I had asked him about perspective on breakup sex as closure... but maybe, he's answering something else, maybe he's typing out responses to all the questions I have now. First and foremost, what the hell is he talking about?

As quickly as the three dots appeared, they disappeared. Amanda and I watched this dance of the thought bubble for almost ten minutes, each time it reappeared, sure that it would ultimately result in a pinging of my phone. I never knew him to be indecisive. He has always been bold and didn't regret things he said, so watching the literal push and pull of his thoughts was the first indication that I unintentionally pulled the pin in a mental grenade and tossed it into his life.

After ten minutes, the bubble never reappeared.

———

I run my fingertips mindlessly across the keyboard and click my tongue against the roof of my mouth. Eyes darting between the computer screens trying to make sense of the latest reports that were submitted, pushing back the completion date by another three months. *Wrong, this is so wrong.*

It's going to be a long Monday; I can feel it already. Especially after the last 24 hours and yesterday's great revelation. As if there isn't enough going on, enough to deal with, enough to prepare for, now I have to comb through every little detail to ensure we keep this project on time.

This morning when I settled in at my desk, looking around my office at the collection of items, photos, moments of my life I have around me. I'd be lying to myself to say I didn't also think about him. About his message. But I shook away the distraction, knowing I hadn't come up with anything to say in response to his *'but-I-didn't-dump-you'* text, and he didn't seem to have anything else to say either. So we left it where we leave all of our history. In the past. Distraction or not, I need to focus. Nineteen year old me might be incredibly impressed with the career I've made for myself, but none of it will matter if this turns into a massive dumpster fire on my watch. I draft an email to get some clarity around this latest mess, in the hopes some of it can be resolved without too much pressure or worse, more delay.

Team,
Let's discuss incentives or resources needed to rectify the latest hurdles. We cannot afford another three-month delay.
- ABS

I always sign my name with my initials. It feels like a subtle feminist power move. My initials are ungendered and detached; they let me email with the power of a man. A habit I started a long time ago–the anonymity behind initials, protecting a bit of yourself, and also, as someone once told me, it *'just sounds cool.'* So it stuck and my initials became my moniker in my adult life. Hitting send, I close out the window and move back to these reports to see what needs reworking.

I catch the flash of the new email notification on my cell phone sitting face up on my desk not even thirty seconds after hitting send. *Oh great, at least someone's working today besides me.* Clicking back to my computer screen and checking my email looking for the latest incoming finding nothing in my corporate inbox. *Looks like I spoke too soon.*

I swipe the notification on my cell and the notification from my personal inbox and see the familiar name of the sender, the subject line a signal to the contents of the email. None of it is what I expected.

Subject: Different sides.

DIFFERENT. SIDES. After yesterday's brief exchange, I was also able to deduce that we have very 'different sides' to the breakup story. One where I clearly remember him ending it and walking away, but he seems to think he wasn't the one to break up with me? After his lack of response, I spent the rest of the afternoon, and much of this morning thinking through absolutely everything that I remember, and worse, the parts I don't. When I think back to the breakup and the breakup sex— the question that started it all—maybe I missed something, maybe I didn't know any better, or maybe he just didn't care. *Different sides?* I'd say so.

Looks like that mental grenade detonated. Maybe for both of us.

AB,

This conversation is years too late, but I need to be clear. I did not end our relationship, *you did*.

I am taking this trip down memory lane because I know you have no ulterior motive, and now I am interested to know how we ended up with different understandings of what happened. Dredging up old love can be a slippery slope, and in all the years since, we've preserved this friendship by staying away from that edge.

You wanted my perspective. Here it is: My intention that night was not for closure. It was to get you to settle, to calm down, to focus on us, to just wait until morning. Until we had sobered from the alcohol and argument. I thought if I had gotten you to stop focusing on the noise created by those around us, we would have been fine. By the next morning, it was too late. I accepted what you were saying, and that we were done. You were so sure, kept repeating the need for closure, who was I to argue with you about your own mind.

I don't know what would have happened if we had taken a minute to understand each other that night. We were so young, and while I would say nothing lasts, our friendship certainly has.

We have known each other a long time, and I have no regrets about where we ended up. Only now that you spent half your life thinking I dumped you.

Your friend
P.S. Thank you for the sufficient mind-fucking yesterday.

You always would do anything in the name of literature. If any of what happened is referenced in your friend's book, I expect to be included in the dedication.

After reading it through his email twice, the words take shape. The curtains of my memory pull back to reveal the stage set for the first act.

Chapter Two

HER

There's something ironically spacious about an extra-long college twin bed. It's not that I have room to stretch out beyond the width of it, but that doesn't matter. It's not about the bed. It's about the freedom that comes with it. This entire space is mine. The items decorating my dorm reflect the person I'm here to be, not just the amalgamation of things I've collected since childhood. Many of the things I've left behind in my bedroom back home.

There is an academic undertone to Cambridge, Massachusetts, unlike anywhere else in the world. *At least that's what I've always imagined.* It's likely due to all the universities in the area. Which is the second reason I chose it. Students. People. Life.

The first reason having more to do with what Cambridge, Massachusetts, is not, it's not Miami, Florida. The weather outside is still a balmy summer day, but it's a far cry from humidity that swallows you whole. It's a far cry from a lot.

———

Walking into the main lecture hall, it's already packed; of course it is. I spent fifteen minutes trying to find the right building. My suitemate, Stella, should already be here, *somewhere*, but I can't spot her. So instead of trying to find my friend, I settle for trying to find a seat. Standing here in the double doorway, frantically looking through the rows trying to find an opening, everything is filled and the shuffling at the front of the hall means it's about to get started. *Shit. Shit. Shit.*

"Hey...*HEY YOU*...Community Chest!"

A quick glance down at my shirt, one of my favorites. The Urban Outfitters graphic tee with an illustration of the Monopoly treasure chest and the words 'Community Chest' scrawled across my, well, chest. I didn't miss out on the irony of the shirt when I bought it as I certainly fill it out, but that's what makes it so funny.

Though maybe not the wisest of shirt choices today. The day I am congregating with the entire Freshman class, the day first impressions and nicknames are made, and I may have just inadvertently stuck myself with Community Chest. *Great.*

"Here." My head whips around and lands immediately on him, somehow loud enough to cut above all the chatter and movement in the room. He has a hand up in recognition as if we know each other, beckoning me towards him, where, yes, there are a few empty seats. Perhaps the only ones left. Though he doesn't seem inclined to point that out to anyone but me.

We're both standing a distance apart, but his voice was an arrow shot through the crowd landing right at my feet. The invisible rope tied to the end of it served as a guide back to its origin, right to where he stood coolly, in the row, casually leaning against the back of seats waiting for me to take a step.

He spots my hesitation and dramatically gestures in a Vanna-White-game-show motion to the empty spot beside him, his eyes dropping down to the seat in indication before looking back up at me with a devilish pull of his lips. Less an invitation, more a challenge. I return the smile, one made to mirror his, and take steps toward him while he takes his seat and joins the conversation to his left. Leaving only his arm draped over the empty seat to his right in reservation for me, waiting like he knows I've already made the decision to join him.

I make my way, shimmying past people in the row. As soon as I've situated myself in the seat next to him, he turns his head slowly, giving me a not-so-subtle once over. Which is fine, considering I managed to assess him in the five paces it took for me to get here.

"Are you a really big Monopoly fan or something?" He delivers the question with a smirk and a cocked eyebrow.

"Or something." I respond with a shrug and chuckle. I laugh far more than I ever actually mean to. Nothing is ever as funny as the frequency of giggles, chuckles, or faked hysterics truly implies. Paired with a shrug, I've offered up this stranger a taste of validation and indifference in one interaction. Now, to seal the deal, deliver the wit and tease that keeps people wanting more.

"I *am* a monopoly fan, games in general, but mostly, I enjoy the innuendo."

"Cute."

"I know. My name is Arden, by the way. For the next time you need to scream for me across a room."

"I think it's more likely you'll be screaming for me..." His sentence hangs there, the pause at the end leaving a space where my name would perfectly fit, but instead of using it, he fills the air between us with the innuendo I just outright claimed to enjoy. A test, I think—one I'm not only used to, but take pleasure in. The challenge of people being one of my most favorite games.

"AR-DEN." I articulate my name slowly and point to

myself as you do when you teach a small child a new word. An intentional patronizing jab at the apparent ego next to me. Something I was able to make note of the second I saw him as it filled his glare, looking to me to feed it.

His voice is honeyed and smooth, toned lower now in conversation than when he had used it to lasso me across the lecture hall. Separated only by the arm rest between us, I can get an even clearer look at him, an assessment he has already made of me, one he is still working through. He has the arrogance of someone who had that good boyband hair growing up, probably played a sport in high school, perhaps even now. And looks like a character who just stepped out of the O.C. The kind of guy who had always been emboldened to flirt maddeningly without reproach, as he clearly charmed people with his attention.

Frankly, I was no better, batting Maybelline coated lashes over blue eyes, always the easiest way to reel someone in long enough to get a read on them. People found me disarming, especially ironic given the mental armory I possessed.

Where I am light, he's the opposite. My eyes are bright, my hair is tones of blonde, some enhanced, some natural, not too dissimilar to my personality. Though for all the exuberance and sunshine I expelled with effort, the glow I let people warm themselves under, my skin is ironically fair considering where I grew up. The only indication I have ever even been in the Miami sun are the freckles that sprinkle across my face, shoulders, and virtually any part of me, the same way other people were left sun kissed. I was marked.

His eyes are almost cat-like, dark irises surrounding even darker pupils. They are mischievous but piercing in a way that I find instantly intriguing. His skin slightly bronzed, the remnants of a summer tan. I'd wager he lifeguarded or had some other kind of summer job where he spent most of his days shirtless and in the sun. All the while, his dark hair falls in his face in a way that's made to look careless, but something tells me there isn't one part of him that isn't intentionally constructed.

"I like the shirt, *AR-DEN*, but I'd prefer it if it wasn't false advertising."

He volleys it over the net, landing on my side of the court as his eyes brighten in challenge, curious if I will play.

"I'd say I like yours too, but then I'd have to compliment everyone else here wearing the same one." Glancing around the large lecture hall, there are handfuls of other students sporting the identical collegiate class of 2011 tee shirt he was. The same one I have sitting back in my dorm room.

"Oh and..." I gesture my hand out, waiting for him to supply his own name.

"Joshua, *Josh*."

"Well, Josh. I don't believe in false advertising." His lips part readying himself to say something, to spike the ball back, but missing the chance as the high-pitched feedback from the microphone cuts him off. Instead, his lips press together with annoyance at the interruption, he pats the bare skin of my knee twice with a combination of condescending praise and personal defeat before he faces front for the first speaker.

Two hours later, after listening to the codes of conduct, speeches from professors, the Dean of Students, and even presidents of different clubs encouraging freshmen to join, I really needed to stretch my legs. The row exit to the right was completely blocked by clusters of people. But I stand ready to make my escape to the left, preparing to climb over the handful of people still seated, Josh puts his palm on my hip to stop me. Still seated, he finds himself eye level with my *community chest*, needing to tilt his head up for his eyes to catch my face.

"Not so fast." He stands from his seat and blocks my exit from our row. Now I'm the one needing to crane my head up to meet his gaze which lands about six inches above my own.

Without breaking the connection he forced between us, he casually throws a wave over his shoulder in a way of saying goodbye to his friends. Keeping his focus locked on me.

My senses take in the rest of him. Whether it be his body wash or his upbringing, he smells like licorice and pine, and he's taking up the aisle entirely. I can tell by the way his tee shirt clings to his torso he's in good shape, and I can tell by the look on his face he would be oh-too-eager to prove it. Reaffirming my high school athlete theory.

"What do you think?" he asked.

"A lot of things–any topic in particular?"

"Campus, classes, codes of conduct..."

"I think... you're a fan of alliterations."

"I guess so," he laughed, "pretty much all I got out of the last two hours."

"Campus–still confusing, classes–really exciting, codes of conduct–to be expected."

The path out of the row had cleared, making an exit easier. His body shifts with mine, readying to move.

"Let's get lunch." His teeth peek through a half smile, as the corner of his mouth pulled upward like it was tied by string to the eyebrow he cocked at me for a second time in question.

Not outright asking me if I was a.) hungry b.) wanted to go.

That face, that challenge. There is no subtlety in it. I recognize it, the warning it is. I don't hide from it, but I've seen enough of those looks to know exactly the paths it can take if I choose. In response to his offer. No, not offer, *command*. I lift one shoulder with the same calculated indifference of our earlier exchange.

"Alright." And walk off ahead of him. As the double doors open to the central courtyard of campus, I feel the heavy weight of an arm thrown around my shoulders and I'm wrapped in him like we've known each other far longer than just a couple of hours as we walk through the quad toward the Student Center.

There are students all over, different groups clustered on blankets on the grass, seated on benches with coffees, and making their way through the common area meant to act as the nucleus of the campus. Very much a scene out of any college movie. I spot the library and make a mental note of its location.

"So...Where are you from?"

"Miami."

"Miami." He stretches the word as the smile stretches across his face. "That explains it."

"And what does that explain?"

"You. You don't exactly give off small-town-vibes in a shirt like that. You also keep looking at the historic red brick of these buildings like it's impressive, so I'm guessing not a New Englander. You have no accent that I can make out. Not Boston or New York, and not Southern belle. And despite the blonde, you seem to have more devious wit than a standard valley-girl. So L.A. didn't seem likely, and Californians don't usually come east. All that and the fact that even though it's easily 75 degrees, I'm pretty sure I just felt a shiver run up your spine. Miami makes sense."

"You seem pretty confident that you have me all figured out."

"What can I say, I'm that good." He lets out a Cheshire Cat chuckle, the kind that slips out through grin, thanks to years of being called good looking. He drops his arm from around me to reach into his pocket for his cell phone, firing off a text before pocketing it again. I wiggle my shoulders at the freeing loss of the weight that was hanging over them just a moment earlier, though now lacking the body heat I didn't know he had been providing. Because as much as I don't feel that being from Miami can be the single brush stroke of my personality, he was right about one thing: Even at 75 degrees, I feel a chill.

"And what about you, Josh?" I feign a bit of thought, he thinks I'm easy to read? He tipped his hand far more than he realizes in his assessment of me.

"Let's see... where might you call home? You seem pretty certain that West Coasters stay west, which makes me think it's actually how you feel, being rooted here." His eyes focus, and whether he notices it or not is full of tells.

"Okay, so East Coast. New Englander, close enough to Boston that you're *not* impressed by three- hundred year old buildings. *Which you really should be by the way.* And while I also don't hear an accent, the judgment and ego around being from a small town tells me that's exactly the case."

Without noticing, we've reached our destination, stopping in front of the glass doors to the Student Center. He looks at me shaking his head in response to what I said. Not because I'm wrong, because we both know I'm right.

His hand is outstretched on the handle to pull it open, but he doesn't. Instead, he paused, as if the gesture of opening the door would open a lot more between us, set an expectation of sorts. Not that I expected anyone to open any doors for me, literally or figuratively. Though throughout my life, the expectation of both has been more than possible.

"You're mighty quick to jump on my *ego*."

"Consider it the only thing of yours I'll be jumping on, Josh."

"You see, I knew it was false advertising."

He tipped his head down in direction towards my tee shirt, messed my blonde hair with his free hand, jostling it out from where I had it tucked behind my ears and threw me a smile.

Draping that arm back across my shoulders and walking me through the now opened door, to friendship.

"Let's get burritos, Miami."

Chapter Three

PRESENT

HIM

Sitting at my desk, I check the clock: 8:42 p.m. I could lie and tell myself I am here working late. The truth is the middle of my day was spent distracted, just like yesterday.

I was excited to hear from her as I usually was, but nothing could have prepared me for what she said. That was more than 24 hours ago. And here I am, rereading the texts. The thread I had abandoned in need of a more composed response, one she replied to within minutes after I sent it. I sit here reading and rereading her reply. Rereading her, *everything*.

Mind-fucking. That was the term I used. To a woman I haven't fucked, mentally or otherwise, in years. At least not in any way that didn't involve my own fist in shower, and that was only the first weeks after she left. *Fuck, or after she thought I left*. If she mind-fucked me with this, what would you call what I've done to myself since? Mental masturbation? Because here I am, *working* late at my desk. Scrolling up in the texts that were all so innocuous, never leaving anything open for misinterpretation. But now, it's her latest response that has me stuck in my chair.

> Hey!!
> It has always been one of our unspoken rules to leave the past in the past. I hope that I didn't throw too much of a mental grenade, but you're right... I will do anything in the name of literature!
> If you've ever read a romance novel, you'll know this is what they call the dreaded miscommunication trope. (It is my least favorite trope.) But normally, it's figured out during the third-act breakup before the happily ever after.
> You shared your version, I guess now it's only fair that I share some of mine. That night you said you were done, that you were better than that, (which you were) and then you left. I thought you left me. When I came by later, it was in a I-need-to-make-sure-this-relationship-wasn't-bullshit kind of way. Just to remind myself there was something real there. I asked for closure because I thought that was all you would give me. And when you did, I thought that it was a goodbye from you.
> It has all worked out, you're right, but you have to admit, this is kind of insane.
> - ABS
> P.S. Can't guarantee a dedication, how about a signed copy?

For all the years we've known each other, I've appreciated our friendship. We'd exchange occasional texts or emails, and we've had coffee a handful of times. It's always felt natural to have her as my friend, even when she was my girlfriend–even when she stopped being my friend, she had been my friend. I'm guessing she felt the same. Otherwise, she wouldn't have felt so comfortable to send that text to begin with. She is right. This is insane.

We never talked about what happened. She had texted after the breakup, but by that time, she had already moved me from the boyfriend column to the friend column. I remember it clear as this morning; she sat across from me and told me she wanted to be friends. She was always so sure of herself. Who was I to push her in another direction? Who was I to grovel for forgiveness for something I didn't do? *Even though as it turns out, maybe, somehow, I fucking did.*

How could she have known what that text would unravel? She obviously didn't. Which is why I am here, at, *fucking great,* 8:58 p.m. Pressing the heels of my hands to my eyes, attempting to rub away the computer screen, the lack of sleep, the now confused memories, and the mounting list of questions. The biggest one, *what fucking happened?* And how did I, of all people, get it wrong?

I tried to respond after the revelation that we somehow both had different sides to this story, but nothing felt clear enough to text. I couldn't even answer the question she originally asked about my perspective on breakup sex as closure. She hadn't asked for a thesis; I'm sure anything would have sufficed. But no, I read what she wrote, and all I could focus on were three words: 'you dumped me.' And it left me with two painful thoughts.

One, I didn't dump her. Two, these are very different from the three words we used to say.

Rather than waste time texting, allowing more to get caught in the *'miscommunication trope'* or whatever she called it. I replayed what happened and decided to sleep on it, or lay in bed and stare at the ceiling until it was finally time to get up and pretend that I hadn't just tortured myself all night. That was until I found myself at my desk ignoring the voice coming through the speaker phone, unfocused on the phone call that required my attention. I owed her an explanation, at least whatever fragment of one I had, and if not an explanation then at least what she had asked for, my perspective. Though the perspective she got was not to her original question but the mind fuckery grenade she dropped instead.

I click back to her email for the tenth time. I laughed to myself earlier as I googled the term miscommunication trope, something we are apparently living through. But I physically cringe every time I reread the line, 'to make sure this relationship wasn't all bullshit.' Could she have seriously thought that? I might understand now that the 'dreaded miscommunication trope' is heavy on the miscommunication, but she couldn't have thought everything before that night was just run-of-the-mill college bullshit. I meant what I said, I don't regret where we ended up. Keeping in touch over the years. Our friendship. But this idea that she had any doubt about how I felt? *That* I regret.

I need to go home and come back to this tomorrow. Work. I need to come back to work tomorrow. But before I go, I need to make a call. It's 9:18 p.m., scrolling through the contact list in my phone, there's the one I'm looking for. A is at the top of the list.

"Hello?" A voice I haven't heard in years.

"Hey, Austin... I know it's been a while, but do I have a story for you."

Chapter Four

2007

HER

The assorted furniture of the Student Center is set up to serve as different types of shared space. Much like my dorm, designed primarily for function but gives the illusion of independence. Though, I don't think anyone is *independently* buying industrial stain proof furniture, just for the fun of it. But illusion or not, I like it. The independence. The adulthood college provides. The feeling of being surrounded by students, people I haven't yet met.

I make myself comfortable with my feet curled up under me wedged into the corner of a couch, surrounded by empty chairs as if I am about to hold court. For as much we are all meant to feel like adults, this feels like a set up not too dissimilar from a high school lunchroom. Ripe for setting up a *cool* group. Me, the not-like-other-girls-cool-girl. *Ha. Because that's what I'm supposed to be. The water-off-a-duck's-back cool girl. Even if your feet are paddling frantically below water.*

I thumb open my book, the comfort read I often carry around because it fills any void I have in time or interest. So I usually jump back in during moments like this. I don't make it to the bottom of the page before I hear that newly familiar voice approaching behind me. He's not alone–it's interlaced with that of others prattling away about dorms, parties, class schedules–but his voice is still above the rest, getting closer, closer, closer... and then in one swift move, Josh lands on the empty couch cushion to my right. He tosses a plate into my lap; the contents are just a large foil wrapped log. One I can feel the heat of, penetrating through the wrapper and plate and warming the skin beneath the fabric of my mini skirt.

He snatches the book I've been holding and chucks it on the table in front of us, kicking his feet up, his heel clipping the spine before landing. I jolt forward.

"Don't you have *any* respect?" I ask as I clutch the book to my chest, hugging it closely. I might like Josh, but my new friend has to understand that this book is one of my *best* friends. Rather than answering my mostly rhetorical question, he leans over to the plate on my lap and starts unwrapping the foil from the top, exposing a clearly overstuffed burrito, before shifting back to the plate in his own lap and doing the same.

"Got you my usual. I can tell we have a few things in common, and this will be a good test."

"Are you in the habit of testing your friends?"

"How do you think they *become* my friends?" I lift the burrito to my mouth, understanding quite clearly the phallic graphic nature (and impossibility) of wrapping my entire mouth around it–so excessively thick–and instead opt for a more demure bite as I stare him down, locking my eyes with his and moaning as I chew, putting on the theatrical review of this burrito. Sounds escape my closed lips, never breaking contact with him until I close my eyes, rolling my head back across my shoulders, and finally swallowing down. End scene. My very own When-Harry-Met-Sally moment, earning me gimmicky applause from audience members. I hadn't noticed the small group filling the previously empty chairs as I had been too distracted by whatever this was. *Entertaining. That's what it was.* And he reveled in the display. Similarly to the way I do. The showmanship. The praise. And with that, what I have recognized in him becomes clear. It's elements of myself.

Straightening up in my seat, taking a napkin to dab the corner of my lips where some of the *truthfully delicious* burrito juices remained. *He was right.*

"I've had better."

"Whatever you say, Miami." As he bites into his own burrito.

I know the girl sitting to my left. Marlie, *I think.* Though the guy she's leaning into looks to be a new addition.

"Marlie, right?"

"Yeah! You're Arden..."

"Mhmm."

"My suitemate didn't looove the midnight welcome from you and Stella." She laughs just as she did when we met during our first night on campus. When Stella and I knocked on every door to be sure we had *'super cool neighbors.'* Surprise, surprise. Even in college people aren't super cool when you knock on their door in the middle of the night. Marlie and her suitemate, whose name I *can't* remember, and now don't want to, opened the door and found us in the hall handing them each a beer, curtseying an introduction, before moving on to the next door.

Marlie looks like the epitome of college freshman with her leggings, Uggs, and Class of 2011 tee shirt. She has an attainable kind of attractiveness, but I like it–the floppy ease about her. In our short time on campus, it looks like she already found her way into a relationship and the college merch store. And while I am looking for the full blown college experience, I think I'll stick to casual hookups and punny graphic tees.

"Sorry about that. We just got a little over excited on our

first night." Marlie laughs it off, clearly unbothered, and I make a mental note that she might be a good friend while I'm here.

"This is Jack." Nodding to her left. Jack and Josh are entangled in their own conversation. And Marlie introduces the rest of the group. "That's Lindsey, Ethan, and Lucas," she says, finishing out the group of people around us. "And you seem to know Josh."

"I wouldn't say we *know* each other." *That's a lie.* The more time I spend around him, the clearer it becomes. Every action, every mannerism, every time he called me *Miami* rather than my name. I knew him.

I feel long fingers cover my eyes from behind, "Guess who?!"

"Hmmm..." I muse. "Well it can't be my favorite suitemate because she was missing during the entire orientation even though she told me she'd save me a seat."

"UGH! Fineee." She drops her hands, freeing my vision from the obstruction and comes to sit on the arm of the couch next to me. "I was planning on going, but then my boyfriend called and said he was driving up tonight because he misses me already!" I'm not sure on the exact stats of high school relationships lasting in college, especially when he's still living in the same town and she's moved into one of the greatest collegiate cities in the world... but I suppose time will tell. Until then, I had the pleasure of meeting him on move-in day, and he seemed nice enough.

I repeat the introductions Marlie had just done for me, and she seems to be relieved at the reprieve, clearly uninterested in being the default ring leader. And we all spent the next couple hours exchanging the basic deets about ourselves. Where we were from, what we wanted to study, classes to take, professors we'd heard to avoid. I learned that Ethan is Josh's suitemate, Lucas has a girlfriend back home, Lindsey doesn't talk much, and by some miracle, we all had the same English Lit class. That is, except for Jack who is an upperclassman.

Eventually, the group dissipated. Stella fluttered off back to our dorm, everyone trickling out one by one. But Josh and I stayed put. Sharing the space and a bit more about our lives.

"What was it like growing up in Miami? What are your friends like? What do your parents do? Why did you leave Miami for college?" He asked so many questions. Seemed so interested in me and there was sincerity in his tone. The kind that allowed me to melt a layer of my exterior and respond in kind.

"As much as I love my parents, I just wanted a chance to be myself without them and their expectations." It's a simple enough idea, not unique to me in any way. Just that maybe my familial expectation might be a bit more intense than most. The kind you hear for so long that becomes so deeply ingrained you dilute yourself into believing it's your own ambition, your own life-plan, not the external pressure of others. He nods like he gets it. Gets *me*. Maybe he does in part. *The parts I've let him see so far*. But as I sat here on this couch, asked why I chose this school, or better yet left Miami, it's because it gave me distance to decide who I wanted to be away from the weight and commentary of those around me even if a lot of that had been prewritten.

Josh wraps his hands around my ankles and pulls them gently to extend them into his lap, stretching my legs out across him to indicate he doesn't mind the invasion of space, in fact he welcomes me into it, laying his arm across the exposed skin of my legs.

"So, I showed you mine..." Prodding him gently both in question and with my foot.

"I'm from Hanover, New Hampshire. It's a nice place, great place for some people, but not *my* place, ya know?" Be it the burrito test or the banter, he seems to be less attention seeking and more sincere. Waiting for a reply from me, maybe even my agreement, even though I don't think he needs it.

"Yeah, I know." I say, giving into what he needs.

"So, who are you away from your family and outside of Miami, *Miami?*"

"Still working that out. I'd like to think I am who I always was, just maybe able to be myself without that extra weight of what everyone else wants. Isn't that what college is for? To grow and learn, to experiment, and expose yourself?"

"Is that what you're here to do, experiment and expose yourself?" I know what he is trying to do. To pull on the innuendo I laid out, this time unintentionally. But rather than give him the opportunity, I just move on.

"As I was saying... college is supposed to be like this great awakening, this opportunity to make friends, build relationships. Well, I have friends and I've always been able to make them easily, I am already incredibly well informed politically, so no need for an enlightenment on that front. I have an eclectic taste in music, so I didn't need a musical awakening. And sexually? That ship had sailed in high school. But I want to just *do college.* I want all the parties, the 3:00 a.m. cram sessions. I want to take a bunch of classes even though they have nothing to do with my major, like Music Theory or Russian Lit! I want all the cliché college experiences, and I want the freedom to do that without judgment or input. I just want to be that person fully."

He's looking at me intently, as if all the things I named are things he intimately craves. Attention, power, knowledge, sex. My feet are in his lap, his forearms laying across my legs, but his eyes are on me. I just sit here, letting that sink in for a minute. Not for his benefit, but my own. A moment of candor around my goals here. Before I turn the table back to him.

"Okay Josh... It's your turn, why isn't New Hampshire *your place?*"

"New Hampshire is just," he paused, trying to think through his next move. "It's just... I need more out of my life, so much fucking more." And with that, his dark eyes sharpened, something fiery and bold behind them. I saw it then, how ambitious he was.

And some of the darkest parts of me related to it.

———

"I can't believe there are tunnels beneath the school!" Standing at my door, my one hand plunged into my bag, blindly searching for my keys.

"They connect to a lot of the buildings, obviously not all the way to this one, but they'll still save you from frostbite in the winter getting to and from classes when you're scheduled on the main block of campus."

"And where is your dorm? Does it connect to the tunnels?" He had mentioned it earlier, so I know he is in a different hall than this one but can't place on a map what that actually means.

"I can get 99% of where I want to go without going outside. Or I could before now." Smiling at me as he leans against the wall. As I made no progress on the missing key front. But he doesn't seem bothered, he seems enchanted. Perfectly happy to stand here as I foolishly dig about looking for a key that I may well have already lost.

With that, the front door swings open, "Tah-Dah!" *Stella.* "I figured it would be easier to let you in rather than listening to you struggle outside the door." Her assessment of Josh may be silent, but it isn't subtle. Her eyes rake over his body before bouncing back to me.

Objectively speaking, Stella is gorgeous. There's no other way to describe her. But it's an effervescence, a buoyancy about her, that is addicting to people, and I saw it the day we met. It doesn't hurt that she spends most of her time half dressed. Even that's a stretch, as she stands in the doorway in nothing more than her boyfriend's tank top and a pair of athletic socks for no other reason than it was just what she decided to wear. Completely unbothered by the passersby in the hall.

She steps out of the doorway back into our shared common area of our two-bedroom suite. I wouldn't say the dorms were a factor in picking this school, but it didn't hurt. A main room that was outfitted with the same brand of standard utility furniture from the Student Center, a small three-seater couch, and two small armchairs. A corner kitchenette, with a microwave and mini-fridge. And the best part? A private bathroom.

When we moved in, Stella and I took one look at the set up, and she immediately pulled a large, patterned tapestry out of her bag and draped it over the couch to cover the lifeless gray fabric. She seemed to do that. Cover the dullness. Later that night, we went out and bought all the twinkle lights we could find, hanging those above the couch and in each of our bedrooms, as well as a collection of polaroid pictures we affixed to the walls, after spending the entire day snapping them, then shaking them, in addition to our asses, as we danced around our new space.

The friendship between us was immediate. She said it was because Libra (her) and Scorpio (me) make a great match and could even be soulmates. Friend-soulmate might be just what I'm looking for, considering I'm not actually interested in anything more serious in terms of *romantic* relationships.

"Are you coming to Welcome Mixer tonight?" I ask her as I sink down into a chair tucking my feet underneath me.

"Nah... I think I'll be good here." She winks, grabbing a couple of water bottles from the fridge before slipping back into her bedroom. The muffled voices of two people wrapped up in each other barely escape beneath the door. *Looks like her boyfriend did miss her already.*

"I thought you were joking about Russian Literature." Josh is holding my printed course schedule. The one Stella and I had taped to the door so we could keep track of where we were at any given time.

"I would *NEVER* joke about Russian Literature."

"You really are packing your schedule. *Jesus Christ!*" He scans the sheet once more before looking at me.

"How will you have any time for anything else? You're taking twice as many classes as an average student."

"Well, that's your first mistake... I'm *not* the average student. And secondly, I'm not looking for anything else–nothing that requires commitment, at least."

"Is that so? Lucky for me, I'll be seeing you in some of these, Miami."*Miami.* A nickname not earned or indicative of anything other than where I came from. It irked me the first time I heard it, but it seems to roll off his tongue with endearment, so I didn't bother correcting it now.

"Josh! Have you checked the time?"

"Not once." Cutting me a look but checking his phone finally to see that it's almost 8 p.m.

"I thought you of all people wouldn't mind being fashionably late."

"I'm always fashionable, never late." I scrunch my face realizing the irony. That running late is exactly how I ended up sitting next to him this morning in the lecture hall.

"Okay, I'm never *usually* late," I amended with a smile. "While this has been fun, I have to get ready to impress the rest of our graduating class, so I'll meet you there in a bit?"

Josh stands, pops a kiss to the side of my head. "I'll see ya."

Chapter Five

HER

I have just enough time to change into something I can dance in and throw on a fresh coat of mascara and lip gloss before shoving my phone in my purse and heading out the door alone. Stella had decided to stay in tonight, barricaded behind her bedroom door, holed up with her boyfriend. I wonder if she will spend the entire year like this, being in a relationship that prevents her from experiencing the fullness of our Freshman year.

I leave the thought behind me as I shut the front door but don't make it two steps before I walk right into him. The familiar shape and smell of him already logged in my brain.

"I thought I was meeting you there?" I collect myself a bit from the frontal assault of slamming right into him, brushing my dress back down and smoothing out my hair. I doubt I am nearly as disheveled as I suddenly feel, but the surprise of literally running into him knocked me back. It almost *physically* knocked me back.

"I thought fashionably late wouldn't be good for a booze

cruise, considering late means the boat leaves without you." He takes in my change of attire, from the graphic tee to the fitted black dress. "But at least you are fashionable." His arm lands in its earlier resting place, back across my shoulders, as we exit the building to where some of the earlier group waited, passing a few flasks between them.

Ethan extends and without thought or hesitation, I take a swig as the fiery burn of whiskey fills my mouth and slips down my throat. I swallow it and wince; I've had whiskey before, usually better quality than this, but even still it's never been my first, or second, even third choice. I let go of the warm whiskey breath in a long smooth exhale.

"I didn't know this was a booze cruise." Laughter breaks out among them, that kind of laughter that comes from everyone being in on the same joke.

"It is now," Josh says, taking the flask from my hand and taking a sip before handing it back. As we all begin to make our way towards the harbor, I take another drink from the flask before capping it and reaching out to return it to Ethan. He shakes his head, the thick curls that sprout from his head fall gently into his face. But he just ignores the distraction of them and pulls another flask from his pocket. He tilts it towards me with a *cheers* motion.

"You can keep that." Bringing it to his lips, he takes a drink.

———

Okay, so we weren't the only ones who decided to turn this Boston Harbor party boat into a full-blown booze cruise. What did they expect when throwing a couple hundred college students on a boat with a DJ and calling it a Welcome Mixer? I've been on the dance floor for the better part of an hour. You can make best temporary friends on a dance floor, and that's what I am doing. Moving throughout the crowd letting the music pull me in the right direction. Marlie and some random girls and I had formed a circle, hands clasped moving in tandem, singing, or more correctly screaming, to the Killers 'Mr. Brightside.' I can feel the music thrumming through me, so I keep moving my body amongst all the other bodies, breaking away from the girl band that I had accidentally formed on the dance floor. It's when I find my flask empty that I realize I am more drunk than I planned to be. I scan the space looking for someone I know, Marlie and the backup dancers already lost in the crowd. I don't see him, but I feel him as he comes up behind me. I feel his large hands run around my waist, pulling me into him to dance. When I lean my head back, the broadness of his chest feels especially foreign. I force my eyes to adjust to the man behind me, and I take in the fact that I have absolutely no idea who this is. I sway a moment longer, considering my options with this clearly interested party. And while I don't know him, I decide that tonight I'm not interested in knowing him, either. *Sorry, pal. Maybe I'll see you in class one day, but you won't be seeing me in bed tonight.*

Nights like this are what I came here for. The expectations of others might still circle me, but at this moment, I have what I want. *Fun. Freedom. Choice.*

I dance away from the stranger and cross the deck to the railing of the boat. There are still people around, but significantly fewer. The members of the party I arrived with dispersed when we got here. And while I thrive with people around, there's a peacefulness in solitude I let myself sink into when I'm alone–or at least the illusion of being alone–as everyone else bounces and bops, grinds and mingles, getting to know each other before classes begin. I stand here, looking out at the city, wrapping my hands around the cool metal of the boat railing and letting the bar slide through my grip as I stretch them out to either side. Leaning forward as I do, until I release my grip and let my arms dangle overboard, hanging the weight of my body forward over the edge. My head hanging down, hair fallen, blowing in the breeze coming off the water. The pressure of the railing against my ribs is comforting in a way it shouldn't be. My body folded over the railing like a rag doll, letting the blood flow to my hands and feet as they dangle. Half of my body forward over the dangerous edge, half safely behind the railing just a few inches above the floor. My feet brush just above the floor, giving me the illusion of far more danger than there is. Knowing I just need to lean back to land on the soles of my feet. But instead, I like this sensation.

I feel it, the pressure of his fingers splayed across my back, a somehow *familiar* hand, and the familiar voice to go with it.

"Is this your Titanic moment?" He pulls me upward and sets me down on my feet, turning me so my back is against the railing as he stands to my side. His arm connected to the length of mine, standing there, leaning into each other side by side.

"Does that make you Jack Dawson?"

"I think that makes *him* Jack Dawson," Josh says as he gestures over to the man who I had been dancing with just a few moments before. Catching the attention of our new classmate, Josh blows him a kiss with one hand and drapes his other arm around my shoulders pulling me close. The weight of him has become recognizable in the hours I've known him. I glance up just in time to see my temporary dance partner flip us off, and that's when we can't contain our laughter. Real laughter. Be it the alcohol, or the ridiculousness of the scene, we're doubled over in a hysterical fit.

And we laughed our way all the way back to the dance floor where we stayed the rest of the night, jumping and singing with our friends.

———

I emerge from the bathroom changed into pajamas, my face washed, teeth brushed, and hair pulled into a messy bun. Possibly: Through my bedroom door, I see him already settled comfortably leaning back in my bed with one of my books in hand.

"What's going on over there?" I ask as I make my way over towards my bed.

"Just reading," he says as he flips the book over, glancing at the back cover. "Did you know she went to school here?"

I roll my eyes as I reach out to take the book from him. *Did I know?* This book. This author. Both favorites of mine, and she walked these halls, lived not far from here. Of course I knew. That might have been another reason I felt this school, this city, was where I could become myself. Because *she* did. The novel has been one I go back to time and time again, so much so that the pages themselves are tired from how often I've turned them, but my fingertips know the weight of the paper and the imprints of pen marks and ink upon it more intimately than anything or anyone else. I set the book down on my desk, grab my laptop to queue up a movie, and climb into bed next to him.

He hops down from the bed, which is slightly higher than standard to accommodate the storage beneath it, landing on his feet with a thud. He stands there in the center of my room, reaching his arm over his back and pulling his shirt off. His cocked eyebrow pulls up the corner of his mouth into a smirk, and a test, before moving to the undo button of his jeans, taking them off and getting into bed with me.

"What are you doing?"

"I just spent all this time warming up this spot, so I'm staying."

"You want to watch a movie?"

"I don't think I'll make it through a movie."

I know that I might be pouring fuel on this fire if I let this go any further. The banter, the touching, the shallow intimacy, he's the same as me. He looks to other people for connections, and he is energized by them. Energized by *me*. I saw it the first time he looked at me. And because I could recognize myself in that, I knew what it meant, and it meant that this can't be more than what it is. Instinctively, I knew almost upon first meeting that this guy laying next to me now, he and I could be a dangerous pair. Combustible.

And the way to prevent it? Remove temptation. I'm not a virgin, and I dated in high school enough to know when I have feelings for someone. But what I am feeling now feels more like a connection to someone in a different way. A look at parts of myself. Maybe that's what appealed to him also. *Maybe I am overthinking his intention.*

With him in only his boxers as we slipped under the covers and only the laptop and a potentially dangerous dynamic between us, it felt like all the banter earlier was for the show we were both starring in. And this moment? This moment is honest, so I will be honest.

"Josh," I say with more caution than I've expressed around him yet. "It's all just noise, you know. It's just deflection, entertainment. I'm a terrible flirt, and it might get me into a little trouble, but me and you, we aren't going to be anything more than friends."

"That's where you're wrong, Miami. You're an excellent flirt, and we're going to be best fucking friends."

Chapter Six

2007

HER

He got into my bed like it was the most natural thing to do, like I should have expected it. I hadn't even known him a day, and yet it felt like more than that. There was a closeness and vulnerability sharing a bed with someone, and that closeness did not just come from the fact this was a college twin. We were close physically, but also in the way that you let your guard down when you sleep. Which is why I didn't have much intention of sharing a bed with anyone. At least beyond the alternative activities meant to occupy them, and that would surely be temporary.

Sleep is something I do inconsistently at best, having been dubbed everything from a night owl to a full blown insomniac. The irony is that I do it best when I'm not alone. I'm not sure when exactly the insomnia started, around the same time as the external pressures of growing up. I had wondered what college would be like in that regard, and the first few nights were pretty standard, by my account. Last night, with someone next to me,

I was able to let myself get lost in the comfort of sleep, the way most of the world does, for more than four hours.

We were both on the tail end of inebriated by the time we got back to my dorm room. My suitemate was already asleep (or otherwise engaged) with her boyfriend behind her own closed bedroom door. So, when we fumbled our way back in, there was nothing to shock us into sobriety, or perhaps have me send him on his way. We slept together last night. But we didn't sleep together last night.

'*Best fucking friends,*' he had said. Like elementary school kids making a pinky promise.

The boundary had been established, and even though we reached for each other while we slept, we didn't cross it in a conscious way. Sitting up on my elbows and looking to my side, I watch the man still sleeping there. He seems comfortable and content. All that bravado exhibited during the day is gone now. Handsome even in slumber, though far more boyish. His dark hair against my light blue pillowcase, with my comforter kicked down around his feet. But looking at him as he slept was something different. His eyebrows were not pulled together in thought the way I had seen him throughout the day, but instead they were gently resting high above his closed eyes. Like he could have been surprised. Everything about him seems softer while he sleeps, everything except his body. His body is fit, exposed in nothing more than boxers, and given that he just stripped and crawled into bed, I didn't notice at the time.

Instead, last night we just laid there side by side watching a movie, talking and laughing about the night, eventually letting the leftover whiskey lull us into a shared sleep. I wonder how the hell I ended up on this side of *my* bed. Trapped with the hard wall against my back and the hard body to my front. Both immovable. He doesn't stir at all when I move to glance at the alarm clock on the dresser. *Wow, seven hours is practically a record.* I am never going to be one of those people who can sleep the day away. Not without physical sickness or pure unadulterated heartache.

Sitting up, I brace my arm across him so I can swing my leg over and hopefully land my foot on the floor, but instead of the smooth move I played out in my mind, my hand slips from the corner of the mattress, my other elbow buckles, and I collapse directly on top of him. Our chests press together, and the air is knocked out of me. My face lands in the crook of his neck, a leg straddling either side of him.

He smells like sleep, the groggy way the scents become muted. But the smell of him still overwhelmed me as my nose pressed against his skin. And I realized it was far more the smell of years spent in New Hampshire than any scent he purchased. Though it surprised me he didn't spray on something more popular to mask the woodsy musk of the small-town upbringing.

He lets out a laugh deep from his gut that shakes his whole body and mine with it. I quickly move to brace myself up on my hands and knees so our bodies aren't connected down at the core. Though I'm fully clothed in pajamas, he's not. I feel him, the hardness of his body, of him, and in terrible judgment, I look down. The sleepy softness of his face is now gone, and something else awakens as he cocks his brow and presses his lips together with a slight shake of his head, swallowing down the rest of his laugh.

"I thought you were only going to jump on my ego, Arden." His mischievous mask back in place. Wrapping his arms around me and pulling me back into his chest, with a kiss on my temple, he rolls me off him, back onto the mattress, and he climbs out of my bed. Picking up his clothes from where they laid from the night before and chucking me my phone at me from where it had been charging.

I skim the messages I missed, one from my mom checking in. *I'll update her later.* One from Stella, *guess she wasn't sleeping when we got back.* And one from Ethan, who I didn't even realize had my number, let alone would use it given we've exchanged all of fifteen total words since meeting.

Mom: Have you registered for enough science classes?

Stella Suitemate: did I just hear you come in... NOT alone?

Ethan: Dining Hall @ 8:30

"Looks like we have breakfast plans." I wave my phone in response to the confusion on his face, as an answer to the unspoken question of *'what are you talking about.'* He checks his phone and sure enough has notifications of his own.

"Ethan?" he tosses the name to me to check that's what I meant about breakfast.

"Mhm, and I desperately need coffee and carbs after last night."

"Hungover? I expected more from you, Miami." *Well, that nickname seems to have stuck.*

"Yeah, whiskey isn't my drink."

We all took seats at a big round table in the center of the dining hall. Stella hopped from bed to join us at the mention of breakfast, and it was nice to see the two people who I had formed immediate bonds with connect now over coffee. It wasn't just Stella who joined us, Marlie and Jack, who are *definitely* on their way to a relationship, Lindsey, and Ethan, of course, plus some other strays who I learned were also on the soccer team with Josh and Ethan. *I knew he was an athlete.*

And now in the clarity of daylight, looking at Ethan, there is no hiding the shape of him either.

"Didn't know until this morning that you didn't come back last night," Ethan says to Josh, bringing a forkful of scrambled eggs to his mouth as a full stop to the sentence. Stella let out a chirping giggle as her eyebrows jumped to the top of her forehead. As if silently acknowledging to him that she too had a morning shock finding him in our room.

"Seems like you were able to figure out where I was just fine... based on who you texted for breakfast."

"Maybe I'm just seen as more reliable," I tease. I couldn't tell if there was actual tension building here or just the natural arrogance of him that I unfortunately seemed to thrive off.

"I'm getting more pancakes!" Stella jumps up from her seat, snatching my hand in the process. When she feels we've taken enough steps from the table, she lets go of my hand, trusting I'm not about to abandon her on this pancake mission. Though it's obvious to everyone we left sitting this is far more of an ask-a-question-in-private kind of mission than one motivated by Mrs. Butterworth.

"What's going on with you guys? I thought you weren't planning on dating anyone?" She jumps right in. Something I have come to adore about this girl in the matter of days I've known her.

"I'm *not* dating anyone. He just crashed in our dorm."

"I think you mean he crashed in *your* dorm. I know he wasn't in my room."

"Either way," I brush off the distinction she felt it necessary to make, "we talked about it. He knows the deal. And he's the same. It was just friendly, and that's how it's going to stay."

"Okie dokie artichokie." I turn to head back, knowing she feels I sufficiently answered her line of questioning, before she grabbed my hand again to halt me.

"Wait! Pancakes!" I guess Mrs. Butterworth did have something to do with this after all.

———

The next weeks passed with a full chaos that I found balancing. My schedule was about twice as many classes as most of my peers, and my social life had begun to take shape as well. *At least, it began to take the shape I molded.*

I had found my way into a groove here, and Josh was right, we did become *'best fucking friends.'* Sans the literal fucking, of course. Which is probably the reason why our friendship works. Walking to and from class, we'd trade stories about our lives. Both what they were and what we wanted them to become. We talked about high school, Mr. Homecoming King, Ms. Valedictorian. Though his high school glory days weren't enough to keep him there.

Some nights we'd go out with our friends, often serving as each other's wingman for the temporary companionship we both sought out in other people before eventually finding our way back to each other to sleep. We talked about relationships, the ones we had in high school, and the ones we were looking for here. Seemingly on the same page, neither of us looking to fall into the first romantic pairing we could find. *If we did, that likely would have been each other.* He said he had been casually seeing someone but that she got a little too clingy. *'Did she get in your bed the same night you met; I wonder what that's like,'* I teased and just got that Cheshire Cat smile in reply.

The more time we spent together, I saw the cracks in his mask. The one that put off the cool and confident exterior and hid the insecurities of who he was trying to be. Not visible to anyone else, and perhaps not even on purpose. I used it as justification to trust him, knowing his vulnerabilities a little more, something I was better than him at protecting.

We had said we were going to be friends, and at the time, I didn't know if either of us truly believed it, but that's what this was. There was a kinship here between us; the ambition we both had for ourselves, though shaped differently, was something we could recognize in one and other.

Chapter Seven

PRESENT

HER

Arden,

Number one, thanks for my lesson on tropes. I have googled miscommunication trope and understand why it is "dreaded." Hate to break it to you, but it doesn't really encourage me to read romance.

Number two, Austin Becks says hello. Had to share the "mental grenade" as you phrased it. Who better to experience the detonation of it than someone who was there?

Number three, and most importantly, I'm sorry you had any question about if it was "all bullshit." None of it was, AB. I'll amend my earlier email to include that as a regret.

Your friend.
P.S. I accept the terms of a signed copy.

Amanda places my phone back on the table and slides it to me, pinning me with a stare that I've been on the receiving end of more than once since the start of all this. Having received this email a few days ago, I decided to hold on to it, to wait until we were back in our Sunday seats for her to read it, without the interruptions of our real lives. It's obvious she's trying to decide what she wants to do first: Ask a question, or tell me her thoughts. She settles for a combination of the two.

"You know what I'm going to say, right?"

"No, I can't say I do." Probably one of the things I've thought about and dismissed myself.

"He still clearly has feelings for you... *and* who the hell is Austin Becks?"

Amanda became my friend later in life. The irony of our meeting is that, for a romance novel, our first encounter would have been classified a meet-cute. Bumping into each other at a coffee shop, both interested in the last pastry, and instead of deciding who should have it, she asked for two plates and we shared it. It only took two coffees and half of a chocolate croissant for Amanda to become a part of my life. But that was years before this moment, and years after the one in question. Which means she doesn't know the story beyond what was playing out between us now. The cast of characters names she's never heard. Parts of my life I don't often revisit beyond, 'Yes, I went to college in Massachusetts,' or 'My college suitemate, Stella, got married recently.'

But as Amanda picked up the story after this chapter, after him, there was so much here she didn't know. But then again, there are only two people who know what really happened *after* it ended, only two people who never talked about it after that.

"It was a long time ago," I say to her, as if time alone could answer her question. "He doesn't have feelings for me, at least not in the way you're reading into it... and Austin was just another supporting character in our story. I just haven't gotten to that part yet."

After all this time, I have no intention of upending anyone's life, and we both knew it. He had said as much in his first email. '*No ulterior motives.*' Had everything just been as I had thought it to be, it would have been a normal conversation, reminiscing about funny scenes from our movie, a highlight reel, rather than rewriting the entire ending.

There was something in this latest email that did make me question it though. I believed what I said, that it was different now. Any feelings left are just those of friendship. But I think now, for the first in all these years, one, or both of us, felt regret.

"He doesn't have feelings for you? You're kidding, Arden. Are we reading the same email?!?"

"Considering I'm showing them to you, yeah, I'd say so..." I like answering rhetorical questions. I think that if I answer rhetorical questions with the same sarcasm in their delivery, maybe people will stop asking them and instead ask something useful.

"Smart ass. And what time did *this* latest one come in?" She looked back at me with that glare. This I won't answer, because I know the late night timestamps don't look as innocent as I want them to be. Even knowing we ended up in different timezones, I could still determine that this last email was sent close to 1 a.m. his time.

"Okay, AB," she says, evoking the nickname he used, one that followed me long after we weren't together, "As much as I am loving this and will gladly use it as fodder for a novel in the future, do you seriously think it's wise, you know—"

"I know, I know," I cut her off. There are so many ends to that sentence. So many things I know, so many things I don't. So many things I am now that I wasn't back then. So, whatever she intended to say, I don't need to hear it. Bringing my hands from where they lay on the table and resting them against my stomach so I can feel the slow, long breath I pull in from the abdomen and deep into my lungs.

"We've been friends far longer than we were ever anything else, this is just that, us being friends."

Chapter Eight

2007

HER

The change in seasons isn't something I'm used to. There's a magic to fall that I never experienced outside of Thanksgiving commercials and pumpkin flavored things. I always thought it would be a slower progression. The way the word indicates it happens. *Fall.* Like a slow collapse from one season to another. But I guess when you're more focused on the exciting moments of your life, it's easy to miss even the most obvious of things, like the world changing around you. Like the trees stripping bare. Because I swear one day I woke up and stepped outside, and I stepped into October in Cambridge.

The tones of the city matched the smell in the air. And now, walking to class this early in the morning, all I can think about is the jean jacket I should have brought. Instead, the only warmth is coming from the body keeping pace next to me.

"What's the plan for tonight?" Josh takes a sip of his coffee and hands it to me as we cross the quad.

"Ethan said it's 80's night at The Commons."

"Sounds good, Miami Vice. I'll catch ya later, this is my

stop," he says as he reaches the building where his class is, knowing mine is a few over.

"Wait!" I call after him, already a few steps off. But he spins back on a heel.

"Miss me already?" he says, cocking a familiar brow.

"I just... I need...I need y–" His face contorts, skeptical for a moment as I approach. "I need your hoodie. I'm freezing!" I nab the sweatshirt he had draped over the books in his grip.

"It's true, you can take the girl out of Miami, but not Miami out of the girl."

"Thanks for the hoodie!" I throw it on for the last few minutes of my trek to class. And I am immersed in the smell of him, one I recognize in all its versions. Sleep. Morning. Drunk. Gym. Post Sex, *though that one is similar to gym, and never involves me.*

Josh and I spent most of our time together, magnets stuck to each other's sides. Everyone was used to it by now, and no one questioned whether we are actually together. The only sexual energy between us is that which we created verbally, especially in situations with others where we preferred to seem as unavailable physically as we had both learned we were emotionally. He was always a great buffer. Intervening when I indicated I needed a rescue from some forward classmate or bar patron. And I could play the perfect role of a scorned and clingy girlfriend when he'd need a reason for someone to move on.

We've both casually been hooking up with people since we got on campus. People we'd meet at parties, in college bars, in classes, *though that posed to be a problem when later assigned any kind of group work.* It's a far cry from dating. Dating implies expectations beyond sex, and I had enough of those already. So we cursed the word, the only consistent relationship with each other, often laying in bed together directly afterwards, scrolling through social media looking at the poor unsuspecting victims of ours, knowing that they were just physical distractions. Never amounting to anything more.

The emotional dependence we shared didn't just tether us together, it served as the noose for any other relationships. And we preferred it that way. He and I identified a need in each other early on. And we filled it. The companionship, the sex-free chemistry, that let us lean into each other in ways beyond the basic boy meets girl, boy loves girl, boy loses girl, rom-com relationship formula. We had a complex dynamic that no one got, and that's fine for me, because I make a point of preventing people from getting me. And when I do let them get me, it's whichever part I am willing to expose, usually only skin deep, whichever part they are in search of.

———

I love any reason for a costume. Any theme night or specialized attire, count me in. And walking into The Commons with Stella, clearly I'm not the only one.

Stella is decked out in all the spandex she could find and topped it off with sweatbands and leg warmers. The bright colors and jazzercise look wasn't what I decided to go for. Besides the fact that having someone else peel down a leotard at the end of the night felt incredibly unsexy, I also have a secret weapon for 80's Night. Curly hair. Full glam-metal-hair-band hair. While I usually polish it straight, going for more of a Cher Horowitz from Clueless style, naturally, my hair was wild. It has volume and curls I opted to contain. But tonight, with a fresh shower and a little hairspray, I might as well be in the Whitesnake music video, dancing on the hood of a car. I paired my big curls with an old band tee shirt and tight leather pants, both of which I already had in my wardrobe. And voilà, 80's Night!

The Commons has become the default hang out. The

Central Perk to our group. Just less coffee, more beer. Always different themes or events on schedule. Last week, we kicked everyone's asses at Trivia Night and earned ourselves a free bar tab and loaded nachos.

As soon as we walk through the door, Stella bounces her way over to her spandex twin, finding Marlie. The room was filled with different versions of googled 80's costumes dancing and drinking as I scanned the crowd. For someone I know, or maybe someone I don't. Still undecided.

I find Josh and Ethan leaning against the bar. Chatting with each other, likely surveying their surroundings as much as I am.

Ethan had cobbled together a version of Marty McFly, likely from his own wardrobe. Next to him, Josh, ever the showman, didn't hold back. And neither could I restrain the laugh that burst free as he tossed my hair as a means of hello.

"What's so funny, Miami?"

"I didn't realize you meant you were coming *dressed as Miami Vice.*"

"And you are?" Standing there in a suit jacket, sleeves pushed up to his elbows, with a pastel tee shirt and hair perfectly quaffed as he rattles the ice in his glass, Josh looks me up and down as slowly as he did that first day.

"In need of a drink..." He hands me his cup, two fingers worth of amber liquid remain, and I take a sip. Wincing as I do. *I knew it was whiskey. It's always whiskey.*

The Commons *is* a bar, and I *am* eighteen, but between the mixed ages of people in attendance, fake ids, boobs, and the fact that it's a *college* bar, getting a drink isn't hard. It just means that sometimes ordering my own drink isn't possible, and I have to be at the mercy of those around me. And those around me, for better or worse, drink whiskey.

I feel it warming my skin as it slips down my throat. *Wait, no, that's someone's breath.*

"You should bring your own flask if you hate whiskey." Ethan had leaned in close enough that I could feel the words against my skin as he spoke them. It was noisy in here, but not so much that he would need to be so close. He chose to be though. And I welcomed him into my space, knowing it was only a physical invasion. For all the things I've learned Ethan is, loquacious isn't one of them.

"I would have, but that would have been an insult to these pants." I gesture up and down. My leather pants are practically a second skin; there was no room to fit a flask.

"That's why I had to put my money and phone in my boot!" I say, kicking one foot up on the leg of the barstool in front of me. Ignoring the fact that someone is sitting there.

"I would never insult *those* pants." His smile is different now than I've seen it before. More focused than in the past, focused on me, and I think that it isn't just the whiskey warming my insides.

"Two shots. Tequila." Ethan calls over to the bartender, produces his own fake id, *apparently tonight he is Michael Hathaway from Rhode Island,* and looks back at me, "It's tequila, right?"

"Yeah," I say as he steps closer to me, handing me the glass, lime perched on the rim, salt shaker in hand. I glance up at him through my thick 80's style eyelashes as I lick my hand.

"Salt?" I ask, extending my saliva slicked hand as he shakes the salt onto sticky skin. Before he licks his own hand and does the same.

"Cheers!" I tilt my shot glass towards him, and we clink our glasses, lick the salt, and throw them back before popping the limes in our mouths and sucking ferociously, pulling in the tart citrus taste. His eyes dip from mine and drop to my mouth, where I expose my bright green lime smile, and he releases one of his own.

I'm acutely aware of those around us caught up in

conversations of their own. Josh has moved closer to a girl at the bar. Marlie and Stella have made their way to the center of the dance floor, moving to 'Let's Get Physical', crowded by other Olivia Newton John look-alikes.

"Another?"

"Absolutely."

Gesturing back to the bartender, before turning back and moving his body further into mine, only a few inches between us, as he holds the two shot glasses in his hands. Extending one forward to me, I take it, his now empty hand, not lowering back to his side as he did before, but instead comes down on my bare skin where my tee shirt's cut off neckline hangs off my shoulder in a very Flashdance-esque kind of way. His eyes meet my own in question, one he doesn't outright voice, and instead runs his thumb across my exposed collar bone. We are suspended momentarily in a dynamic different from one we have shared previously. And it doesn't take any words besides one to confirm the next move.

"Salt?" He makes the offer this time, softer, leaning in close to my ear and my skin warms under the heat of his breath.

"Definitely," I say in clear answer to the questions he's not asking.

He leans forward and drags his tongue across the same line his thumb previously traced, shaking the salt, a few grains falling down my shirt in the process, but a collection remains waiting. Unbothered by the noise and closeness of us to other people in this moment of display. He then shakes the salt against the soft flesh following the curve between his thumb and forefinger and holds the lime between his fingertips, waiting for me.

"Cheers."

"Cheers."

We clink our glasses. I lick the salt from his hand, sucking the skin and pulling it between my lips at the same time I feel his mouth come down across my collar bone. Taking in the grains of salt, but also the taste of my skin. I throw the shot into my mouth, and swallow as my head falls back, his right arm wraps around my back and his mouth makes its way across my skin.

"Suck." Pulling back, and snapping my attention to him, he feeds the lime between my lips, running his thumb across my tequila-soaked bottom lip and watching me closely as he takes his own shot.

Having both downed the liquor, he sets the empty shot glasses aside, and brings his remaining free hand to my ribs, and moves in closing the final space between us.

His mouth is salty and warm, mine is tart and sour, and as his lips take mine, the tastes mingle, and I throw my own arms around his neck, his broad shoulders offering stability, as I press my body closer into his. A body I had never considered an option.

The kiss was deep, and full of more passion than I had expected. We've spent weeks hanging out, sharing meals, trading class notes, and this caught me by surprise.

He brushes the wild curly hair from my face, so his hands can cup each cheek and pull me into him. Though he seems wholly unbothered by the length of his own hair falling in his face, blocking his vision, instead more focused on his need for access to mine.

My hands fisting the sides of his red Back-to-the-Future-style puffy vest, steadying myself in front of him.

"I didn't know Marty McFly would do it for ya."

"*He* doesn't, but you are." As I step forward again and tilt my head upward to align my lips with his. It was all the indication he needed to pull me into him once more deepening the kiss between us.

As Guns and Roses starts to play, Ethan's lips pull away from the swell of my own, his hands settle on my waist and he looks at me, like it's the first time he's truly been able to. I see his eyes move past my face and over my shoulder.

"I don't think we have to worry about anyone's opinion." He juts his chin in a direction over my shoulder. He said *anyone*, but I know who he meant. I glance over and see Josh having progressed to a similar stage of companionship for the night with someone he's got nestled in the corner of a booth off to the side of the bar.

"I *don't* worry about other people's opinions, and you certainly didn't seem worried a moment ago."

"I'm not. But you guys have a thing or some shit, I've been giving it space to play out."

It's not like Josh and I didn't know we gave off a *vibe*. But all of our friends have also seen us with other people on nights out in the past that my availability shouldn't have been a question. Especially not a question tied to Josh. Ethan was different though, I suppose. Different because he is Josh's suitemate and independently had become my friend. Meaning that when this inevitably shifts back to just friendship, be it tonight, in another week, or the next time I find myself in Josh's bed again trading stories about our latest classmate hook ups, what would that mean for our friendship, *all* of our friendship?

I look back to Josh and the girl by his side, only now recognizing Lindsey. Someone I peripherally hang out with and share a few classes with. While she's pretty meek, she's always seemed sweet. *Good luck to her. Josh doesn't do well with sweet.* I notice then that his attention isn't on her, but he's locked eyes with me, when he presses his fingers to his lips and blows me a kiss. When his hand leaves his mouth, all that's left is the remaining smirk and shake of his head, before turning back to his booth-mate and leaning down to whisper something.

"There's nothing to let play out between me and Josh," I say, wondering who I am convincing. I'm not jealous of Lindsey, nor have I been any of the others. But, have everyone's perceptions of the situation between us made us into something else? Am I somehow a pariah? Unfuckable in our in-crowd because of him? Was he? Doubtful. It's never the same for men. But there is nothing between us besides this bond we had crafted. The one I leaned into. We had the best of both worlds, as is evidenced by the way Lindsey moved her hand underneath the table to his lap. Even in a dark bar, off in the corner, it's obvious the way his hand gripped the table in front of him with his eyes closed, she had a grip on something also. *And I doubt it's his intellect.*

The friendship we had crafted might have more intimacy than most, save one critical element that would shift it. And even though I slept in the crook of his arm multiple nights a week, it's never more than that for either of us.

"Ethan, I'm ready to get back to the 2000s."

"Thank fuck."

"I don't have keys, I came with Stella, and she's... well, she's still doing *that*," I say and wave over to where she is on the makeshift dance floor, bopping around with her arms above her head.

His hand moving from where it had become glued to my waist, sliding it down the curve of my hip, running it over the black leather. So tight, he might as well be running his hand over my bare skin. *It will be soon. And we know it.*

"I have keys and my dorm is closer." *I know that too.*

Chapter Nine

2007

HER

He couldn't keep his hands off me as we walked back. We didn't use the time to exchange any words, but touches. And we walked back like we were tied together in a three-legged race. Intertwined. Fumbling. And ready to race across the finish line.

Finally in sight of his front door, he turns me to face him and brings his mouth over mine. The ferocity of our earlier kiss rebuilding, knowing it will soon have the sanctuary of his bedroom. My eyes are shut as my feet follow his, leading me backwards until my back hits the solid door behind me. He steps back leaving the door to brace the weight of my body leaning against it and drags a slow look over me, as my eyes shift to where his hand reaches into his front pocket for his keys, but my line of sight is caught on something else entirely.

I hear the door click as he turns the key in the lock, bringing his mouth back urgently back over mine and guiding me into the familiar living room. Never breaking our connection. I've been in this room dozens of times, but never like this. There was always light and noise when we were here together. There were always people, *certain people.* There was always space between us. None of that was here now. Now, it's different. There is no light, there are no people. Only muffled music escaping from his bedroom.

The music is louder now, as he opens the door, 'Sex and Candy' by Marcy Playground.

"I don't like coming back to silence." His mouth forming the words into my skin between the kisses on my neck.

"Well, I'm glad because I like this song."

"Good. It's one of my favorite songs to fuck to." He moves his fingers to the button of my leather pants. Moving us deeper into his bedroom and shutting the door behind him.

I feel him; his hand slips into the front of my pants, and he pushes deep inside of me. I throw my arms around his neck, a grip he welcomes, to offer support as my legs weaken with the deepening of his fingers inside of me.

"I need you." I know he does. I know when anyone does. But that need isn't something I resolve without interest. Without control. And even with his fingers dancing inside of me, my legs unstable without his arm braced across my back, the grunt of his words proves that we both know, I remain in control, to participate in this exchange between us.

I can feel his hardness pressed against me, my forehead fallen on his shoulder, my leg intertwining his. I can feel him nipping at the exposed skin on my neck, and with each drag of his teeth my body tightens. It tightens in his arms, and it tightens all around him.

I lower my hand to him, gripping him tightly through his jeans, his groan and fingers, deepening in response.

"I fucking *need* you."

I can hear the desperation and feel the words roll through my body. A need I want to fulfill; a need I have of my own. I wrap my fingers around his wrist and remove his hand from my pants, guiding it up my side to my breast as I sweep my tongue into his mouth. A kiss left to hold him over momentarily as I step away from him, giving myself space so I can toe off my boots and socks and unzip my pants. In the absence of his lips on mine, I pull my bottom lip and pin it beneath my teeth. Desperate in my own way to feel the pressure of something on my mouth.

His lips trying to stay connected to mine, until the moment he realized by letting me back away he would ultimately get what he wants. I peel the leather pants down my legs and step out of them, standing there in front of him. He closes the space between us once more. Hands on my bare thighs, running them up my sides, under the looseness of the shirt where they catch on my bra, as he reaches behind my back and smoothly unhooks it with one hand. Freeing my breasts while his teeth drag down my neck. The strapless cups release the hold they have on my breasts, freeing them of the constraint. A feeling I desperately want to be replaced by the grip of his hand. His fingertips climb up my ribs, blindly searching for my nipples, as the soft cotton of my vintage tee shirt brushes against them in wait.

Yanking me towards him and grabbing me under my thighs, lifting me up and setting me on his bed. Much like mine, his is also slightly lofted, so my feet dangle over the edge. His hands on my waist, holding me in place. With the extra height, I am eye level with him, even requiring me to lean down into him to reach his lips. My fingers in his hair, big soft curls not too dissimilar to my own. Though his are always free. Much like the rest of him.

His hair is also longer than most of his peers and much darker than mine, a multi-dimensional brown with flecks of caramel and whiskey tones that become visible in the way it moves, and his eyes mirror the natural pulled colors of him. A golden brown patterned like tree bark. There is no denying he is attractive, but he is more than that, he is organically beautiful.

I've seen him shirtless before, lounging on the couch in the main room, or if we all ventured to the gym. But I've never seen him like this. His body shifted now, sculpted for a different purpose. His muscles and tanned skin were not just crafted for visual appeal, but developed naturally from all the time he spent outside. Hiking, swimming, climbing, playing soccer. And his touch on my skin felt as if he was clinging to the side of a mountain. Hand rough, and fingertips gripped on my waist like he's holding on for dear life. Maybe he is. *And maybe I am living for it.*

Having me perched on the edge of the bed, he settles himself to stand between my legs. Hooking his fingers onto the fabric of my panties and dragging them down, slipping one leg out and letting them go until they dangle from my other foot before falling to the ground between my feet where he stands.

There I sit, bare, on his bed, his navy sheets soft against my skin, as he makes quick work of removing his own clothing. Returning to the place between my legs only once he's completely naked. I realize how comfortable he is totally nude. Like it wouldn't surprise me if this was how he spent most of his time. Doing homework, sorting laundry, just himself naked as the day he was born. While I was lost in thought at the idea of Ethan sitting at his desk studying naked, he had reached for a condom. Wordlessly, he tears open the package and guides my hand rolling the condom down on to him.

I lift my arms above my head and discard my shirt. The remaining piece of clothing serving as the final boundary, the last bit of consent I tossed amongst the rest at his feet. And he accepted it.

He had no words, never particularly verbose, so instead, he filled his empty mouth with my nipple, arms tightly wrapped around my back pulling me down, so he was braced at the entrance, until he slid me down fully onto him... and then he moved.

I was right; he is comfortable in the nude. Animalistic. Primal. Wild. Fucking like it's his sole purpose on this earth. A purpose he fulfilled with passion, delivering on some fundamental need.

Our bodies were glued to each other most of the night. Stuck together by sweat and exchanged need. It was close to 4 a.m. when I hopped out of bed and checked my phone for the first time all night. Fishing it out of my boot where I had hidden it earlier, to find the slew of missed text messages. I saw the notifications, the texts from Josh asking where I went, if I was heading back to my dorm or his and the winky face from Stella, who knew exactly where I went. I don't bother responding to anyone now, instead just crawl back into bed. He slept naked, but I threw back on my tee shirt and underwear.

I curl into his body, and his body responded. Lips moving to mine even in sleep, I thread my legs through his and join him in a slumber, at least for a couple hours.

———

I wake up and peek around the room, just after sunrise, in a different light than I've ever seen it. I am slightly sore, slightly hungover, and in need of caffeine and a shower. As my head rests on the pillow, hair splayed out wild from 80's Night, and more so from post-80's Night sex. Seeing the man still asleep beside me, his own hair mixing with mine. I slip out from the arm snaked around me, out from under the covers and make my exit. Tiptoeing across the living room and into the bathroom he and Josh shared.

This isn't the first time I've been in this bathroom. This isn't the first time I've showered here. *It feels different, but does it have to?* I turn on the water, blindly, just spinning the knob as far as it can go. Knowing that even the hottest setting is never hot enough. As the room steams, I step into the shower, letting the water run down my skin. I scan the shower for any kind of product that isn't a 3-in-1, but I know better and just reach for it anyways. I wash and rinse off the remaining smell of bar smoke and tequila, the stickiness of the sweat and the grains of salt that had clung to my skin. As the water runs over me, my mind is thinking back on the events of last night while my body aches for more of it. But for now, I leave that desire asleep in bed with the man who filled it.

I wrap myself in a towel and I emerge from the bathroom. There he is, sitting on the couch in just his sweatpants and the abs that soccer built, soccer and maybe his ego. Feet up on the coffee table in front of him casually sipping his coffee.

"Sit with me," Josh says as I move over to the couch to join him. He extends the cup out towards me, the smell of a fresh coffee reeling me in. I plop down next to him and take a full sip of the overly sweetened, whole milk, coffee. *I wouldn't have turned down caffeinated mud at this moment.* I sit there in just a towel and kick my bare feet up next to his on the coffee table and lay my head on his shoulder as I have dozens of times before.

"I didn't know you were here."

"I can tell..." A laugh sputters out, as he takes his coffee back from me to down another gulp.

"Where's Lindsey?"

"In her bed, where I left her."

There's a beat of silence. Something that doesn't usually pass between us, it's always filled with banter, nonsense, or conversation. Trading pieces like baseball cards.

"Is this gonna be a thing?" He motions his head toward the door, behind which I know Ethan is still deep in a sated sleep.

"I'm not sure," I say honestly, glancing over as if I can see through the door and catch a glimpse of him still in bed.

"Maybe for a bit."

"You know what they say, 'don't shit where you eat'... and in case you need a reminder, you eat here plenty." His tone is incredibly calm as he hands me back his mug the remnants of the sugary coffee mixture at the bottom. He says nothing else, just drapes his arm across my bare shoulders, pulling me into the crook of his arm.

Chapter Ten

2007

HER

It's been a couple of weeks since I climbed into Ethan's bed, and it wasn't the last time, either. We'd found ourselves entangled more than once, sneaking away from those around us and escaping into each other. After Josh's less than subtle warning, I knew it was best not to broadcast it more than necessary. I'm not keeping it a secret, why should I have to, but I also hadn't been looking for anything serious, so there really isn't anything to say. And considering Ethan didn't say much of anything at all, I don't have to worry.

Like me, Ethan was not on the hunt for anything more than a physical escape. He chose physicality as his preferred form of communication, and I devoured it as he devoured me. Using all parts of himself to worship and distract me, and I did the same for him. All without knowing what it was the other one needed distraction from. We know the boundaries of what we are doing. And it fits perfectly into my schedule, with a *more than* full course load, different campus clubs, and a pretty epic social life. *A social life he is deeply a part of.* We existed to each other solely in this place, and whether he recognizes that I restrained his access to me, only allowing the physical transaction, or whether he doesn't care, I appreciate him for it.

Ethan and I hooking up didn't change much surrounding our friend group. And when Josh followed suit, actively dating Lindsey, in this case a differentiator without a difference, his time was occupied as well. Meaning his whole *'don't shit where you eat'* remark fell by the wayside. Though, even though we found ourselves in other people's beds, *our* relationship didn't change, not the way it likely should have.

The nights I spent with Ethan usually resulted in me waking up early, leaving him deeply slumbering in bed while I showered and got ready, and then Josh and I went on to one of the classes we shared.

———

Walking across campus, coffee cups in hand, headed to class we usually ran through the updates on our nights. Chatting about the people we knew, what work we had to do for our classes, what next year might look like, and this morning wasn't that different.

"I need to end it with Lindsey."

"Come again?"

"Only if you ask nicely, Miami." I shake my head, dismissing the innuendo.

"I didn't realize there was anything to really *end*?"

"Of course, you didn't."

"What happened?"

"Nothing, that's just it."

"NOTHING? Then what have you been doing over there?"

"Trust me *THAT'S* happened. It's just... it's not enough... *she's* not enough. And she's looking for more. That I just can't give her."

"*Oooph*," I let out the noise and my whole face pinches together like he elbowed me in the gut. I can't imagine hearing anything worse than being labeled not enough. Finding that sweet spot of being 'enough' but not too much is exactly the kind of high I spent most of my life chasing. Looking to be the perfect bowl of porridge. Not too hot, not too cold. *But if you have to be one or the other, always be more not less.*

But as he said the words, I understood what he meant, and in some ways, I could apply the same reasoning to my own current situation. That even though it's what I wanted, needed even, it's not sustainable, and I never planned it to be.

"*Jesus*, Miami. Why do you look like that? I'm not breaking up with *you*."

"I am just thinking how I would feel if someone said that about me." He makes a face like he doesn't believe me.

"Ethan's not saying that about you." Again, my face responds more quickly than my words can.

"I didn't *say* Ethan."

"That's what you meant. He's not saying that. He won't say shit to me about it, period. But I don't think you need to worry about being inadequate."

"Aww, thank you!" Bringing my hand to my chest, feigning surprise, and overly sweetened gratitude. He takes the nearly empty coffee cup from my hand, polishing off the final sips of the coffee-sugar mixture before chucking both of our now empty cups in a nearby trash can and using the strength of his arm around my shoulder pulls me into his side for a hug.

"We both know it's him who should worry."

And that was a different kind of elbow to the gut, one I had been pleasantly avoiding. *Fuck.* I know the situation with

Ethan has no real legs to stand on, no real substance. He accepted what it was, for both of us. Just sex. And it works well because he is purely physical and never questions why when he'd wake up, I would often have moved to Josh's room or already been gone. Why whenever we hung out, it was as a group.

I haven't been looking for substance though, not in that way, and not from Ethan. And neither had he. Not beyond what we sought out to take from each other in bed. Josh knew that as well; we had that conversation the day we met when he laid next to me in my bed.

'Tell me, Miami, do I have to worry about you finding some douchebag boyfriend?'

'Nope.'

'You've already got one?' He asked with a cocked brow, lips pulled to the side, assessing my answer. A question I think he realized he probably should have asked sooner. Though it didn't seem like it would impact the current set up.

'Nope.'

'Can't catch one?' The corner of his mouth begins to curl, the smirk forming on his lips as he delivers the taunt. Meant almost in the way of negging, a challenge, an insult, a question to test the water.

'Nope. I'm just more of a catch-and-release kind of girl.' And there was that Cheshire Cat smile. Apparently, my answer had passed his test.

My catch-and-release mentality wasn't just because I wanted to have the same sexual freedoms as the men I knew but had far more to do with the fact that whoever I did manage to catch was usually lacking. I could find pleasure in someone for a short while as long as the expectations were lowered. And this wasn't just romantic relationships. I claimed it had more to do with scheduling, more to do with prioritizing school work. It wasn't wholly untrue, but the reality that I never found the balance between challenge and rest that I needed in someone, to be more myself, was far more accurate of a reason.

Josh pulled out his phone, and on the remaining walk to class, his arm still hanging across me, he broke up with Lindsey and I felt the full weight of it.

———

The autumn air is cool as Josh and I walk to The Commons, heading to the college bar to meet the rest of our friends. Dressed in a black turtleneck, short skirt, tights, and boots, I am finally getting the hang of dressing for fall. A lot of that had to do with remembering to bring a coat. Something that no matter how cold it got, Josh never seemed to actually put on.

'I have thick New Hampshire blood,' he'd remind me every time I would shiver and inevitably reach for the hoodie he wasn't wearing. I knew that tonight, with the Lindsey chapter closed, Josh would be on lookout for something, specifically *someone*, new.

"Ready to have some fun, wingman?"

"Absolutely, it's time to spread 'em." Josh barked a laugh as I held up my hand to halt him from speaking while trying to stifle my own.

"I meant the wings... time to spread your *wings*."

"Whatever you say, Miami."

We spot the large back booth with our circle. Stella and Marlie sitting close together, wedged next to Jack and Ethan who are deep in conversation–based on the expressions, the topic was soccer. I've learned to spot those looks on their faces and to never get involved. Mostly because I didn't care about sports beyond when they had a game. And seated next to them, Lindsey. Taking a sip from her beer, softly smiling as usual. She'd integrated herself more deeply in the last few weeks.

"That gonna be a problem for you?" I nudge Josh with my elbow and tilt my head toward the table where Lindsey sits, our friends around her not bothered, or unknowing, of the fact that she and Josh are no longer an item as of this morning.

"That gonna be a problem for *you?*" He retorts, acknowledging the same direction, and I see what he's referring to. Lindsey looks entranced by Ethan. I'm not a particularly jealous person, typically considering myself far more possessive. But neither of those emotions bubble to the surface right now. What I feel considering the prospect of them together is far more peculiar.

"I actually think *that* makes a lot of sense." I slide into the booth and look at the small stage in the back of the bar, there are six chairs lined up, and the emcee, dressed in a tacky costume tuxedo, shuffling around finishing the set up.

"What's the deal tonight? Is the entertainment a game of musical chairs or something?"

"The Newlywed Game," Josh says as he lowers himself into the booth seat across from me, a whiskey glass in one hand and a beer in the other and holds them up for me to choose.

Ugh, I don't want either, but going through the trouble of getting something else doesn't seem worth it.

I point to the whiskey glass, knowing that while I hate the taste, I will at least feel far quicker, and won't leave me with the inevitable burping and bloating a beer would. *Not very cool-girl of you, Arden.*

"Oh this *should* be entertaining." As I throw the full contents of the glass back draining the liquid and return the empty glass in a slide back across the table for him to catch.

"It will be..." *uh oh*" when we win." The table erupts in laughter, and I drop my head to my hands.

"Are you nuts?"

"Nope, but you are if you don't think a gift card to this place isn't worth it."

"It's the newlywed game..." I repeated like he wasn't the one who had told me to begin with.

"And?"

"...and I don't think we are exactly newlyweds, we aren't even a couple."

"This is a college bar, no way are they looking for actual newlyweds, and if you think anyone else has a better shot to take this home than you and me, feel free... *Ethan?*" Josh turns to face Ethan, tossing the challenge to him but Ethan just shakes it away. His hair falling in his face as he laughs it off.

"Nah, man," he says to him. "Sorry," he says to me, incredibly unbothered.

I know Josh is right. The truth is, Ethan and I couldn't really answer questions about each other beyond *'what does your partner's orgasm sound like?'* Even in spending time with him almost daily, we still never opened ourselves up beyond the casual friendship we all shared. Him, because he might not have much more to share, and me, because I had no interest in sharing it at all.

"If you want to enter with him, Miami, or anyone else here, good luck. But if you want to win, and I know you do. Remember, I'm the one who knows you."

With that, an amplified voice booms through the bar, "Participants please approach the stage," and the noisy rattle of glasses and chatter soften momentarily while the other two couples, *and us,* apparently having already been fully signed up, head toward the chairs. I feel far more like I'm heading to take a seat in front of a firing squad than play a drunken bar game.

"If we're actually doing this, we should have a strategy.

"This isn't strategy, Miami, it's just how much we know each other, *which we do.*"

"That's where you're wrong; everything's a strategy. For

example, if they ask a question that requires a color for an answer, say blue."

"Like your eyes," he says and romantically blinks his own at me in mockery. But his stare is hooked on mine until I forcibly break it.

"Sure, whatever. Or if there's something that would be a number for an answer, we just agree now to say..." I gesture quickly with my hands, "I don't know, Josh, just pick any number."

"Eight," he says.

"Okay, any question that requires a number for an answer, we say eight."

"Food?" he asks.

"Yours is burritos." I could have answered that one from the stage and gotten it right. "Damnit, it's starting... You really should have asked me, you know."

"Maybe, but where's the fun in that?"

We take our seats, cue cards, and permanent markers in hand, and I assess the couples on the stage with us. Looking at them, they certainly *look* like couples. Then again, I know we do also.

"Welll hellloooo to our lovely newlyweds, can I get a round of applause from the audience?" The emcee calls out to the crowd and applause and cheers erupt across the bar. Even through the crowd, I can hear the identifiable cheers of our friends.

"What lovely couples we have here. Now we've decided to make this version of the Not-really- married-Newlywed Game a little more *interesting*. After all, we aren't expecting any of you to have taken a run down the aisle yet... but let's test that young love of yours anyways."

"Let's start off with an easy one... How did you meet?"

Oh, this is easy. He summoned me across a lecture hall by

calling attention to my tits, or, um... my tee shirt? No. It was tits. Well, I can't say it like that...can I? Of course I can, and the crowd will eat it up.

I scribble something down on my cue card, I glance at him out of the corner of my eye, trying to catch a glimpse of what he said.

"Nooo peeking!!" The emcee chides, and I snap my eyes back down to my card, and the only thing I catch is a glimpse of the smirk overtaking Josh's face.

Starting to the left of the stage, the emcee moves to ask the first couple to reveal their answers. We were in the seats all the way to the right, so I had to sit through all the real couples' answers before we bullshitted our own.

"I'm sorry, looks like you both might have different memories of your first meeting." I take a look at the first couple. She looks furious. They *do* have different memories of how they met and by the substantial differences in their answers, I think if they don't know where their relationship began, they will at least know where it ended.

The next couple's answers were in sync, 'HERE!' both cards said. Were they proud to be the poster couple of this bar? It's not like they get extra points for it. These two might be a problem for us. Though, we haven't even shared our answers yet, so I really have no idea how this is going to play out.

"And now onto couple number three, why don't you tell us how you met..."

I flip my card,

CALLED ME ACROSS A LECTURE HALL BY POINTING OUT MY TITS

The hoots and hollering from the audience coming from our friends, the same ones who were also there that day.

"HUH, welllll, I am sureee lookin' forward to what you have to say, buddy."

When his knee knocks mine, I know we have it in the bag. Beaming smile and a wink as he flips his cue card.

SCREAMED COMMUNITY CHEST
TO GET HER ATTENTION

While our answers weren't identical to anyone else, we needed to tell the story and then get an audience vote to determine if we got the point. It was unanimous: We did. We also quickly became the crowd favorite.

There are going to be ten questions total, and they started out neutral enough, but as Louie the emcee pointed out, this is a college crowd, and the rules to this game are a little different. If you get one wrong, you take a shot. And as the questions progress, they also get increasingly dirtier. We have done well so far. Our strategy came in handy when asked what color underwear I was currently wearing, and we both were easily able to say 'blue.' *Even though nine out of ten times the answer is black.*

The only question we've gotten wrong so far: 'Who initiates sex?' We both put ourselves. Which isn't technically wrong, neither of us had ever initiated sex with the other, but we certainly had with other people. We just couldn't exactly explain that to the audience. Josh was right, though; we had a chance to take this thing. And when we removed the idea of sex from the questions and instead just answered them honestly, *or our version of honesty,* our answers made sense. 'Whose bed and what side do you sleep on?' Easy. We've shared a bed enough that we didn't even have to lie. My bed. I was always by the wall on the right. As the questions got dirtier, our answers made less sense, but with only two questions left, one point separates us from the other couple. Couple number one hadn't recovered from their false start, and I really doubt they are walking out of here in a relationship.

"Currently in third place, couple number one, Alex and Jamie, with three points." Light obligatory cheers from the crowd.

"In second place, couple number two, Becca and Robbie, with six points." More cheers took hold across the bar.

"And with one point keeping them in the lead, couple number three, Arden and Josh, with seven points." The difference was undeniable. Whether or not we would win this thing (though I had a suspicion we actually might), we won this game in the court of public opinion. If this was a vote-for-a-winner thing, we would have already walked out of here gift card in hand. It wasn't hard to see why, either. While the other two teams on stage were likely actually couples, they seemed to lack any real companionship, they weren't having fun like we were, spilling our not-so-dirty-dirty secrets to the crowd and laughing while we did it.

"Next question: What's one food you like to enjoy in the bedroom, wink wink?" I have two thoughts, one, I can't believe he actually said wink wink.' And two, I know exactly what our answer is going to be.

Couple Number 1: "Chocolate" *Lame*

Couple Number 2: "Whipped Cream" *Cliché*

"Arden, Josh, you need to get this right to stay in the lead... Josh, what food do you most enjoyyyyy in the bedroom?"

He flips his cue card.

X-LARGE BURRITOS

"Arden... I'm afraid to ask... what food do you most enjoy in the bedroom?"

BURRITOS!!

As the bar fills with chaotic sounds of laughter and cheers, I lean in close.

"Come on, Josh, we both know it's only *average*." I tease.

"Only one of *us* has that answer," he retorts. Just one question left. If we get it right, we win. If not, there's a chance the actual couple Becca and Robbie might steal this out from under us in a 'lightning round,' or so we are told.

"Final question, and this one's a dooooozyyy folks, let's see how honest our couples really are. You see, I know a few ladies who aren't so honest, and a few men who are too stupid to notice. So let's find out how our beautiful couples stack up...How many orgasms did your *wife* have the last time you had sex?"

A FUCKING NUMBER QUESTION.

Without hesitation, we uncap our markers and commit the pre-agreed upon number to paper. We are going to win, because Robbie, of Couple-Number-Two-Becca-and-Robbie, doesn't look like he knew about anyone's orgasms but his own.

Louie the emcee is hyping up the crowd. Dragging this out longer than necessary, really earning his paycheck for the night, also kind of getting on my last nerve.

But my eyes cut through the crowd and across the bar, and I can see Ethan. Beer bottle hanging in his hand, elbows on his knees, perched on the back of the booth so he can see above the crowd. Watching me with such desire, maybe thinking like I am about the *actual* last orgasms I'd had, and who had given them to me, knowing that we could have answered this question. *It was this morning, it was him, and it was two.*

"On the count of three, let's have all the couples lift their cards... One... Two... Three..."

Couple Number 1:

ONE
ONE

Respectable. Consistent. Not enough to pull them through and win this thing, but at least they could know they were on the same page about *one* thing.

Couple Number 2:

ONE
THREE

I knew it. Something tells me the 'one' Becca held up was really a pity orgasm she faked for his benefit.

Couple Number 3:

EIGHT
EIGHT

There are literal gasps from the crowd before screams and laughs break out. Everyone suddenly looking at Josh like he is a sex god. Which, I have no actual gauge of. Plus, I can't help but think how fucked up it is that he automatically gets all the credit. Sex really is a team sport, and more often than not, women do a lot of the grunt work in getting *themselves* across the finish line. Yet here he is, getting all the praise.

Robbie, Mr. I-Can't-Actually-Count-to-Three, of Becca and Robbie, Couple Number Two, also now officially Second Place, stands from his seat and rushes over to Josh. Clapping him on the shoulder and leaning in, whispering something in his ear. I can tell from Josh's face it was some sort of compliment, maybe even a question asking for tips. But Josh just smiles and nods in gratitude.

"I think we have our winners! In more ways than one, am I right folks??" *Ugh, someone take this guy's microphone away.*

"Arden and Josh, come here take a bow!" We stand, he offers me his hand in gentlemanly fashion, and I place mine in it in a ladylike return, curtsying dramatically as he bows. Performed in such unison that you would have thought we rehearsed it.

"And just like your wedding day," *Louie laughs like he's funny,* "let's have our newlyweds seal this celebration with a kiss!"

This was not part of the strategy I had accounted for. And just like that, Josh drops my hand and grabs my waist, pulling me flush against his chest. Hovering only a moment for dramatic effect and lowers his mouth to mine. There's force behind it, the way he holds me against him. Our bodies reacting in recognition from countless nights sharing a bed. Though this is new.

He's taken control. His arms move around me. One to better grip my back, the other running down my hip to pull my upper thigh up to him. Our bodies are firm like the kiss, my breathing heavy as his lips are still pressed against mine, not moving, not exploring, but building the same pressure as his fingers are digging into my leg. With a flair for dramatic, he pulls my leg tighter around him, leans forward and dips me back in a sweeping motion that has the crowd crying out for more. *Gotta give the crowd what they expect.*

He pulls us back upright, not releasing me from his grip. My arms are still knotted around his neck, as he leans into my cheek, and I feel the devious warmth of his words as they are whispered directly into my ear.

"You think they enjoyed the show?"

"I think *you* did."

We head back towards our friends, excited to pick up everyone's bar tab tonight with our newlywed-winnings. My lips still stinging from the remnants of his kiss.

"Josh, this isn't one of those moments, you know."

"What moments?" He takes a pull from a beer that someone must have handed him in congratulations as we walked off stage.

"You know, like where the main characters fall in love." He says nothing, just stops his steps and halts mine as well with an exhausted look.

"You know what I mean, like a moment where we look deeply in each other's eyes after one staged kiss and feel the earth shift and realize we're madly in love, and we've just been lying to ourselves all along."

He lets out a sigh, and slowly shakes his head as he drapes his arm over my shoulder.

"Of all the nights, do you really think I'd let it be this one? When you just sat up on stage and told a room full of people I'm a mind-blowing fuck, Arden?"

"Well, *you* just told everyone we're a couple, *Josh,* so good luck getting someone to go home with you."

"Lucky for me then, we aren't a couple. Look around, there's no shortage of women here who'd gladly test out the lucky-number-8. Don't worry, Miami. I'm sure you'll do just fine without me tonight."

I meant what I said, standing my ground post public kiss, that we were still just friends. Even 'best fucking friends,' as he had dubbed us that first day. But while I was reaffirming our friendship, he had pointed out something else entirely.

Of everything I know about him, I know his ego got him off better than anything or anyone else ever could. And I just played the ultimate wingman. I was the one anointed him a sex *god*, and there are more than a few women here eying him eager to see for themselves. I hadn't noticed Ethan next to me until I felt his hand run down my spine. Landing perfectly in the curve of my lower back.

"You're all set." Josh hands me his half empty beer as he kisses my cheek. Clapping Ethan on the shoulder in some kind of bro-handoff. And walked off, over to the bar to be greeted by his new fans.

"Let's see if we can beat eight," Ethan said, wrapping his arm around my waist. The shift between men was subtle, but I leaned into the warmth of his hold and the delicious temptation of the rest of the night spent with him.

On our walk back, Josh sent Ethan a text that he wouldn't be coming back to the dorm. Translation, he found someone to help him take full advantage of his post-newlywed-game-fame. Which had worked out perfectly for us, as we got back with the sole intention of fucking until we beat the fake-8 or passed out trying. Neither really happened. Instead, the next morning, we had another non-conversation that just resulted in the shared understanding that this was done. Neither of us upset, perfectly content removing sex from the equation, knowing we couldn't go on much longer without looking to level up to anything more.

I walked out of his room, through the main space, and didn't hesitate to open the door of the adjacent bedroom. Hopping into Josh's empty bed and pulling out a book from my bag, figuring that in closing the chapter on Ethan, I could find comfort in reading a different one, one that someone else has already written, to avoid trying to write my own.

Josh wasn't surprised to find me in his room when he turned up a few hours later. Instead, just scooting me over towards the wall and taking the seat next to me, positioning his laptop between us as he has countless times before to watch a movie.

"What happened?"

"That's done." I jut my head back towards the wall they share.

"Is he heartbroken to be back in the friend-zone?"

"First of all, the friend-zone is some bullshit term made up by dudes who want something they can't have. And second of all, considering no one's hearts were in it, I'd say he's just fine."

"Well then, it was only a matter of time, Miami."

Chapter Eleven

PRESENT

HER

"All of this really happened? With Ethan? With Josh?" Amanda types away on her laptop, barely looking up, as if by not looking at me directly I might divulge more of my secrets than I already have.

"Yep. I mean, there were some people in between," I smile, thinking back to some of my wilder college days, where I could lean into the immediate gratification of a casual hook up without the pressures or expectations of a relationship. "But yeah, it all happened. And you don't even know the half of it yet..." I snag the remaining piece of croissant from her plate.

"This whole thing is just too good to be true. It's the second chance romance that needs writing."

"Well lucky for me, I'm best friends with a bestselling author." I wiggle my eyebrows at her, and she just sticks out her tongue.

I like to remind her of her status, especially in situations like this where she can see things through a literary lens in a way I don't. It's why I know she wants to talk about it, what happened since I reached out to him a couple weeks ago, why she's even more interested in what happened before that.

I might love to read, to experience it, but she views the world as a story waiting to be written. Where for as long as I can remember, the only story I was interested in writing, was my own.

So here we are, laptops open in front of us, as she works diligently away on her novel, and I do whatever it is that I do on Sundays. Oftentimes, I used to just sit here and get a head start on the work week. *Today is one of those.* Other days, I'd bring along my kindle and sit here as the official coffee refiller and occasional thesaurus as Amanda writes away.

Two weeks ago, it was different. Two weeks ago, she pulled me into her research. *Actually, I think I did that entirely myself.* Little did I know I would be opening Pandora's box. If I was different, if he was different, maybe it could have been the world-ending monsters that crawled out. Instead, it was just long overdue truths belonging to two people that would be barely recognizable to our younger selves.

This was our *new* Sunday ritual. Where we had started this journey together, she asked to hear the whole story. So that is what I did. I've gone back to the very beginning. The one that started before our romance ever did, but she needed the full context to try and understand how everything ended. Why regardless of time, or opportunity, we never ended up back together.

"You loved him," she softened her voice, not actually asking as she looked up to me. Whoever's benefit she was whispering for couldn't hear her anyway. But she spoke in such a way, as if mentioning an old love was inviting a curse on a new one. She might have had a point.

"Yeah. I loved him. Whatever that even meant to me back then. Whoever I was... yeah, I loved him." I take a slow steading breath as I think about it. "I just don't think I always made it easy for him to love me."

I had also hushed to a muted tone, knowing that even with a whisper, there was no escaping my own voice. Who I was when we were together, and even before, it was someone who spent years trying to live up to others' expectations. I loved to be loved in a way that didn't require anything from me, but I chased validation the way young people often do. Academically performing for my family back home and being the shiny mirrorball for everyone else. All while enjoying the thrill of people and unapologetically seeking out physical pleasure along the way.

I'm not that person anymore, and looking back, retelling this story from the beginning, made me wonder how much of that was because of him. Eventually getting to a place where I no longer needed the external superficial validation and finding freeing peace within the silence. The only expectations to live up to—my own.

"You really don't think he could still be feeling any of that?" Amanda nabs the remaining piece of scone from my plate now, clearly retaliation for my croissant thievery, though my attention is more on what she asked

"No. Whatever he's feeling, *if he's feeling,* it's just the memory of the short-lived romantic part of our relationship, the *old* intimacies. He's not feeling anything real, nothing current, and I think he knows that. I know that." And I *do* know that. We have shared enough texts, emails, coffees, and even lunches to look into each other's eyes and know there was no great unrequited love there. It was mostly just us sitting on the outskirts of friendship.

My phone vibrates on the table, and we both jump, the thought that we willed the spirits of relationships past into a message from him.

As soon as I realized we weren't the witches conjuring up

ghosts of boyfriends' past, *technically we had already done that,*
I muted the vibration and flipped it down on the table.

Chapter Twelve

HIM

She hasn't written back since my last email. Now is not the time to overanalyze, though I wish I could have stepped back from that ledge before I went into the mind-fuckery that has been the fallout post 'when you dumped me' text. If that wasn't enough, her last response to me included the 'was any of it real' fucking gem.

It's not like I hadn't wondered what happened. How it had gotten so far from recognizable in one night. How, in all my self-righteous glory, I thought it would be better to let her go. That she'd made up her mind. All that 'when you love something set it free' bullshit. I loved her, I set her free, and she flew off, and we all know how that worked out. What she flew off to.

I tried to be impeccable in my emails to her. Tried to be composed. Knowing that I couldn't let her see the scattered nature of the detonation of her mental grenade. It wouldn't be fair for her to have to wade through the collateral damage in my life. To watch me replay the chain of events that happened

87

after that night when we both walked away. Honestly, I don't even know how much of it is about the relationship itself. I don't have any motive or some grand arching plan. We know each other differently now. We know each other through career updates and maybe a biennial coffee if we happen to be in the same city. We've had about three-thousand miles, fourteen years, and a big fucking misunderstanding between us. We didn't just end up on different sides that night, we ended up on different sides of the country, different sides of our lives.

The casual texts we exchange only in the event of a request, or something relevant. All specific, thoughtful, none of the old intimacy. Perhaps that's part of the reason her text was also so unexpected. It broke the mold from what we normally exchanged. Even the friendliest of notes, never went back in time to relive *that*. Our relationship was friendly, and I haven't thought of her as anything more in an exceedingly long time.

About two jobs, five apartments, six girlfriends and one terrible cat of a long time. And because of our casual contact through the years, I know her numbers also. Four jobs, three moves, two dogs, and... *fuck* this is a stupid game to play.

I called Austin after she emailed me, to have him confirm what I remembered. He was a friend of mine at the time and he knew her. He saw it all play out. He was there for me after she left, trying to console me, telling me it wouldn't stick, going so far as to put $100 bucks on the fact we would be back together by fall. I didn't agree.

Now, he feels that because we were both grossly mistaken about what happened, that I should pay it as a stupidity-fine. I Venmoed him the money without argument.

Talking to Austin didn't do anything to settle the questions I had. The ones that go beyond the breakup. Would I be sitting at this desk right now? After what happened, I finished my degree and left, taking the first job I could get in New York, eventually leading me here to San Francisco. When we were young we had talked about staying in the area together. But the city lost its appeal.

My regrets are few and far between. In general, I live my life in such a way I don't often look back and lament things of my past. But I have regrets now, and it has been hard trying to decipher if that is my ego for misunderstanding, if it is for how she must have felt, or if it is for feeling like I missed out on something. *It's not that.*

I look around my office and take it in. The success of my life is most visible here. This corner office on a high floor has all the comforts and luxuries someone in a position like mine would have. I've done well here. Made my life here. This is my life, a life I worked hard for, one I *don't fucking regret.* But I do have unanswered questions. Ones I haven't been able to shake since she texted me about her friend's book. That's what this was all about. Her friend is writing a book about this?

I need to read it, even if it's far from my normal genre.

I pick up my phone with the resolve that I am not going to make any of this awkward. I am going to text my *friend.* Without hesitancy. As she did to me. *And maybe this will get her to reply.*

me: Is it embarrassing to admit I have been wondering about this book?

Knowing it's the middle of the workday, I set my phone down on my desk. Taking comfort in the fact that she's probably too busy to engage in this game right now. But also knowing that a question about a book isn't one she can ignore forever. *ping*

her: It's my fault you even know about the book. Though I should put you out of your misery and remind you it's not a book about us. It just INCLUDES a breakup sex scene. And I just err.. shared some of our breakup sex scene. Which now I understand was maybe not exactly how it went... lol

How can she 'lol' at a time like this? Alright, not about us per se, that's disappointing.

me: Then is it embarrassing to admit I'm disappointed?

Oh fucking God. What are you doing? You're not disappointed.

her: Since when are you so interested in having your dirty laundry aired lol
her: But I'll admit, this whole miscommunication trope thing is far too good to not be a novel
me: It wasn't all "dirty" and it was better than "good"

Get it together. Didn't you just tell yourself that this wasn't about her. It isn't, is it?

I had made such a point to stay composed and thoughtfully distant in talking about this, not going down the breakup sex road, because I do think that those things should 1. Remain private and 2. Should be avoided as a topic by people not in a relationship with each other. Looks like number one is out the door. I practically flung the thing open and punted it through. As far as dangerous topics for exes, we are far past that.

her: Careful there—sounds like your emotions are showing.

She's witty as ever. No point in lying about how you feel now.

> **me:** I told you. It was a mind fuck. I've been thinking about it.

Stop saying mind fuck. Stop saying mind fuck. Stop saying mind fuck.

> **her:** Should I take the bait and ask what you've been thinking?

Might as well...

> **me:** I'm not baiting you. You opened the door to a conversation I never thought we'd have considering all the times in the past it could have been raised. This miscommunication trope may be good for a romance book, but I've wondered what other events it triggered in my life.
> **her:** FIRST OF ALL–no one likes the miscommunication trope.
> **her:** Secondly, I never thought there was a conversation to raise... Why the hell would I ever bring up the ONLY TIME I EVER GOT DUMPED.
> **her:** And lastly, I think imagining the alternate paths of your life could only do more harm than good.

I chuck the phone on my desk and run my hands through my hair. She texts just like she speaks. Full of thought, authentic, and excited. I've never met anyone whose punctuation of a text could mimic the gesticulation and how they speak so well. I can practically hear the inflection of her tone and see the circling of her hands as I read it.

I'm stuck somewhere between laughter and anger at her messages.

'Only time I got dumped.' Well, glad to reset that score for you, baby. You are officially undefeated. *A lot of good it does now.*

> **me:** Please. Stop saying you were dumped. You were not dumped. It makes me fucking furious.
> **her:** You think YOU'RE furious? Imagine how I felt! Haha

Did she just really ha ha me? Am I missing the funny part of this?

> **me:** Arden, imagining how you felt, is what makes me fucking furious.
> **her:** I just don't want you to romanticize something that happened a long time ago to consider the what ifs, and cause you any more of mind-fucking.

She's right. It does do more harm than good. Imagining the options of your life. For someone who doesn't have regrets, that's a surefire way to get some. While I might be here replaying the choices I've made in my life, I know I don't regret them, and it's important she understands that, too.

> **me:** It's not just about you, there were implications beyond that.
> **her:** Trust me, I know better than anyone what happened beyond that.

Am I reading too much into it, or is she annoyed now? The truth is whatever happened after our breakup wasn't much I knew about, not beyond what I heard from friends. Deciding I didn't want to know more. Sure, we eventually reconnected, but she didn't open up about her private life, and eventually I knew it was because she moved on.

It's like my brain and my thumbs have an arrangement where they bypass all logic and before I know it, they hit send on something I might soon be able to add to my regret column.

> **me:** Tell me face to face. I'll be in town for work. 3 weeks from now.

I watch waiting for the message to say delivered. Instead, the blue text bubble turns green. She doesn't answer.

Chapter Thirteen

2007

HER

I've spent the first half of October barricaded in my room studying for midterms, only receiving visitors bringing sustenance or support. Given my over-preparation and obsession with study materials, my suite became home base for the makeshift study group for our English Literature exam, which by all accounts, is known for being notoriously difficult. Josh, Stella, Ethan, Marlie, and Lindsey all committed to the biweekly study session.

Now, with only hours until the exam, fueled on burritos and beer, we shifted our study strategy to focus on the hundred-question multiple choice section. Covering everything from Geoffrey Chaucer to Alice Walker.

"You've been through this 100 times, I think we've got it." Josh stands from where we're all seated on the floor. Taking a long swig from his beer, he stretches to his full height. Stella is passed out with her head in my lap, usually able to sleep through anything. Marlie's busy texting, probably her boyfriend Jack, who took this class a couple years ago, though he had no advice for us besides *'pray the old man is in a good mood.'* And Lindsey, who is busy ferociously highlighting passages in the textbook, cross referencing them with the study guides, and pointing them out to Ethan as she goes.

We have been going at it for a while, and I feel good. Feel confident, even. But there's no way to know what to expect. And if you don't know what to expect, prepare for it all anyway.

Not everyone agreed with my approach, but we were different types of students. Would be different types of people later in life. They just forgot that because I could exist in both worlds. In a classroom, I'm often seen as Type A, an overachiever, *the girl who sits in the front of the class.* But the dichotomy to who I am outside of an educational setting always seemed to surprise people. For every perfectionist characteristic I possessed, there were other parts of me bursting at the seams.

Josh recognized my ambition as something he too had; it was different. He lacked a lot of the patience needed and just wanted to get to the finish line. While for me, I enjoyed running the race.

"The whole point of this is to really hammer it in," I say as he extends a fresh beer to me, but I shake my head. Not interested.

"Trust me. I know how to hammer it in."

There it was. The game of verbal volleyball we've been playing for months now. I prefer to play when sober, not only because I'm sharper when I'm not intoxicated, but also because I feel like it's easier to keep everything clear. He, on the other hand, is the exact opposite. The more he drank, the bolder he got. His confidence while sober was replaced by alcohol induced confidence when drunk. That buzzed boldness is exactly where he is now. Blurred vision is one thing, but blurred lines is something I prefer to avoid, so as he pinned me with a stare, the smirk playing on his lips, I said nothing in response.

"Oh, that's right, you wouldn't actually know." Bringing the bottle to his lips and downing the contents of the bottle in his hand.

"What I *do* know is that in less than twelve hours, we have an exam that is worth 40% of the total course grade."

"Come on, Miami. This is fucking boring, let's play a game or something, Never Have I Ever?" He ignores everyone around us, focusing instead on the bait he set, knowing how much I love a game.

"How about this, Josh. I'll quiz you. For every one you get right, I take a drink, for every one you get wrong, you take one." This feels somewhat safe as I've only had one drink in the last few hours, so I am effectively stone cold sober. A beer won't hurt.

"Fine, but we're doing shots." *Shit. Shit. Shit.*

He walks the two steps to the kitchenette, pulling the bottle of whiskey from its hiding spot. It's his bottle for the nights he ends up crashing here.

He lines up four shot glasses between us as he settles himself across from me.

"This is a new game; I call it, Study Shots," he announces to the room. "Four questions only, one from each of you," he points to Marlie, Ethan and Lindsey, as if we've all ganged up on him. Stella, the only one offered any reprieve as she sleeps.

"If I win, study sesh is over. If you win," he points back to me with the neck of his beer, "well, you can play study group dominatrix until you're blue in the face."

While he pours out the shots, I scarf down the rest of my burrito. If I do end up taking a shot, or two, at least I will have something to soak it up.

I really shouldn't even be going through with this; he's already buzzed, and certainly another shot would push him into drunk territory. But of all places to start, Lindsey is ready. With the index cards in hand, she clears her throat with a smile. I think she is going to enjoy besting him for a moment, a form of retribution for the abrupt way he ended things with her. *Though she seemed to bounce back just fine.* She flips through the cards looking for one she likes until she reads the question aloud.

"In which Charles Dickens' novel do we find the characters Bentley Drummle, Joe Gargary, and Herbert Pocket?"

A dangerous laugh comes from his direction, cracking open yet another beer and taking a pull from it. Not for anything to do with this game, just his own enjoyment.

"Starting with the easiest I see," he says looking straight at her. "I'd say I expected more from you, but that wouldn't be right, would it, Linds?"

For having been seated cross legged on the floor, she straightened her shoulders with such resolve, showing off the backbone I didn't even know she had. She looks ready to reply. Instead, the response comes from elsewhere.

"Don't be an asshole," Ethan cuts in. "If you know the answer, let's hear it." I glance over at Ethan, who has inched closer to Lindsey than he had before. *I think there might be something there.*

Josh picks up a shot glass from between us, eyeing it carefully, looking as though he's going to drink it. Instead extends it out to me as he answers with ice cold calm, "Great Expectations." *Fuck. Fuck. FUCK.*

I take it and chase it with water. *Stay hydrated.*

I can see by the look on his face, there is no way this ends well. Painfully aware we are playing two very different games. Ethan is up next. Taking the cards from Lindsey, I catch as their hands still on each other for just a second longer than necessary, but more than that I notice how her eyes stay focused on him.

"Elizabeth Bennet acts as the protagonist of what Emily Brontë novel written in 1813?" *SHIT!* What is Ethan thinking, I don't think that's even a question I have written. And then the delay of the words finish penetrating my brain. *Emily Brontë novel.* Emily Brontë didn't write Pride and Prejudice, Jane Austin did. He's thrown a trick question. Maybe I never gave Ethan enough credit. It wasn't that I ever doubted his intelligence, I mean, he's here in some of the same classes I am, though I had always wondered how much of his college career was centered purely around athletics. I had gotten to know parts of him intimately well, in all ways but one. And it seems like he had far more to offer than I had originally thought.

"I thought the point of this was to prove I didn't know the answers... Pride and Prejudice."

I sink my teeth into my bottom lip to keep from laughing, though it doesn't stop Ethan from huffing out a chuckle in satisfaction.

"Elizabeth Bennet *is* a character in Pride and Prejudice, but I'm afraid it wasn't written by Emily Brontë... *shot?*" I lift the glass to him, and he snatches it, the anger of his bruised ego spilling some of the liquid onto the papers below.

He takes it without a word and chases it with his beer. I don't see anyone walking away here a winner. For him? He's either going to be victorious or drunk, and both count as a win in his mind. He's no longer taunting, instead, just turns slightly to face Marlie, waiting for her question.

"What literary character had a little sister named Phoebe, wore an iconic red hunting cap and saw expulsion from school?" His face is pulled in thought. I can tell he doesn't have confidence in the answer, but he stills his expression anyway before giving it.

"Jo, Little Women." *Wrong.*

"It's Holden Caulfield, Catcher in the Rye. It was literally the first book we read this year."

Silence. He reaches for a shot and throws it back before flipping the empty shot glass on top of the stack of study notes. The liquid drips from the walls of the glass, staining the papers beneath it. *Fine, after tonight I won't need them anyways.* We are seated directly across from each other, one shot glass remains between us, and I *really* would prefer not to take it. He's gotten two out of three wrong, so the odds are against him, but I don't know what he may or may not have retained through all the studying.

I don't need the index cards. I wrote most of them, and have been studying long before tonight, so I don't need them as a reference now. Instead I just fold my hands casually in my lap.

"Name Shakespeare's four greatest tragedies." There's a flash of concern on his face, quick, so that I'm not sure anyone else even saw it. I've seen it from him before when he talks too much about home. There's always a small concern brewing in him that he will end up back in the small town he fought to leave. But that look hardens. His lips are pressed together tightly when he picks up the remaining shot glass and downs it. Flipping it over and slamming it next to the previous one.

"The only great tragedy, is what a fucking waste tonight has been." He stands and moves over to the couch, crashing down and extending his body across the length of it.

The next couple hours ticked on. Marlie headed out early, giving Stella reason to scurry off to bed seeing as the party was breaking up. Ethan and Lindsey left together, under the guise he would walk her back to her room, *even though it was just down the hall,* and Josh passed out on the couch. I draped an extra blanket over Josh, letting him sleep off the effects of the alcohol and embarrassment, and headed to bed myself with just enough time to get four hours of sleep.

———

Walking through the living room this morning, I noticed the index cards and study guides that had been left scattered across the floor were straightened and left on the table, the beer bottles all in the recycling bin, and Josh was gone. Left in his place, the blanket folded on the couch.

As I stand in the hot shower, the room is thick and full of steam around me. The water coats my body and I continue to flip through the mental index cards I have stored. One last time in preparation. More out of expectation and habit than actual need.

Interrupted by a knock, I quickly wrap a towel around my body and open the front door cautiously. *I am not trying to flash everyone first thing this morning.*

"Hey." Freshly showered himself, in jeans and a clean shirt, here he stands. Different than he was last night. The lack of sound sleep visible in his eyes, as well as maybe a little embarrassment. Whether it be for his general behavior, or ego, I don't know. But he's shown me flickers of this vulnerability before. He extends the large coffee cup in his hand, like he always does, sharing it, connecting us, this time more of a peace offering than a tether of friendship. "Figured you could quiz me some more on the way to class."

I take a sip of his coffee, *whole milk, too much sugar, way too sweet.*

"You like coffee with your sugar in the morning?" I open the door so he can come in, "I have to get dressed, but the note cards are on the table while you wait."

"Thanks, don't know what I'd do without you." He walks in, drops a kiss on the top of my head, and takes a seat.

A week later, we got our midterms back. I passed with a 96. Stella, Ethan, Lindsey, and Marlie, all passed above 70s, and Josh said he did fine.

Chapter Fourteen

HER

With midterms over, we can all relax a bit more. Which is such a funny concept for me because my mind never really settled. I can never clear it out long enough to truly relax. Instead, the closest I can get is a controlled rest. Shelving away the stresses of the day, the expectations of my life, and instead letting myself fall into someone else's life, one that exists between the pages of a book.

Unable to escape into sleep the way normal people do, books have been a comfort, the security blanket, therapy I refused to go to. They ask questions but don't require answers. They make me think but expect nothing in return. And when I wake up in the middle of the night, they are companions that never complain, either keeping me company as I lay awake or lulling me back into a temporary state of rest.

Stella's even been known to come fall asleep in bed with me if I was especially restless. We'd lay there and talk about her current boyfriend, and she'd ask about my next 'lover-boy.' *As she always called them, though there were no real candidates at the moment.* We'd talk about classes, or this new band she heard about. She'd ask if I heard the latest about our group of friends. She would talk until she fell asleep, or I did, usually the former, and then eventually I would turn off my reading light and let myself rest also.

My relationship with Ethan post hookup never missed a step. It really had been just sex between us, and there was nothing lingering now in a way that prevented our friendship. He wasn't friend-zoned, the idea alone misogynistic, he's just my friend and never expected more than what I wanted to give him. He didn't begrudge the idea of being benched. He was grateful he played the game at all. Kind of how he lived his life, with thrill and gratitude.

And while I still crash in the suite he shares with Josh regularly, the whole thing is very Dawson's Creek. I am Joey climbing in the window, *okay walking in the front door,* and sharing a platonic bed with my best friend. The fact that Ethan shares a wall with him has zero impact on either of us.

Both men are still asleep in their respective rooms, but as usual, I'm the first one up and ready for the day. Having spent another night here last night watching movies on Josh's laptop instead of finding my way back in my own bed for the night. *Or someone else's for part of it.*

"Are you making coffee?"

I hear the soft voice and spin from the small corner kitchenette. Identical to the one in my suite across campus.

Lindsey asks as if I had some right to be here, like it's my coffee pot. When in fact, given the suspicions we've all had, and the fact that she just emerged from Ethan's bedroom, I think the hierarchy would dictate *she* has seniority in this situation.

"Just made it, do you want some?" Her face is sweet as it usually is, and I'm sure that's a reflection on how she takes her coffee. She nods in reply, dressed in a tank top and a pair of Ethan's sweatpants that absolutely drown her petite figure.

In all the while Ethan and I were sleeping together, and she was with Josh, I never saw her stay the night. I hand her the mug I've just filled and slide the container of sugar towards her on the counter.

"There's milk in the mini-fridge." She shakes her head and brings the steaming coffee to her lips.

"No thanks, I prefer it black." *Well, well, well. I might have been too quick to judge Little Miss Lindsey after all.*

"Can I ask you something?" Whenever someone prefaces a question by asking a question, I always get equally concerned and annoyed.

"Sure." I fill another cup for myself and reach for the almond milk from the fridge, the one I keep stashed here for myself.

"Do you think it's weird, you know, that I'm here? That Ethan and I are," she pauses looking for the right word, "dating?"

Dating. Good. We never actually dated. We socialized with our shared friends and had sex. We blew off steam and never committed to anything beyond that. *I also never gave him the chance to.*

"First of all, I think that if you and Ethan are a thing, that's great, really great, and there's nothing *weird* about you being young and dating or fucking or doing whatever it is you want. These are our best boob years, and we should get full use of them."

Her shoulders eased, releasing tension either from the question or the person she had decided to ask.

"Second of all, and I realize this is contradictory because I just told you what I thought, *but*, don't worry about whatever anyone else thinks. I promise you, Ethan, Josh, the whole fucking male population, don't spend their time worrying what may or may not be considered weird."

A bigger smile than before brightens her face and I think about how much of herself *she* keeps protected behind her docility. She lifts her coffee to mine and clinks the mug.

"Cheers to that."

The bedroom doors open behind her in surprising synchronization. Ethan, barely dressed, leaning against the door jamb, watching Lindsey. While Josh steps out of his own room, trading places with her as she retreats back into the arms of her *boyfriend*.

———

We sit in our usual formation in the Student Center, not too dissimilar to the original arrangement of the day we all met. It's amazing how much first meetings and the roles you fill in those initial moments become who you are. That immediate imprint becomes the shape you take in people's minds. *Which means, on day one: Be sure to pick a good seat.*

I've spent the last twenty minutes going on about an upcoming lecture, and yet, no one seems an ounce more convinced to join me than they did when I began. My favorite author is coming back to her alma mater to speak to one of the graduate classes. As soon as I heard the rumor she was coming, I went to work. Immediately tracking down the TA responsible for managing the lecture and spending the last two weeks aggressively flirting with him for the details. *It worked.*

"It's going to be phenomenal! It's Bronwyn Fox!" I say as I wave around my favorite novel of hers, the one that lives in my brain *and* is within arms reach of me most of the time.

"Noneeeee of you want to come with me? It's going to be brilliant! Josh? Stells?"

"Definitely not."

"Nope."

"No thanks!"

"Come onnnn..." My feet up on the short table in front of us, knocking into Josh's in a desperate plea for a companion.

"You guys. She's brilliant. She's written so many books, but her first one, *this one,* this journey of self- discovery, and it's just..."

"Okay, okay, Miami, I'll go." He laughed and stole a fry from the plate in my lap.

"Yes! You're gonna love it!"

"I'm sure he will." I look and see Stella, who just shrugs.

———

This lecture is being held in a different building than I've ever been in. Most of my classes are confined to the main freshman campus. Not here. And this is a big lecture hall, expecting a large turn out. The rows of seats ascend so the massive space can accommodate the views of everyone in attendance. Each row with a long-shared table, and individual chairs tucked underneath them.

This isn't a class, so my seat selection doesn't need to follow the same rules I usually do. I don't need to sit close to a power outlet for a laptop, nor do I need to prioritize the chalkboard. I don't want to sit in the first row, but I *do* want to be close. That's how I finally pick my seat. Third row up, center-right.

Taking a look around the room at the others in attendance. There are students already here, despite the fact that I am incredibly early, but if I wanted to get premium seating, I *had* to get here an hour ahead of time. Clearly, I wasn't the only one who thought so.

Settling in, arranging a notebook and the newly purchased copy of her novel on the table in front of me. Other attendees had continued to trickle in, taking seats all around me. I'd placed my bag on the chair to my right, reserving it for Josh. *He's been hanging outside the hall killing time and promised to bring me a coffee.*

I'm thrumming with excitement, my eyes bouncing around the room waiting for it to begin. *This* is the reason I chose this school. This city. Sure, there's a program here that feeds right into med-school, which is *of course* the plan, but really, it's this.

I'm surveying everyone else in attendance.

Doubt anyone here has read her book more than I have.

But when I glance to my left, my eyes are hooked on the man just two chairs over. I hadn't seen him take his seat. But he looks as intentional about it as I was in selecting mine. Unlike me, though, he's not focused on anything besides the book in his hand. Reading, with a pen cap hanging from the corner of his lips, as he runs the pen over the page underlining a section before writing something in the margin. He slips the pen back into the cap, and removes it from his mouth, tucking it behind his ear as his eyes move rapidly across the page.

I can tell he's reached the bottom when he brushes his thumb across his bottom lip, pulling it down so slightly so he can subtly and smoothly, gather the smallest amount of moisture onto the pad of his thumb before lowering it back to the corner of the page, and turn it to the next. *Fast.*

I look down at my watch and note the minute and second hands... Am I *really* about to time this stranger? *Yes. Yes, I am.* He continues like that, minute after minute. He'd occasionally uncap the pen, underline, and tuck it back behind his ear, before casually gliding his thumb across his bottom lip again and using the moisture to grip the page to turn it. When he didn't underline anything, he was reading almost two pages a minute, when he had annotations, it was half that.

Some people find pen annotations in books to be sacrilegious, others treat them as gospel. To me it feels like the most intimate way to read. Like a blood oath between reader and book. The book gives of itself so selflessly with the printed words, as the reader takes them page by page. The notes I leave written in the margins are my exchange, a way I can return to the pages that have given me so much of themselves.

Which is why most of my books have notes in the corners, dog eared pages to mark passages or sections, and written on the back cover, my overall review.

His face didn't attempt to mask any expression, as I watched his eyebrows draw together and nod in agreement with something he read. It's like I was experiencing it with him. He plucked the pen from behind his ear, uncapped it with his teeth, underlined the section, capped the pen, back behind the ear, touched his thumb to his lip, turned the page, rinse, and repeat. And I am entranced by the incredibly methodical way he progressed. And he's enraptured by whatever he's reading. I want to talk to him, I want to know what he is reading, and I want to see what thoughts of his own he returns to the page.

Perhaps I haven't realized just how obvious I've been. Constantly glancing at my watch, keeping tick marks of his page turns, jotting down in the notebook in front of me. I might as well have been doodling *Mrs.-Random-Hot-Reader-Man*. I wonder if he has one of those brooding literary names, like Heathcliff. I don't realize until it's too late. Until he closes his book, and sets it down, turning to face me with a smile broadening on his face as he does.

His eyes are the color of smoke, but behind the smoldering is a sheet of the clearest silver. The contrast is breathtaking. So much so that I don't want to look away. His face is warm and welcoming in a way that is almost disarming. And while his hair might be categorized as a dirty blonde, I don't think there is a single messy thing about him. As he looks at me, even with the darkness that billows in his eyes, he doesn't look like a brooding Heathcliff at all. Not a melancholy Mr. Darcy, either.

The smile he offered me was sincere, brightening the space instantaneously.

"If we're going to be sitting next to each other, I should introduce myself. I'm Reid." He extends his hand across the empty chair between us.

"Arden." I slip my hand into his and his grip tightens immediately. His long fingers wrapped wholly around the back of my hand.

"Your fingers are ice cold, Arden." His left hand joins his right, encasing mine between them. Giving one more squeeze of his grip, this time for warmth, not introduction, before slowly pulling his hands away from mine. His smooth fingertips linger just a fraction of a second longer than necessary as they dragged away from my skin. And though only there for the briefest of moments, I felt their absence immediately.

"I'm told it's my weak Florida blood, I'm still adjusting to the weather."

"Maybe, but there's no shame in a good pair of gloves."

"But I'm trying so hard to do the cool-Cambridge-girl look. You don't think I'd immediately out myself a non-local?"

He laughs lightly at that as his eyes narrow just the slightest, but there's humor in them as he shakes his head in light friendly disagreement.

"Number one, there's no prize for frozen fingers. Number two, something tells me you don't have to try that hard. And number three, I'll let you in on a little secret—most people are non-locals; it's a college town, after all. No point in being too proud for a pair of gloves."

He's casual in his manner, but direct. There's something nice about the sincerity that dripped from every word. Spoken in an unrushed, patient tone, one with interest so thick I can easily recognize it, I can taste it. But it tastes differently than it typically does from men. Less singular.

I've never met anyone so young that just seemed to be so

naturally confident and transparent, in a way that wasn't aggravating. His face is readable, and I wondered if that's a choice he made, to let people just see him and what he was thinking. It's the opposite of the one I typically make, and it absolutely enchanted me.

"What are you reading?" I'd wanted to ask for the last fifteen minutes. Instead I sat there clocking his page turns. Something I'm not sure if he politely ignored to save himself the second hand embarrassment, or if he had been too deep into his reading to truly pick up on what I was doing. Either way, I was grateful for the reprieve.

"I'm glad you asked." He slides into the empty chair to my left, cutting into that space that had been reserved to keep a comfortable distance between strangers, and I immediately warm as he shifts his body so we weren't just seated side by side, but he angles himself towards me so he could look at me without the added effort of constantly turning his head.

"The Metamorphosis. Have you read it?" He places the book down on the table in front of us. Not disturbing the things I had in front of me. Gently sliding it, inch by inch, further in my direction.

I flip open the cover, and on the interior left flap is a list of numbers in ascending order. I look down at his pen marks with unspoken questions, he reaches up between us, his arm brushing past mine as he does, and runs his index finger down the list of numbers.

"Page numbers," he says, offering me the answer to the question I didn't ask out loud. I had assumed they were page numbers, but there were smaller dots and tick marks next to them I couldn't figure out.

"If the number is underlined, it's the whole page I wanted to reference, otherwise the number of vertical lines and dots tell you the paragraphs and sentences."

There is something so intriguing not only about his system

for reference, but also about his willingness to share it. It felt private in many ways. Like a code to access parts of him, that's what it would be for me, sharing the notes within the pages of my books.

"I've never seen anyone do that," I tell him as I begin to flip through some of the pages he has marked. The first page number, early on, chapter one.

"Is this a metaphor, or does this guy actually wake up as vermin?"

"You'll have to read it and find out, that's kind of the point of the book."

"Maybe I will then. But if you won't give away the ending, then just tell me why you marked *this* quote?"

"It's a reminder how quickly you can wake up and everything is different." My head turns toward him, where I had been focused on his pen marks on pages; I know that he's been focused on me.

"What about you?"

"What about me?"

"You're sitting here waiting for Bronwyn, and yet you have an unread copy of her book in front of you. Are you here for class credit, or maybe an unrealized fan?"

"I *HAVE* read it!" My response is defensive. "It would feel like fraud sitting here otherwise, like I'd be taking the seat from someone who appreciated it more. I mean, I haven't read *this* copy. I just bought it to have it signed." Reaching in my bag, I pull out the more loved copy of the book that I had read dozens of times in my life and place it gently on top of his book.

He reaches for it, and as he begins to flip through the pages, stopping when he sees my own scrawled handwriting in the spaces between.

"Wait!" I say, louder and more forceful than I mean to. As I slam the book closed, my hands on top of his on the now closed cover. "Sorry, I just mean, those notes aren't academic or anything, it's personal, I wasn't expecting you to read them." *Great, now I have effectively snapped at him twice in the span of four minutes.* But there is an eagerness I have being in his presence, that has words tumble out of my mouth without the normal calculation.

"No matter how much I want to know what you wrote, I don't expect any part of you that you don't want to share." He lifts the book, and hands it back to me where I settle it back in my bag for safe keeping. My eyes drop to his lips, full, as they pull into a soft smile. "Although, Arden, I did show you mine." And the shape of his mouth shifted to something more playful, suggestive.

We are somehow locked in this moment, and despite all of the excitement I had to be here, I somehow had forgotten about everything but the man next to me. That is, until his eyes narrowed, and I felt a hand on my back alerting me to a familiar presence. A cup of coffee landing on the newly purchased book in front of me. Reid snatched his book out of harm's way just in time, as a few drops of coffee spilled from the lid and landed on the *thankfully* still plastic wrapped cover.

I twist my neck to see him, standing there behind me. Fully contorting my spine rather than shift completely. Not yet ready to release my body from the space it shared with Reid. But he has no such hesitation. Straightening in his chair and pulling back from me entirely. So the closeness our bodies had assumed in looking into the same book, was back to a respectful distance.

"Josh, this is Reid."

"Good to meet you." Reid is the first to extend his hand offering it to Josh as casually as he did to me.

"Yeah man, you too." Josh slips into the seat I had saved for him and drapes his arm over the back of my chair.

"When does this show get started anyways?" I think he was asking me, maybe just asking a question rather than saying what he wanted to. *That he doesn't really want to be here.*

With that, Reid retreats back to his original seat. Parting us again by the empty chair.

"Should be any minute. I hope you both enjoy the lecture," he says looking between us, and I wonder if the subtle emphasis on the word *both* felt like emphasis to anyone but me.

"Bronwyn is wonderful, I saw her when she was here before speaking about her last book. Be sure to stay for a bit when she's done. She does a meet and greet." *I had absolutely planned to stay. As in, I-bought- a-new-book-to-get-it-signed level of planned to stay. But now, knowing he would also? No-brainer.*

"Thanks! I'll catch you after?" He offers a wordless smile and nods in return. Unlike the others he's given me, this one has his lips pressed together more firmly, and his lips barely turned up to reach his eyes. *Maybe I misjudged the situation.*

"New prospect?" Josh takes a sip of the coffee before handing it back to me.

"Hopefully."

"Unless he's an idiot, I don't think you'll have to hope too hard. But do me a fucking favor this time and bang this one out of your system quickly. He's too stiff to keep around for Stells Bells Big Birthday Bonanza."

The only thing big about 'Stells Bells Big Birthday Bonanza,' *as it has been dubbed,* is that she's been planning the party since we landed on campus and found our favorite bar. In other words, she's been planning it since day one. *'I'm a lover of birthdays,'* she said when we met. Though I didn't realize at the time just how literally she meant it. And while I'm sure she'd love an extra guest, especially one as undeniably attractive as the man I just watched like a literary voyeur, even if there was something between us, if he wasn't interested in sticking around for a conversation, I doubt he would stick around a couple of weeks.

Applause picks up around me and fills the lecture hall, and

I see her. The reason I'm here. Not this man, but her, standing off to the side while introductions are done, she begins, and with that I drown out everyone else, completely. So much so that I can barely notice Josh on his phone next to me, texting throughout the whole thing.

Chapter Fifteen

2007

HER

As the lecture ends, Josh stands like most others in attendance who begin to make their way towards the exits. While I gather up my things, unwrapping my new book, readying it for her autograph.

"Let's go meet the gang at The Commons."

"I don't think so." I look to my left where Reid had been sitting; he stands with his back to me now as he patiently waits for others to move from his path. "I *neeeed* to get this book signed, but you should go without me!"

"Well I could never deny you anything you *neeeed,* you're my best..."

"Your best fucking friend!" I finish the sentence for him. *That's what friends do.*

"Have fun with your Lecture-Boy." With that, and a kiss dropped on the top of my head, he made his escape. Maneuvering around the people in the row, down the stairs, and all the way out the door.

I look back to Reid, who had also begun to progress toward

the exit. Currently stilled on one of the stairs, waiting for traffic to pick up again. His height is surprising, as I hadn't fully grasped it earlier.

I'm not considered *short*, but he had to be at least a couple inches above six feet. And my mind jumped back the hour in time to recall how easily his hand wrapped around mine. My eyes dropping to where it currently hangs by his side, noting the length of his fingers, as they drum in a thoughtful pattern across his denim covered thigh.

I weave through the people that separate us, and land on the step next to him, not yet sure of what to say, more so just interested in giving him the opportunity to make the move I knew he wanted to make.

"Did you enjoy the lecture?" His tone threaded with reservation. I noticed that while his expression didn't seem to hide it, he also seemed to have taken a notable step back from me, literally and figuratively. *Okay, so not quite as eager as I thought.*

"I really did, I'm going to go get in line now to have her sign my book."

"I'm glad you enjoyed yourself. It was great to meet you, Arden. Maybe I'll see you around." With that, his long legs carried him down the stairs and away from me.

"Wait!" I sound more desperate than any cool-girl should, hurrying to catch up to him. "I'm not in the graduate program, I'm never on this part of campus, just for this. Well technically, I'm not really supposed to even be here. Kind of one of those all's-fair-in-love-and-war things. So you *won't* see me around, not unless you want to." I have no problem being forward and flirtatious, but not the one actually doing the chasing.

His face stilled, his eyes hardening with clarity, offering a compensatory smile, as he lifted his hand to my shoulder and let it rest there for just a moment.

"It was great to meet you. I know this is college, but I don't get involved in complicated situations. Though perhaps next time save your boyfriend the trouble of running out as soon as it's over and just let him stay behind." His hand slides down my arm as he speaks until he reaches the end of my fingertips, and the end of the sentence. And the sensation ripples goosebumps over my skin.

"He's not my boyfriend, he's just a friend."

"I know well enough what just a friend means. I've been just a friend, and like I said, I really prefer not to get involved if you're already involved. No matter how much at this moment I want to."

It's my hand that reaches out to him now, halting any more words, or allowing him to walk away. Resting my palm against his stomach. Hard. Also surprising considering that while his shirt fits him well, it appears to do absolutely no justice for the strength I feel penetrating the fabric as if it's my palm pressed against his bare skin.

"Reid," Calmly, regaining some control, some more composure compared to the frenzied version of me he has seen so far. Mirroring back his own. "He's *not* my boyfriend, and he *is* just a friend, in the way the words are meant to be used. Nothing complicated or involved behind them. Just my best fu–, my best friend."

While our version of friendship may have blurred some lines, we hadn't crossed any major ones. The only kiss we ever shared was at the newlywed game, then he went home with some other woman and I didn't see him until he emerged from the sexcapade a few days later. I am being honest. He is just my friend, and even though it annoys me to have to explain it, for some reason it feels critical to me that Reid understands. Because for every second my hand is pressed against him, for every inch his fingers slide down the length of my arm, I am hyper aware of the connection pulsing between us. Even if in this moment he is trying to sever it over semantics.

He's confident in a way that entirely lacks arrogance. I realize that he's drawing a clear line and setting an expectation immediately. It has nothing to do with me, but what he wants for himself, what he feels he deserves. In standing with him, the assurance radiates off of him, and it makes me believe it, too.

I can tell when he's absorbed my explanation, accepting it, because the way he looks at me shifts slightly to allow the reservation in his gaze to relax.

"We should get in line so you can get your autograph."

After waiting in line for ten minutes, I learned he was here as a graduate student, but not in the literature program. He too just came for the speaker, but wouldn't tell me who he had to flirt with to get the lecture invite. He just shook his head and laughed when I told him how I managed it. '*All's fair in love and literature,*' he said.

He's four years older than me, soon to be three, as my birthday is just over a month away. (Though I didn't dare share that detail.) I told him how I am obsessed with reading but had decided to go into medicine. We used each step forward like it was a lightning round of trivia. With a goal of covering off the main topics before we reached the table.

When it was finally our turn, we stepped up and his smile widened when the guest speaker, also known as my all-time-favorite-author-Bronwyn-Fox, received him with incredible warmth, standing from her seat in recognition and making her way around the table to be nearer to him. She was in her early sixties and had silver hair that just brushed her shoulders. One of those women, unlike myself, who leaned into every indication of aging. Living for the beauty of the life story it told.

"Reid! I knew I saw you but was worried you were going to sneak away like last time." She releases him from the hug she stole.

"You know I would never sneak anywhere. This is Arden, she's a big fan of yours." His hand rests softly on my upper back, gently urging me forward. I cast him a sideways glare, and his face beams with the knowledge that I am stunned by his casual relationship with her.

"I–I, I had thought about what I wanted to say, about all the ways your book totally changed the way I viewed the world, and myself, but now, I'm just kind of speechless. And if you knew me, you would know I'm rarely speechless." *Get. It. Together. Arden. You sound like a fool.*

"Is that true? Have I stunned her into an uncommon silence?"

With a look down back to me, his eyes billowing smoke into mine, "I don't know her well enough to tell you yet, but I hope to find out."

This isn't how I normally am. The axis of myself tilted in response to being near him. Leaning me into a version of that was less concerned with perceptions and expectations of others. Instead just tilting me towards him.

Reid's stare doesn't break the connection as his hand softly wraps around mine where it's clinging to the novel as I stand here paralyzed in admiration. He gently pulls it forward, extending it towards her in a way reminding me I don't have to be white-knuckling this book, and I had come here for a reason.

She just smiles and nods, accepting the offering, knowing exactly the request I couldn't voice. Flipping to the inside cover and inscribing something quickly and handing it back.

"Actually... I've seen on the blogs that you are going to write a sequel to your debut novel, even though it's been fifteen years since its first publication, but there's so much speculation around it, and there are rumors it includes an alternate ending to your first, but no one has anything confirmed, and I just, I really hope that's true, because I think you're incredible." *Great, I've gone from speechless to rambling.*

Perhaps for all the articulation I've ever had, I lost it in this moment. In front of someone I had total adoration for.

Someone who I felt understood me in an intimate way without ever having met me. Let alone knowing I existed.

"I don't usually ramble."

She looks back to Reid, who was smiling at me so brightly and full of intrigue, and when he caught her eye, her unspoken question of *is that true,* just received a wider grin and a shrug. A repeat of his earlier answer. *I don't know her well enough yet.*

"Thank you for coming; it means a great deal to know I have readers like you. I also think I have you to thank for keeping my nephew behind. He always tries to dart out of here like I won't spot him, though I always do."

She cups her hand around his cheek, in what I now can see is familial affection. I don't try to contain the sharpness of my glare to him, as he just laughs at the secret he held from me. *I wonder what else he keeps hidden.*

"Let me know if you want to do dinner while you're in town, otherwise I'll see you this summer, Aunt Bronwyn." She wrapped him in another hug, before she leaned in and extended the same kindness to me. Something I earned just by proximity.

While holding me in her embrace, her voice is below a whisper as she says, "I *did* write a secret sequel to my debut, and I *am* publishing it by the end of the year... but don't tell anyone."

My mouth falls open, and I suck in a breath that I'm sure sounds near orgasmic.

"Aunt Bronwyn, you've scandalized her, maybe we should let you get on with the rest of your crowd so I can get Arden some air."

"Thank you so much," I say. "It really has been a dream to meet you; next time, I promise I'll have something better to say."

"I can't imagine anything better than telling someone they

changed the way you viewed the world. I hope one day you get to experience it for yourself."

And with that final exchange, I followed Reid out the door. Remaining at a loss for words, though the reasons behind my speechlessness were growing the longer I spent in his company.

Chapter Sixteen

2007

HER

"Do you want to take a walk with me?"

"Okay!" I answer quickly, and he smiles as if he had doubted my answer would be yes. The sun is high in the sky, and the day is clear, but it's cold the way I've learned Massachusetts in the fall can be. In just minutes outside, I already could feel the warmth in my extremities draining.

"It's only about four blocks from here, but I know you'll love it."

"Oh yeah? What makes you so sure you know what I'll love?"

"I'm not sure, *yet*, but I think I will be soon." He takes the light jacket that had been draped over his chair earlier, that now hangs over his arm, and wraps it over my shoulders to protect me from the bite in the air.

"Aren't you going to be cold?"

"Maybe, but I'll be fine. It's a short walk, and by the looks of it, you haven't mastered warm layers yet. We'll have to practice."

"Thanks." Looking up to him, I feed my arms through the sleeves and he adjusts the collar of the jacket so it settles on my body. I don't care that it looks a touch ridiculous, whether it be the body heat from him holding it, or the kindness of him sharing it, in this moment, it's the warmest thing I've ever put on.

We walked the short distance through the city square, to our mystery destination, turning down a side street lined with brick-faced buildings, until we came to a stop in front of a black door, with a striped awning.

"Do you like hot chocolate?" He pulls the door open and the smell of chocolate overwhelms me. It's a deep and roasting scent. Not the normal smell of chocolate, but richer, coating the entire room. There are a few handfuls of small cafe-style tables and a glass case with the most beautiful truffles, pastries, and desserts. People are sitting in the cafe, sipping drinks, sharing cakes, reading books, as the sound of an espresso machine or milk steamer fires off somewhere in the back. All while soft Parisian music plays throughout. Setting a scene as decadent as the chocolates themselves.

"I love hot chocolate, but rarely drink it. It's always been more of a special occasion drink. A making memories drink. A comfort drink. It's so much less practical than coffee." As I delivered what felt like my thesis on the practicality of hot chocolate, I watched his eyes as they focused so intently on what I was saying. Registering each word, his attention dipping from my eyes to my lips as I formed the thoughts into words that came spilling out. He picked up and pocketed each one, dropping them like coins into a mental piggy bank. Which is good because I am losing my grip for reasons I can't outright explain. A nervousness I don't typically possess in front of people, certainly not men.

"I think this is a 'making memories' kind of day. This is also the most delicious hot chocolate you'll ever have; they make it depending on your preference for sweetness, look…" his long finger pointed to the menu on the counter in front of us, where there were descriptions of chocolates, flavor profiles, strengths, sweetness, notes, like you were looking through a wine list.

"What's your favorite, something not overwhelmingly sweet?" I asked the barista. *Or would he be considered a chocolatier?*

"Mexican Hot Chocolate, it's dark chocolate, more bitter than usual and made with chili powder, so it has a little kick. Topped with freshly made whipped cream and cinnamon."

"I'll take that!" I turned to Reid, waiting for his order… would he order what I did, or did he have a go- to favorite?

"I'll have an Espresso Hot Chocolate, please. And…" turning to me, he interjects his order with a question, "would you like a croissant?", I smile and nod, "…and two chocolate croissants."

"Is that for here or to-go?"

"For here, but we're going to take it to the back." Reid paid, drops a five-dollar bill in the tip jar, and takes the order number as he guides me around down towards the long hallway. I look back in farewell at the cafe, instead approaching an all black door with an unmistakable RESTRICTED sign hanging above it.

"I don't think we're supposed to be back here?" This man has dropped smiles at my feet since the moment I met him, and this one is the kind of smile that contains a secret, that contains the joy of *sharing* a secret.

"Have you heard of speakeasies?"

"Like the hidden bars during Prohibition?"

"Well, this is like that, but… it's not a bar."

"Is this like the doorway to Willy Wonka's Chocolate Factory?"

"Even better…"

He opens the door, and the smell of the chocolate shop

dissipates. It blends with one of my favorite smells in the world. Paper. Printed Paper. Books. The commingled aroma of the dark chocolatey sweetness and musk of the pages was something that suddenly satisfied me in ways I didn't know I craved.

"This is Bardock Books. It was the first thing I thought of when I saw the copy of Bronwyn's book, the one you annotated. The books here are all used, and many have annotations just like yours. Find the right one, and it can be like reading someone's journal."

There is an intimacy to this place; even with other people here, it feels private in a way like you can get lost here behind a stack of books or in one. It's somewhere only we know, a secret garden where he has the key.

The room is longer than it is wide, and navigating it through it is a maze of the best kind.

Nestled in a small alcove of bookshelves is a small table tucked away to the side with two large wingback chairs on either side. I feel like we're the first ones to discover this.

I slide his jacket down my arms, and he catches it by the collar to help me out of it, hanging in on the back of the chair I stand next to.

"I'll leave this here in case you get cold."

He takes the seat across from me, and our cocoas and croissants are delivered to the table. This isn't just a cafe table. Just like this isn't just a book shop. It's painted like a scrabble board. I trace my finger over some of the painted tiles, swirling them on the wood and take a sip from my large mug. The heat and bitterness fill my mouth, leaving behind a lingering tingle from the chili. The cool whipped cream hangs on as I pull away the mug, curling my tongue up to run it across my top lip, licking it clean.

He wears his emotions, we are different in that way, but something about being around him makes me want to lower that guard just enough that he felt it was an even exchange, not just a reflection. There is something about his sincerity, and assuredness, that makes it clear he feels he can be exactly who he is without regret, and it's contagious. He doesn't hide what he was feeling, and that's why I see so clearly the unbridled desire in his smile.

"Looks good," he says, bringing his own mug to his lips. As much about me as the decadent drink.

"Do you like scrabble?" Inclining his head to the board on our table. Shifting the saucers and croissant plate off to the side, making the painted board beneath them visible.

"I don't *like* scrabble, I LOVE it, but this has been such a nice day, it would be a terrible shame if it ended poorly when I inevitably kick your ass."

"As much as I'd like that, *and trust me I would*, we are going to play a different version. Not because I'm a sore loser, but because there's a way we can play and both win." He retrieves a hanging bag from the side of the table, one I hadn't noticed was there. Emptying out all the tiles and handing us each two tile stands.

"What's this version where we both win?"

"We'll divide up the tiles, each taking half. You can put down any word, any adjective, any proper noun, any abbreviation, *anything you want*, as long as it is something to do with you. When you lay down the word, you have to explain it. I'll do the same. We play until we run out of tiles, or I know everything about you, whichever comes first."

"We might be playing for a while then..."

"That's what I'm hoping for." *Me too.*

"What about points?"

"We can track points the same way you do in normal scrabble, but I'll tell you now, Arden," that smile pulling on his lips, "I won't need to keep score to know if I've won, because if

I walk away from this table knowing you more than I do now, it won't matter how many points I have."

I've never felt anything like this. A boldness without arrogance, just matter of fact, and it does something to me. Not just in a way that makes it clear I want him, but I also want to *know* him. Maybe we both can win this game, walking away with a little more knowledge about the other than we had going into it. As his jacket hangs on the back of my chair, the smell of books and cocoa surrounding me, I can also smell him. The fabric from the jacket left the scent of him cocooned around me, even just the smallest amount.

I reach across the table for one of the croissants and take a full bite. My eyes practically bulge from my head as I chew the flakey buttery pastry, and hold back a moan that should only be reserved for something far more salacious.

His elbows on the table, hands folded, and his thumbs tracing the lifelines of his alternate hands repeatedly, so slowly, as if imagining they were touching something else. *The same thought I have.* I imagine what it would be like to be with him. How would all these things translate to him in bed? *Fuck it, how would they translate if I pulled him into that restroom we saw.*

My silence must have come across as hesitation because he says, "I'll even let you go first… just this once."

"In this case, I think *you* should go first, just this once." I say it, not as a gesture of good sportsmanship, but because I wanted to see just how personal we planned to get. We divided the tiles evenly, I lined up as many as I could on the two tile racks before creating little piles for the rest of them. Grouping them together by consonant or vowel. I can tell he does the same.

Taking a sip from his cocoa with one hand, he lays down his first word with the other.

B-R-O-T-H-E-R.

"I have two sisters." He offers an explanation for his word

choice, and this introductory taste makes me more curious about his family, about his life.

"Older? Younger?"

"Both older, both totally nuts, but both really great," he replies with a low huffed chuckle. The laugh coming from a clear memory that he recalled at the thought of them, one of happiness and even contentment. But by asking, I have just committed to this game of scrabble truths.

"Okay, double letter score for the H..." I pull a pen and paper from my bag and set it on the table, ready to add up the points.

"How about I keep score, and you can just focus on kicking my ass." Teasingly, he slides the pen and paper away from me. Pops the pen in his mouth to uncap it, leaving the cap hanging there as he draws a vertical line down the center of the page, and a horizontal one intersecting it at the top. Dividing the sheet in two columns. In the column on the left, he writes RJ, which must be his initials, before he looks up at me and asks, "What's your last name?"

"Bancroft, with a B."

He puts the pen back to paper and adds AB in the column to the right. Caps the pen and tucks it behind his ear.

"Alright, AB, you're up."

Chapter Seventeen

2007

HER

We played our own version of scrabble for hours, laying down words that clued into pieces of our lives. More often than not, the word would trigger a whole offshoot conversation. Follow up questions about our families, our interests, words we would use to describe ourselves.

He played the word T-R-A-V-E-L, and we spent thirty minutes talking about all the places we would like to go. Like me, he was more of a museum traveler than a resort traveler, though he loved any opportunity to get away.

I played the word R-E-A-D-E-R, and while he originally said that shouldn't count, because that was the one thing he knew about me, he did eventually let it slide with the stipulation I tell him about my favorite books. We talked more about his aunt, the author, *because she's one of my favorites,* and he told me what it was like growing up in an accomplished family. When I played the word D-O-C-T-O-R I explained how both my parents are in medicine, and that becoming another Dr. Bancroft has been the plan for as long as I can remember.

He played the word T-E-N-N-I-S. I learned that he played with his dad a couple times a week growing up. He learned that I dropped out of tennis camp after just two days.

"I didn't have you pegged for a quitter."

"I'm not, that should tell you how much I dislike tennis."

He laughed at that, but without judgment. Simply offering the chance to take another swing at it with him sometime. *Yes, 'take another swing at it.'* And I burst into laughter at the terribly cliché pun that lit me up from the inside.

I played the word C-O-F-F-E-E and he asked my go-to order, vanilla almond milk latte. He preferred a bone dry cappuccino, which for everything I had learned about him so far, somehow made sense.

When he played the word H-O-N-E-S-T, I believed him.

When I played the word B-O-L-D, he said he noticed.

We went on like that, learning the big and small things through little wooden tiles. He eventually gave up keeping score, setting the pen and flipping over the paper pushing them off to the side.

It wasn't until he laid down the word P-L-A-Y that my face pinched in curiosity.

"I ran out of letters for the full word."

"Play-er?" I asked, my eyes focused, surprisingly concerned by his answer as I slid two tiles from another word to tack on the -E-R that were missing

It shouldn't matter; up until this point, I haven't bothered worrying about the whos and whats of what people were doing. In many ways, I've been the one who had been eager to play the field. *Or whatever the dumb expression is that men use.* But Reid had made the great proclamation that he 'doesn't get involved with people who are already involved.' Either he was lying then, or lying now.

"Play-*ful*," he responds, and the unease I had refused to acknowledge taking shape in my gut began to relax. The look in his eye *is* playful. As he looks at me, I don't think there was anything boyish about the way he meant it.

We reached the end of the tiles when I lay down my last word. Also missing some key letters, I-N-T-E- R-E-S-T...

"I, uh, also ran out of letters for the full word."

"-ING?" Moving the letters from other places on the board to complete my word from INTEREST to INTERESTING.

"Because I agree." The compliment in those words scratching the itch that exists deep within me, and has for most of my life.

I had tasted it when we first met. When his body first came close to mine under the guise of showing me his book. I could feel the thickness of it as he spoke to me. He found me interesting, which isn't entirely uncommon, in fact, it's something I try to be, but his interest was more layered than any I had experienced.

He isn't just interested in getting me, but in getting to know me, and in sharing himself with me. And he has no reservations in doing so.

I shake my head, and move away the three tiles he added, replacing the I-N-G with an E-D, changing the word from INTERESTING to INTERESTED. As I did, I felt a nervousness I don't usually when flirting. I *am* bold.

"I told you we both would win this round. Next time, however, I would *really* like to see you kick my ass... or at least try." He picks up the scorecard, folding it and putting it in his pocket.

He begins scooping away the tiles, filling them back into their bag for the next players. But I spot his left hand casually flipping one of the tiles between his fingers. Just rolling it over the backs of his knuckles mindlessly. It's hypnotizing.

In the silence, I hear the subtle buzzing of my cell phone,

and my trance is broken. Checking it for the first time in hours to find a slew of texts and a handful of missed calls.

BFF Josh: meet me at the commons
BFF Josh: did you get lost?
BFF Josh: where are you
BFF Josh: wtf Arden what happened to you today

Stells Bells: Josh just stopped by looking for you.
Stells Bells: Everyone is coming over tonight!! Come home!

Mom: How was the lecture? Did you sign up for the Dr. Langley lecture also? Would be a good reference for med-school applications.

"*Shit.*" Not as much of a whisper as I intended.

"Everything okay?" he asks with growing concern.

"Yeah, I think I just kind of fell off the face of the earth today, and people are wondering what happened to me."

"People?" He's skeptical and doesn't hide it.

"Yeah, my suitemate, a few from Josh, whom you met, and my mom."

A flash of something more serious crossed his face, his smile retreating.

"Arden, this has been great, but I meant what I said. I don't want to get involved in something messy. That's just not who I am, and that's not what I'm looking for. If there's something going on there, I understand it, I respect it, but I respect myself enough not to get involved in it."

"And I *meant what I said earlier.* There's nothing going on there. We aren't together. He has just been a good friend. I understand what you're saying, and good for you to be able to be so clear, but I don't want this to be a thing where I'm going to be constantly defending myself to you." My tone might have been on the defensive, even though he wasn't accusatory at all. He was just being direct. Giving me an opportunity to think clearly about the situation.

"You should never feel like you have to defend any part of yourself to me, or anyone else for that matter. You tell me he's just your friend, I'll trust you. I know myself and prefer to set that expectation out of the gate, especially when I am *interested*, that's all I am doing."

'Interested.' His use of it now is a clear intentional nod to the last word I played. A reference to the fact that we both clearly feel something here, he just was unguarded in articulating it beyond scrabble tiles.

"You trust me even though you barely know me?"

The smile broadens on his face, and his eyes brighten, whipping out the scorecard from his pocket and waving it across the table. His reach is so long, I can feel the flutter of air it fans on my face, almost imagining the brush of the paper against my nose.

"I'd say better than *barely*, AB."

I have never experienced anyone like him. So clear in what he means, not standing on ceremony or hiding behind masked emotions. Just articulating what he wants, what he expects, and not asking for anything in return except honesty. And it made me want more of him.

"Maybe you do. But we'd have to play another round or two before you can get to all my deep, dark, dirty secrets." The way his eyes change from silver to smoke, the darkness behind them all lust. I wonder if it's real, the way they shift, or if it's just something I want to see.

"Should I dump back out the tiles? We can change the rules again. This time, deep, dark, dirty secrets only." But I glance down at my watch knowing I've been gone the whole day, that Stella is about to have a room full of our friends.

"I want to, but I should probably be heading back to campus. Can we come back here, though? You were right..." I say to him as I begin to rise from my seat. He follows suit and stands when I do, adjusting himself to his full height.

I look up to him, and it's an odd sensation, to have to crane my neck upwards to see him, but without feeling the slightest bit inferior. Somehow even with the eight inches that separate us, he doesn't make me feel the least bit small.

"What was I right about?" A deep playfulness in his voice.

"You said I would love it..." I waved my hands around, swirling the air around me to indicate it was this place, this time, that I loved. "You were right, I do."

I can sense the smallest shifts in him, and I can tell he feels like he won our game before we ever started playing. The fact he knew me before I laid down the first tile. He walks closer to me, plucks the jacket off the back of the chair, and holds it out so I can thread my arms through.

"I live just a minute down the block. I'll walk you back to the dorms, but I think the temperature will have taken a dip now that the sun has gone down. Do you mind if we stop by so I can grab another jacket before we get you back to campus?"

"You don't have to do that," I begin to shimmy his jacket down my arms, ready to hand it back to him. His hands gripped my upper arms, halting the removal of his jacket, of what feels like him, from my body. He pulls it back up over my shoulders and tugs it at the collar. Sweeping my hair out from under it, brushing his fingers across my neck as he does. I sucked in a breath and the corner of my bottom lip pulled in with it. Biting slightly down on it in response to the unexpected shiver his touch sent down my spine.

His eyes warred between steel and smoke, the smoke in them churning over as he looked at me. He clenched his jaw ever so slightly as the side of his mouth pulled up, warm and inviting.

Our eyes are locked, as his hand snaked around from the back of my neck, up the side of my jaw, his fingertips trace my skin before landing with his hand gently cupping my face. His thumb reached up and plucked my bottom lip, freeing it from my teeth as he ran the pad of his thumb smooth across my slightly moistened lip, before removing his hands from me entirely. Stepping back and putting them in his pockets.

"I know I don't have to. I'd like to walk back with you, and rather than one of us being cold, I can easily grab another jacket. I really don't live far."

"Is this all just a ploy to get me back to your apartment tonight?"

"Arden, you're welcome to come back and spend the night right now, don't think I won't enjoy it. We can order dinner, we can play another game, watch a movie..." he paused as his eyes narrow, taking a step forward again, reaching up and tucking the hair behind my ear, "but I don't do ploys, or scheme, I'm not going to try and convince you to do anything. I won't need to."

There it was again. That confidence unlike anything I had ever seen. Wrapped in authenticity, not arrogance. I knew he meant it, and we both knew he was right.

His apartment is just a block down from my new favorite place. Which explains why he knew it so well. Why he had felt so comfortable there. We approach the brick building, a few front steps and a recess with unit numbers and a call box.

"I'm 2A." He says as he uses the key and opens the door to the mail vestibule. And I log that in my mind. Undoubtedly knowing I'll be back, and I think that's why he said it. Making sure I know exactly where to find him. He makes his way up the stairs stopping on the second floor, his door just right off the landing.

Flipping to a different key in his hand, he inserts it in the lock as I stand back against the wall to his side. Pausing to open it, "I'll only be a minute, but to prove to you this wasn't any kind of ploy," he throws out the word teasingly, "you can stand on this side of the threshold. *Or*, you can come in and look around."

He pushed the door open, and held it there, offering me the chance to come in, which I took without hesitation.

Dramatically crossing through the doorway, extending one leg out in slow-motion, and pulling the other one through behind it.

"This feels like a one-small-step-for-man kind of moment," I say.

He laughs, "You think this is as monumental as landing on the moon?"

"I don't know yet, maybe." I offer him the sincerity of my answer, the vulnerability in it, as he has offered me all day. Though to him, transparency and honesty aren't vulnerable things. To me, I protect myself by limiting them. And that earned me a totally different kind of smile.

Looking around, he's got a quaint one-bedroom apartment. Brick walls that match the exterior of the building. A kitchen immediately off the entrance, with a countertop that divides the space and two tall chairs to match. He has a brown leather sofa with a clear indentation from what must be his default spot, a single reading chair, which I was able to identify by the strategically placed lamp and six stacked books on the ground next to it, there's a desk, and... a standing piano? The top with stacks and stacks of books.

He follows my eyes around the room, watching me, mental assessing his stuff. He was so open with letting parts of himself be known. Whether it be the notes in the novel he was reading or letting me into his apartment without any pretense or expectation.

"The piano was here from the owner; they didn't want to move it, and I happen to play, so I bought it from them at a great deal."

"You play? I didn't see that on the scrabble board."

"I play *some*, what about you?"

"... some." I head over to the piano, and take a seat on the bench, lifting the fallboard and exposing the keys. Before straightening my back like I am about to perform with the Boston Philharmonic, I can see him from the corner of my eye. His arms are crossed as he leans against the kitchen counter.

"I should warn you, I've been told I'm very, *very* good."

His jaw ticked, and eyes narrowed, every indication that it was taking effort not to cross the distance of the room.

"I have no fucking doubt." A voice rougher than I'd heard from him yet filled the space, and as I breathed, I swallowed it down.

I theatrically clear my throat, set my hands in position, and begin to play... *Chopsticks*. The go-to song for every child that sits at a piano. Not anything of skill or talent, and certainly nothing that constitutes 'playing *some*.' It was rudimentary, silly, and I couldn't keep the joke up or halt the bubbling laughter as I turned and to find him fingers pressed to his lips forcing himself to remain composed, perhaps out of concern or politeness. And with my laughter, his burst free.

Then he does it, taking the three steps to join me on the bench. He glances down at my hands, as I do his. I can tell from his structure alone he knows what he's doing, and I wonder if he thought the same thing. I shift my hands, outstretch slightly over him so I can better reach, and resettle, beginning to play again. This time, something a little *more*. Moonlight Sonata, by Beethoven. I felt his eyes follow my fingers, felt them crawl up my arms, until his eyes were on me. I've been playing this piece for as long as I can remember. It's beautiful, a bit haunting, but far from complicated, so it takes little effort for me to turn and meet his gaze. Perhaps part of the reason I picked it. Knowing that the distraction I felt just by his presence wouldn't pull me away from playing, I could do it blindly.

He pulls his lips to the side and shakes his head. "How about something a little more cheerful?" The quickest of smiles flashes across his face when I pull my hands back and he positions himself. We're sharing the small wooden bench, our legs touching from hip to knee, and I am hyper aware of every place our bodies are joined.

He begins to play. It's far more upbeat, downright whimsical, and so familiar.

"Is this..." he inclines his head and looks at me, waiting to see if I can answer, "is this the Little Mermaid?!?"

"Yep! Sisters," he says with a shrug of his shoulders as if that should answer it. "I had to counteract your dreary choice of Beethoven."

"Well next time, I'll come more prepared, especially seeing as it seems you play more than *some.*" I raise my eyebrows at him and give them a little wiggle. *God, Arden. Be cool. Be cool. Be cool.* Emphasizing that he may have been a little too modest in his ability, granted, so was I, but while he may have chosen the soundtrack from an animated children's movie, it was far more technically complex than what I just played.

"I'd like that," he says, closing the fall board and standing from the bench. He heads to his bedroom, and I peer down around the doorway to catch a glimpse. His bed is made, and it's much bigger than my standard dorm room twin; he has a single nightstand on the right-hand side, *guess that's his side,* with a lamp and another stack of books, this one only two high.

He emerges from the room, carrying with him a knit scarf, before opening the hallway closet and grabbing a coat from the hanger. I step closer to the front door, closer to him as he puts on his jacket. Standing there, waiting for me, he runs the scarf through his hands. When he has each end in grasp he drapes it gently around my neck, not releasing the ends, but tugging them, tying us together, pulling me into him and landing my body flush against his. I look up at him, wishing I could think of something clever to say, but the words that were usually so easy for me to find, don't string together as easily in this moment. The instinct to rise on my toes and kiss him is so overwhelming I feel I could drown in it. But all I muster is a fumbled, "Ready to go?"

The smell of him all around me, and I'm not sure if it was actually him, or the sensation crafted by my brain, by today, that made him smell like paper and ink, like cinnamon spice and cedar, but it wraps around me so completely and fills my nose so deeply I can taste it.

He leans down and plants a controlled kiss on my lips. Testing the invitation of it. When I throw my arms around his neck, he releases the scarf, wraps his right arm around my lower back, pulling me up deeply into his chest, my toes the brushing the ground, as his left hand slides up my spine, between my shoulder blades before taking a firm grip on the back of my neck, his fingers tangling in my hair. That hand tilted my head back so he could gain access to my mouth and deepen the kiss that is building between us. He trails his kisses, which intensified the moment they felt the return of mine, moving from my lips to my cheek, down my neck. Where he lowered me back to the ground slowly, steadying my feet. His breath on my skin, not removing his mouth from where it now nestled by my ear.

"*Now,* I am ready to go."

The gruff in his voice was just another part of him he didn't hide. His desire. He lets it come through without restriction, though he still has restraint. His hands pulled back, each one taking an end of the scarf that was left hanging, before looping it around my neck, wrapping me in its warmth. Adjusting it ever so slightly as he leaned in once more and planted another kiss to my lips. This one is quick. Like a dot atop the column of an i. Balanced on the strength of the longer, lingering kiss.

He opened his front door and we descended the stairs, back

out into the cool night, when we walked the mile back to my dorm.

The weather might have had more bite in the air than I'd experienced yet, but as we walked back, wrapped in his jacket and our conversation, I was perfectly warm.

Chapter Eighteen

2007

HER

Reid walked me back to my door. On the way back, he told me more about his sisters; one of them was getting married soon, and he was going to be a groomsman. We talked about politics, and while he disagreed with me on some minor points, it ultimately made for a more interesting and challenging conversation.We talked more about the piano. He started playing when he was ten, I started playing when I was five. I teased that meant we have almost been playing the same amount of time, him being four years older than me. His grandmother taught him how to play when she moved in with him growing up. *'No one else in the family got lessons,'* he said with a mourned smile. Likely missing the woman who gave them, who he told me passed away a couple years ago. I told him how I had a piano tutor, but that my primary instrument was violin, something I started learning at the age of three. *'Intense,'* he said and then asked if I was a little prodigy. To which he earned an eye roll in reply. He said he'd like to hear me play, but I told him it had been a few years. When he asked my favorite piece to play, I was too happy to share.

Knowing his expectation was something classical, but he smiled in surprise when I told him it was the score from Lord of the Rings.

We talked more about my plans for school, and eventually med-school, and while science wasn't 'his thing,' he did rattle off the song that showcased his memorization of the periodic table. He told me about his Master's degree, which is almost completed in Business Administration, and what he planned to do afterwards. There was nothing I asked that went unanswered. Nothing evasive in him. And when he asked me something in return, he was intent on knowing the answer and more. Never just the *whats* he asked but the *whys*.

We hadn't exchanged numbers prior to now, as we finally made it back to my door. Not having looked at my phone since I last noticed the what-the-hell-happened-to-you texts, I realize I've since accumulated a few more of the usual characters. Throw in Marlie and Ethan for good measure. *They are all acting like I had gone missing or something.*

As we stand at my door, my keys in my hand, he steps further into me, like he had all day, closer and closer only after testing the space, being sure I would allow it. I go to remove the jacket, and he stills my arms.

"I think you better hold on to that. At least until I can be sure you have a replacement."

"You sure this isn't just another ploy to see me again?"

"I told you, I don't do ploys, I don't need to. So, I'll be clear, I want to see you again."

"You can always come in now if you want."

"As great as that sounds, and as much as I do *want*..." He clears his throat, but it doesn't clear the desire that's whirling, building between us. "Your friends have been looking for you all day, and I have to get going. I'll talk to you tomorrow, and we can plan something."

He leans in and kisses me, his hand moving to my neck and sliding up to cup my cheek. His fingers trail my jaw, tipping my chin upwards so he could more freely meet my lips, and I release the subtlest hum the moment he introduces his tongue. Parting my lips with it, curling it slowly into my mouth, before he pulls away. Returning just one second more to plant a quick signature against my lips, stepping back so I can see the remnants of our kiss visible on his.

His left hand grips the hanging end of the scarf and unloops it until my neck is bare, and he wraps it around his own.

"You can hold on to the jacket, but this," he holds up one end of the knit scarf and waves it in between us. "*This* is my favorite scarf." His face breaking out in the smile I've become too addicted to in a short period of time. Another kiss, this one on my cheek, as he turns back down the hallway and walks off.

I open the door, and it's surprising I hadn't heard any of the commotion from the other side. Encircled around our coffee table playing a round of Kings. Another game where the sole purpose is to drink. They are downright roaring in laughter and as I come into focus, they erupt in cheers, clearly already drunk enough to be a few rounds in.

"ARDENN! WE MISSED YOU!" Stella throws her arms in the air, spilling the contents from her red solo cup as she does. Raining the bubbly liquid down on the cards on the table.

"Opa!" They all scream in response.

But my interest is singular. Focused on how much I would rather chase after Reid, and I lose myself momentarily in the thought of what the night would have been if I did. Rather than float off in the daydream of it, I'm weighed down by the arm landing around my shoulders and pulling me into a side squeeze.

"Come on, Miami, you've got some catching up to do." Josh guides me over to the group, before landing us both on the couch with a thud. Never releasing me, so I kick off my shoes, tucking my feet up under me and lean into the crook of his arm.

"I'm good–I'm pretty exhausted, and I have a bunch of schoolwork to take care of."

"Booo!" Marlie slurs in response, as Stella pouts her lip at me in annoyance that I'm not going to participate in their plans for the night. I laugh a little to myself as Josh stiffens a bit to my side. Taking a gulp from his cup before handing it to me.

"Exhausted huh? Lecture-Boy that good?" He cocks his eyebrow, and his stare is full of questions. *One in particular it doesn't look like he really wants an answer to.* I cut him a sideways glare in response, "I wouldn't know."

"Whaaat?" he responds with insincere confusion.

"I *said*, I wouldn't know... *yet.*" I chug the rest of his beer and hand him back an empty cup as I stand and head to my room. Passing Stella, who is seated on the floor, I lean down and plant a kiss on top of her head. "Night, Stells!"

I shut the door behind me and drown out the noise with the highlight reel playing in my head from the last twelve hours as I settle in at my desk to do some studying for the week. The vibration from my phone distracts me, but when I see his name pop up on the screen, the whirling that had been around us is now contained within my stomach. Churning nerves, a type of excitement I've never had for someone so intensely. So immediately.

> **Reid:** I was going to call tomorrow, but I don't want to wait. How about coffee tomorrow morning?
> **me:** I have class midday, but YES! I'd like that.
> **Reid:** I also have something for you. me: That should have been your opener...

me: But isn't it a little soon for a new suitor to bestow gifts?

Okay, Arden, so weird is the vibe you're going for.

Reid: Is that what I am, a suitor? Maybe I should have asked about your dowry before getting such a coveted gift?

He's into it. He must really be into me.

me: Don't worry! My dowry is great, 15 cows! Can you believe it?! Might even get a goat if you work for it.
Reid: Trust me, AB. I'll work for it.

The whirling in my gut tightens immediately. My whole body does at the thought of him. The decadent, hypnotic, thought of him.

I begin to type a reply, something to match the indication that has me practically panting at the indecent innuendo. Beginning and deleting several versions of *'why don't you come over and prove it.'* I don't want this to be immediately over. So I eventually settle on something else entirely.

me: Coffee sounds great, meet you at 9, Coffee Haus?

His next reply comes in the form of a photo not more than seconds later. It's his countertop, I recognize it from earlier, with eight scrabble tiles laid out.

Reid: [C-A-N-T–W-A-I-T]

After a few hours of studying, I crawl into bed more sated and ready for sleep than I have been in a while. Even with the eruptions of drunk laughter from the other room, I lay thinking about seeing him tomorrow, ready for those thoughts to carry me into my dreams. Letting my subconscious fill in all the gaps and paint a picture of a man that I could cling to in my sleep. Thinking of him, thinking of the day, I'm exhausted in a way that my body told me to rest. And for once, I knew my brain would for once allow it.

Chapter Nineteen

2007

HER

He carried me into my dreams last night and walked me out of them this morning. So I woke up ready to jump out of bed and right into his arms. The only problem: It was about four hours too early. After back tracking every minute to figure out just how long I had to twiddle my thumbs before I could be on my way, I had finally managed to stall myself as long as possible. Checking my watch for the umpteenth time. *Okay, it's finally 8 a.m. I might as well just go. I can get there early, I'll bring my book, and get a prime seat. That's a good plan.*

Walking into our main room, cups, cards, and beer bottles all over. No idea what time they broke up the game last night, but by the mess, and lack of movement from Stella's room, my guess is everyone is still crashed in their beds across campus, except Josh who I find passed out on our couch.

I've bundled up, wearing my own coat this time, *to prove I have one,* and bringing his jacket to return to him I headed out the door. Leaving the two sleeping beauties, who didn't so much as stir as I moved about the room, in their respective slumbers.

The walk didn't take the fifteen minutes it should have. Could have been the early morning cold air, which had my nose frozen, and my hands shoved in my pockets, or the excitement to see him again, but I got there much faster than I thought possible.

Opening the door, I'm hit with all the sounds and smells of a coffee shop. The screeching of the milk steamer, the dark roasting aroma. I stand in the doorway just a moment and scan the room looking for an ideal seat, before landing on the occupied table by the window. *He's here.*

He doesn't notice me. He looks like he did when I first saw him. Pen cap hanging from his lip, book in hand, as his eyes move intently over the page, he flips to the inside cover of the book, scribbling down what I now know is a page number, before returning to the page he was reading. There is something so incredibly sexy about how closely he focused on whatever was in front of him. Whether it be a book or, well, *me.*

I check my watch, defaulting to the same game I played yesterday, timing each page. But the coffee shop door opens behind me, and I realize I am standing directly in the doorway when I am bumped by its abrupt opening.

"*Shit!* Sorry!" I jump, quickly moving out of the way. Apologizing despite the fact I was the one smacked with the glass door, I had been standing and blocking the entrance since I saw him.

His head picked up immediately at the sound of my voice, catching on me as he capped the pen tucking it between the pages of the book, setting it down, and smiled a big morning smile. The kind of ear-to-ear, can't-contain-it, greet-the-day, kind of smile.

I walked over to the table, and he stood, placing a hand on

each shoulder, and running them down my arms as he leaned down and kissed my cheek.

"Hi, Arden."

"Reid."

"You're early." He's not admonishing, but pleasantly surprised.

"Me?! YOU'RE early." He rubs his large hands up and down arms creating friction and warmth.

"Have a seat, I'll get you a coffee–vanilla almond milk, right?"

"You paid attention during scrabble."

"I played to win."

"I can grab it myself, you don't have—"

"Please, let me," he said with a gentle hold on my arm to maneuver me toward the chair. As I take a seat, he slides his book to me, the same one he was reading yesterday. "If you want to take another look."

It amazes me how freely he shares his thoughts. For me, there was nothing more intimate than what I wrote in the margins, but for him, he had no restraint in letting me see what was in his mind. Something I protected immensely. As I sat there flipping through the book, picking up on the pieces of himself he left on the pages, he returned with two mugs which he balanced impressively well in one hand and a plate of pastries in the other.

Putting the plates on the table, "I thought you might want something to eat. You didn't name a pastry in scrabble yesterday, so I went with an assortment."

"That does look like a delicious blueberry scone..." Eyeing it, eyeing him. He pulls his chair closer to mine, so we aren't seated across the table, and lays his right arm across the back of my chair. His left hand comes up slowly to grip my chin as his thumb plucks my lip from where I had pinned beneath my teeth, before leaning in for a simple, delicate peck. So easy, like he's done it for years. The act of pulling my lip free and rewarding it with his own. It feels so natural I could have missed it. Except for the fact that any time he touches me, it lingers beyond the point of contact. In a way that leaves an imprint long after his touch is removed.

"So, what are you doing here so early?" I ask as I break off a piece of the scone for myself, sliding the plate to him, so he does the same.

"Is it embarrassing to admit I couldn't wait?" He pops the piece of pastry into his mouth.

"You don't strike me as someone who is easily embarrassed."

His lips give the slightest twitch in reaction to what I said. Like the recognition and understanding I had of him already was something his body couldn't help but physically respond to.

"You're right. I'm not. If I am myself, what's there to be embarrassed about, or even regret?" He broke off another piece of scone, and tossed it in his mouth and then slid the plate back to me.

"Yeah, I guess you're right." I thought about that for a minute. I can tell he sees me thinking; I watched him watch me, and it felt like I was sharing something I normally don't.

There must be something so liberating just existing as your honest self. I am by no means a liar, not dishonest in the slightest, but I adapted to those around me. In exchange, it protected the parts of myself I didn't want people to see, as they were too distracted by seeing the mirrored traits they so enjoyed in themselves. But that meant that when I slipped out, as just myself, I felt uneasy. Knowing the judgements being made weren't against the projections of themselves, but of me, truthfully. The quirks of mine, the complexities. They could overwhelm people. They overwhelmed *me* sometimes. But Reid so far seems in search of the right thread to pull, the right key to unlock the door and walk through.

"I have something for you. Not that I used a present to lure you here earlier than planned."

"You didn't *lure* me, Reid. But you didn't have to buy me a present and you could have waited until later."

"I didn't say I bought it. And I told you, I didn't want to wait." He pulls something out of his messenger bag hanging on the back of the chair, a brown paper bag, and lays it on the table.

"*Awwww*. You packed me lunch?"

"I will gladly pack you a bagged lunch, but first you'll have to spend the night."

"And what makes you so sure I'll stay over?"

"I'm not sure, but I'm looking at you, and your face is telling me I can be hopeful." He hands me the brown bag, "Why don't you open this, and tell me if I can be optimistic or not?"

I can tell by the way the paper is folded around the contents that it's a book. I unfold the top of the bag and reach in with unnecessary caution. Slowly teasing my hand in like I might be bitten. But instead, my fingertips brush with undoubtable recognition across a spine, not of a small animal, but a paperback book.

"Feels like a book."

"Very good, Miss Bancroft."

I pull the book from the bag, and it's coverless. No printing, no title. It's bound, and from the size of it, I'd say more than 500 pages, but as I flip it over, again looking for clues as to what it is, I find none. The spine is slightly worn, so it has been read, and I open it to random pages and flip through them, a watermarked ARC soft beneath the printed text. Noticing scribbled notes, and underlines throughout them. I look up at Reid, and he smiles, confirming what I suspect, that this book belongs to him. I flip to the inside cover and find the list of page numbers, tallies, and dots, that he uses as a tracking. *Yep, this book is his. But why doesn't it have a title, or author?*

"What is this?"

"My aunt, Bronwyn, she told you she's publishing a new book, a sequel." My head snapped up faster than the sharp breath I inhaled in surprise.

"This can't be... is this... no way... this isn't it, *is it?*"

"It is. It's my advanced reader copy, so you'll also get my thoughts on it as you go, and more of a borrow than a gift you can keep, but I thought you'd appreciate it."

"Wow. This is the best gift I've ever received from a suitor," I say as I bring my hand to my chest, and fake accent to mimic a Southern debutante. *Why? Who knows?* But there is something about being in his presence that released the quirkiest parts of me as well.

"Yeah? You think your family can throw those goats in for the dowry now?" *And he responds playfully in kind.*

I move to swat at his chest, playfully as I laugh, while the other hand holds this nameless novel close to me. He catches my hand and he wraps his fingers around mine, holding them against him, I can feel each inhale he takes, and it slows my own.

We drank our coffee, I even ordered a second round— his bone-dry cappuccino and my vanilla almond milk latte—and just naturally fell into the rhythm that had us so deeply engrossed in discovery.

We've been here for almost three hours. I checked my phone for the time, knowing I have to head to class soon, but ignored all the missed notifications. Instead just sliding it back into my pocket.

"What are you doing the rest of the day?" I ask, curious about what his days look like, about how I might fit into them.

"I have class later and a lot of work. What about you? You

said you have class today?" I can tell he is trying to make the same mental note of scheduling that I am.

"A few actually, but Russian Lit is soon, but it happens to be one of my favs, and today we are going through Tolstoy so I'm excited!"

"Intense." He throws the word out in compliment not criticism. "Meet me again tomorrow, same time?"

"The time scheduled or the time we showed up?"

"The earlier the better, AB."

We are standing, readying ourselves to leave. I return the jacket he leant me, and he folds it, shoving it into his bag, having brought one with him. He holds out my jacket, letting me slip my arms into it, turning me to face him, and pulling my hair from where it was trapped beneath the collar. Acting like this is a practiced dance we've done numerous times before.

"I'm glad to see you took my advice on the gloves," he says as I pull a pair from my pocket.

"I did, anything else you think I should do?"

"I have some ideas," he responds coyly, leaning in with his hands on the collar of my coat, pulling it tightly and planting a quick kiss to my lips. He pulls away, perhaps because we're in public, still standing in the coffee shop, perhaps to show restraint, but as he straightens, I rise up on my toes and bring my gloved hands to his face, pulling him back down to me for a deeper, desperate kiss. One I've thought about since last I felt it. The one that I imagined each time I sucked on my own lip lost in the thought and memory of his first touch. One I've craved for twelve hours. One that he provides without hesitation.

I am robbed of every thought in my head. His arms wrap around me, relieving my toes of the weight of the kiss, supporting me, drawing me into him, as his hand moves to brace the back of my neck. When we both release slightly, to fill our lungs with air, he settles me back onto my feet. Planting one more quick kiss, like the period at the end of the sentence, before we walk out the door, and he tells me he'll see me tomorrow.

Chapter Twenty

HER

"At eighteen, I was pretending to know who I was, but in reality, I was trying so hard to figure out who I wanted to be. I mean, I knew who I was *supposed* to be. I always had. In high school, I was the textbook overachiever, the perfect daughter, friend, girlfriend even. I checked all the major boxes. And in going away for college, I slowly started unchecking them. I didn't want to just check the boxes when I got there. I didn't care what made sense. If it was all a contradiction. I was finally able to be somewhere and decide for myself, outside of where I grew up, outside of whatever expectations everyone had. The ones that played over and over in my head. There had been a plan for my life, a map to follow, and I was ready to stick to it, mostly, except for a few detours. But all of what happened changed that."

"In a good way or a bad way?" Amanda asks as we sit at our usual table, our Sunday ritual in full swing.

"I guess that depends on who you ask."

So much changed in my freshman year. Maybe it would

have always turned out this way, but who knows. I am happy now. In ways most people search for well into their middle age. More than *happy,* I am content. Happiness, I had always been able to find. Even then. Be it for a night, or longer. I could find it in a man, a book, a game. But eventually, I found it in myself. The peace that comes from being content? That's always been harder to find, let alone accept.

Amanda stands, "I'll get us the next round, but you need to tell me the rest of it when I get back... vanilla almond milk latte coming right up!"

"I switched to decaf!" I call after her, her thumbs up confirming she heard me as she walks off to the counter to place the order.

We sit here every week; sometimes we talk through her books and character development, sometimes our own personal development, but for the last three weeks, there has only been one real topic of conversation. Like we could only talk about it here, where it started. When we sat here and I texted my ex-boyfriend, and current completely platonic friend, out of the blue asking him to explain to me what he felt the night we broke up, the night he dumped me. Only he hadn't dumped me. Not really. Not at all.

And now, replaying the story from the *very* beginning, retelling it to Amanda, all the things I never saw were glaringly obvious.

I didn't think about it often, talked about it even less. Only landing in therapy like most other millennial women around my mid-twenties to deal with a lot of the things I had always refused to admit. The things only the 20/20, *or even* 2020, lens could fully clarify. The gifted-kid-trauma of familial expectations. The coming of age during the tabloid fat-shaming era of celebrities, and of course, the fact that no starlet ever wore underwear in the early 2000s. Pre #MeToo, where the traits of a pick-me girl were encouraged and then vilified. The

155

culmination of it all fueling this need to chase validation in many ways, eventually through something within your own control, productivity. Something in my thirties I still contend with. But going back to the beginning of this story was never just about him. Even if it started out that way.

"Here you go, *decaf* vanilla almond milk latte and a muffin, because you really should eat more."

"Thanks," Reaching for the muffin, *good–she went with blueberry*, unwrapping it, and taking a bite. I really should be eating more, not to mention that I haven't been sleeping nearly as well as I needed to. But I can't handle another lecture on the topic, so I won't be telling her that.

"He wants to meet up."

"WHAT?! Why am I just hearing about this now?!"

I open the thread on my phone and hand it to her to read. I should have just taken a screenshot and sent it to her a few days ago when it came in, but there was something we both had begun to look forward to about our *new* ritual. The one where I share the updates while telling the whole saga in a very *The-Princess-Bride* kind of way. Piece by piece, chapter by chapter. Plus, I wanted to see her face now, and get her unfiltered reaction when I told her that he wants to talk in person. And she certainly didn't disappoint.

"He said he'd be in town in a couple weeks and wants to talk *face-to-face*."

"And will you?"

"We have before; I don't see why we can't grab a coffee now?"

There has been a shift in the dynamic, even through text. His first email was easy enough, even his second, but then he decided to text me. I can't blame him really, and just like then, this is no one's fault but my own. Yet when he texted me about whatever chain of events he thinks were set off all those years ago, about what happened after the breakup, I was mad. It was fleeting, but it was the bubbling of anger of a 19 year old that had been shelved away for over a decade. When the text came in, I was annoyed so I didn't respond. I turned off my phone and tried to turn off my brain. Knowing that surely on the other end it would have done the opposite for him. Finally turning it back on hours later to a message delivered later, challenging me to meet him. It wasn't the normal lunch or a coffee we'd share by universal alignment. He clearly wanted answers for something I'm not sure I can give him.

I've spent the last few days considering it. Meeting him. And maybe I'm foolish to think it could be the same as it has been all the years since.

"Who are you really trying to convince about all this?" She takes a sip of her own coffee, as if using the hot liquid to fuel her next statement.

"He has feelings for you, you'd be foolish not to see it."

I don't say anything, I don't want to. And that silence left an opening for her to continue.

"I'm not saying it's this big secret love all these years later, I'm not even saying he's waiting for you to finally act on it, but from everything you've told me so far, from everything I read in my life, hell, from everything I've *written,* that was instant chemistry, and it doesn't burn out entirely over time, no matter who else has chapters in your story. It might not be that big burning love it was or whatever, but that never dies out completely." She settled herself, confident in what she said.

"You're really telling me you don't think he still holds any feelings for you? I've written this story. This has happily ever after written all over it."

This time I do respond. "Except for the fact it doesn't. We were only together for months, and we've been friends for years. Anything anyone feels is just that."

"What do you mean, *anyoneee?*"

I realize how I slipped up. How *anyone* feels. Not how *he* feels. I had lumped myself in as having the same feelings she claims he must still harbor.

When the relationship ended, I packed up everything I was feeling and shelved it away. I logged things in the mental boxes I tried to never unpack. Instead, just letting them accumulate layers of emotional dust in the attics of my mind somewhere.

I can think of a couple reasons, and a handful of emails, that indicated it might be better to keep my distance at this point. Be it Amanda's inquiry or the settling of the nerves, *or whatever else,* might be bubbling in my stomach, I make the decision.

"Well, how about this: When I see him, I'll ask him."

Chapter Twenty-One

2007

HER

I pull open the door at 7:52 a.m., and there he is, sitting in the same spot I saw him yesterday. Two coffees already on the table, one clearly there waiting for me. I smile when I see him, unplanned and involuntary. His smile exuded confidence, charm, and honesty. Mine always feels vulnerable, even more so when it happened without my control. Instead, I usually opted for a calculated smirk, or pursed lips, smiling more with a strategic glint in the eye than anything else. But for some reason, I lack strategy now, I just seem to respond to him easily.

He stands when he sees me, placing a hand on each shoulder, sliding them down my arms and helping me out of my coat as he plants a kiss on my cheek, his full lips catching the corner of my mouth as it curved up in answer to the feeling of him in my space.

"Morning, sunshine," Reid says. He is clearly a morning person. "I got us our table." He gestures to the small cafe table in the window, the same one we shared just 24 hours ago.

"I didn't realize we *had* a table."

"I figured after today it would be official." That feels weightier than I think he means it. *Right?*

"Don't you think that's a little fast to commit to a... *table?*" Hopefully I wasn't mistaking the implication of what he said. I hadn't been looking for any commitment when I first moved here and had made that clear to everyone else, up until now. Whether I was sharing a meal or a bed, I was direct in explaining immediately that I wasn't looking for a relationship, just friendship, companionship, and maybe a few other things. But I didn't with Reid, in fact, he had opened the conversation the first day by making sure I was explicitly unattached. I had spent the entire day with him. And yesterday morning. And here I am again today. But still the only *official* thing between us seems to be coffee.

"Well, I really like this *table,* and when I like something, I commit. But I think we should come back tomorrow to be sure." Pushing the coffee towards me, the scribbled writing on the side, Van Alm Lat. *He ordered my coffee.*

"I only just sat down, it should be hot, and you seem to always need some warming up."

"Thanks, you're not wrong. But at least I'm wearing gloves now!" I hold my gloved hands up in front of us, showing them off like a child. That got a laugh from him.

I take a sip of my coffee and let out a soft *mmmm* as my shoulders relax and I settle into my seat across from him. I can spot it the moment his eyes start billowing smoke and narrow on me. Shifting the air between us just so slightly, as I swallow my coffee and he swallows down whatever it was that seemed to have him struggle to refocus.

"Tell me about your classes. I know Russian Literature is your favorite, but besides that?"

We went through my courses; he was impressed by the extra workload and seemed to like that even though I had a plan for my life, I was still leaning in to see what else I might like. That I was really making the most of college. He told me about his own favorite classes from undergrad and about the workload he had now finishing his MBA. When I first met him, I assumed he was at the lecture as an English Lit grad, but of course later found out he was there to support his aunt. Whose pre-published book I had consumed in one sitting and then spent the hours following obsessing over it, texting Reid all night. Though, his face now doesn't allude to any exhaustion or regret on his part.

Our conversation is so natural, just an unexpected ease until his phone breaks the flow of it.

He fishes it from his pocket to check, he looks annoyed, but he silences it without saying a word and sets it face down on the table.

I'm not sure what washes over me, but it feels almost like jealousy. Like I could be envious of whoever else might have an ounce of his attention. And more so, who he would hide from me. I look at him but say nothing. Not outright asking what I want to. And I think it's because I don't really want to know.

With a shake of his head, "It's no one," he says simply.

Five minutes later, it rings again. And again, he looks annoyed. Switching it off and setting it back face down on the table. He just goes back to carrying on the conversation, as if there wasn't someone desperate for him on the other line. Pretending there had been no interruption at all.

Until again. The sound extends well beyond the small corner we're tucked in. Garnishing glares from other patrons.

"It seems really urgent—you should just answer it."

"Arden, it's really *no one*." He picks it up and illuminates the screen. SNOOZE with a countdown. My face must have said it all because he smiles. "It's an alarm. I have to get going, I'm already a few minutes late, but I set it because I knew I'd be too distracted to leave on my own."

I think the same relief brushes across both of our faces. That is until I check my own watch and see the time.

"Shit! Shit! Shit! I'm sooo late!"

He lets out a loud deep laugh, standing as he does, pulling on his jacket before moving and helping me into mine.

"See? That's why I set an alarm."

We exit the coffee shop and stand on the corner of the street. Both knowing we are heading in different directions, each getting ready to cross the opposite streets.

"Same time tomorrow?" Leaning down, finding my lips fully this time.

"Absolutely, we need to check on *our table*." I say it and wonder just what I have committed to.

––––––

While I saw everyone the other night, I hadn't updated Josh on the details of Reid. Not beyond their original quick introduction at the lecture. So, after my classes finished for the day, I decided to make my way over.

We'd become so close since the beginning of term. Regardless of the annoyance he might have projected because I ran off to bed early, abandoning whatever other drinking games they had planned, I know he's curious about Reid. He's always curious. Since day one, we've been trading the tales of our hookups. But the sheer fact that he'd chosen to crash on our couch rather than in bed with me last time I saw him was an indication that he, too, felt something was off.

I don't knock. I never have. Opening the door to find them both on the couch, feet kicked up on the coffee table in front of them. Shirtless, maybe from the gym, maybe soccer. Maybe just because they looked like that and knew they could.

"Look what the cat dragged in."

"Come on–"

"You want me to come on... *what* now?" That eyebrow pulled up into a mischievous look. Mouth pulled to the side, waiting for my reply. A litmus test of our friendship, to see how I respond to the sexual banter that had made us magnets that first day. So, I play. Volleying it right back across the net to him.

"Oh, me? Nothing at all. It looks like you have done fine for yourselves without me here." I gesture between them. Both throw their heads back in laughter. Ethan grabs Josh by the face and plants a big wet kiss on his cheek. As you would imagine a golden retriever licking an owner who had been gone all day.

"Had to make do without you." Ethan says as he stands from the couch and I land myself right in his seat. Josh throws his arm around my shoulders and pulls me closer to him. Pressing a kiss on top of my head.

"Missed you, Miami. Didn't see you last night or at breakfast today?" I *had* intended to spend time with Josh and some of our friends last night. That was the plan. But after spending the morning with Reid and an afternoon full of classes, I couldn't motivate myself to leave my dorm. I just didn't want to get caught up in the conversations or drinking games. So instead, Stella and I ordered in and then I curled up with my new favorite book before texting Reid every thought in agreement or argument I had on the notes he annotated.

"I've been busy." I offer a coy calculated smile and a shrug in return. Ethan takes a seat in the chair opposite and hands us each a beer.

"Yeah? And *who* is keeping you so busy, the Lecture-Boy?"

"That would be the one," the calculated smiling warming to something sincere just at the mention of him. I duck out from under him and lean back against the arm of the couch, stretching my legs out across Josh's lap. "What can I say, I've never met a *man* like him." The emphasis offered to try and counter whatever superiority Josh tried to drive home with the new nickname. As if tacking on -boy made Reid any less of the man he clearly is.

"Well, cheers to that." He leans over, stretching his bare chest across me and taps the bottom of his beer bottle to the top of mine. Causing the carbonation to bubble up to the top and overflow all over me. The beer soaks and stains my shirt, and I feel it running down my skin.

"DICK!" I push him off of me and storm into his bedroom. No need to stand on ceremony, I just reach in and grab a tee shirt from his drawer.

I'm standing in the middle of his bedroom in just my bra and jeans, holding his shirt against my bare stomach, giving me the illusion of modesty. This room is dark, it's always dark. Blinds drawn, lights off. But the polaroids of us, of all of us, pinned to the corkboard by his desk, light me up. A shot of the guys after a soccer game, one of Stella and I losing at beer pong, but my favorite is the two of us on stage at the newlywed game. Frozen in a moment of total joy, eyes locked on each other with we-know-we-are-about-to-win grins across our faces. *Best fucking friends.*

Out of the corner of my eye, I catch movement in his bed. Completely startled, I bolt out of his bedroom and back to the main room where Ethan and Josh are holding back their laughter as I stand there, hurriedly putting on the tee shirt I had just been holding against my front.

"What the hell?! Who is that?!"

"Eh, that's who's been keeping *me* busy."

Our laughter mingles as I land myself back on the couch and we move onto more important topics... like Stells Bells Big Birthday Bonanza.

We lost track of time, of ourselves, and the count of beers. Only realizing after the nameless body from Josh's bed emerged. He kissed her as he walked her out the door, though unlike me, I don't think she realized it was a kiss goodbye.

I fell asleep on the couch. Josh woke me sometime after midnight, and brought me a blanket when I didn't take him up on his offer to join him in bed as I have done dozens of times before. I said it had to do with the fact he had fresh-sex-sheets, but the only thing I could think of was Reid. Someone I spent a day with once and had coffee with twice. And even half awake, I realized what that might mean. And that scared the shit out of me.

The whole suite is quiet when I wake up. The boys are still asleep in their rooms, so I flip on the coffee pot for them, knowing that, like me, they probably have some version of a hangover they'll be nursing when they get up. I check the time and know there's no way I can head back to my room, get ready, *and* make it to the Coffee Haus in time to beat Reid there. So, I make the game time decision to just shower here knowing I still smell like last night's beer.

Freshly showered, with barely any minutes to spare, I sneak into Josh's bedroom, and there he is sprawled out in bed, facedown, blankets kicked down by his ankles, just in his boxers.

My shirt is beer stained and smells like it was used to mop up a frat house, so that's not going to work. Time for game time decision number two. What to wear. Borrow a tee shirt. It's totally fine, you'll look fine. Lucky for me, he likes his black tees fitted. So, tie it off at the waist, it will be like a Tim-Gunn-Make-It-Work moment.

"What are you doing, it's too fucking early." I hear the grumble from behind me.

"I'm running late, I'm meeting Reid for coffee." The only response from him is the groan muffles with his pillow, annoyed at the early morning disturbance.

"You can go back to sleep in two seconds. I'll be out of your hair. I just need to borrow a tee shirt."

With that, he rolls over, and breathes out the sleep he'd

been holding in his lungs. There's drowsiness visible on his face, but it ends there. The rest of him tightens as he props himself up on his elbow.

"You really think showing up in another man's shirt is a good move?"

"I think..." *I had thought, but it doesn't matter now.* "I think that I don't want to be late... So, I'll see ya later, alligator."

"You're too fucking chipper in the morning." He turns away from me to face the wall, pulling the pillow over his head to block the smallest fractures of light coming through the break in the blinds.

I'm wearing my jeans and boots from yesterday and tied his tee shirt into a knot, accentuating my waist. My hair dried naturally, which means it's a little more unruly than usual; the curls I usually contain with a flat iron and some anti-frizz oil are out on display. So focused on getting there on time, *okay, getting there early,* I ignored the fact that I am a much more disheveled version of myself, the version that was reserved for the morning after, or the inner circle, the version no one typically sees.

I made it with a couple minutes to spare. Just a few minutes before 8 a.m., and I knew as soon as I walked through the door he would already be here, at *our* table. Two coffees waiting. And he didn't disappoint. I saw him and wondered if he ever could. His smile greets me before anything else, as he helps me out of my jacket and brushes the hair from my face so he can see me. Wrapping a curl around his finger. I take full advantage of the connection twirled in his hand as his long fingers find themselves deeper in my hair. I take a step towards him, into his embrace. One he opens to me without realization or reservation.

"Morning, sunshine," he says, the kiss he pressed on my lips still lingering with an invisible touch.

"I think *you* might be the sunshiny one here. You are

practically beaming every time I see you." His laugh is sweet, almost sounds shy, but I know better.

"Of course I am, because it's every time I see *you*." As he says it, his eyes roam my face and down my neck to the neckline of the shirt that hangs a little too wide to be mine. He undeniably assesses the upper half of my outfit. What is very clearly not my shirt.

The words come out in unsolicited explanation before he verbalizes the question, bubbling up from my gut full of nerves. *But there's nothing to be nervous about.*

"I crashed in a friend's dorm last night and I didn't have time to go back to my room, so I just showered and stole a shirt."

We both take *our* seats at *our* table.

"I'd like to hear about your friends." He had begun to tell me about his friends yesterday, said I would meet them soon, and I wondered if the connections I've made in the first two months of school would last through graduation. Or even beyond that.

I told him about Stella, or Stells, as she is almost exclusively known now. I shared some about the other main characters, covering off the core group, even talking a bit about my friends from high school. And of course, Reid had already met Josh. He seemed to take it in, nodding along, asking polite questions along the way.

"And last night? Who's down a shirt today?"

"I just crashed on Josh's couch after we all had too much to drink." His lips pressed slightly together as he nodded in understanding.

It may be Josh and Ethan's couch, but it's only Josh's shirt. Introducing Ethan as someone else he's going to worry about seems like the only thing that could take this miscommunication from bad to worse. *Especially considering, of the two men, I'd only had sex with one of them. And that's not whose shirt I'm wearing.*

"Does it bother you?" I'm skeptical to ask, but he's always so direct. If he isn't now, if this is going to be a problem, I need to be the one to outright ask the question. Even if the answer made me more uneasy than I care to admit.

"Does what bother me?" He looks at me warmly but wants me to clarify. Wants me to be clear.

"That I'm wearing someone's shirt?" I'm not in the habit of being nervous around men. I don't often find reason to be. But saying it out loud made me nervous. I do the only thing I can to distract myself from the tightening in my chest as I wait for his answer. I suck in the corner of my bottom lip, pinning under my teeth. Giving me pressure I need as they dig into the soft skin.

"Yes," Succinctly, clearly, standing from his chair.

My heart drops to my stomach instantaneously, but he doesn't make a move to leave. He plants his left hand flat on the table, his long fingers sprawling out between us, his right hand reaches across and grips my chin as his thumb plucks my lip from its bite and pulls me up to replace the pressure of my teeth with the tenderness of a kiss. One that tugs on every ounce of desire, sucking it from my core with each movement of his lips merging mine. His mouth hovering above mine as his fingers grip my chin holding me in place for his gaze.

"Because I keep thinking the only man's shirt you should be wearing is mine." He presses another kiss to my lips, ending the sentence, and sits back with a smile as I stare at him like a deer in the headlights, my hair having fallen into my face. Because a moment ago, my heart fell into my stomach sinking into the fear he was readying himself to leave, and right now, it has fallen even lower. Landing somewhere deep and desirous. Sitting back in my chair, I press my legs together tightly, and I know I need him. In more ways than one.

Reid and I met for coffee every morning for almost two weeks. Each day, we shared more about ourselves, every day getting harder and harder to leave the small table by the window. He asked about me in a way people usually didn't. He seemed interested in the layered parts of me, not just what was outwardly facing, and he didn't hold back in repaying the truths with his own. There was something special about this morning coffee ritual. What was building between us, what brewed each morning, was a lot more than coffee.

Chapter Twenty-Two

2007

HER

We cut up some limes and put out our saltshaker, taking two tequila shots in the birthday girl's honor to get us started. Our suite is packed with all the usual characters, plus a few supporting ones we don't see as regularly, but still we had opened our room for pregaming before we head to The Commons for the full kick off of Stells Bells Big Birthday Bonanza.

The thing making tonight especially *big*, not just the guest list, it's who else is on it. Reid. I invited him days ago, excited that we'd be able to see each other now that both of our schedules allowed for a bit of fun. But the more I think about it now, looking around this room as the group that gathered, I'm not sure if this is really his scene. From what I've learned about him, he isn't uptight by any means, but he has a level of self-respect that dictates his actions, his expectations. And as I look to the corner of the room where the beer can pyramid is underway, and to my other side where Stella is planting lipstick kisses on people's cheeks, I just don't know if I can really visualize him in this setting. And I don't know if that's a bad thing.

"Come on, Miami, have another drink with me!" Josh calls from across the living room, as he pours out two shots of whiskey.

"I can't, I'm trying to keep it a little together, at least until we get to the bar. I'd rather not be totally shitfaced *before* Reid shows up."

Josh crosses the room, parting the crowd with a huffed laugh aimed directly at me.

"What the hell," he says, glaring at me with incredible irritation. "You've spent the last two weeks with this guy, who gives a shit if he's coming or not?"

"Careful, Josh... you sound jealous." It's not the right thing to say, but I mean it. He *does* sound jealous. And it makes me more nervous that I invited Reid. Knowing that Josh's supreme ability to scare away unwanted suitors has always been used to my advantage. But now? The fear washes over me that he will use those powers of his that I've encouraged, for evil.

"Jealous? I've seen you fuck enough of these guys; I don't have anything to be jealous of. You always end up back here." He opens his arms, extending them to his sides, gesturing to our surroundings, but I can't help but wonder if he means *him*, as the one I return to. He's not entirely wrong. It's been part of our dynamic. And the same can be said for him. There is consistency between us as the only regulars sleeping in each other's beds. But I can see him, he's clearly already tipped towards intoxicated, so I don't dignify his claims with an answer. It wouldn't seem like a fair fight. But I can feel his breath as he exhales in frustration. As if my lack of answer annoys him more. "Or wait a minute, you *aren't* fucking him yet, are you? Put the poor man out of his misery, it's been all of what," he holds up his wrist, pretending to check the time despite not actually wearing a watch, "it's been a whole 13 days, might as well get it over with and move on already so you can rejoin the party." *Was I a fucking idiot to invite Reid?*

It's just a party, and sure, I haven't slept with him yet, but that's scheduling, not lack of interest. Trust me, the interest is palpable. Something delicious I taste every time his tongue slips past my lips and curls into my mouth.

I have no doubt that Reid can handle his own, and I am glad to have him come tonight, but it looks like I had lured him right into the lion's den. Josh's arm is around my shoulders, and I can feel his chest rise and fall, the heavy breathing exhaling the warmth of whiskey breath which mingles naturally with the licorice and pine smells of him.

What are you doing, Arden? Say something back.

He might be roaring the loudest, but he isn't the lion here.

I am.

And now is a good time to remind him of that. I softly wiggle out from under the weight of his arm, and smile up at him, where his stare is burrowing down into me. As his arm falls from around me. I adjust myself closer to him, propping my elbow up on his shoulder as he has done to me countless times before.

"You misunderstand me. I didn't say you were jealous of him." His body is full of tells, maybe not visible to anyone but me, but they all react, and I know I hit a nerve. The one he exposed early on in our meeting. He moved to shrug me off his shoulder, but I held my place and lowered my voice.

"You're jealous of the fact that in the last two weeks someone has found me more interesting than they have *you* in the last three months combined."

It's not kind. But why should I hold back? Not when he doesn't. I see the moment where his eyes flash, and I know I'm right. Only confirmed when he knocks my arm from him and walks off to join some of his other friends.

Ethan steps up from where he'd been watching it play out.

Standing off to the side and out of the line of fire. Never one to really get involved.

"I've been waiting for that for a while." He extends me a soda and offers me a smile. Though whether it's in consolation or victory, I'm not sure.

———

We've taken over the entire back area at The Commons. Josh is back to his saccharine self, grabbing me a drink as soon as we got here, and not leaving my side. As if his presence is an apology. Which to him maybe it is. *Maybe that's enough.*

Despite all the distraction, I saw him as soon as he walked in. Through the noise and the crowd, none of that mattered when there was a pulse in the way his presence called to mine. My eagerness to see him, even after leaving him just ten hours ago, is substantial. *How much I want him is substantial.* The few inches he has on most people makes him easy to spot, but he seems to find me just as easily. Especially as I hurry my way across the crowded space and throw myself up into him.

My arms twine around his neck, pulling myself off the ground just because of his sheer height. I feel him wrap his coat around me, pulling the sides of it over my back, cocooning us both inside.

"Excited to see me?" he breathes into my ear, ending the thought with a lingering kiss below my jaw. He holds onto me tightly, suspending us in this moment, before easing my body down the front of his. I can feel his eyes rake over me, dripping thick and slow like molasses. And he doesn't shield the desire that pours from his stare when he meets mine again.

"You look fucking incredible."

"You too." He laughs, though I said it without an ounce of humor.

I return the smile he's given me. It's hard not to. He wears them so freely, never afraid of running out, and it's amazing how natural it feels to mirror that warmth right back to him. Not in calculation as I usually do, but natural reflection.

We make our way back through the crowd, to my crowd, which has somehow grown in only the matter of minutes since I've stepped away.

"EVERYONE!" I call the attention of the group, "This..." gesturing with my hands to the charmingly handsome man next to me, "is Reid!"

As if in a prepared chorus everyone sings a version of "*Hiiii, Reidddd.*"

His left hand is resting on my lower back as his thumb runs back and forth slowly, reminding me that even amidst this crowd, he's focused on me. The silk of my dress follows the path of this thumb, and I imagine the touch of his fingers crawling up my bare skin.

He sees Josh, just a couple feet away, and without hesitation steps towards him to make the first move.

"Good to see you again." He offers him his hand, a repeat gesture from their first introduction, and while Josh accepts the handshake, he cuts his glare to me. Something I can tell Reid notes by the way his hand strengthens against my back, but he says nothing.

"You too, man. We are about to play a round of Never Have I Ever. If you're going to be hanging around our girl, we should get to know you." His tone is smooth and charming, but the challenge and possession is clear.

Our girl.

"I don't know if that's the game we want to play..." I interject, not wanting Reid to be immediately bullied into a drinking game when I don't even know if he drinks, also unsure of which way Josh is going to try to steer this. But rather than protest, he simply soothes his hand up and down my back twice and looks over to me rather than in response to Josh. Having removed his hand from Josh's grip and using it to gently curl my hair behind my ear, before casually putting it in his pocket.

"Who wouldn't want to know everything there is to know?" He looked back to Josh and ended the sentence there.

"Arden, why don't you grab us a couple seats, and I'll get you a drink. What would you like?"

"Tequila soda, please!"

"Got it... Josh, what are you drinking?"

"Whiskey," I answer for him.

"I'll get you my favorite." Reid walks off to the bar; he doesn't need a fake id given that he has a few years on me, though he isn't the only one.

"Never Have I Ever, *really*? I'd rather not give him anything to worry about here. Joking aside, you can tell I actually like this one."

"Ouch, poor Ethan. This will be fun, it's one of the few games you lose." His laugh is mischievous and dark. "What are you even so concerned about, afraid he'll be scared off when he hears some of your dirty secrets?"

"I don't think he scares off easily." *But yes. I'm scared.*

"What is it then, it's not like there's anything you have to hide here." He gestures between us. Knowing that Reid had been curious about our relationship from everything I've shared.

"I'm not hiding anything. I just don't want him to get the wrong idea."

"Oh, Miami, you're always hiding something, he just doesn't know you well enough to realize it yet."

Our group has broken off and gathered in a large booth, readying for the game. Lindsey and Ethan are nestled tightly together, as he leans down to nip at her ear. I know him well enough to know he's not whispering much unless it's to do with whatever plan he has for her later. They are seated in the middle of the booth. Tangled together and trapped by people to either side of them. To Ethan's left, Stella and Josh. To Lindsey's right Marlie, Jack, and Lucas, who is also seated next to me, and to my left, Reid. Who has one hand holding his glass and his right hand resting gently on my thigh under the table. His thumb moving back and forth again, reminding me he's there, even though he's got Josh wrapped up in conversation. A conversation that seems to have Josh wholly engaged, perhaps impressed, even pacifying him. *Good.*

"Hey, Stells! Why don't you kick us off in Never Have I Ever, birthday girl honors!" Stella, like a lot of nineteen year olds, is a lover of drinking games, and while I enjoy most games, *usually ones that require more of my mind than my liver,* I want to get this one over with.

The tension at the table may only be detectable to me, but I'd rather not delay the inevitable challenge I see taking shape in Josh's smirk, not a single minute longer.

"Okay! So, just a reminder of the rules. We all take turns listing different experiences we've never had. If someone *has* done the thing, they take a drink! If no one has, then the person who said the thing has to drink... and remember, it's my birthday, so nothing boring! In fact, new rule! If you're boring, you drink!" Golf claps go up around the table, Reid obviously unaware of the inside joke that the theatrical response stems from. But he seems comfortable sitting on the sidelines of it.

"Before we get started, a round of Never Have I Ever that I'm sure will devolve into madness... Let's all raise a glass to the birthday girl, may this be the best year yet–and maybe by the end of the night, we will have some more experiences to cross off the list for next year's game!" I raise my glass, and the resounding CHEERS goes up around us, extending well beyond our booth spreading across the bar, and Stella lights up at the attention.

"Never Have I Ever... gone skinny dipping." Her smile wide across her face as she giggles to herself. It's not that it's the most scandalous of experiences, but I know it's something she had said was on her bucket list, so it makes sense this would be where she started. Looking around the table…

Josh, *drinks.*

Marlie, *drinks.*

Ethan, *drinks.*

Lucas, *drinks.*

And before I move to bring my own glass to my lips, I feel the movement to my left and realize Reid, too, *drinks.*

I didn't think Reid was boring by any means, but I wasn't sure if I thought he was a skinny-dipping- kind-of-guy. I realized that even though our get-to-know-you-scrabble was thorough, I was going to learn a whole bunch more about him now. *And I can't fucking wait.* He seems to have the same thought, as he leans down to me, to whisper in my ear.

"That's something I'd like to see."

"I was thinking the same thing."

Ethan begins, "Never Have I Ever… stopped sex to get a snack." He bursts into laughter as Lindsey drops her head in her hands, shaking it fervently in embarrassment. Clearly, this was a very targeted attack, solid strategy, Ethan. *I really did underestimate you.*

"Drink, babe," he says, and Lindsey picks up her head, her face blushed with shame, and *drinks.* No one else joins her.

I look to my left. A different kind of smile plays on his lips, as his grip on my thigh tightens ever so slightly and I'm incredibly aware of each fingertip and how far they reach across my thigh. Leaning in again to hover his mouth above my ear to whisper words only for me.

"I've never had to get out of bed to find something I wanted to eat." My mouth must fall open, as he pulls away and releases a dark hungry laugh. One different from the normal brightness he exudes, but it's delicious.

Lindsey responded to Ethan's targeted challenge with a

specific one of her own, which meant that only the two of them took drinks the last two rounds. Though really it seemed like a specific brand of foreplay. *Good for them.*

Marlie takes her turn. "Never Have I Ever... smoked pot."

Josh, Stella, Jack, and Ethan *drink.*

Reid *drinks.*

So do I.

"Never Have I Ever... had a threesome." Jack looks at Marlie, not subtle in the slightest clueing us all into a conversation that none of us wanted to be a part of.

Ethan *drinks.*

Stella and I *drink.*

And Reid's grip on my leg tightens in a desperate way. *I wonder if he would consider this 'messy?'*

Lucas is up next, "Never Have I Ever... had a one-night stand." Makes sense. I know from conversation he's dating the girl he lost his virginity to. *Not sure where you'd fit a one night stand in that timeline.*

As a select few people around the table begin to move their drinks to their lips, rather than taking the drink I know I should, nervous for some reason, I call a point of order, asking for a question that will be a distinction without any real difference.

"How are we defining one-night stand?" I prompt the group, not too interested in answering myself, but knowing any clarification of definition won't really matter.

"One and done, Miami. Drink."

Josh *drinks.*

Ethan *drinks.*

Stella *drinks.*

I *drink.*

Reid doesn't.

"Never?" I look up to him and he shrugs so effortlessly, so casually, like it's not the slightest care in the world. His fingers move against the patterned fabric of the tights on my thigh.

Catching the skin between the threads of lace threads as they dance, no, they play. Like his right hand is playing the melody to a song. It's not a song he knows, but one he is improvising, writing it as he goes.

"Nope," he says coolly and unbothered. "Not my thing. I think you're up."

It's my turn. There was a reason Josh chose this game. Not because he wanted to learn about Reid. But because this is a game I have lost more than once. There aren't many things I haven't done, and I'm not embarrassed, in fact, I want to do more. But it makes my turn a little harder.

"Never Have I Ever... had someone say the wrong name during sex." It's a regrettable move, but it's the only thing that came to mind. I know from one drunken night trading sex horror stories that both Ethan and Josh would have to take a drink. But on my left, Reid moves to lift his glass, hesitating only slightly, "Hang on, does role play count?"

"Oooh, good question, let's ask the judge, Stells Bells? Does role play count as having someone call out a different name during sex?"

With a laugh and a sweeping *OUT* arm gesture, like an umpire at a baseball game, she decided. Reid releases his glass, safe from this round. I know he would feel no humiliation in any version of an answer. Though the only thought I have is the desperate one that is curious about the details of whatever role-play scenario he was referencing.

Reid's turn brings about a different type of unease. This man who had no cap on his confidence, and felt no reason for embarrassment or regret, could say anything. Everyone around the table stilled, to focus on this make-or-break-it moment.

"Never Have I Ever... gone commando." And as his eyes are on mine, he winks.

Around the table, all but he and Lindsey take a drink.

When I bring the glass to my lips in admission, he looks to

be readying himself to ask me something, to whisper something. As he has throughout the whole game. Teeing me up, teasing me, knowing how I've inched closer to him throughout the night of sheer craving. This time I make the move. Leaning up to him, answering a question he doesn't ask.

"Right now." Kissing his cheek and lowering myself back into my seat. His grip on my leg tightens. His whole body seems to tighten. Technically, I'm wearing tights, but given that I opted to go underwear free, I stand by my answer as definitely counting as the official rules of commando.

I've been nervous at every turn, but Reid is more layered than I originally thought and he held no reservations about showing it. Nor has he expressed any judgment at the things I said.

"Hmmm..." Josh muses, as he sloshes his drink around, swirling it in his glass. Even with the normal darkness of his eyes, I still see it. The spark that flickers there. That tells me he's about to set the whole thing up in flames.

"Never Have I Ever... fucked someone at this table."

Reid's hand released from the glass knowing he won't be taking a drink as we haven't slept together yet, and he isn't the kind of person who needs to pretend to impress anyone around him.

But I look around the table, and Ethan catches my eye for the briefest of seconds. Reid doesn't know there's a history there, why would he? I don't have his sex roster, and I had no reason to share mine.

Ethan and Lindsey *drink.*

Jack and Marlie *drink.*

I *drink.*

And then Josh *drinks.*

But this doesn't even make sense, Josh *had* been with someone at this table, Lindsey. We all knew it. Well, *almost* all of us knew it. One person, the only one without context, didn't. And I realize, as usual, Josh is playing a very different game.

The fingers that had been curled around my thigh release immediately. I know why. He thinks I've been dishonest, that I lied to him when he had asked about my relationship with Josh. Looking at the situation, Ethan and Lindsey are curled so tightly into each other, and from their ultra-specific Never Have I Ever challenges, it's clear they are together. Marlie and Jack outright proclaimed they are in a relationship.

That just leaves me and *Josh*.

"You're not supposed to say something you've done." I deliver sharply in his direction.

"That's right, my mistake." Josh winks as he takes another sip from his drink. Neither the admonishment or his response helps my case. One I know I'm about to have to plead.

Reid's body shifted ever so slightly from mine, but he's not said a thing. Instead, he polishes off the rest of his glass, removing his hand from underneath the table.

"I'm going to get another drink." He stands and runs his fingers through his hair, casually, and while I know what must be running through his brain, he shows none of it to anyone else here. It amazes me how clear he can be one moment, how totally unguarded, and yet, presently, rather than openly ask me what I know must be one question he's swallowing down, he steels himself completely.

"I'll come with you!" I say, quickly standing to follow him. He nods and smiles, different than his normal, this one more forced, and heads toward the bar. His smile indicating that while in this moment he might keep himself restrained, his closed lips are containing what he wants to say. Ready to be right behind him, I give him a few steps lead, hanging back only momentarily knowing there are two things I need to make clear before I take a single step.

I place my palm down on the table in front of Josh, and I

lean down to meet his eye. My dress hangs low, and while I know my position puts my cleavage on display, he doesn't break his focus from my face. Which is closer to his than I intended. So much so I can feel the breath he exhales.

Preparing himself to combat whatever I am about to say, as if he is excited for it. His eyes darken, more than usual, and narrow. Momentarily staring each other down, waiting for the other to take the first step into the no-mans-land of this verbal battlefield.

"What's wrong, Miami? Lecture-Boy not up to the challenge? I told you to get him out of your system before tonight, it's not my fault that you didn't listen."

"I'm surprised your ego allows you to play dumb, Josh. But you know exactly what you just did, and don't think anyone here doesn't know why you did it. This isn't about him. You wanted to make me look like a liar? Well, you failed. The only person you'll have made look like a *liar*, is yourself."

His hand comes down on top of mine, pinning it to the table as I move to step back.

"I guess we'll see, won't we?" As he said it, there was that same flash of something in his eye from earlier. He releases my hand, and I don't give him the chance to say anything more. I spin on my heel to hurry after Reid.

Despite what I said to Josh, I don't *really* know why he did it. Not beyond the usual Josh bravado, the arrogance and possession he liked to flex. Even when I was with Ethan, while he had expressed annoyance, he hadn't ever seen Ethan as any kind of legitimate threat to our friendship. I think that might be different now.

I'm not sure exactly where to start, but I know I have to clear up the confusion.

"Reid, I know what that looks like, but it's really not." That's where I would start. It looked like I lied to him. When he had asked me about Josh, *more than once*. And for all the things I am, a liar isn't one of them. The unrevealing face he possessed when he stalked off, relaxed now, knowing it's just us in this conversation despite the people all around us.

"I don't care what things look like; I care what they are. I told you what I am. *Who* I am. I like you, but I don't put myself in situations like this. Not just messy ex-dynamics, but dishonest ones. Not situations where I am being queued up for a public argument, something I downright *loathe,* by the way. I asked you if there was something going on there, you told me no. Please, tell me, Arden. What am I missing?"

"I was with Ethan." His eyebrows draw together, clearly in thought, shocked even. Maybe he's assessing me for honesty. I can't be sure. But when he doesn't speak, I can tell he is leaving the space for me to continue. "We were hooking up, it wasn't anything serious. Josh was with Lindsey, which is why he drank. I mean, I don't know why he drank, he wasn't playing by the rules." I can't stop myself from saying the words that are strung together so quickly it is like they are spoken in cursive. It wasn't the alcohol, but the explanation I wanted to get out that threaded them together. "But I know what you've asked me, I *know* what I told you. There's no history between me and Josh, just friendship. There's just a little bit between me and Ethan, but you don't have to worry, he's moved on, I mean, there wasn't really anything to move on from, but it's nothing now. Maybe I should have mentioned it, but I really didn't think I needed to. I promise. But there's no messy history there."

He takes a slow inhale. One that I think is meant to steady him but manages to soothe me where I stand in front of him. So I continue, "I'm sorry about Josh. I know he was an asshole, I told him. But he's just drunk. He's harmless, he can just get possessive as my best friend."

His eyebrows relax, as do his shoulders. I hadn't noticed the tension he was holding in them until it was released.

He brings his hand to my shoulder, where my skin is

exposed, and slowly drags his fingers up and down my arm as I can see the words beginning to form in his eyes. The apology he was preparing himself to make.

Still, I can't help the feeling that I am about to lose something I haven't even had yet. Something I want in so many ways. *Please, please, please. Not yet.*

"Baby," he says, his voice is low and firmer than I'd heard it yet. His gaze holds onto mine, looking back and forth between my eyes, as if there's something unique to what each of them might tell him. "I don't think he's a very good friend."

My eyes drop down to the floor as I step into his body, and he pulls me in the rest of the way. My cheek pressed against his chest. Even in this crowded bar, I can hear his heartbeat. And despite his cool exterior, it gives him away, beating nervously.

"I'm sorry." I look up to him, in a voice meeker than my usual. The arms he had wrapped around me keeping us close now pull me away from him so he can see me more clearly, or maybe so I can see him. *Which I do now.* I am blushed with shame, though I can't actually name what for. As each of his large hands comes to rest on the sides of my neck, his thumb tracing my jawline as he steadies me in front of him.

"You don't owe anyone an apology, and I don't need you to apologize for anyone else, either. I wasn't bothered because you have a history, I'm not looking to read an empty book. Arden, you're brilliant, and you're gorgeous, you *should* have fucking history. I was bothered because I have a hard rule to avoid messy situations. I told you that when we met, and when you said you were single, I was thrilled. And in that moment just now..." He so subtly gestures his head back to the table of my friends and his smile softened in relief of the inner battle he was preparing to have with himself. "I don't know what upset me more, that I thought you weren't honest, or that whatever this could have been between us was about to be over."

I had never in my life met anyone so open. I can't think of

what to say in response, so I don't use words. I reach my arms up, wrapping them around his neck, and draw him down into me. With a kiss full of the want that had been burning between us all night. He slips his tongue along the joining of my lips, parting them, and building the strength of it between us.

For a man who refuses a public argument, he seems to have no problem with a public display. This one ready to border obscene. I can feel it, the physical reaction his body has to mine. If it weren't for the bartender, I'm not sure we would have come back to reality. Perfectly able to block out all noise around us and just be tangled tongues. My mind is empty of everything that normally occupies each corner of it, replaced with the pure fantasy of what comes next. *And I want it to be him.*

Reid collects our drinks from the bartender, closes out his tab, and leaves a bill tucked beneath the empty glass as a tip. He dips back down, planting that signature kiss, the one that acts as a period at the end of the sentence, lingering just a second longer than usual so we both know it's not a period at all. But a comma, *a pause*, he's ready to return to.

"How about we finish off this round, say our goodbyes, and get out of here. You can show me what other songs you have in your piano repertoire."

Chapter Twenty-Three

2007

HER

By the time we finished our drinks, the game had naturally ended and no one seemed bothered. We got back to the table, and Reid was collected and unflappable. Conversations went on casually like Josh didn't intentionally try to ruffle him and like I didn't call him out for it.

It's just after midnight when I can finally pull myself away from the birthday girl. Telling Reid I am ready to go. The amateur singers participating in karaoke are now the sole entertainment. Josh eventually found a companion for the night and neither his performance nor Ethan and Lindsey's karaoke rendition of Grease, needed an encore.

We've been standing off to the side, away from the commotion and crowd. And his body is angled in a way to shield me from some of the chaos of a college bar. His hand rests somewhere between my waist and hip, his grip a firm presence on me, one he has kept most of the night, as his thumb rubs back and forth, sometimes catching the fabric of my dress and pulling it up just slightly higher before lowering it back down on the next stroke. I want him, perhaps haven't wanted anyone so badly before, and I have since he first kissed me, so deeply in his apartment, wrapped in a coat smelling of him. And now, after the last two weeks, when we sat together each morning at *our* table, chairs inching closer each day, until this morning when he first placed his hand on my leg, where it stayed the entire duration of our time there.

"Reid, let's go somewhere." His smile brightens this dark corner of the bar. The one that allowed him access to me teasingly while he patiently waited for those words.

"Your dorm or my apartment? I've been thinking about you walking back through my door since the moment you left, but it's your choice."

"Here I was thinking you would carry me across the threshold this time." His grip on my waist tightens and jerks me ever so slightly forward, closer to him. An uncontrollable flex, as if the idea of it triggered a physical reaction that he was eager to unleash fully. I lift myself onto my toes to reach his mouth, and his body responds immediately. His right hand runs across my lower back until his forearm is there in its place, lifting me up, bracing my upper back against the wall, moving his body in front of mine completely. His left hand flat against the wall just above my head, caging me in as he intensely moves his mouth with mine. His kiss is deeper than any touch he's given me before, fervently, passionately splitting my mouth with his tongue. Pressing me into the wall, and himself into me. And I let him. Holding most of my weight against his arm, his right leg sliding into the space between mine. Leaving me nearly seated on his upper thigh, my back arched against the wall and his body curved over me, shielding me. Consuming me. The skin on my neck and shoulders are exposed by the simple black dress that hits me well below the collar bone and high on the thigh. He moves from my lips slowly, trailing kisses down the uncovered skin he's seeing for the first time tonight. A sprinkling of freckles across it, he marks them with his mouth before settling me on my feet, planting a gentle punctuated kiss on my lips, another comma, a pause before what's to come.

The walk back to his apartment isn't far at all but felt desperately long. We eventually make it back to the same brick-building lined street, passing *our* hot chocolate spot with the secret bookshop in back, until we arrive at the familiar alcove, his keys already in hand. It's not until we arrive at his front door that I step out of his way. Waiting for him to open the door and remove the final barrier keeping us apart.

The smile that crosses his face looks like the only secret I've seen him try to withhold. The flash of silver spinning around his long finger, his swinging keychain, the only thing that could distract me from the look in his eyes. It spins twice more, and he catches it in his grip on the third whirl, and in one fell swoop, while I was busy looking at his keys, he bends down and throws me over his shoulder. His forearm braces across the backs of my thighs as the wind knocks out of me. My hair falling all around me as my whole world turns upside down. My dress now hoisted up higher than it had been, his hand palms my upper thigh, the tip of his thumb so close to my now somewhat exposed ass. The only thing covering it, a pair of patterned lace tights which I can't imagine will last much longer.

He chuckles deeply as he pushes open the door and the warm air of his apartment hits me.

"That's not exactly what I meant about being carried over the threshold." Bouncing on his shoulder with each step forward he takes.

"Next time, tell me exactly what you mean, and I promise to do exactly that." And I feel the smallest pinch against my skin.

He pinched me.

"Ouch!" His chuckle becomes thicker, and from my

upside-down view of the world, I can tell we've stopped in the kitchen. His hands come up to my waist and slide my body down the front of his until my ass hits the cold kitchen counter, and I am looking at the world right-side up. Right at him. And he settles himself between my legs standing in front of me.

His hands running from my back to my hips and down my thighs, I swing my left leg out from where it hangs. His large palm follows the length of it until he can wrap his fingers around it wholly and trap my booted ankle in his grip, before releasing it, and stepping away from me entirely.

Suddenly, he turns his back to me. *No. No. No.* I want him closer, not farther.

"How about a glass of water." He reaches for the fridge and asks a question that begins to suffocate the mood. The fire that was burning between us just now, all night, *hell, all fucking week*, is being cut off of oxygen as he plays host.

Could I have misread him? Misread this?

"Sure, okay... thanks?" I just want him back next to me. His hands back on me, the places they left an imprint. I shrug off my coat and take off my gloves, shoving them into the pocket. Just leaving his scarf around my neck, the ones he wrapped around me on the chilly walk back. With the smell of him around me–not just the wool, but this place. I leave the length of it hanging down the sides of my breasts, to leave my cleavage on display and lean back resting my palms against the cold countertop, my back arching and my legs left dangling there, ever so parted from where he had stood between them. Awaiting his return.

He wordlessly removes a Brita filter and fills two glasses before turning back to me.

"Fuck."

The word dangerously escapes him, but he restrains himself quickly. Shaking his head, as if to snap him back to a more controlled state and handing me one as he comes back to the place he previously inhabited between my legs.

He drinks his water down, I sip on mine, lowering it from my lips, the glass still mostly full when I reach for him.

"Nope. Keep drinking, baby." Bringing two fingers to the bottom of the glass, tilting it back upwards towards my mouth, watching the column of my neck in movement swallowing down each mouthful. Something so routine now feeling totally erotic. And despite the next words out of his mouth being fairly innocuous, it is the intention behind them and his tone that make it sound downright indecent in the most delectable way.

"You haven't had any water since I've been with you,"

"Actually I–"

"No, the *soda water* from your tequila soda doesn't count."

My mouth snaps closed, with nothing else to argue. Not when he was so easily able to find the thread of my next thought and unravel it before I said another word. He just watches me intently.

"I'm fairly certain you and I are on the same page about what's about to happen, and I intend for you to be at least somewhat hydrated."

I haven't seen a Brita jug since I came to college, which means he's together enough as a person that he remembers to change the filter. And now stands here as an undoubtable desire burns through both of us in an uncontrolled-forest-fire kind of way, but doesn't make another move until he's sure I wont pass out from dehydration.

He's un-fucking-real.

My eyes stay on him even as my head leans back. I slowly drink the rest of it down, and he slowly drinks me in. A hand braced on each of my upper thighs, the hem of my dress pushed up high.

"Tell me something..."

His fingers moved across the lace of my tights. My skin catching glimpses of his fingertips between the woven pattern.

"What do you want to know?" I hook my left leg around him and yank him closer to me. I can tell the move seems to catch him off guard by the way his fingers dig into my skin in reaction.

"I guess it's really two things..." He says leaning forward, pressing his lips to my jaw, trailing kisses to my ear, as his hands make work to remove the scarf the rest of the way.

"I can handle two things." His fingers return my thighs. Higher now, his thumbs pressed against that place where hip joins leg.

"Number one," he pulls back to look me in the eyes. His own completely hypnotizing. The smokiness behind the burning desire he makes no effort to hide. "Are you really not wearing any underwear right now?"

What a serendipitous round of Never Have I Ever. Perhaps the highlight of the game. Now knowing that this thought has tormented him since he heard it.

"Yep." I say, popping the -P on the end of the word for dramatic effect before bringing my lips back together containing the smile that tells him how badly I wanted him to know.

"Good answer." He muses and nods along. Moving his mouth to the other side of my neck. Planting the seeds of small kisses along the trail of my jaw, before again pulling back and locking our gaze once more.

"Number two," leaning his mouth closer to mine, as if planning to speak the words directly into it.

"How much... do you like these tights?"

I suck in a breath as his hands move to my inner thighs. Any closer and he could without a doubt feel the wetness that has been gathering with every brush of his fingers against my skin. I have to answer, I have to speak. He's looking at me, waiting for my answer, he's not going to make a move until I say something.

"I fucking *hate* them." I spit out with stinging disgust, but it broadens a wicked smile across my face in hopes of what he's going to do next.

With that, his fingertips curl between my legs, gripping the lace fabric at the seam of me and splitting them open. Ripping it down the middle, exposing *my* middle completely to him. In the same moment, his lips meet mine wildly, ardently, possessively, and my arms wrap around his neck, bringing him as close to me as possible.

For a man who seems so in order, there is a beautiful uncontrolled chaos in how he reaches for me.

His hands move over my body with such intention, and my fingers work their way into his hair, and when I tighten my fingers around the soft strands that I've messed out of place, he smiles devilishly into my mouth. His tongue invades the space with warring purpose. Seeking out mine, and conquering.

His left hand moves to my rib cage, holding me there firmly, the length of his fingers long, leaving the tip of his thumb in a place to follow the under curve of my breast. His right hand running delicately up the inside of my thigh. Moving so slowly towards the throbbing, wet, center of me. His kiss slows as his fingers move, like I could feel them hovering in the warmth between my legs.

That feeling when someone is in your shared space, I can feel it now, knowing the tips of his fingers are the smallest movement aways from knowing the deepest parts of me, as is he.

He moves his kiss down the invisible central line from my mouth to my chin, using the force of his kiss to tilt my head back, as he makes his way down my neck, between my collar bones, landing right at the line of cleavage where my breasts were pressed together. Dragging his tongue across the curve of my upper breast, and back up towards the flimsy strap of my dress keeping me covered. My breathing is heavy. Breathing him in, sharing the air. I've never felt such a pull to have anyone in my life. So strong I almost don't know how to fill such desire.

"Tell me," he says commandingly.

"Tell you, what?" I ask in more of a whisper than his, though I have no idea whose benefit I feel it necessary to whisper for.

"Tell me what you want, Arden. Tell me what you want, and I'll give it to you." He doesn't whisper. He doesn't shy away from words. He looks at me when he says them, as his left hand moves from clutching the fabric of the dress at my ribs, and climbs up my arm, his fingers hooking the strap keeping my breast hidden. Running them underneath teasingly but keeping it in place until I say the words. For the second time tonight, he waited. His fingers moving back and forth under the thin strap like a metronome keeping perfect time but the rest of him is still.

He doesn't move anymore, just waits for me to respond. And for the second time tonight, I find myself nearly speechless at the sight of him, at the thought of him, at the fucking *feeling* of him. What I want is *all* of him. And I am beginning to realize I don't just mean physically. I see him trying to contain himself, patience battling desire.

"Arden." The single word. My name. The depth in tone is something I can feel reverberate against my skin.

Letting the strap fall from his fingers down the side of my arm, lowering the neckline of the dress, exposing my skin a bit more... I don't say anything, I just flicker a smile at him, as he lowers his lips to my now fully exposed shoulder. Adding a small nip in frustration at my lack of answer.

"...Arden." His voice feels like it penetrates me completely, sending a jolt through every nerve ending in my body. A question and warning as the fingertips he had hovering between my legs brushed across me like playing strings of a harp. So delicately, capturing a bit of the moisture building there waiting for him. My breath hitches on the feeling, and he straightens himself again.

"If you want me, you have to say it, baby." This time holding me in place with his glare alone.

"I want you."

I finally let the words go, and the moment they reached him, he spreads me open and plunges two fingers into me, curling them inside of me. My knees lock on either side of him, holding *him* in place, not wanting him to escape me even an inch. Though I have no real fear of that. His mouth takes mine as his fingers play deep within me. His thumb applies slow pressured circles as he pulses his two fingers deeper, and my body begins to melt into him. He wraps his arm around my back, supporting me, and he leans in deeper to the kiss. With his palm splayed wide across my back, he yanks me forward, making his fingers hit a spot deep within me, increasing the speed and work of his hands and bringing me closer to the edge. The edge of the countertop. The edge of my orgasm. And the edge of being lost to him entirely.

His hands work independently but so coordinated. Not mirrored actions of each other, but like two hands playing the piano. My head rolls back and catches the base of my neck, straightening it forward to look him in the eyes. I reach down to feel him, and he's impossibly hard. I knew he would be. I felt it at the bar, as he held me in the dark corner and kissed me. But now, in the comfort of his home, I reach for him more intimately. Using the heel of my hand to stroke his shaft through the denim of his jeans. And he lets out an unfettered groan. One that sounds more feral than I ever imagined he could be.

His eyes keep mine locked, his hand moving within me, and I can feel my walls closing around his fingers. As his one thumb strokes the side of my neck, the other drawing pressured electric circles between my legs.

"Can you come for me, baby?" His voice softened in tone but not in volume. I can only nod in reply. And he smiles and nods back. There is something so reassuring about the way he speaks to me now. Coaxing my orgasm out mentally, patiently, pulling it from me gently, not forcefully, a contradiction to the movements of his hands. He was not demanding it like it was owed to him, but something he knew was not as easy as most of the male population assumed it to be. With my acknowledgment, his speed quickened. His mouth back to my skin, speaking sweetly into it.

"I want to feel you around my fingers before you take the rest of me. Come for me, so I can hear you. So I can prepare myself for what you're about to do to me."

He tugs me closer to him as he tugs the thread from me, and I tighten around his fingers, in his arms, my breathing labored, locking my legs around his back as he adjusts his movements to the reactions of my body. Until the tightness of my core releases and I soften within his hold, melting against him. I simply lay my head on his chest and my eyes close in submission, in safety.

He removes his fingers from within me and brushes his thumb against my bottom lip. I can feel the wetness of it like a coating, as I open my eyes and he kisses the spot he just painted with me.

"Tell me." Not a question, but I know the answer.

"I want more," I whisper up into his ear.

"Good. It's yours."

My legs lock around his back, and he hoists me up off the counter and into his arms. He begins to take a step before turning back around and grabbing the jug of water and a glass. *His concern for my hydration even now, both incredibly endearing and almost alarming.*

I can tell from the way his Adam's apple bobs against my

lips that each step is taking focus; his stride is long, but nothing could carry us into the bedroom quickly enough. He instantly drops the water jug and glass on the dresser, the first flat surface he sees, before making it to the edge of the bed and landing me right on my back. Catching himself with his free hand so he doesn't immediately crush me beneath him.

And I have two thoughts at the exact same time.

I want you to crush me and *thank fucking god this isn't a college twin bed.*

Leaving me on the bed, he stands at the foot of it. Assessing me. For the first time, I look down at myself as well.

One breast almost entirely escaped from the silk slip dress I had worn braless. The hem of it high on one side bunched up around my waist, exposing the ripped lace tights, the tear running all the way down the leg disappearing into my black boot.

I look down at myself, disheveled but dripping with desire. Thinking about the touches I've collected from him up until this point. The first moment I pressed my hand to his stomach, knowing there was a strength that was hidden beneath his clothes. I can see it more clearly now as I look up to him.

Despite the earlier frenzy, we both are basking in the moment, recognizing we have only a few fabric layers that remain between us. Still pulsing from the feeling of his fingers inside of me, imagining the feeling of what I see clearly bulging against his zipper.

His hands make work of undoing his belt buckle, and in one fluid motion, whipping it through the loops and tossing it to the floor. I lean back on my elbows. Sitting up slightly to get a better view, I let the other strap fall from my shoulder and slip my arms through the loops, so my dress slips down from my torso to hang around my waist. Leaving my breasts uncovered. Exposed.

His eyes, breath, and brain all react at once. His eyes

widen, trying to take in more; he inhales the deepest breath, as if it would allow him to breathe in all of me, and his brain fed just one thought tumbling out his parted lips.

"Fuck."

His hands had stilled where they had been. Having made way to unbutton his jeans and give himself some relief. But the sight of me forced his brain to reprioritize what needed to happen next. He reaches for one of my legs, to yank off my boot before moving to the next and doing the same. Tossing them carelessly to the side. His fingers then crawl up my skin, under the hem of the dress, and catch the waistline of my torn tights before pulling them down the rest of the way and tossing them also into a pile on the floor. He pushes the hem of my dress up, so now it bunches entirely around my waist, exposed on the bottom, exposed on the top, just a loose silk fabric belt hanging around my middle, and that was the beginning of our undoing.

He doesn't wait to remove the rest of his clothing, working so quickly I barely caught sight of him. My eyes struggle to land on a single spot.

His smile is telling, bolder than I've seen it. His body is prepared, but visibly strong, and hard. And when he finally frees himself from his boxer briefs, my entire body responded to the sight. Throbbing from the inside, imagining the feeling of him, remembering the orgasm just moments ago. So I dig my teeth into the corner of my lip, keeping me focused on the pressure of it. Sinking them in so hard, I'm surely leaving marks.

His body comes down on top of mine. This time, I do feel the weight of him on me, and I revel in it. The substance and strength of him, knocking the air from my lungs. But of what air I am able to inhale, all I breathe is him. The illusion of cinnamon on my tongue. The imagined taste my mind assigned to each of his kisses. Feeling the length of him against my leg, I wiggled beneath him to move him into place, nearer to the entrance. Making clear what I want. *Him.*

His hand grips my face firmly, his thumb plucking my lip free, as his mouth takes mine in a punishingly wild kiss, one that has his tongue plunged in to explore, and has my body thrumming with the intensity he seems to inject directly into my bloodstream. His teeth catch on my bottom lip. Biting down and tugging, sending a small pang of pleasured pain deep within me.

"Baby, if you want the feeling of teeth on your lip, say so. Because every time you do that. It doesn't matter where we are, it makes me fucking crazy. And I don't know how I'm supposed to control myself."

He reaches up to the side table, stacked books rattling as he pulls the drawer open, and retrieves a condom. In the swiftest motion, sitting up onto his knees, rolling it down onto him. I swear I must have licked my lips, because he let out a deep throaty chuckle in reply. He is large, and I am desperate to take him. I need him urgently, and I told him. Knowing there would be nothing I could tell him that he wouldn't respond to. He wouldn't give me.

"Reid," His name forms on my lips like it's been meant to be there. I let out a staggered breath, the next word a short, fragmented plea for him, "Pl–please."

He wraps his arms around me, tossing me up higher onto the bed so my head lands between the pillows. He takes both of my hands, keeping them interlocked with one of his as the other remains wrapped around my back, keeping our bodies sealed together. He raises our joined hands above our heads to grip the headboard behind me. Not looking back, just at him.

"Please," I say again. *Maybe it's considered begging. I don't care. I've never craved someone like this before, and waiting even seconds has me pleading for him.*

"You can beg me if you want, and don't think I won't get off on every fucking second of it, but *baby*, I'm the one who should be on my knees begging to have you."

His eyes narrow on me in the quickest of flashes as he plunges into me fully. Fulfilling my desperate pleas for him. And it's as if our bodies are so perfectly attuned to the others' needs, that he let out a grunt of air as I sucked in a gasp of one. All of me taking in whatever he would give me.

He removes himself teasingly slowly, before slamming back in. My fingers clawing at the headboard, gripping it so tightly, his grip still covering mine, holding them there in place. He fucked me deeply and without reservation, his mouth owning mine and he thrust into me, I could already feel the tightening in my core, the slickness of his skin, as his chest pressed against mine, our sweat commingling, our tongues locked in dance, and him, charging me, deeply from within.

I lock my knees up to his sides, and he releases my hands from above my head, moving to grip my bent leg, wrapping his hand around my calf, pressing it down, opening me up for him, as my heel digs into his side. The other hand reaches behind me, his palm at the small of my back, giving him access to deepen his thrusts.

"Reid," I let out, his name louder than I thought it would be. The intensity within him is so unleashed now that my entire self-tightens around him.

"Fuck," his voice full, his next words punctuated by his breath and motion of driving into me, "I'm going to come for you now, baby, but I want you to come with me."

I have no control over the sounds that escape me, and sink my teeth into the muscle of his shoulder, trying to muffle myself. He reacts to the bite with a groan but pushes his skin further into my mouth, letting me lean into what I need. I finish explosively, and I can hear him chasing me across the finish line, feeling the pulsing of his cock, before spilling himself completely into the condom and slowing entirely. His muscles relax, lowering himself gently onto me and kissing away the sweat that has gathered at my brow.

Planting a kiss on my temple, he peels himself off of me, and the absence of all the places we were joined now painfully bare. He removed the condom and poured a glass of water bringing it to me where I remained in his bed, sitting up on my elbows as sweat dripped down between my breasts.

I look around the room, my eyes landing on my discarded clothing, wondering if I should head home. But it's as if he can read the look on my face, not making me ask.

"I'd like you to stay, but if you want to leave, I'll walk you back." He situates himself against the headboard, having pulled on a pair of boxer briefs at some point. He makes no reservation in communicating what he thinks, and beneath the initial shock of it, it comforted me, and I decided I would give that sincerity back in kind.

"I want to stay."

The desire to sleep in someone's bed is not the desire I often have when it comes to sharing a bed with a man. Usually, I might rest for a short period of time before finding myself in a bed for comfort and companionship, *only*. This is different. I want to be here nestled next to him, and not just for the morning sex I can already imagine.

Stay hydrated. Get the flu shot. Pee after sex. Stay hydrated. Get the flu shot. Pee after sex. Stay hydrated. Get the flu shot. Pee after sex

The weird post-sex-mantra on loop in my head never fully clears until I've completed the *pee after sex portion* of it. It's a weird post-sex-mantra, but I can hear my mother on repeat, the advice she's drilled in most of my teenage life, both as a parent and a doctor. As if those three things were the only pillars of health needed. Well, sorry mom, I'm terrible at staying hydrated, I've been slack in getting the flu shot this year, but at least I am religious about peeing after sex! Not that your mother is the first thing you want to think about when you crawl out of someone's bed, but I grabbed the glass of water he had waiting on the dresser and made my way to the bathroom, for a ritual post-sex pee. I pulled off the rest of my dress and stood there naked in front of the mirror, assessing the signs his body had been on mine. My skin is sensitive, and I can always see the marks left as signatures of the person who had held me. And right now, my skin was a map of the places he had touched. And I wanted to follow it again.

"There's a spare toothbrush in the drawer," he offers up, unsolicited.

"A lot of overnight guests, Reid?" I pop my head through the bathroom door to look at him, not in judgment, but curiosity. Especially after his Never Have I Ever admission about sexual exploits. *Or lack thereof.*

"No, baby. Toothbrushes usually just come in packs of two." He laughs a bit to himself as I splash some water on my face and walk back to join him. Leaving my dress hanging on the back of the bathroom door. I walk back in, and there on the edge of the bed, is a folded tee shirt, and I thought back to that moment in the coffee shop. *The only man's shirt you should be wearing is mine.*

"I didn't know you were good at trivia." I pull the *high school academic decathlon* shirt over my head. That kind of soft tee shirt material that comes from years of wear. The print faded, but not enough to hide the word *champion* in big letters on the back. "Now that I do, you can be my partner during trivia night at The Commons."

"I'm good at a few things you don't know about yet." He lifts the comforter, welcoming me under it, under his arm, and I curl into him, ready to rest.

"As long as one of them is trivia night, I can't wait."

"Okay, AB," and I can hear the smile in his voice as my check lays against his chest, "one of them can be trivia night."

We settle in, meeting in the middle of the bed. His fingers run through my hair. The hair along my sweaty temples beginning to curl at the roots from the moisture. But he seems content to just play with it. Twirling the early curls around his fingers as I yawn against him.

"Tired?"

"Yeah, actually. But I'm a bit of an insomniac, so I don't usually get to sleep too long."

"How about this, if you wake up, wake me up. I'm sure we can find something to do." He brushes the hair back from my forehead and plants the seed of a small kiss there to grow overnight.

I slept straight through to the next morning.

Chapter Twenty-Four

2007

HER

I wake up Saturday morning in a bed that isn't mine. *Okay–not the first time.* But usually that means there was someone next to me, someone still sleeping as I sneak out.

I'm wrapped up in the warmth of the bed as I soak it in. There's an actual comforter, clean striped sheets that are not the standard navy sheets of every college-aged man, there's more than one pillow, and all have matching pillowcases. If I thought the Brita filter was impressive, this makes him practically a unicorn.

I draw my arms and legs into my chest, curling tightly into a ball on a deep inhale. Existing just in the middle of this big empty bed. Before stretching them out as far as they can reach with an equally long mirrored exhale and morning moan. Not realizing how trapped I had begun to feel in my own bed until I finally began to stretch out in this one.

Leaving the cocoon of bedding doesn't seem to unwrap the comfort of being here. Still cloaked in the smells of his high school tee shirt. It's quiet here. I imagine it always is. No rowdy games or dirty-toasts to a crowded roomful of drunk college students. But it's almost too quiet, and looking around the living room I realize he's not here. The confusion of it floods my mind. I mean, I know people leave after sex, but that should have been me. But he wouldn't leave *his apartment*. Not when he asked me to stay. Maybe I was mistaken. Maybe I misunderstood. Maybe he just meant to stay for a little bit. *Shit. Shit. Shit.*

You should have known better. Now what are you going to do? The walk of shame? Such a stupid name for something that shouldn't be shameful at all. Except again, another example of assigning names to things just to criticize the sexual choices of a woman. *Okay, okay. Focus.* Just get your stuff, text your friends, and head back.

Nerves churn in my stomach. I think it's nerves. Maybe being that I had hoped this was going somewhere. Maybe I wasn't thinking *somewhere-somewhere,* but at least, maybe somewhere this morning.

We've been collecting all these moments. Dropping them into a piggy bank, accumulating the coins to amount to something. But where I was interested in more of him, it looks like he made the decision to smash it open and cash out.

Despite last night, despite the extra toothbrush, and despite everything else he said. *I don't know why I'm surprised. Maybe because for the first time, it's not me running out. And someone else has made the decision before I ever could.*

I see my purse sitting on the kitchen counter, my coat, his scarf, hanging over the back of one of the two chairs tucked under the bar. Waiting for me. But when I reach for my purse, ready to fish out my phone and deliver the 'I'm alive and coming home' messages to the necessary people on the phone tree, I see the scrabble tiles laid out adjacent to where my bag had been strategically placed.

S-T-A-Y – A-B
I – W-I-L-L – B-R-B

Okay, he will be-right-back. So *maybe* I was wrong. And immediately the whirling chaos that escalated from nerves, dissipated. Becoming only fluttering excitement rather than the spiraling fear of rejection.

For the second time in twelve hours, he told me he wanted me to stay. Maybe he didn't escape me this morning. I'm not sure how long ago he left, so I have no way to know when that would be. He left me alone in his apartment, not to leave, but to return. He is either a crazy person, or really trusted that I'm not. *That remains to be seen.*

Barefoot, pantiless, and in his apartment, I take another look around. His desk is orderly. Make sense. *Far more organized than mine.* Everything here makes sense. *Except me.*

The only things that seem to have a sense of randomness are the books he has in stacks across the room. Three in this corner, five stacked high on his desk, a few on the floor by the sofa. Textbooks, reference books, novels, even a small stack of moleskine notebooks on his desk. He has a blanket thrown across the sofa, and I imagine him there. *I try to imagine myself there.* His entire space feels as practical and transparent as he is. Nothing hidden or out of place. *And he left me here, so maybe to him, I, too, am not out of place here.*

There it is. The standing piano that we played together when he first brought me here. I wonder if he played often. I think I would. *My memories of the way his hands played me last night tell me he does.*

I snag the blanket from the couch and wrap myself in it before taking a seat on the piano bench. Quickly adjusting and pulling the tee shirt down to cover myself a bit more when the bareness of my bottom hits the wooden bench. I tuck my feet up into a criss-cross position to warm my toes and notice the books stacked on top of the piano are music books. Different collections, so I pull one from the pile and begin flipping through, wondering if he leaves notes in here like in his novels. *He does.*

I lift the fallboard and begin to play. Like a doodle on a notepad. Mindless movement of my fingers on the ivory keys, not following any of the music, just the hodgepodge melody of this morning and years of muscle memory coming together.

The front door opens, and I stop the intuitive playing that my fingers had taken up. Too distracted by him.

His post-sex-good-morning smile is the best one I've seen yet. So much so, that I barely notice the fact that he's carrying a tray of cups and a paper bag.

"Morning, sunshine." *He* is sunshine. I am cold and curled up, he is vibrant, and it bounces off him, despite the grayness outside or the glistening remnants of rain on his baseball cap and jacket. "Don't stop playing on my account."

"I was just messing around, nothing too special."

"Oh, I don't know about that." He purposefully makes his way across the room to me in two easy steps. His hands hold either side of my face, the lingering coldness of them from the outside world, as his mouth claims mine in eager greeting and deep recognition. He pulls away from the kiss, hovering slightly above before planting one more small one.

"Good morning *indeed.*" I whisper against his lips.

"I picked up hot chocolate and croissants." He tugs on the ends of the blanket. Bundling it tighter around me. Gesturing with his head towards the cups he left on the counter.

"You didn't need to do that, I could have grabbed something on my way back to campus."

"I'm sure you could have. But I knew that once you woke up, I wouldn't want to head out and brave the elements. I have every intention of staying in all day, *all weekend in fact,* and would like it if you stayed with me."

I nestle deeper into the cocooned blanket. How could I have thought this man woke up and *made an escape?* It's clear from the look in his eyes to every word out of his mouth, he wants me.

"Do you always just say what you mean?" I look up to him as he stands, forearm leaning against the piano, towering over me where I sit.

"Yes." So straightforward. Like it's bizarre to even ask. I can't think of what to say. I should probably head back to campus. My friends would expect me back by lunch at the latest, my parents would expect me to be studying. But what would Reid expect? He told me what he'd like. And he'd *like* me to stay. It doesn't take a moment's thought to admit, I'd like that too. So, instead of planning my day based on what was expected of me, I decide to just do what I want.

Granted, I have no clothing besides the party dress and a pair of ripped tights from last night, but something tells me, whatever he has planned for this weekend, I won't need it.

"Scoot." I feel the back of his hand swat at my thigh. Urging me to move over. I make room for him, putting my feet back on the cold floor, as he takes a seat to my right, sharing the space of the bench.

Cutting me a glance from the corner of his eyes, a hint of a challenge. His fingers move to the keys, and he begins to play a melody.

I know it. I've heard it before. But I can't place it. Flipping frantically through the rolodex of possibilities stored in my mind, and I'm turning up empty. I'm so frustrated, and he can see it on my face. My mouth forms a pout of annoyance as my eyes watch the movement of his fingers, teasing me differently than they had last night. His playing slows, giving me more time to try and name it before he reaches the end, and perhaps giving him the chance to lean into my ear, not worried about the keys.

"Morning Mood, Edvard—"

"GRIEG!! OF COURSE! It's Morning Mood by Edvard Greig! I knew it, I swear!"

His laugh is hearty as I practically screamed the answer at him, the answer he basically spoon fed me. It might have been on the top of my tongue, but my tongue was clearly far more interested in being tangled with his than providing any correct answer.

"Well done, you're up." His breath is warm even as his skin is still cold from being outside. The cold tip of his nose grazed my neck. His lips moving across my skin as he says, "But maybe something a *bit* more upbeat than last time." He nips at my shoulder as I position my hands on the keys, his hands move to my lap.

By the first few measures he was laughing into me. The song picking up speed and despite my best memory of the music, my desperate attempt at focus, and the desire to win, I couldn't keep up with tempo. The song built far faster than his choice. That coupled with the fact that his laughter shook the entire bench we shared, had me eventually fumbling the notes and laughing with him. I finally just slam my fingers to the keys in my own fit of laughter. Knowing I was never going to make it to the end. *Knowing I didn't really want to.*

His arms come around me and pull me on top of him. Straddling him where he sat. My back against the keys playing its own cacophony of notes as he runs his hands up my spine, leaning me forward into him. Totally exposed beneath the hem of his comfort-tee- shirt, but he is solely focused on my mouth. Looking at my lips like they are about to be his. *And they are.*

Bringing his mouth to the edge of mine, "Hall of the Mountain King is not what I consider a morning song."

He smiles, knowing he was able to correctly identify the piece of music. He's sexy in a way I'm not used to and it makes me respond to him in a way I'm not used to. Extending beyond physicality or a flirtatious boldness.

"But it's Grieg?!? I should get bonus points for playing follow-the-leader and choosing the same composer!"

His exhale is warm, like he's breathing out unfiltered desire.

"I've told you. I'm not worried about keeping score, AB. You can have all the points, but I get you."

And he took me. His arms are strong and muscular, knotting around me, bringing us together, as I feel him harden beneath me. Just like Grieg's Mountain King, our pace quickens impossibly fast. I am frantic, and he is full of fervor as his hands run under my (*his*) shirt.

"Arms up." At his command, I release my hands from where they are locked in his hair. Lifting them above for him to undress me. The tee shirt being pulled over my head is the only break of our connected stare. When he throws it off to the side. Woefully uneven, as I am now stark naked on his lap. On display. Where he remains completely clothed.

His hands quickly land back on my skin, each making their way to my breasts. Nipples peaked with interest, and perhaps exposure to the cool apartment air. His right thumb drawing familiar circles around one as his left hand played my skin, leaving fingerprints like a melody he already knows how to play.

"*Fuck,* Arden."

He lifts my back higher, so he can take my breast into his mouth. Teeth dragging across the skin, and tongue swirling, taunting a nipple clearly meaning to represent another throbbing and delicate part of me. I'm desperate and starving to feel all of him, pulsing deeply from within. Wet. Needy.

It escalates so quickly, my need for him, and not just in this moment. From the first moment. I reach between my legs, fumbling for the button of his jeans and yanking down the zipper.

"Hang on, baby." He snatches his wallet from his back pocket to retrieve a condom, shoving down his pants and boxer briefs in the process. Putting us on more equal footing now.

His cock is hard between us, and I grab a hold of him. The soft humming from his lips, as my thumb brushes across the beads slipping from the top of the smooth head. His breath is short as I pump him in my hand tightly. His large hand wraps around my neck, pulling my mouth down onto his. Before breaking the connection and releasing my lip that he held between his teeth and replacing it with the condom wrapper. Ripping it open.

This time, I reach for the hem of *his* shirt.

"Arms up." A command mirroring his. And he obeys without me hesitation as I pull it over his head and throw it to the ground.

I sit up on my knees, leveling my breasts to his face, something he does not ignore, as I line him up to me. The wetness collected there, waiting for him. Urging him to the entrance. His fingers dig into my back as I swirl my hips on top of him. His head is perfectly placed, waiting to be completely immersed within me. His hips try to buck up slightly, but I slam my hands back down on his shoulders, pushing him back into the seat. Tugging his earlobe with my teeth. He'll wait for me. I know he will. Waiting for me to decide when to settle him inside of me. But that doesn't mean that his desire to have me isn't fully palpable.

We're staring at each other, wordlessly. In a standoff, a tug-of-war. Knowing that he could win easily by just standing and carrying me off to bed. But he gives me the illusion of control. And when he takes a breath to steady himself, to temper the aching vibrations that are permeating from his chest... I decide.

Without warning, my hands braced on his shoulders, I slam

down, taking him all the way into me, filling me at once. My body immediately recognized the fullness from hours ago, squeezing around him in familiarity. His pupils dilate in response, and I fall into the darkness of them.

"*FUCK!*" This time the word falls from my mouth. Reacting as if my spine has been ripped from my body, leaving no support to keep myself upright. But he doesn't let me collapse, bringing me forward to press closely against his chest, serving as stability I need as my body melted into a new euphoria. And once we both acclimate to the sensation of being soldered together, I move on top of him. And each time, he meets me with a thrust. Whimpering and panting as I take him in deeper and deeper. Our pace is crazed and frenetic. Building as rapidly as the song had been.

"Can you..." He tries to get out the words, but I can see him unraveling in the most amazing way underneath me. I know what he wants to ask me. It's what he asked me last night. A question. Not presumptuous. '*Can you come for me, baby?*' He had asked me. *And I answered.*

He wants that again. *I* want that again. I want more.

"Yeah, Reid. *Tell me.*"

"Arden, I'm going to come." Rough, each word punctuated with his breath. I had been holding on to it, struggling to hold it back, but letting it build like a wave beginning to crest, letting it build within me, and then I came crashing to shore. My body stiffened, and his final jerks up into me were aggressive and uncontained, using one hand braced against the piano frame to steady him.

Watching this man come, watching this man come apart, *for me*, is magnificent. And I wonder if he knows just how undone I am in his arms.

Chapter Twenty-Five

2007

HER

"Guess the first time wasn't a fluke," I say, still straddling his lap, him still inside of me.

He had closed the fallboard on the piano so I could lean back and not crash into keys, and that's exactly what I did. Leaning back, stretching my arms side to side, laying them across the wood. On complete display to him. *And I feel like there's nothing I have to hide.*

"You thought the first time was a fluke?" His right hand holding the frame of the piano by my head, his left palm open on my chest, his thumb and fingers hanging lightly around the base of my neck. Slowly running it down my sternum, between the channel of my breasts.

"You never know!" I say with false concern.

"I knew." A hand landing on each of my hips, giving them an indicating squeeze, "Baby, I've got to get rid of the condom."

I pouted, *actually pouted,* in reply. And he lets out a chuckle. Because I have no interest in disconnecting us where we are joined. But I know better.

Time for a post-sex-pee, and probably a shower.

Especially given that last night I crawled into bed still sticky from sweat and smelling like a bar. He didn't seem to mind, more focused on having me next to him. But before another layer of smells cling to my skin, I need to clean off.

"Can I use your shower?"

"You don't have to ask. But if this is a *shower-after-sex* thing... I'm thinking it won't be the last one you take today."

"It's not a 'shower-after-sex' thing. It's more of an 'I-was-in-a-bar-last-night-and-you-definitely-took-one-this-morning-because-I-can-smell-your-freshly-washed-hair-and-I-don't-want-to-be-the-only-dirty-one-left-in-this-apartment' thing." I get the run on sentence out in one deep breath.

"You are not the only dirty one in this apartment."

"That's not what I–" He stole a kiss, and the rest of the sentence.

"There should be whatever you need, and I'll leave out some sweats if you want them. Or you can spend your day perfectly like this." His eyes and hands run the length of my torso to indicate what he means. As if the words were unclear. I just kiss his cheek and skip off to the bathroom.

"Wait a minute..." he calls after me, handing me the to-go cup, "shower hot chocolates are the best."

I washed my hair, scrubbed the remaining makeup from my eyes, and washed off any remnants of beer and smoke I might have picked up from the bar last night. The parts of last night and this morning I couldn't wash off were him. And I didn't want to.

Where he touched me, where his fingers played me, how his lips left a trail of kisses.

There is such a decadence in sipping the warm drink in the steaming shower, the spicy sweetness down my throat, filling my belly and my brain with the memory of the first sip.

Wrapping myself in a towel and running it through my hair

so I don't drip water across his apartment, I exit the bathroom and find him dressed at his desk. Studying maybe. There's nothing about him that is unfocused. Always paying complete attention to whatever it is he is doing.

When I first saw him, I noticed it. The intensely methodical way his eyes roamed across the page, and I think that's what I found so engrossing. The speed in which he seemed desperate to consume knowledge. *Although, I have learned that hunger translates to other interests as well.*

He hears my footsteps and sets down his pen, closing it in the moleskine notebook, turning his head to me.

"Feel better?"

"I felt pretty perfect before. Now I just feel perfect *and* clean." He looks ready to say something, but I speak before he can.

"What are you doing?"

He removes the pen from the pages, closing the book flat, realizing he won't be returning to it now. And adding it back to the stack of its brothers. He's not at all annoyed that I interrupted whatever it was, but just tucked it away for later.

"I keep journals. Notes and thoughts of the day." I don't know if it's his ability to read me or my transparency around him that allows him to find the right thread to pick up and tug when I don't say anything. Knowing I have a question on the tip of my tongue.

"What do you want to know?" Still seated at his desk, he adjusts his body towards me.

"Everyday? You keep journals everyyyydayy? What do you write about? Does anyone read them? Do you write about, like... *this*?" I gesture between us.

"Not always every day, no one reads them, not even me when I'm done, and no, not always things like... *this*." His gesture is a mimic of mine. "But, sometimes." I love his smile.

The one he gives me that drips with indecency. Though he might just be the most decent person I've ever met.

"Why do you do it?"

"It started when I was younger, we had an assignment in school to keep a journal for a week, and I never stopped."

"Oh, is that your M.O., Reid?? You start something and just don't stop?"

"Only when it's something I enjoy, Arden."

"And you enjoy it?"

"I do. It helps me clear my mind, remember details, and say things I don't want to say out loud. It's the perfect captive audience."

"I thought you always said what you meant."

"I say what I mean, I don't say everything I *think*. I have *some* self control."

"Well, I'm glad one of us does..." I say as I drop my towel. It barely hits the floor by the time he's up and has me wrapped in his arms, carrying me back to bed.

———

We spent the weekend holed up in Reid's apartment. He had gotten a couple calls from friends seeing if he wanted to venture out, but he made no attempt to hide his lack of interest. Instead, opting to stay in, only interested in me. I checked my phone a few times, called my mom once, texted Stella and Josh letting them know I would see them back on campus by Monday.

There was something about his space that was comfortable and easy. It was familiar because he had spent days getting to know me and showing me himself in the process. The scrabble game was just a small piece of it, each morning as we sat at the sun soaked cafe table, he gave me more and more about himself. So much so that now, being in here feels intuitive.

On Sunday evening, we both knew I had to go back to my dorm. I know he would have let me stay despite the workload he had this week. I felt like it was time to check back into my real life. Plus, I have classes tomorrow, and I will need my books.

Hell, I'm going to need my clothes.

"You're going to need to borrow something to walk back in. It's too cold for just that dress."

"Are you sure you want to do that? I don't know if you've heard, I've been known to steal clothes." His jaw clenches slightly, I wonder if this is one of those things he thinks but doesn't want to say.

"Come on, let's get you presentable."

He says it in jest, but he isn't entirely wrong. My hair is out of control, something I typically tamed. But the big blonde curls that emerged naturally, falling in my face, somewhere between Shirley Temple and wild bed head. But Reid said more than once this weekend how much he loved it, usually as he twirled a curl around one of his long fingers, or tucked a mess of them behind my ear.

I don't have on a lick of makeup and was going for a no-bra look, given that the outfit I arrived in was without one. I probably could have asked Stella to drop off a care package of some kind, but it felt like in doing that, it would have burst the bubble we created this weekend. And I didn't want to emerge even for a breath away from him.

Despite my begging, he wouldn't let me keep the academic decathlon shirt that I've lived in for the past three days. *'When you're here, that shirt is yours. But it doesn't walk out that front door.'* Instead, handing over a pair of sweatpants and a long sleeve henley for the walk back. I look about the farthest thing from presentable. But still, we put on our coats for the first time in three days and headed back to reality.

We stand outside my door as he plants a kiss on my lips, one deep enough to last the few days until I see him again. We traded schedules and knew Monday wasn't in the cards; Tuesday, though, we had agreed to meet at our *official* table.

When I finally step into my suite, Josh, Stella, Ethan and Lindsey, all laughing through a movie, stacks of pizza boxes on the table. Their night looking every bit the cliché college set up I longed for in high school. The people you become attached to faster than logical purely because of forced proximity and shared experiences. And I love them for it, and everything they represent.

I sit on the arm next to Stella, throwing a kiss on the top of her head as she wrapped her arms around my waist.

"Missed you!" She says, as she laid her head in my lap.

"What, they haven't been good company?" I reach over her and swat Josh's shoulder.

"You know I'm the best company. I have a few names if you need to check references–" I hold my hand up to stop him mid sentence.

"I'll take your word for it, wouldn't want to make you double dip."

Double dipping. Sleeping with the same person regularly. God forbid we just call it dating, but this diminishing term kept us from having to call anything what it really was. And we both seem to find that preferable to the alternative of commitment. Although, he seemed to have been willing to compromise that rule in the past, landing himself a *steady* hookup buddy, usually when I did.

"You know..." he teases the words out, "we could use a few references for Lecture-Boy. No one heard from you all fucking weekend, Miami, we don't even know *this one*." The emphasis on *this one* perhaps a nod to *that one* just a few feet from him. Because as much as I think he was annoyed by the brief Ethan chapter (and the fact that it was a chapter at all), he always knew where I was. Usually just on the other side of his bedroom wall. This was different, and we knew it already.

Friday night had been strange, and sitting amongst my friends now, the contention we had just a few days ago felt like it happened a lifetime ago. Stella's birthday party, the game of Never Have I Ever. Josh had intentionally tried to stir the pot, to throw Reid off, rile him up. His petulance and ego needed to be fed the attention.

By nature, I was a grudge holder. By practice, I tried to be better. It was always a great struggle to subdue the parts of me that wanted to be more volatile. Knowing there was no benefit to it, not really.

And that's what I decide now. Not focusing on Friday night when I was so mad at Josh, but just accepting that our dynamic always was a challenge, and that's part of why I was always so addicted to the thrill of him.

Stella scoots over just a bit, and I slide down and wedge myself in the spot between her and the arm of the couch. My back leans against it as I stretch my legs across Stella and Josh. Prodding him with my toe. Which he catches and restrains easily.

"Well, I'm back now, so no need to check any *Reid-sources*... get it? Like resources?" I pause there, waiting for him to laugh at the play on words. But he just huffs and shakes his head while I laugh at my own joke. "Anyways, if you hadn't taken your chance to get to know him and turned it into some dumb let's-spill-Arden's-secrets pissing contest, maybe you would have learned he's a pretty decent guy."

The Cheshire Cat grin widens devilishly across his face.

"Decent is what kept you occupied all weekend? Tsk. Tsk. Tsk... I expected more from you."

"Oh no, he's much *much* better than decent."

Stella bumps shoulders with me in question for the dirty details. I settle in between my two best friends, catching everyone up on some less intimate details of the weekend, though that doesn't stop them from asking for more.

Chapter Twenty-Six

2007

HER

I wake up at an ungodly hour, this time not from insomnia, but nausea. I had made my way to bed a few hours ago, leaving the party going in the other room. I felt fine when I came to bed, *alone,* just a little tired, but now, my skin is covered in a cold sweat. I cling to my blankets, shivering cold as my stomach wildly churns. *UGH! I have food poisoning!* I barely allowed the thought to break through my rattled consciousness when I feel the urgent need and run to the bathroom dragging most of my bedding with me. Landing harshly on my knees and gripping the toilet bowl, throwing up violently, until everything left within me is gone.

I feel the cold ceramic of the tile deep within my bones, but I can't move from where I'm curled on the floor. Wearing nothing but a large tee shirt, I'll just stay here, hugging the bowl, trying to think about what I am supposed to do.

I've never been sick away from home, away from my mother. And suddenly, that terrifying thought takes hold.

Who is going to take care of me?

That's right. Me. The future doctor. Not sure how my science courses would help me now, as I lean forward to throw up again. Do I even have medicine here? Can you take medicine for food poisoning?

God, my parents would be disappointed.

I spent my night back and forth between my bedroom and the bathroom. Stella is a heavy sleeper but found me when she came stumbling into the bathroom early the next morning.

"Are you okay?!" Her face is full of worry as she fills a glass of water and hands it to me.

Damnit, Arden. Stay hydrated.

"I think maybe something was off with the pizza." I had my comforter wrapped around me as she helped me up, grabbing a few plastic bags and the trash can from the bathroom and guiding me back into bed.

"I don't think so, we all ate it, and I'm fine. Plus," she says, extending her hand to my forehead, "you're burning up. You definitely have a fever." My eyes begin to close, drifting into a sleep-like state, though not feeling restful at all. My body is in full battle mode.

"What the fuck, Stells? Why didn't you call me?" I hear the voice in the other room, and not seconds later, my bedroom door swings open.

"I got her back to bed, and she's been asleep for the last few hours."

A few hours? What time is it? I have to get to class.

I feel a hand on my cheek, on my forehead, and I feel a presence hovering over me.

"Hey, Miami... you're not lookin' so hot. I hear there's a bad flu going around." The voice was softer, smooth, the hand brushing the sweat drenched hair from my face. I groan, my throat sore from throwing up, my skin covered in cold beads of sweat, my head tight and pounding, barely able to comprehend the weight of what's happening.

221

"If I-I-I have the f-f-flu, what's your e-e-excuse?" My teeth are chattering with undeniable fever. He laughs, and it sounds like a bit of relief. Knowing that the litmus test of our friendship was always the banter we traded.

"*I* look like shit because I'm worried about you." His hand runs calming strokes through my hair and down my back. He's soft in a way I don't usually know him to be.

"But, I-I-I...h-h-have c-c-class." The uncontrollable shivering as a result of the fever makes it nearly impossible to string together a thought, let alone form a sentence.

Good job with the food poisoning diagnosis, Doctor.

"You missed your morning class. But you're not in any shape to go anywhere." I can feel him, his presence, and the quick work he made to tuck my comforter around me to keep me warm.

My eyes finally open, and there he is; Josh is standing over my bed, and he searches through his phone for something but pauses when he sees my eyes are open and alert.

"There you are." I don't think I've ever heard his voice so passive, looking visibly concerned.

I try to shake my head, to indicate I don't want him to worry, but as I do, the churning begins to surface. Panic washes over me as I hurriedly sit up and reach down beside the bed grasping for the trash can. "Hey, hey, hey... here..." His hand on my back, he lifts the trash can, allowing me to grab it as I lean over, holding tightly and retching into the bin as his other moves to pull my hair back.

"You're okay." Taking a seat next to me on the bed, I lift my head and wipe my face on the sweat-drenched tee shirt.

"You're fine, Arden. I'm here, you're alright." His hand on my back rubbing circles, as my stomach clenches and I lean forward again.

I've expelled everything my body was holding on to, so I let myself fall back into bed. Josh stands from where he was seated beside me and picks up the trash can, as I see him pull his phone from his pocket and hold it to his ear.

"Hey man, you have class with Arden Bancroft today, right?" I don't hear who's on the receiving end, but I'm guessing by Josh's reply, they confirmed. "Can you let the professor know she's not making it to class, and I'll grab whatever notes and assignments so she can have them... mhm... she's in bad shape... mhm... looks like that flu... nah, I got the flu shot."

God, Arden. Get the flu shot. Thats fucking number one on the list. Get the flu shot. Stay hydrated. Pee after sex.

He made three more calls just like that one.

I was watching this play out through a foggy lens as Josh took off the cocky mask he normally wore and replaced it with this *nurturing one?* Whatever it is, I am grateful.

"Thanks." It comes out in almost a whisper. Whatever subconscious grudge I still had from the other night loosens and is released entirely knowing he's here and taking care of me because he's my friend.

My best fucking friend.

"You need to change." He grabs some miscellaneous pajamas from my drawer and helps me step into the bottoms. Handing me the top, before taking the trash can and heading back into the main room leaving me to change, returning a few minutes later with a washcloth, a clean trash can, and a bottle of water.

"Here's the plan, Miami, you're going to get back in bed and get some sleep." He brushes the cool washcloth across my brow and down my face. Pulling my hair up with a scrunchy he found on the table beside my bed, leaning me back, tucking me in, and settling next to me, until my eyelids lose their battle and shut.

I don't know how many hours pass before the next time I open my eyes, but my head is throbbing. There is light coming from my desk, and I spot the figure sitting there. Josh is working away on the computer, the desk lamp the only thing illuminating my room. I can tell from the window the sun has already set, which means I've been asleep all day. *I think it's the same day.*

"Hey," my voice rasps, raw from the ordeal today. The word vibrates within my skull.

His head whips around, "Heyyyy," he drags it out slowly, cautiously. "You look a little more with it."

I chance a smile, but it doesn't fully form, as he stands and walks over to the bed where I've managed to sit up to face him, my back still against the wall for support. He presses the back of his hand to my forehead.

"You're still burning up," he says as he slips a thermometer in my mouth. "What are you doing?"

"Stop talking and keep that thing under your tongue, otherwise it won't get a good read."

"Is this my thermometer?" It hangs from my mouth as I speak, ignoring his direction, just dangling there between my lips like a lit cigarette.

He snags it from my mouth, resets it so it beeps. Taking my face in his hand, and squeezing my cheeks to part my lips, before slipping it in again.

"I'm being serious here, Arden. I need to see your temperature. And if you can't keep this under your tongue... There is always another option." I oblige and keep it pressed beneath my tongue, knowing the alternative is a level of intimacy he and I will never share.

I hate this. I hate being taken care of like this. I hate being so wholly exposed in this moment that even my body temperature is up for discussion. Yet, I don't know what I would do if I were alone.

Ironic, isn't it? I should be able to handle being sick.

But being sick is a type of vulnerability that leaves me at the mercy of others, and I hate it. Yet, like everyone else in this world, I can't avoid it.

But Josh isn't here to exploit that vulnerability, he's here to take care of me. My eyes drift close. And I have no idea for how long, only realizing it couldn't be more than a minute when the thermometer still held between my lips beeps in completion.

The shrill sound slicing right through me.

"102. You need to take some Tylenol, and take a shower to help with the fever." My eyes open from their defeated state, to look at him as I ask, "How do you know all this?"

"I called Dr. Bancroft." *Which one, mom or dad.* I want to ask, but I don't need to. "She gave me a list of very specific instructions to follow. Which means now she has my phone number, and she is definitely not afraid to use it." He points to the desk, where there is a collection of items. Medicines, Gatorade, saltines, a practical how-to guide.

"You called my mom." Not a question, but there's something about needing your mom when you're sick, *doctor or not*, and he called her. I know this was beyond normal medical advice when I look over to the desk and see a bunch of lollipops, something she no doubt would have told him I needed, not to manage any symptoms, just because.

"Yeah, I called your mom."

I move to sit up straighter and my vision tunnels out, blurry at the edges. I feel dizzy as my head tightens. It must have been visible because he steadies me with his hands on each arm. Standing in front of me. My strength is completely gone from the last twelve hours of vomiting, and he helps me off the bed, grabs some stuff from my drawers, and supports me on the short walk to the bathroom. Turning on the shower, the steam already filling the room.

"Come on, Miami... you have to get in the shower. You can get in like this if you want," he tugs the pajama blouse, reminding me I'm dressed, "but if you're interested in a wet-tee-shirt situation, we should find a contest where you can actually win a prize."

"I like to win," I rasp out with a congested laugh.

"I know." His grip on my arm tightens as I sway slightly. I'm more out of it than I care to admit, but the first step to feeling better? Faking it.

"I'm okay, Josh. I've got it from here."

"You don't have to prove anything, Arden. You can barely stand." He puts the clean clothes on the bathroom counter. I stabilize myself, slip out of my pants, and muster everything I have to show him I'm fine.

"You're so fucking stubborn," he mutters. "Leave the door open, I'll be right out here." He steps out of the bathroom, and I focus on staying upright, as I finish undressing and step into the shower. I rub my face clean and let the water wash away the sickness of the last day, at least on the outside.

I hear their voices as soon as I shut off the shower, Stella and Josh, the two of them trading details like nurses switching shifts.

"I'm staying, Stells."

"You don't need to, I can keep an eye on her."

"Doesn't matter, I've already grabbed what I need, her mom calls me every couple hours, and she listens to me." Stella just laughs in reply, like I would if I had the energy to do anything more than breathe.

They must have heard the silence when Josh's voice penetrates through the bathroom door.

"I'd ask if you're decent, but I know better."

"As decent as I'll get." I was standing there, wrapped in a towel, but had already managed to put on underwear. The heat I felt moments ago was replaced with a desperate need for warmth as I shivered in place. He helped me dress as I held on to him. A vulnerability neither of us really ever exchanged. Him offering himself sweetly, me, allowing the help.

My entire body trembles, and my head feels like it's losing the battle to stay alert. I let down another guard, as I drape my arm over his shoulder and lean my head against his chest.

"Okay, Miami. Come on." He bends down and picks me up slowly, dressed in my clean, warm pajamas, he places me back into my bed and pulls the clean navy sheets up over me. Before settling himself next to me.

"You changed my sheets... wait, are these my sheets?"

"My spare set. Yours are in the hamper. You weren't here this weekend for laundry day."

That's right. Laundry day. Our Saturday morning ritual. That way we always have clean underwear and clean sheets for Saturday night.

I lay there, leaning into him, when Stella enters with a bowl of something clearly steaming.

"Soup!!" She squeaks. Handing Josh the bowl, and settling herself at the foot of the bed, laying her arm across my legs. They stayed there with me as I swallowed down, spoon by spoon. Not sure what I found more comforting, the soup or my friends.

Josh's head was resting back against the wall. His eyes closed, but with none of the vulnerability of sleep. Just resting next to me, listening to Stella go on about her boyfriend and other miscellaneous campus gossip. Even strategically asking about Reid along the way.

Reid. Shit. I am supposed to meet him tomorrow morning. I hadn't spoken to him since he dropped me off at my door. *Had he called? Texted?* Either way, I have to tell him I won't be able to meet him for coffee. My two nurses, and my tele-doc mom, already decided that I was to make my way to the Campus Health Center first thing in the morning, not happy with my progress so far.

"Where's my phone, I need–?"

"What do you need?" Josh's eyes open, sitting upright ready to respond.

"Tomorrow, I have class."

"I have that class with you, already emailed the professor."

"And I'm supposed to meet Reid at eight."

"Already texted him." I move my head to look at him, but every move causes my body to ache.

"It's fine, *AB*." He looks at me tightly as he says it. Draping his arm around me and letting me lean into him completely. "He knows you aren't coming. Lecture-Boy will be fine as soon as you are."

———

The trip to the Campus Health Center proved it was the flu and I was dehydrated. *Sorry mom. Guess you were right.*

I spent the next three days in bed, and never completely alone. I'd wake up to Josh or Stella, or *both*, depending on the shift, after strict instruction from the doctor, *and my mother*, to keep me hydrated.

Day by day doing better. Eating more, throwing up less by Wednesday, fever completely gone by Thursday. And by Friday morning, I awoke with more clarity in vision and thought than I had in days. Rubbing the sleep and sickness from my eyes, I check the clock. It's 10:00 a.m., so Josh will be in class. I swing my legs from the bed, momentarily feeling like a baby giraffe as my legs adjust to the ground, as if I hadn't learned to walk.

Grabbing the hoodie hanging on the back of my desk chair, *Josh's*, and making my way into the main room where Stella was standing in our small kitchenette making a cup of tea. She brightens immediately when she sees me.

"You look sooo much better!"

"I'm feeling sooo much better!" This time when I say it, I finally mean it. No longer feeling like I'm lost in a daze.

"Thanks to you, Nurse Stells."

She hands me the cup of tea I now know she was preparing for me, part of whatever sick regimen she had been following. *And I remembered the countless cups of tea and broth I had been forced to drink in the last days.*

"It was more him than me, you know."

I think I did know. I have hazy memories of him carrying me to bed, sitting with me in the bathroom, steaming the room to break my fever. I remember him on the phone to my mom.

I move to the couch and curl my feet underneath me, holding my mug of tea to warm my hands as I sip it down.

Stella joins me and looks on the verge of saying something. She's usually the first one to say what she's thinking, so her hesitation has me curious. I jab her in the thigh with my toes.

"Just say it..." Her face pulls to the side and her eyebrows pinched together. Teetering on the thought.

"It's not anything..." She presses her lips together to contain the thought.

"Then why does it look like something?" And it does. She is noodling it through, I can tell, but I don't know why.

"It's just that, I've never seen him like that. Like he wouldn't leave your side. It was incredible, but I..." she trailed off, cautiously. "I just think he might be feeling more than he's let on."

"Oh," I laugh, and she looks shocked at my dismissal. I don't know what I was expecting her to say, but it wasn't that.

"No, Stells, I don't think so."

Her head whips to me, "You didn't see him, I'm *telling* you. There's something there. He's just not saying it."

"Stella, that's how I know it's not anything, because when does that man *not* say something? *Especially* if it could have the ability to stir up a reaction. I know he cares about me; I care about him. But hey, I remember you also nursed me back to health."

"I don't know, Arden, just keep an eye. Especially because it sounds like you might be jumping into something with this Reid guy."

Shit. Reid.

I haven't picked up my phone in days, so I have no idea the status of the *Reid-guy*, but he was at least warned I was sick and couldn't make it. Though it's almost strange to me he didn't show up here. It's not that it was expected for him to drop by, but we had spent nearly two weeks meeting for coffee, talking on the phone, texting, and then three days totally tangled together, it seemed out of character that he wouldn't.

Or at least the character I thought he had.

He had said this would be a busy week but had still made plans to see me Tuesday morning. And I just couldn't shake the feeling that if he had felt the way I was beginning to about everything that was happening between us, he would have been more concerned that I was sick, or at the very least that he hadn't heard from me in a few days. *And this is why I don't do labels.*

While I didn't have an expectation for him to be here, to be the one taking care of me, based on what I knew about him, it seemed like something he would have done. Something feels wrong at the thought that even if he does care, it isn't the way my friends do.

With that, disappointment and doubt took root.

Chapter Twenty-Seven

2007

HER

After being down with a flu, I had immense amounts of work to catch up on. Josh had made sure I'd gotten notes from all the classes we didn't share from mutual friends or classmates of mine he hunted down, and provided his own for the ones we did. His notes are more thorough than I've ever seen them before, and I suspect it was for me.

It wasn't just schoolwork, I had gone M.I.A. from my entire life, and it was time to get back into it. I called my mom, who was relieved that I was better. Apparently, she was close to hopping on a plane and coming up, but between Josh and Stella her concern was slightly assuaged.

Despite not having heard from Reid, I wanted to talk to him. Not that I was looking to *'jump into something'* as Stella put it, but I definitely thought there was something between us that could have merited a quick drop by, or even phone call in the last few days.

Like me, his schedule is packed with a working internship, graduate courses, plus friends and a social life which he referenced regularly enough for me to believe he actually had one. But, even still, he had made a point to find time for me to fit it. I made time to fit in.

He answers on the first ring, and I can hear his smile through the phone. The eagerness in the single word of greeting nearly knocked me down in surprise.

"Hey!"

"Hi..." I'm not sure what I called to say. Just that I knew I wanted to call. I probably should have thought about it for longer than a second. But he doesn't leave a fraction of silence between us.

"I'm glad you called. I was wondering when I'd hear from you." He sounds it, too. Enthusiastic and sincere. But his tone doesn't stop me from asking.

"Really?" My voice is still soft, perhaps because my vocal cords are still waking up after being so infrequently used this week. Perhaps because I'm surprised he wanted to hear from me at all when I haven't heard from him in days.

"Yes, really. Why? What are you doing?" His eager tone is now curious.

Let's see, what am I doing? Laying in bed thinking about you? Taking my temperature for the millionth time confirming I'm no longer sick? No, I'm looking at a stack of a week's worth of reading I need to do in two days.

"I'm just getting ready to jump into some reading... I have a lot of work to catch up on. What about you?"

That's smooth. See what he's been up to that's kept him so busy that he didn't call.

"Finishing an analysis for a class. Wait, why are you behind?"

"I wouldn't say *behind*..."

"Why are you, whatever it is you would say you are, that's got you needing to *catch up*?" His tone shifted again, this time from curiosity to confusion, maybe even concern.

"Well, that's what happens when you don't go to classes for a week."

"I need you to be clear, what happened?" *Yes, that's full blown concern in his voice now.* It escalated differently than most people I know. He didn't dial it up in volume or frenzy, but strength. Like he wants to jump through the phone to make sure everything is alright.

"It was just the flu."

"You've been sick? And you're alright now? I thought you just needed some time because you had a busy week. You could have called me. I know this is a new thing between us, but I hope you know you can call me if you need something. I'd prefer to have known what was going on, rather than you just canceling our date."

Wait. Did I cancel our plans? I don't remember that. Now I'm the one who is confused. Not remembering the details.

"I'm fine now, perfect even, but yeah, I was in pretty bad shape; the doctor kept me in bed." *The doctor, my mom, and my best friends.* I switch the phone to speaker and look over my text messages. There it was, the texts that were sent, and one that had been received.

> **Reid:** I like having you here, AB. ;)
> **Reid:** When can you come back?

I checked the timestamp. He sent it as soon as he got home Sunday night. Then he sent three more follow up messages that came through on Monday.

> **Reid:** Can't wait to see you in the morning.
> **Reid:** I wonder if our table will be mad that we abandoned her for a few days? (Yes, I'm calling our table a her. I think it has something to do with the legs.)

Reid: Then again, she'll be fine without us. I have a perfectly good coffee pot here...
me: Can't make coffee or anything else this week. Will call when I can.

Nope. Not me. Didn't send it, and I know who did. I can't even be mad. Josh had told Reid I couldn't make it. He wasn't wrong. He didn't just disappear on him; he preserved the notion that I wanted to see him again. *Kind of?* It just wasn't as friendly as I would have hoped. I look at the messages Reid had sent. He *was* playful, in a way that I don't know he let a lot of people see. But here it was in writing as he personified a small cafe table, *our table.* And you know what, it absolutely made me smile. Until I again look at the response he got.

I don't try to explain it all, knowing the tangled explanation of who took care of me, and who canceled our plans could go over poorly, it's just not worth it. Reid doesn't seem mad; in fact, he gave me the time he thought I needed based on the message.

"Sorry, the whole week has been a fever dream. I'm finally back to myself."

"I feel bad that you were sick and alone. Next time, tell me and I'll be there. I can make a mean cup of tea."

"Oh yeah? *How* mean?"

"A downright bully. Complete asshole if you'd believe it. But with a little honey, it can be just what the doctor ordered." We both chuckle, and even hearing it through the phone warmed me as if I just sipped one down.

"I'm alright, my friends were here, my mom called a lot. But it was really weird being sick away from home."

I hear him clear his throat, not sure if it was a reflex or him containing one of the things he didn't want to say. Instead, opting for something he did.

"I remember the first time I got sick on my own, it was the

worst. I also called my mom. I think I kept her on the phone the entire time. That was also the last time I ever ate a lobster roll." He huffed a little laugh as if recalling the memory of what sounded like a traumatic food-poisoning experience. Offering it up to me in exchange. And I laughed lightly with him. Both at the shared experience and the visual of him begging his mom to stay on the phone. *Okay, he didn't say he begged her. But in my mind, that's how it went.*

He breaks the laughter with something else entirely, unabashed honesty.

"I've been thinking about you." There it is, the thing that spreads a smile across my face because even in the feverish state, he occupied a place in my mind.

"You can bring whatever work you have to catch up on and do it here. Might be quieter than a dorm on a Friday night. I'll make you a deal, you can even have the first choice between the counter top and desk for your workspace."

"Giving up your desk? How selfless."

"Not entirely, I'd like to see you. It's a worthy price to pay. That is, only if you're feeling up for it."

"I really am all better, but are you sure *you're* up for it?" He lets out a dark laugh that flutters my stomach recalling him.

"Arden, number one, I wouldn't offer if I didn't mean it and I can guar-an-tee," he enunciates every syllable, "I'll be *up* for it." We let that sit there a moment. And for the first time in a week, the flutter in my stomach isn't from nausea.

"That sounds great then, I'll be over in a little while."

"Buzz when you're downstairs, I'll be waiting."

We hang up the phone, and I feel better than I had. I pack up some things, the books I need, my computer, the items he'd lent me last week, and an actual change of clothes this time. He hadn't asked me to stay over but it was implied, wasn't it? And I didn't think he would want to give up another set of sweatpants for me to walk home.

Stella is going home for the weekend to spend it with her boyfriend, so our suite will be completely empty. Truth is, it would probably be a perfect place to catch up on schoolwork, but it is missing one key thing, *him*.

The walk to his apartment has become familiar. Feeling like I've done dozens of times, though it's only been twice. I wonder what other muscle memory might be triggered when I get there.

There is comfort in seeing him, lacking a lot of the anxiety around a crush, but the familiarity that comes from knowing someone. Someone I hadn't truthfully known all that long. There were layers of myself that I had built up, layers of ice that I let come down only when someone worthy put in effort to thaw them, and that seemed to be Reid. He began to thaw them instantly. His sincerity washed over the sheets of ice like warm water. Until they eventually would be melted away completely. We aren't there yet. Not everyone could be as barefaced as he was. But it didn't seem to put him off, it seemed to challenge him.

The notion of being a challenge for someone was not new. It was one of the things that drew people to me. One of the reasons I was always able to collect friends. Because I kept parts of myself tucked away like prizes for only the worthiest of contenders. My closest friends have barely made the inner circle, but in just a couple of weeks Reid was making it his personal mission to get through them all. But it was different. It wasn't the thrill or challenge he was after nor the prize. It was the knowledge, the learning. He wanted to *know* me, not *win* me. He said it from the beginning. The moment he sat down and pulled the bag of scrabble tiles with the intention of only playing words that would allow us to get to know each other.

My mind keeps pace with my feet as I turn down the brick lined street. Passing the striped awning of our chocolate shop. By the time I get to the brick alcove and buzz his apartment, my head feels heavy and overflowing in thought. Like things I had picked up along the way, collecting them, and tucking the thought into whatever empty corner my mind had available.

He buzzes the front door open immediately as I hit 2-A, and as I climb the stairs two by two, he comes into view. Standing there, front door open, leaning against the door frame waiting casually. Though the smile on his face is anything but casual. It's eager and bright, everything he is, and it hits me immediately.

I dive into his chest. Head first into the deep end of him. Enveloped entirely. Every one of my senses are completely overwhelmed by him. He wraps his arms around my back, lifting me into a hug, squeezing me tightly as my feet hovered above the ground. The pressure around my ribs from his embrace doesn't restrict my breathing, but slows it to follow his.

I lay my head into the crook of his neck. *Was he this tall last week?*

He lets my body slide down his so slowly until settling my feet back to the ground. His hand curved around the back of my neck as he brings his mouth to mine. Gentle, but intentional. Always testing the waters of my comfort.

My mind had been full but when his lips found mine they pulled every single thought out of me. With each tug of his kiss, he empties my mind of clouded thoughts and replenishes it with new ones. Ones of *him.*

"Missed you, AB."

"You really just always say what you want."

"No, I say what I *mean.*" Planting one more soft kiss on my lips, the signature at the end of the sentence. He grabs the bag I had dropped at his feet and walks me inside.

"Are you sure you're feeling all better?" He appraises me, at face value I must pass inspection, but he wants to hear me say it. The clarity he always asks for.

"Yes, all better. Scouts honor!" I say holding up three

fingers to signify some kind of boy scout symbol I didn't actually know.

Standing in his space feels like being in his arms. It's such a representation of him. Dropping my bag next to his desk, I can see he had his own laptop open next to books, notebooks, and a stack of sticky notes. Methodical. Having been in the middle of something before my arrival.

"I think we have a couple options..."

I had taken a seat at the kitchen counter and propped my chin on my fist, batting my eyelashes in a blatant display of false naivety, as he rounded the counter and placed himself across from me on the other side. As if the forced distance between us on the countertop is necessary until we choose just which option we will pursue.

"I'm listening..." My voice is lyrical and sweet.

"We can start with studying, set a goal, and not let ourselves get," he clears his throat, "*distracted* until we've completed it. Pros include the incredible motivation of reward. Cons, it will be hard... not to be distracted."

"Hmmmm," I muse. My tongue curls up around my lip tauntingly. I see his eyes narrow on me, dropping to my mouth instantly. "That sounds like it has its benefits, and I really *do* like a reward."

"I can see how you would say that, *Miss Bancroft*," His tone is stiffer, more academic, yet playful in a way I was learning he could be, straightening his stance to that of a professor. "But I must remind you *not* to answer prior to having all the information." Even in just a tee shirt and sweatpants, even knowing his tone is in jest, his presence is commanding, and I want to eliminate the distance between us. I giggle at the display. But beneath the counter, my legs are pressed together impossibly tight.

"Yes, *Sir*, and what is my other option?"

His throat bobs with forced restraint, anticipation for

what's building. My mouth aching for the feeling of his, I pull in the corner of my bottom lip, pinning it under the pressure of my top teeth. Slowly releasing it, letting it glisten with wetness from where my tongue grazed it, before pulling it again slowly.

"Arden." His voice is slow, deep, and has a rough smokiness to match his gaze. Not an actual warning, but it feels like I am teetering on the edge of one. And my body prepared itself.

This habit that was so second nature. Grounding and focusing. It wasn't intentional, but his reaction was going to make it so. I remembered what he said last week when he saw me do this same thing, for the first time in private. Not having realized the tension that had been building for him. Each time we were together in public, the restraint he exercised seeing me do it.

'Baby, if you want the feeling of teeth on your lip, just say so. Because every time you do that, it makes me fucking crazy.'

Instead of responding, instead of releasing the skin of my lip, I cock my head to the side and pin him with a stare of my own. Waiting in provocation.

His inhale is deep and slow, commanding his body to still.

"Option two." His professor-voice is replaced with one much darker, the deepest keys on the pianos. One that drips of intensity and tastes like desire. His hands tightly gripping the edge of the counter, trying to maintain even the smallest amount of control over his body as he watches me drag my lip under my teeth one more time in pure taunt. "You can get your ass over here. *Right. Fucking. Now.*" His lips pull into the most indecent smile.

I had kicked my shoes off, dropping them beneath the counter. Pulling my feet onto the seat and placing my hands on the counter in front of me, I lean forward and begin crawling the short distance between us, my shirt hanging loosely, and I see him chance a look down the collar at my breasts, before he looks back to mouth, something else he's ready to claim.

I move impossibly slowly. It wouldn't have taken long to cross the width of the counter, but no one has ever looked at me the way he is, and I'm in no rush for that to end.

I stop right in front of him, not altering the animal-like position that has me on my hands and knees. His hands on either side of me, his face looks down at mine.

"Good answer." He looks ready to take me, but instead, the corner of his lip pulls higher into a deviant smirk.

"I like you like this, on your hands and knees."

"Then you should have me like this. *On my hands and knees.*"

I'm pulled off the counter and into a deep kiss. A forewarning. My feet back on the ground, we begin to frantically undress.

I take off my jeans, he drops his sweatpants to the ground, not before pulling a condom from the pocket and letting it dangle from his lips as his hands remove my bra.

Our clothes leave a scattered trail from the kitchen to the living room, where he guides me with each of his steps.

There we are, again, both completely naked, as he palms my breast with one hand, and drags a long finger across the seam of me, feeling the wetness that waited for him. I take him in my hand, and he's hard, throbbing as I tighten my grip, and move aggressively, causing a groan so deep that I am brought to my knees by just the sound of him.

Before he can fully register it, I take him deeply in my mouth. His hand gripping the top of my head with the same force my fingers had around him.

He yanks my head back.

Is this not what he wants? Is this not good? Whether it be the thought he had or the one he could read on my face, his next words answer it for me.

"I said I want you on your hands *and* knees." His voice is smoke surrounding me. The words swirling from his lips curled around me where I kneeled at his feet by the brown leather sofa.

"I want you to come so furiously that your fingernails leave marks in the leather." His hands under my arms lifting me back to my feet. As he tears the condom wrapper and rolls it on.

"I want to hear my skin slap against yours while I fuck you relentlessly." He pulls my back to his front and moves us onto the couch. Leaning me forward so I can brace my hands against the arm as he cloaks me with his whole chest.

"I want to feel you come around me so hard that your body rips the orgasm from mine." He trails kisses on my back, lining his body up against mine. Grabbing my chin and turning my head towards him, over my shoulder taking my mouth with his.

"And baby, I won't have your mouth around me until I've had mine on you first." He ends the sentence with a kiss as he slams himself into me. My core tightens around him immediately, my elbows buckle as I almost collapse forward from the incredible pressure of having him inside of me at this angle.

His right arm wrapped under me, around my ribs, supporting me as I lose myself in total physical rapture. The grip of his arm is solid, his palm takes ownership of my breast, as his fingertips mimic my own, digging into whatever they can.

I feel his teeth on my back. Nipping at my skin as his body is leaned over mine, possessing me completely as he slams into me, having deserted any of his self-control. And like he predicted, I come furiously. In the final seconds collapsing forward and sinking my teeth, not nails, into the arm of the sofa, muffling the sound of my orgasm. And with it, he chases me over the same edge he pushed us to. "*Fuck.*" He grinds out as he comes. Our bodies collapse completely onto the couch. I can tell it takes more strength than it should have to lift himself onto his elbows, completely spent, doing his best not to crush me under him.

"You fucking have me," he says through panting breaths. Answering something I didn't ask. At least not out loud.

I thought *I* was lost to *him, my* body owned by *him,* but that isn't it.

We are completely lost, together.

Tangled in this, in a way I couldn't have predicted, a way neither of us could have expected.

I wasn't sure that he wanted to say the words out loud, but I know well enough he meant them all the same.

"Good, because I fucking *want* you."

Chapter Twenty-Eight

PRESENT

HER

Amanda is typing away on her laptop; we've been here longer than normal today.

It had all started four weeks ago when she asked a simple question about breakup sex. Looking back, one I probably shouldn't have answered. Because in doing so, I took a first step down a path I thought was familiar, but I had no idea where it would lead. That's the bizarre part of it. I thought I had read this book before–several times, in fact. Over and over for weeks after everything first went awry.

The story began before we ever started dating, and the end of our relationship was not the end of the story. The real end is one that no one *actually* knows, aside from the people involved. But now, this book I had thought I'd known so well has become a story I can't predict the end to. The main character, a first draft to the main character now. Who I am as I sit here, so different from who I was when he was him. When we were together.

I had begun to tell Amanda the details of the story. She

knew all the relevant characters by now, and while I know she wanted me to jump to the end, to the part of the story that explains what unraveled that night, there were reasons I wasn't ready to yet. As if my body responded to the thought, and a small wave of nausea rolled through me. Swallowing it down with a sip of water.

"You feeling okay?" She asks delicately, looking up from her computer. I nod my reply, taking another small sip of water. The only thing that seems to help. I rest my hand on my stomach as if I can feel the nausea churning, taking a deep breath through my nose.

"Yeah—totally fine. Where was I?"

"Josh is clearly in love with you, and you are definitely falling for Reid. The good-ol'-fashioned love triangle trope." Her laugh is one of disbelief, and thrill. To a novelist, this story with its layers and real life tropes was too good to be true. *For now.*

"But I don't understand how you end up—"

"I know, I know, trust me, I'll get there. You need the whole story to understand it. I lived the whole story, am still living the whole story, and I don't fully get it." This time, it is my own disbelief that has me shaking my head from side to side.

"And you guys have stayed in touch all this time, didn't let your friendship go, it's gotta mean something to both of you. And after all that, you don't talk to—"

"No."

"I know you like to think you're psychic, but you could let me finish a sentence," she teases.

"I'm sure I could, but then how would *you* know I'm psychic?"

The truth is, I am far from psychic. I'm not even sure if I would call myself intuitive at this point. I have years of anecdotal evidence to prove just how wrong I could be. This being a perfect example. It's no surprise that I am different now than I was then.

That is just the nature of growing up. And I had done some growing. At the time, I was so afraid of losing myself, but I didn't even really know who that was yet. So I focused on not losing the person everyone expected me to be while I figured out the rest of it. I focused on the fleeting happiness, the kind it was easy to find in other people.

The start of my college career catapulted me immediately into an inner circle of friends, created these codependent relationships and then practically overnight the entire thing shifted under my feet. Cut to 2022, and here I am. While many people look around and want more from their lives, mine was about as fulfilling as one could get.

"How's your book coming?" I ask Amanda, changing the subject from the topic that has monopolized our conversation since it happened.

"There's been some interesting developments, I think this is going to be a good one." She smiles.

"Well, I'm still waiting to read it."

"You'll get the full draft soon! But you're gonna totally love it. I already do."

She moves her hands back to her keyboard and begins to type away when my phone pings in alert. It appears we are not the only ones who find ourselves reliving this. Seems as though, he too, has fallen into this Pavlovian response to a Sunday afternoon, where he jumps back into the conversation just like we do.

It all seems to come to a head on Sunday, as if he can hear it, the story I'm telling. The details I've included as I paint the picture for Amanda.

Despite the fact that his last text to me remained unanswered. No matter that he is across the country, there's a tether between us that keeps tugging on his attention.

Arden-

I went through some old boxes from my time in school and found some photos I thought you might enjoy.

See attached.

I scroll through the half a dozen attached photos, some of us on campus, at The Commons, me playing in the snow, and a photo I have never seen before, taken by someone else obviously. We weren't even the focus, it was a shot of the lecture hall, but there we were, luckily caught in this moment. Seated next to each other engaged in deep conversation, surrounded by people and ignoring everyone completely.

Looking at us, at them, they had no idea what was going to happen. How hard they would fall in love. She had no idea how much she would change because of it. But looking at us so much younger than we are now, I can see it. She was enchanted, *I was enchanted.*

HIM

I never heard from her when I asked her to see me. The only response I got was her turning off her phone. Fuck, for a good hour I thought she might have blocked my number. Only accepting that as an over escalation after checking back later that night, drafting another response, and seeing the option to send as an iMessage. Knowing the blue bubble would send, and not turn green upon delivery, was enough to take comfort in the fact that I hadn't crossed the line beyond repair.

But it's still been a week and a half and she hasn't responded to the invitation to meet. Had I invited her to coffee prior to all this, I have no doubt she would have shown up. Now? She won't even text me back.

From the moment we met, there was something that pulled us together, and we still have some semblance of a friendship because of that, even with the short romantic detour. It's not that I am wildly sentimental, but I do think it is important to remember the important things. She was an important thing. I knew it immediately when I saw her. Even in a room full of people.

I pull down the box from where it has been tucked away in the side hall closet for years, COLLEGE written in marker on the side. I have an idea of what is in here. It's a lot more than just her. But it is her I am looking for when I open it. I pull out an old college tee shirt that is thread worn and smells of mothballs. Some tickets to Red Sox games, notebooks, a paper hat from that obnoxious restaurant where they heckle you while you eat an overpriced burger, and just what I was looking for... stacks of photos. *Thank god I kept photos.*

She told me once that she got rid of everything after a breakup. I guess it makes sense, you wouldn't want to keep mementos from someone who you thought dumped you. *Even though I did.*

There is one photo I am looking for. One I haven't thought about in years. As I flip through the stack, many of them are stuck together, not having seen the light of day in at least a decade.

There it is.

There we are.

Day One.

Seated next to each other in the lecture hall, waiting for it to begin. Waiting for it all to begin. I had spotted her immediately that day but had no idea what would come of it. How it would land us in a relationship so deeply intertwined, until we both just... weren't. That's what happened. I've thought through it enough, played the options out numerous times. Through the eyes of who I was then, and who I am now.

The thing that doesn't change, no matter what context is added, is that we both effectively walked away and didn't challenge the other to stay. We let ourselves bury the romantic part of our relationship, only preserving a more structured version. A structure that has been crumbling now.

I have photos of friends, Rocky Horror night, and then one stops me completely. I took it during the first snow of the year. She said she had seen snow before, but never in the way I had growing up somewhere cold. Growing up in Miami meant she only ever saw snow on a planned vacation. Not the surprise joy, or more often the inconvenience, of waking up to a fresh snow flurry.

The photo was taken one morning when we woke up, and overnight, six inches had fallen. She ran outside to the quad, grabbing her roommate along the way, barely dressed in a way that wouldn't result in frostbite. She's holding out a snowball like it's her prized possession, meanwhile snowflakes are clustered to her eyelashes, forming an angelic crown atop her head, and her nose is bright red from the cold.

How could I not have kept these memories?

Making quick work to attach several of these photos to an email, including my two favorites, I send them off to her. Maybe this will get a reply.

This is the most dangerous game we've ever played.

I know it, but I can't control myself. *Can she?*

Chapter Twenty-Nine

2007

HER

"I really have work to catch up on, I didn't come over here just for this."

"I'm sure, and you can absolutely spend your weekend with your face in a book. But as an expert, I can tell you study breaks are a necessity." He had put back on his boxer briefs, I pulled on my own underwear, and grabbed the hoodie from his desk chair. It smells like him, I smell like him.

"Okay, but I'm not ready to get up yet."

"Good." He whispers into my skin, ending the thought with a kiss pressed to my temple.

It all happened so fast; we were happening so fast.

He pulled me into him in every way. My body against his, my mind into his, me, into his space. That we lay here my back to his front, his arm tucked under my head, as the other draped over me keeping me close on the sofa.

We were ravenous just moments ago, feeding from each other in an insatiable way, and now we lay here peacefully sated. I roll in his arms to face him, the profile of my face lines up to his throat, my nose brushing against his Adam's apple as he tightens his hold around me. And I breathe him in that cedar and cinnamon scent that might exist more in my mind than on his skin. I inhale this moment of uninterrupted comfort. Where my head is clear but not empty.

"Tell me something," I whisper into his neck, with my lips against his skin.

"Anything you want." I can feel his mouth move on the top of my head as he answers.

"Hmmm... tell me... about your plans and what you're doing next."

"Oh, what I want to do next is right here," nuzzling his chin into my hair, "and as for my plans," a low laugh breaking up his thought, "with you, it seems all my plans go out the window."

There is so much charged energy between the two of us, and while we lay here, bare legs intertwined, it would take nothing to have him inside of me again. I can feel him, hardening pressed against my leg. He takes a long slow inhale, something I'm constantly mesmerized by. The control he exhibits over himself.

Another deep inhale, as he drags his hand up and down my back in rhythm with our shared breath.

"I have a few potential job offers lined up after graduation. One is at the consulting office that I am currently interning with..."

"Mhmm," I mewled into his neck. "Tell me more..." wiggling my hips into his as I slide my right leg up, laying my thigh over his.

Another slow inhale.

"Well," *it's a game, he knows this is a game,* "it seems like it will be a good fit, I have a good friend already working there, and I've learned a lot so far, but would require me to stay in the area."

"Oooh, and don't you like it here?"

"I am loving it here." He palms my ass and runs it down my thigh. "I originally planned to move to New York, or maybe Chicago, depending." I drag the tip of my tongue with painful slowness up the length of his neck. And the groan that vibrates from his vocal cords reverberates down my core, and he feels the involuntary jerk, squeezing my thighs together on impulse.

"Baby, you need to tell me what to do right now."

"Oh, yeah?" I move myself deeper into him and pull my head out from under his chin so I can look up to him.

"*Ohhh, yeahhh?*" he mocks as he pinches my chin and locks his eyes into mine.

I say nothing. I know what he wants from me. He wants me to tell him I want him. I was the one who made the point about having work to do, but it's only Friday. I have two more days. *Granted, I have enough to do that I could fill the time.* But right now, the only thing I want to do is him.

"I can always study later. Don't you *want* to distract me?" He leans his mouth over mine. His tongue moves slowly, patiently waiting for allowance into my mouth.

"Arden," he pulls his face away from mine to catch my eye clearly. "I won't ask again because that's not my responsibility. I'll trust when you tell me what you want, that it isn't at the expense of something important... But *fuck*, if it isn't clear to you what I want right now."

It is clear. Crystal fucking clear, and hard pressed against me.

"I'll study later."

"Good answer."

He moves on top of me and grabs the hem of his sweatshirt that I had stolen, pulling it up and over my head. Exposing me again completely. My back hitting the leather of the couch, my nipples peaking as soon as they are exposed to the cool apartment air.

He lips on mine, beginning his map of kisses. Unhurried.

The pace is entirely different than before. Languidly marking each spot like a trail of breadcrumbs for him to find his way.

His hair, usually brushed back, until moments like this when he comes undone. A strand falling to his face, as his tongue drags between my breasts, a finger following the glistening trail. The slow movements in direct contrast to the ones before.

At first, the desperate need was primal, uncontrolled, it was hunger. This is pure pleasure. Leisurely, deliberate, decadent. I thread my fingers into his hair and tug his head up. Halting his movements. Annoyed at the disruption, but curious at the cause.

"Reid."

His hands wrap around my waist, kneading my skin, stabilizing himself as I have control of him.

"What was it you were saying before," my hand softly running down his cheek, "about having your mouth on me?"

He places a kiss on the skin between my breasts.

"I said," he pauses, letting the anticipation hang between us, "I won't have *your* mouth on *me* until I've had *mine on you first*." It may have been a whisper, but there is nothing quiet or subdued in his tone.

"And did you mean it?"

"I always say what I mean, baby, and with you, a little too much."

"Well, I usually hate second place. But in this case..." and I raise my eyebrows at him in response. Not the move to match the sexy display he is currently putting on, but one he responds to without hesitation.

Kisses pepper the laugh that he breathes against my skin as he makes his way lower down my ribs, and presses another kiss to my belly button. His palms run down my sides until his fingertips grip the waistband of my underwear and he moves his fingers playfully underneath them. Pulling my underwear down over my legs, sliding them off, and dropping them on the ground to our side.

I am fully exposed to him, at his mercy in a way I usually held reserved. Sex was different, *this?* This is a level of intimacy I did not always allow access to. As was the reciprocal act. And even still it did not stop me from dropping to my knees like his fucking pet. Looking up to him eager to take him in my mouth.

I always felt that my mouth was my most powerful attribute next to my brain. It was the vessel I had to deliver thought, spoken word, and developed language. And I did not freely strip myself of the ability to speak. Not without wholly trusting the person. And trust isn't something you get regularly from a casual hook up. Which meant most times, I didn't trust my partner enough to hand over control while I was at my most bare.

This is not one of those times. This time, not only do I lay there, as I succumb to him, as the warmth of his breath plays against my skin. It also infuses me with a sense of power, and control.

Owning the vulnerability I had spent so many years hiding.

He sits up on his knees and looks down at me, laying there, my cream-colored skin against the dark brown leather sofa. Moving his palms across my thighs, his eyes with mine, as he slowly drags his bottom lip into his mouth, releasing it glistening with moisture as he roams his tongue across his top lip, before smiling at me with unbridled intention.

His fingers wrap around my left thigh, and he slowly opens me up to him. Not breaking his locked gaze from mine, a silent agreement of what we want. He spreads me further, letting my left leg fall off the side of the sofa, until my foot lands against the floor. That earns a smirk.

He leans down and adjusts his body so he is positioned to try me. It is the last glimpse I catch of his eyes before he lowers himself completely.

His right hand lifts the corresponding leg over his shoulder, and I feel the gentleness of his tongue teasing me at the line of moisture down my center. I wonder if he can hear the throbbing emitting from my core. The pulsing hidden beneath.

He uses his tongue to split me open, and when the tip of him encircles the pulsing part of me, my back bows from the couch in involuntary response.

He takes his time, reacting to me as I react to him. Reading me. Following my lead to pleasure.

His fingertips dig into my skin as his lips close around me, sucking, teeth grazing, and I whimper out in reply.

He pulls back from me, releasing his lips where they'd sucked on a sensitive part of me. But he didn't leave me without him, his thumb replacing his mouth, swirling the wetness dragging it from within me, encircling me with the moisture, applying a firm pressure at my entrance, rimming the edge of me with the fingertip positioning it to push inside.

My breathing is staggered and short, as he watches my chest move up and down. His fingers toying with me thrumming them across me as his thumb moved with building speed, building me as he watched, consumed, *learned*.

In complete contrast to me, he is completely controlled. Slow, deep breaths. Dragging in a long inhale as his palm runs up the length of my left thigh, only coming to a stop on the lowest boundary of my stomach, and as his eyes narrow, he slips two fingers inside of me. Curling them up upon entry to stroke the innermost wall. I jolt up to lean into it. To be closer to him, as his hand slides up the center of my torso pressing me back down into the sofa now sticky with sweat.

His fingers moved in and out of me with deliberate accuracy, pulling the wetness from within me. His body lowered, his hand returns to the place it previously rested, and as he pumps his fingers deep into me, the heel of his palm presses down on my lower abdomen, making the feeling more intense than I had ever felt by just the use of someone's hands.

I'm not sure if it is him lowering himself out of sight, or my eyelids lowering, heavy with the weight of ecstasy pulling me towards it. But I slip my fingers into his hair as his mouth works in tandem with his hands.

I'm transfixed.

This is a hedonistic existence, I lay here with a deep satisfaction that I have not experienced before.

His way is unlike anything, in all aspects. There doesn't seem to be any slowing. Nothing *fully* sates the urge between us, as he moves between my legs and fucks me while I still cling to the edge of my previous orgasm.

Being with him is like running downhill. That feeling where your feet can't keep up with the force, picking up speed, no idea what happens when you make it to the bottom.

Chapter Thirty

HER

By nature, I am not an easy person.

I am a fun person.

An entertaining person.

An outgoing person.

An adaptable person.

But not *easy*.

Not easy to be with, and not easy to understand. And because of that, I often find myself surrounded by people who only ever operate with a partial comprehension of the complexity I keep contained. It didn't often feel easy to sit in someone's space, to let myself relax in someone's space completely. In part due to the well-mannered nature I was raised with, and the rest, fear that I would be too much. I could be bold and brave and keep that projected. But in truth there was underlying fear that it was all too much. A caricature of who I really am.

Which is why, sitting here at Reid's counter, the one I literally crawled across a few hours ago, *stop thinking about it, stop thinking about it, stop thinking about it,* it's bizarre how incredibly calm and comfortable I feel. My laptop in front of me as I outline a paper for school. My books to my side, as I highlight the relevant passages.

And *him* sitting at his desk, focusing on his own work. Our backs are to each other, as his desk faces away from the kitchen, as I stare at the invisible handprints I am sure I can see on the granite counter from where I moved on all fours towards him. *Focus. Focus. Focus.*

Despite the distraction, the memory, the smell that still lingers on my skin, I am comfortable here studying.

I glance over my shoulder. He looks like he did when I first met him, and I love that this is his default state of focus. Pen cap hanging from his lip, as he underlines something of importance in the text. His head peered over his shoulder, and he caught me. Capping the pen and tucking it behind his ear.

"Are you watching me?"

"I wouldn't say watching..." *I am, I am watching him,* "but I am almost done with this outline, how about you?"

"I've been done for almost an hour. Didn't want to disturb you." He runs a hand through his hair, brushing it back as he laughs.

"I *want* you to disturb me... but I also want to know what you're working on... or is this more journaling? Oh my god... Is this sex-journaling? Can I read it?!"

"Come see."

I practically fall out of the chair and jump on his lap, where he kisses my shoulder and brings his arms around me to flip open the notebook in front of him.

He brings his mouth to my ear, "*Not* sex journals." He says with another kiss to my temple.

"This isn't your journal at all! I've been bamboozled!!"

"You haven't been bamboozled. You asked if you could read

it, I said yes, it's not my fault you thought you'd be reading... what do you call it, five-pepper-*smut?*"

I do call it that. Not his journals, though I had a sneaky suspicion that might be classified as five- pepper-smut as well. But he was talking about the romance novels that I sometimes read, the ones where they talk about 'velvet-wrapped steel' and 'throbbing members.' We laughed together over coffee when I sat next to him and read him a passage for the first time. And despite the dark chuckle it exuded from him, he said he could '*see the appeal.*'

"Well, if it's not a sex-journal, then what is it?"

"It's notes for a case study."

"What's this acronym? EBITDA?"

"Earnings Before Interest, Taxes, Depreciation, and Amortization... If you look here, you see the whole point of this case study is to determine if this is a good business for a potential investor. EBITDA helps someone do that, looking at the value of the business."

"You're basically playing Monopoly."

"Something like that, you have to weigh the investment to see if it's worth it... What do you think, according to this, should I buy *Park Place?*"

I look at his notes and the textbook next to it–by Park Place he obviously means Company A, the example listed in the case study as the one being positioned for sale.

"Okay, well let me think... Company A is showing an EBITDA margin of 17%, and that looks really good based on the industry in the chart..."

"That's right, I have that here," he says, coaxing me, wrapping his hand around mine as he slides my finger towards his notes. But I look back at the textbook, the table of data for the companies' profits, and the industry standards over the last years.

"But no, you shouldn't."

"Tell me, why not."

"I would buy the Boardwalk instead."

"The Boardwalk?"

"Come on Reid, *Company B*, B for Boardwalk. I thought we were playing Monopoly?" He laughs, and I move with him, still seated in his lap, his chin resting on my shoulder, able to see all the books in front of us.

"Okay, AB, I'm listening."

"It looks great that it's so much higher, but it's been dropping for the last five years, see?" I tap my finger on the data table.

"But what does that matter if it's still above average?"

"If I was buying a business, I would want to buy one that has potential for higher margins, not declining ones. So, I would go for Company B. They aren't above average, but at this rate they will be. And three more years with growth like that, they will be equal to Company A anyway."

"You're fucking incredible, you know that?" He flips to the next page of his notebook, where I see he landed on the same conclusion I did. Company A is not worth the investment, Company B has better long-term potential.

"I had to spend thirty minutes explaining to my study group what you picked up in thirty seconds."

There is something about his praise that feels different. It isn't like he has low expectations, but still, he's so wholeheartedly impressed. *The only problem with being impressive, is eventually people become less impressed.*

But for now, even I'm impressed with myself. I enjoyed that exercise, that feeling of piecing together information to chart out potential decisions. Immediately my brain wrapped around it, and played out the scenarios, until coming to a solution. It's not that there was an outright *wrong* answer, but there was a *better* one. One that I seemed to have found.

"Can we do another one?" I ask, leaning back into his embrace.

"As many as you want." He flips open the book to another problem, this one relating to project management. We sat there, sharing the seat, sharing knowledge, at times arguing over whose assessment was correct.

"Have you thought about a business degree?"

"I've thought about business classes, but no. The plan has always been medicine."

"Why?" It's the simplest question, but the biggest to unpack. I like science, and I've always been one to meet the expectations set for me, becoming a doctor has been one of them, like my parents.

But right now, I really, *really*, like this.

I don't have an answer for Reid, so instead, I just shrug and smile. I think he notes there's more to it but doesn't press. Just flips to another page and offers me another problem to solve in place of solving any of the bigger ones of my life.

The rest of the afternoon is much of the same. Fucking and focusing. Balancing between being wrapped up in each other, and eventually breaking apart and returning to our respective study locations.

"How about, you finish up whatever you're working on, and I can make dinner?" He stands from his desk and walks into the kitchen, placing himself back on the other side of the counter, gripping the edge of it. A barrier I already crossed. He smiles knowingly, both of us replaying the recent memory, but he doesn't dare me to him this time.

"You can *make* dinner?"

"What, you didn't know you are dating a chef?" He feigns insult. But *chef* isn't the part of the sentence that has me frozen.

I'm not sure if I am worse at controlling my expression around him, or if he is just more focused on reading it. Because his shifts also.

"Come on, AB. *Tell me.*"

Tell me. Simple. His tone is soft and sincere. Looking for me to offer up the words or explanation I typically hold close to my chest.

Tell me. He said, so easily.

Tell me what you want for dinner.

Tell me why you made that face.

Tell me your fear.

Tell me what is going on.

Tell me something. Tell me everything.

"I didn't know we were, um, dating... *not really.*"

I've never felt such immediate regret as I do right now. The words that tumbled from my mouth tasted sour in a way I didn't know they could. Having not been interested in a relationship, I didn't realize how it would feel now, denying what we both know is obvious.

The smile I was so used to seeing across his face is empty. His mouth presses sternly in a flat line; I can read it. The emotion, it's frustration, disappointment, maybe even a little hurt.

"What did you think we were doing?"

I raise my eyebrow and pull the corner of my mouth into a partial smirk, the distraction of the shiny thing between us, rather than just answering the question.

Wrong fucking move.

His annoyance takes center stage at my passive dismissal. But why am I being passive, I'm not really. I'm not indifferent—in fact, it's the complete opposite. There is no doubt in my mind what this is, what I *want* it to be. I just had not admitted it yet, not to anyone and definitely not to myself.

"I thought we were still figuring that out, that we were just hanging out?"

"Did you really?" He has me frozen in place with his stare.

"I guess, I was still figuring that out. In case you're... um...

hanging out with other people too?" *God, I hope that's not the case.* My stomach bubbles in reaction, jealousy, an emotion I never feel, churning at the thought.

"I'm not. Are you?"

I shake my head no.

"So tell me, what were you trying to figure out exactly, if you liked spending time with me?"

"That's not it," I respond.

"If you liked *fucking* me?"

"No." I say it clearly this time.

"Then what are you trying to figure out, Arden? Because it feels like I jumped in while you are testing the water."

It only seems that way, though; if I thought about it, if I was honest with him, with myself, it would have been that I had cannonballed into the deep end the minute he played his first scrabble word. And regardless of how well I thought I knew how to swim, this current was pulling me under in a way that terrifies me.

I close my laptop, shut the book, and stand from the chair. He wants clarity. Here it is.

"No," I say again, clearly, this time as I approach him. Making my way around to his side of the counter a little more efficiently than I did last time. "I'm not testing anything, and if I was, I'm not anymore. It's just been a few weeks. I didn't want to assume what you wanted from me."

My sentence stopped right as my feet did in front of him. I've been afraid of this moment, knowing that my feelings for him are developing faster than logical. And that perhaps his logical mind wouldn't accept that. For the first time I feared rejection, something I hadn't been ready to admit. So I kept the illusion of indifference in place. But here he is pulling the thread again. Tugging on it to get the truth.

His arm snaked around my waist slowly and softly.

"Then don't assume. If you're not sure, ask me. But right

now, I'll be clear so you don't have to ask. I don't do casual, I don't do open, I don't just consider 'hanging out' when I'm sleeping with someone. That's never worked for me, and I don't like the idea of it now. Especially not with you. You're going to need to tell me if that works for you. If it doesn't, I'll be disappointed, but I'll understand, and we can remain friends."

"You want to be my friend?"

"I do, it's not the only thing I want out of this *relationship...*" he paused, waiting to see the impact of the word as it landed against me. "But like I said, if that's what you want, I am not going to pressure you into being with me." He is earnest in his delivery, and it thaws a bit more of my insecurity, intentionally or not.

Until this point, that had been my preference, non-committal. I was committed to too many other things in my life that a relationship and the requirements of it, felt unnecessary to fulfill the actual needs of what I was looking for.

We haven't known each other that long, but every time I'm near him, I don't want to emerge from this bubble he creates around us, and I know exactly what would pop it.

I run my palms across his chest. He isn't an overly broad man, but he is strong, and I can feel it even through his shirt. Resting my hand finally over his heart, my thumb rubbing back and forth. I'd like to say I can feel his heart skip a beat, but I'm fairly certain that is my own pulse picking up speed.

"I bet you make a really good friend." I still my movements and look up to him. He wasn't lying and didn't try to hide the combination of disappointment and skepticism that overtakes his face.

"I do." He is clearly willing to accept whatever boundary I establish. Always the one to ask me to define the next step before he took it.

"But I bet you'll make a better boyfriend."

His fingers curl around my jaw to pull my face up to him

for a gentle kiss. One I return in kind. Our signatures on this contract of commitment we just entered.

"I'll do my best." With those words the smile that brightened his face thawed my defenses even more.

"How about a rewind?" I suddenly reverse my way out of the kitchen, walking backwards moving my face and hands as if someone is rewinding a video. He laughs with me. Breaking a bit of the more serious nature of the conversation. Until I hop back onto the seat and look up to him.

"Wow," I say, feigning surprise and clutching my non-existent pearls. "I didn't know I was *dating* a chef!" The emphasis on dating is unmistakable. And I don't try to contain my smile.

Watching him in the kitchen is mesmerizing, like most things. Much like that first moment I saw him, I should have sensed it then, that there was a pull to him, more than the usual passing enjoyment.

I sit back at the counter, open my laptop to complete the bit of work I have remaining. But before diving back into it, check my phone, realizing how much I disconnect from the world the second I walk through his door.

BFF Josh: Open your door, I'm outside.
BFF Josh: Where are you?

Yikes, that was a couple hours ago. I bet he'll be pissy about that, especially because Stella wasn't there either.

me: hey! Sorry! Not home. w/Reid @ his apt.

My reply was two hours later; his was instantaneous.

BFF Josh: You sure that's wise? Must be feeling all better then?

me: More than better! The best! Thanks for making sure.
Stella told me how much you did.
BFF Josh: Staying with Lecture-Boy for dinner or want to
grab burritos?
me: –friend
BFF Josh: ??
me: Lecture-BoyFRIEND.
BFF Josh: Sounds like you're there for more than dinner
me: ;)
me: Have fun without me! BFF Josh: Don't worry, I do

Reid turns on some music, and I watch as he moves throughout the kitchen, preparing for something more complicated than a frozen pizza.

"Wait, do you eat meat?" He turns a bit frantically.

"Of course not!!! You *do?!*"

"Oh my god, I'm so–"

I wipe the serious expression from and burst out in laughter. The sound has his shoulders relax.

"Reid, I'm just kidding. It's fun to keep you on your toes."

"My toes can handle it, my heart might not."

"Here I was trying to impress you..."

"I don't think you have to try that hard." He really didn't. I was impressed by him before he even noticed me. Impressed by him as I counted each turn of the page and kept tally before he even knew I existed. Impress me? He enthralled me. More so now.

"Do you want to help?"

"Only if you'll teach me."

"Of course, anything you want."

I round the counter to join him in the kitchen and get a better look at the workspace he has set up. Cutting board, a bowl with ground meat, a pot already filled with water on the back burner waiting to boil, and miscellaneous seasonings.

"What are you making?"

"We are about to make meatballs." He brings the bowl of meat closer where we stand in front of a parchment paper lined tray. *Seriously, who is this man?* Before taking a spoonful of the meat mixture in his hands, rolling it lightly and placing it on the tray.

"Got it?" he asks. *No. No, I don't.* I have been too transfixed watching his large hands work that I didn't realize he was telling me what to do.

"Sorry, I got... distracted," I say, pulling my bottom lip under my teeth as a contrite reply.

So quickly, he moves and takes my mouth into his, and digs his own teeth into my lip, pulling it free before sealing it with a kiss. Looking down at me, my moistened plump lip free from its self-induced cage. He looks pleased with himself, managing to free it despite the fact his hands were covered in ground meat. *Okay, now I am really distracted.*

"As I was saying..." he elbows me gently, "the spoon is to measure the amount, it's pretty basic, just grab some, roll it, and drop it on the tray."

"Okay–got it."

We stand side by side, Billy Joel playing in the background as he hums along.

"This song reminds me of you."

"Is that a good thing, it's kind of depressing, isn't it?" I roll a meatball in my hands and drop it on the tray.

"Sure, everyone wants to be Uptown Girl, but Vienna? Vienna is beautiful in a way that makes you think about your life." *Is that how he sees me, like I am the crazy child who was too ambitious that Billy Joel was singing about it?*

"I don't think there's anything wrong with ambition," I counter with more defense than necessary.

"There isn't anything wrong with ambition, but you shouldn't let the ambitions of other people prevent you from enjoying your life now." He's incredibly perceptive, and while I had given him enough context about my life for him to know these things, he also understood them beyond the context I provided.

We went back to discuss his plans following graduation, *the conversation we didn't finish earlier.* We talked more about our families and what my plans are. And while he's encouraging, motivating with judgment or self interest, he also tells me I should take advantage of every opportunity now.

We sat at the counter and ate dinner, and shared a very Lady and the Tramp meal of spaghetti and meatballs. After an incredible domestic scene of dish washing, I sat with him on the couch as I read through the advanced reader copy of his aunt's book for a second time.

His thoughts were left in the margins like secret notes passed to a friend in class. He handed me a red pen, to distinguish from the blue markings he already left, and sat there as I returned my own thoughts to the book. Even though I texted him the first time I read it, arguing some of the points he's annotated, we sat there again discussing the notes on every single page.

"You know," he says, before I started again, "if you ask me about every little thing I wrote, you'll never beat my reading time." I jolt up from underneath his arm where I have been curled and turn to face him. The smile that caught me barely contained the laugh he tried to keep behind it.

"What do you mean?"

"Well, right now, I can tell that you might be able to read at an impressive speed, but if you keep talking, you'll never beat *my* time. Which you have recorded as what...?"

"Two and a half pages per minute. But, that's not fair, you weren't talking to anyone when I timed you."

A deep laugh rumbles through him, one I now think he has been holding on to since the day we met.

267

"I didn't think you would just admit it! I had a feeling that's what you were doing, and then when I saw your notebook had all the tick marks on it, it was all but confirmed!"

He hadn't accused me of timing him, hadn't mentioned it when we first met. But now, he brings it up *now? Hell I brought it up and threw it right in his lap.* But for all the embarrassment I should feel, I don't.

Instead, I just feel seen.

"*Welllll*, maybe if I didn't have to point out how incorrect some of your interpretations are, I would be able to read it faster."

"Oh, baby, if you do that, I won't be able to explain why I'm right."

"And what makes you so confident that you're right..."

"Come back here and I'll show you."

He wraps his arm around my waist and pulls me into his lap. Flipping to a marked page, I watched his finger scan the words. There was something about the way we bantered. It wasn't a game of ping pong, but wit. It made me think, positioned a challenge, and a thought, unique from my own, not just clever word play.

We just flowed so easily. He made it feel so easy. Made me feel at ease.

Chapter Thirty-One

2007

HER

In a matter of weeks, I was swimming in the deep end, introducing him, *again*, more officially as my boyfriend to our inner circle of friends. Though, everyone remembered Stella's birthday with crystal clear accuracy. Well, except maybe Stella, of course.

The Sunday after I called him my boyfriend, when we talked about exclusivity and what the expectations of our relationship would be, he walked me back to my dorm as he had before. Stepping outside of his apartment, leaving the brick bubble we created always felt like a shock to the system. Somehow, we found ourselves in a groove that flowed so seamlessly that we just got to absorb each other without any distraction. The more time I spent there, the more I melted away the icy walls I spent the last eighteen years building up... well, technically almost nineteen, with my birthday just around the corner. Something Stella let slip, though you can't convince me it wasn't on purpose.

I was dead set against any kind of birthday; I don't mind

being the center of attention if it's something I earned, but for being born? Anyone, and everyone, has done that. What's the acclaim? But Reid, Stella, and I were all sitting in the Student Center, sharing a basket of fries, as they bonded over whatever shared interest Reid had found to connect them. I've seen him do it before, always finding some middle ground to make people feel comfortable. He's naturally disarming. And she was obsessed, more than once sneaking me a thumbs up in approval when he looked the other way. *Little does she know, as I have learned, he's more observant than he lets on.*

"We are having a party." Stella says matter of factly. Plucking another fry from the basket as I shake my head aggressively in disagreement. "We areee!" She says again, looking to Reid as if he would help her. Instead, he raised his eyebrows and shrugged in reply. Knowing it's not his decision to make.

His arm is draped over the back of my chair as his thumb runs back and forth across my shoulder.

"You don't want a party?" He asks, looking at me. His voice is soft, coaxing, as opposed to Stella's forceful eagerness.

"Oh no, we can have a party, but there's no reason to celebrate *my birthday.*"

"I don't know about that, AB, it sounds like a good reason to celebrate to me."

"Yeah, listen to your boyfriend," I hear the voice from behind me and see him come into view as he pulls out the chair next to me. "I can't think of a better reason to throw a party, *AB.*"

"Hey, man." Josh tosses the greeting over the table to Reid, who responds in kind.

"Good to see you, Joshua." No one calls him Joshua. *No one except Reid.* It's his name, but I don't think I've heard it outside of formal settings, a class maybe. Josh just grabs a fry from the basket and continues.

"We've been talking about your birthday for weeks, you're not just going to leave everyone hanging, are you?"

"First of all, *you all* have been talking about it, and I really don't want to do anything birthday related."

"It's not just birthday related, it's Rocky Horror related!" Stella practically screams it as if the volume of her voice will be a deciding factor.

"It's what?" Reid pulls his attention from me to ask her what she means, but Josh jumps in eagerly to explain something that gives him the leg up.

"Rocky Horror Picture Show, the cult classic, not sure if you know it, but there's a theater in the square that plays it at midnight on Saturdays, and our girl's birthday just so happens to land on a Saturday. Soo, we thought, what better way to celebrate than dressing up?"

"Saturdays, hmm? And what Saturday would that be?" Reid directs his question to me as he tucks the lock of hair behind my ear, as if he is preparing himself to whisper into it.

"The 17th," Stella and Josh answer simultaneously.

"Is that so?" This time his voice *is* lower. Closer to a whisper. Closer to me. I wouldn't say he sounds annoyed, but I don't think he likes being the only person at this table without that piece of information. Particularly because it really is just around the corner. And while we had already made plans for next weekend, it would have made sense for me to tell him the following weekend was my birthday. I just didn't.

The Rocky Horror Picture Show *is* a lot of fun. Midnight showings are known to be outrageous, with audience engagement and costumes. It had been the birthday plan because it was less to do about my birthday and more to do about the movie.

The movie where a buttoned-up couple get stuck in a storm and end up at this spooky mansion, with a strange collection of people, including a creepy butler and a lab-created muscle man, and they all sing and dance.

Getting dressed up meant you could put on any manner of underwear, corset, and fishnet stockings and pass for a cast member. All while the movie played in the background and you used your bag of props to participate in the showing.

I went on and explained it to Reid, who nodded like he got it, though I don't know if he'd enjoy it. Can't imagine him in fishnets. *Because yes, the men wear fishnets.* But he looked up the movie and decidedly came up with a plan for himself.

"I know this theater, it's only a few streets over from me. Who else are you inviting?"

"I really hadn't thought about it."

"The usual gang, you'll remember them all from Stells' birthday a few weeks ago," Josh answered in my place.

Reid's fingers play mindlessly with the ends of my hair, as the conversation goes on around us, *though there's nothing about him that feels mindless.*

"How about you guys come over before the movie? I'll invite some people, we can have a cake, and it's a short walk over to the theater."

"That's perrrfecttt!" Stella sings her reply.

But I turn to Reid and ask, "Are you throwing me a birthday party?"

"More like he's hijacking a birthday party."

———

The week before my birthday was spent on campus. Reid has his own projects to focus on, and while he said I could come set up camp at his apartment, I felt like it was important I keep some semblance of my life preserved. And that's what it was, just part of it. The appearance of my day to day. Because every time I found myself with the whole gang, I felt like I was only the outline of myself. And I don't think they realized.

It was amazing how easily things snapped into place. How I could just take my seat at the round table, and everything felt normal. Josh would be texting some random girl, Ethan and Lindsey never separated by more than a couple inches, Stella fluttering on about something, always the only one to ask about Reid by name. The nickname he sometimes let slip, had now made its way throughout the group. My friends having picked up on it, perhaps originally in jest, but it stuck. Now threading it throughout the normal conversation.

'AB, another drink.'

'How about that test, AB.'

'AB, can I borrow your notes?'

'Let's get burritos, AB.'

Things have changed somewhat in just a matter of weeks. I stopped showing up at Josh and Ethan's door, Josh stopped waking up in my bed. It was inappropriate now, though it meant that the nights I couldn't spend with Reid my sleep was erratic at best. I could get a few hours if I got in bed already feeling tired, otherwise I would toss and turn, never resting for more than an hour or so at a time.

It's not that I could always sleep when I was with Reid, but either I was already exhausted that my body could rest, *or* he would wake up when I moved from the bed. The first time he woke up without me in bed, I had snuck off into the living room, flicked on a reading lamp and curled in the chair with a book. He found me some time after midnight, and brought out his scrabble board and we played until I was tired enough to rest my brain. That's how it went. Sometimes scrabble, sometimes trivia, and sometimes, my favorite times, he would open his course work and test me on the textbook problems. The hypothetical business strategies that didn't have *wrong* answers, which meant we often ended up debating approaches, until one of us caved.

He realized early on there were two ways to get me back to sleep—physical or mental exertion—but he was really a master of both, knowing that draining my body of energy and my mind of clutter meant I could sleep through until morning.

As much as I always wanted to stay with him, it felt selfish. Even if I tried not to bother him, he'd wake up soon after, like his body's rhythm was out of sync without mine to balance it out in bed.

But the weekends were ours.

And this weekend is my birthday.

The party I didn't want, but all the people who cared about me here, *did.*

Reid and I had planned our Rocky Horror outfits. Opting for the main couple Brad and Janet. He realized, unironically, how easy it would be for him to dress up as Brad. Given that his general appearance was already that of an attractive man with a polished exterior, he just needed a pair of glasses which he picked up from a costume shop. As for me, Janet had a couple versions of her outfit, one a demure pink dress and cardigan, *or* the version I opted for from a specific scene where she was stripped to her underwear.

I wore a white bra, and white slip with white pumps. And this was how I was going into my nineteenth year of life. Half-naked, and already a little buzzed. Reid had invited a few of his friends over as well.

Had I originally planned to meet Reid's friends in a white bra? Definitely not. Is that what's going to happen? Yes. Yes, it is.

But the second the door opened to Austin Becks, all of my anxiety faded away. His friends were here, mingling amongst my own. *Here. In Reid's apartment. Where he hung a birthday banner and picked up a birthday cake.*

Austin strolled into this apartment like he owned it, and everyone froze. One of the most classically attractive men I've ever seen, and it's obvious from everyone's reaction they felt the same. Though it wasn't just his good looks, it's the fact that he showed up in nothing more than a gold speedo, his body chiseled, and covered in shimmery body oil, calling attention to every cut of his abs.

He's Rocky. In The Rocky Horror Picture Show, Dr. Frank. N. Furter creates a beautiful man, blonde, tan, cut like a Greek god, wearing nothing more than gold briefs and gold boots. *He created Austin Becks.* Though something tells me it doesn't take a costume party to get him to remove his shirt. He's the kind of man who strips regardless, just because he can.

Meanwhile, Josh, never to be outdone, had decided to dress up in full Dr. Frank N. Furter regalia. He loved to shock, and that he did.

Compared to the two of them, my outfit felt tame. It was strange, the melding of our worlds, my friends in his space, a space I had become entirely comfortable in, now felt more rigid. Maybe it was the insanity of the corsets and fishnets juxtaposed next to the wood piano, or the fact that Josh sat on the leather sofa, drumming his fingers against the arm where my teeth had muffled a scream.

Josh and Austin hit it off immediately, I think because they were equally charming, and Josh no doubt would have seen him as another human conquest, a game I wasn't unfamiliar with, just one I had become far less interested in. Josh and I were different in that way, he sought to collect people like trophies. Not sexually, though that counted, too. But a collection of people he could claim to know or have on his shelf of acquaintances. All building his network for his escape-from-New-Hampshire plan. He wore masks, faces and traits he picked up from the people he collected. He came here as a reset for him. He came here with the intention of establishing himself as something more. He had confided that in me early on, looking to bond I think. That's where we were different. I didn't need to borrow someone else's face, or traits, or clever anecdotes, I had my own, and I restricted it. His persona was crafted, created as needed. Mine was curated.

Or at least it had been.

That changed lately. Until now, when I sat here watching them all interact and wondering where I fit. Reid and I were seated on the piano bench, his arm wrapped low around and resting on my hip, as we chatted with Stella and her boyfriend. Stella was always a lightweight, and it never took more than a single shot to open her up, and she was well on her way to making the most of her French maid costume. *She's dressed up as Magenta.*

"We need a birthday toast!" Josh calls to me from across the room, expecting the toast I am normally all too happy to deliver. It was the part of me they love, *The Showman, the Entertainer.* I enjoyed it, at times. It was the part Josh saw first and latched on to with my Community Chest shirt. But Reid, Reid had gone deeper than that, *okay literally deeper as well,* but he had almost bypassed the enchantments of the extrovert and jumped right in to see how it all worked together.

"Yeah!" Stella jumped in. "How about some birthday wisdom."

My friends are drunk. I am a little drunk. Is Reid? I can never totally read it, he seems looser than usual, but he's never someone I ever saw as *loose* save one exception. When we were alone. I just decided to be exactly who they expected me to be. I stand with my beer bottle in hand and clear my throat, indicating that I have something important to say as the room hushes.

"Thank you all for coming to celebrate my birthday, something I didn't really want to celebrate but you all make it worthwhile. So tonight, in honor of my birthday, in honor of all of you... let's toast to that...

Here's to *honor*.

To having *honor*,

to getting *on her*,

and if you can't come *in her*, come on her."

The rowdy laughter completely fills the room, but I feel his hand grip my waist and pull me to stand between his legs where he remains seated.

"You're fucking incredible, you know that?" He says with a low rumble in his voice. Pulling me into a kiss earning a collective *'awwww'* from the crowd. His fingers crawled my bare skin, as I was painfully aware that I was in nothing more than a white bra.

"Hell of a speech, I'll be sure to use that one at your wedding," Austin says as he claps Reid on the shoulder between whoops of laughter. I can see how Austin and Josh would become fast friends. Both dressed truly to elicit a response, and full of the same cocky sarcasm.

A few rounds more, and a chorus of 'happy birthday' later, we bundled up and headed to the movie, where we were no longer the only costume-clad attendees. I know it's normal for guests to dress up for the midnight showing, but right now, it feels like it was all for me.

I sat in the retro theater between my boyfriend and my best friend. As the film rolled, the audience engaged. Throwing rice at the screen during a wedding scene or screaming key phrases at the screen during certain exchanges.

This might have been the perfect birthday.

Eventually, everyone scattered back to their own beds or whoever's they could convince their way into.

"Tell me, birthday girl," he says, sitting on the edge of his bed, watching my every move.

I don't need to ask his meaning. Reid constantly asked what

I wanted. And in doing so he made sure to find the right thread to pull. Knowing that my complete unraveling would come at his hand with the right tug. But he wanted me to tell him, not for him, but for me.

I just step out of my silk slip and let it pool at my feet.

"Technically my birthday is over."

"We're going to celebrate a little longer."

Chapter Thirty-Two

2007

HER

There was something so different about waking up in Reid's bed. A bed he made sure I was comfortable in. He was always clear when he wanted me to stay over and that he preferred his bed to mine. *Obviously*. Besides the fact that it was more than two times the size, there were also far fewer interruptions.

Having a boyfriend didn't stop people knocking on my door in the middle of the night. And as I learned, my boyfriend didn't like that. *'You already barely sleep.'* He had said after pounding on my door woke me up one night, and I just ended up staying up, unable to settle back to sleep.

I became more comfortable in his apartment, he made sure of it. It felt familiar the first day I walked in, even after only knowing him a few hours. But now, I am able to exist here. I was slowly being woven into the quilt of his home. It became clearest when I went to bed one night and noticed a new nightstand on the left side. The side I always landed on. There had only been one in the room before. On the right, his side.

It didn't match his, and that made it even more endearing.

This wonky little wooden end table with brass knobs. The only thing sitting on top, a reading lamp. *'I figured your side could use a lamp.'*

Your side. *My side.* He had designated a full side to me. Maybe I had claimed it, night after night, staying here rather than heading the mile walk back to the dorm. But either way, he had set up a nightstand, and lamp for *my side. For me.*

Insomnia pulled me from my sleep. There wasn't any reason, it just happened from time to time. Not a nightmare, just an alertness that switched on suddenly. My reaction is always to bolt upright and run to the other room. As if there is an urgency to my new awakeness. *There isn't, there never has been.*

I look over and Reid is pulling in slow steady breaths. Laying on his stomach, arms tucked under his pillow.

It's a slow-motion avalanche.

Looking at him like this.

Like this building, a powerful feeling, rolling through me. In just a matter of months. *I think I might love this man.*

It was then I moved, not wanting to get too tangled in the thought that I couldn't yet comprehend. And like numerous other nights, when I moved, he woke up.

"Anything particular tonight?" he asks, like always. Running his warm hand down my bare arm. As if one day there's going to be an answer that might have more of a solution. There hasn't been yet. And there isn't now.

"Nothing. Just enough sleep I guess." I shrug casually, but it wasn't *really* casual. Because there were times it was horrible, when I woke up exhausted or drained and needed sleep even though my body rejected the idea. It was clearly at war with itself. But tonight, my body just woke up. Filled to the brim with sleep and no longer interested in being suspended in a state of rest.

He rubs his eyes and checks the alarm clock he has by his bedside.

"Go back to sleep. I'm going to just go read in the other room. I'm fine."

"I know you are, but I have an idea. You're going to need to find something warm to put on."

I had some miscellaneous items stashed here, but nothing seemed to be warm enough for whatever Reid had planned. *He clearly has a plan.* Handing me a big knit sweater, and scarf. He put together a similar outfit before grabbing us our coats and hats, and heading out the door.

"This is nuts! Where are we going?"

"Have you ever been to the law campus?"

"No, all of my classes are on the main one. Wait, you're taking me to law school? Is this my Elle Woods moment?" His large gloved hand squeezed around mine three times in quick succession. A little morse code of *'just you wait.'*

"Kind of, I'm taking you ice skating." It's a short walk from his apartment to where we now stand in the center of the law quad, and sure enough, an ice rink is nestled right in the middle of it.

"Seriously?!?"

"Seriously. It's small, can only hold a few people, but when the temperature drops, they freeze it. People skate randomly day and night because it remains open."

The ice is like a perfect piece of glass. No one is here, why would they be at this hour. There are a few big plastic trunks off to the side of the rink, and the smile that spreads across Reid's face wipes out any of the lingering sleepiness in his eyes.

"Let's see how good you are with a pair of skates."

Flipping open the trunk and pulling out a couple pairs of skates. This is surreal. This is a perfect rom-com date, right out of a Nora Ephron movie.

"What size?"

"8, please!"

He brings them over to me and helps me lace them up moving quickly to his own.

"Now the important question, do you know how to skate?"

By no means would I consider myself a *good* ice skater, but as I wobble my way to the rink, the blades see-saw my ankles with each step on solid ground as he holds my hand and guides me on to the ice. Letting his phone balance on the banister, and turning on Billy Joel, as we leisurely skated under the moonlight. Our skates cut paths in the ice, as he holds my hands and pulls me into him. The unsteadiness I felt as I glided through eased away, like everything eventually did with him.

I no longer felt like I had been jolted awake from a dream, it felt like I was skating through one. I looked at this man, the warm light from the surrounding lamp posts bathing his face, the moon chaperoning overhead. The only witness to this moment, where I knew what it meant to love someone who was previously a stranger.

All of the seeds he planted had bloomed in this moonlight.

My body was tired by the time we got back to his apartment, yawning my way as we climb the stairs. My legs still feeling the illusion of the ice beneath my feet.

We land on the sofa, our scrabble game from the night before still set up on the coffee table in front of us, *real scrabble this time.*

Sitting here, fitting into the curve of his body, fitting into the curve of his life, he brushes my curly hair from my face and leaves a kiss on my temple.

As I turn up to him, my nose grazes his chin. His head resting back against the sofa, eyes closed, beginning to drift off.

It's a slow-motion avalanche.

I love you. I think.

"I love you." I *say.*

I can't gauge time in this moment.

It crawls.

So. Slowly.

He doesn't immediately open his eyes when the smile overtakes his face. He doesn't try to hide it, not his smile, and not the emotions feeding it.

Slowly lifting his head, bringing his hand to cup my cheek. The pressure of my teeth in the soft skin of my lip keeps me focused on that feeling, and not the one I just laid bare to him. His thumb so tenderly runs over my lip and plucks it free. Immediately landing his own mouth against mine in replacement.

His kiss, *our kiss,* builds, slowly. His hands pull me deeper and deeper into him. Stealing breath from my lungs and clearing the chaos from my mind.

He cleared my mind so he could fill it completely. So, there would not be noise or distraction when his hands held my face, and his eyes held mine.

"I love you." Replenishing the silence with only that singular thought.

It's no longer slow-motion. The rolling waves of snow no longer thundering down the mountain. They reached the bottom, and we are buried together under the weight of the words.

Chapter Thirty-Three

PRESENT

HER

"I was so in love with Reid. I had said it before, the 'I love you' to someone I dated in high school, but that was more in response. Reid was totally different for me. I didn't even want a relationship, or at least what I thought a relationship was. I thought it would be a distraction from school. I thought it would hold me back from having fun. I thought a lot of things that were wrong. I was so young, we both were, but all my experience prior was high school romance. Where we existed in the same space and already knew the same people. This was a conscious effort to learn someone, and it meant I had to let him learn me. Something I only ever had done in small parts because I was so afraid of not meeting the expectations people had of me in their minds."

Amanda takes a sip of her coffee; she's closed her laptop and is listening intently. I had been giving her the high-level overview of everything, but there was so much more, and she wanted the details. Both as my friend and the author, I swear she looked like she was taking notes.

"So you loved Reid."

"I really did."

"And Josh?"

"My feelings then were complicated. I never had any intention of anything changing between us. But I ignored a lot of signs because I was more focused on preserving what I thought was just friendship."

"But it did change."

"Eventually."

"You haven't responded to the last messages, right? Maybe it's time?"

"Maybe..."

My phone in hand, why does this feel more dangerous than it used to? Why in this moment does the idea of seeing him have my stomach turn over... who am I kidding. I know exactly what's got it churning.

In talking about what happened, it would mean talking about *what happened.* And that is a box I had never intended to take off the shelf. He brought out his college boxes, sent me photos of the life we had begun to build, maybe it's time to unpack some of the reasons that never happened. I hadn't responded to his last email, the memories of us when we were together. I hadn't responded to his texts from last week, either. Quite literally left on read. As he challenged me to meet him. To talk face-to-face. But it worries me now that there has been a shift, this new understanding of the misunderstanding.

It feels like the slippery slope he wanted to avoid. And yet, even still. For as much as every intelligent fiber of my being would advise against my reply, I send through a delayed response. This one powered by the part of my nineteen year old heart that I never let see the light of day.

HIM

After the radio silence when I sent the message, and the follow up desperation in sending over those old photos, I was beginning to think I wouldn't hear from her again. I had begun to accept that, just as I did all those years ago.

But as she'd done before, she surprised me. Her text today, responding, *finally*, to the offer I extended to meet in person. *One I had no real proof even got delivered.*

For whatever conversations she needed to have, to motivate herself to see me, it looks like she finally decided it was worth it.

her: Let me know what your schedule is when you're here.

My reply is immediate. We usually grab lunch or coffee, because it fits so well into the boundaries of our friendship, something tells me this is a glass of wine, or better yet a double whiskey, kind of conversation.

me: Dinner Thursday?
her: Perfect, I'll send you the deets.

Looks like she agrees, this *is* a double whiskey conversation. It isn't that I had intended to chase the white rabbit down the rabbit hole, but here I am.

Chapter Thirty-Four

2008

HER

Time changes when it's shared. And that's exactly what happened.

It moved more quickly, waking up some mornings and wondering how the months had come and gone. We celebrated my birthday, the end of the semester, and so much had changed since my first week on campus. January and the new year now in the rear view mirror.

Once we exchanged those three words, everything sped up.

I woke up the morning after to find I-LOVE-YOU written in scrabble tiles, and it was clear, whenever he thought it, he just *said it*.

He would take me ice skating when I would wake up in the middle of the night.

I learned some of the Little Mermaid score to impress him.

We traded books, traded notes, traded *I love yous*. There was rhythm to us. A consistency, and ease. Even our friends had melded, and we'd spend nights at The Commons, Josh and Austin becoming each other's ultimate wingmen, as Reid and I hung back and watched them peacock their way into someone's bed. And night after night, I crawled into Reid's.

———

I'm buttoning up my coat and packing up my bag, as Josh does the same. We share a few classes again this term, which is always nice to have a backup set of notes and someone to walk with. *At least when I was coming from campus.*

"What are you up to?" He looks at me as I loop the knit scarf around my neck, assessing the question with interest.

"Let's get lunch." He drops the weight of his arm around my shoulders and pulls me into a side hug. "It's cold out, we can take the tunnels."

We call them the tunnels, but it's really just the lowest level, the basement hallways that connect the buildings. I didn't often use them. Usually because I forgot, but the few times I did try to navigate them on my own, I found myself lost, only ever able to turn up in Josh's hall.

But Josh is an expert. Because they connected *most* of the dorms to the main buildings, they worked to his advantage when sneaking back to his own room in the middle of the night.

The poorly lit hallways all look the same to me down here, but he navigates them with ease.

"I can never find my way around down here."

"Maybe if you actually lived on campus, you would." The tone of his voice is sarcastic, but surprisingly honest, letting the irritation cut through.

"Come on now, I still live on campus... don't act like you miss me, I'm always here."

He barks a laugh so loud and uncontained I hear it echo down the hallway.

"That's what you honestly think? That you still live on

campus? That must be why Stella and Marlie are so close now, because you're around *alllll* the time."

"So, you're saying Stella misses me, nothing to do with *you?*"

"I'm saying, Arden, you're just not around much. You don't have to worry about me, I'm keeping myself busy. But you know I prefer *keeping busy with you.*" He chuckles lighter this time. The laugh sneaking out through the smirk that has his lip pulls up as he cocks his head to the side in challenge.

We pick up some burritos and, as if to prove a point, decide to take them back to my dorm. We sit there, my feet curled up on the couch like we had dozens of times, and Stella squealed with excitement when she opened the door to find me there. Throwing herself between us on the couch. Grabbing a bite of my burrito and settling into the conversation.

The text alert from my phone is barely heard over the laughter, as Josh goes on about how he and Austin are the 'Bachelors of Boston.' *I'd watch that show.*

> **Reid:** How was your exam?
> **me:** Nailed it.
> **Reid:** Of course you did. What time will you be home?

Home. Did he mean MY home or his? Was this a Freudian slip, or just another example where he didn't feel the need to hide whatever it was he was thinking?

> **me:** At the dorm now. Catching up with my friends, I think I'll stay here tonight.
> **Reid:** Okay baby

Sitting there with Josh and Stella was like a sitcom. Not that it was scripted, though elements felt like it could have been.

It was just standing in the shallow end of a pool on a hot day. Whereas being with Reid was losing yourself in the deep end. But sometimes you need the security of standing ankle deep and not floating away. Or the comfort of a rewatching sitcom you've seen before.

"Lecture-Boy looking for you, AB?" Josh, standing and grabbing a couple beers from the fridge, tosses the question as he usually does when talking about Reid. Dismissively and with a hint of sarcasm. It's not like we didn't talk about who we were hooking up with, usually immediately following. But Reid was different from the first meeting, and Josh knew that.

"*Reid* is just asking about the exam, considering he watched me kill myself studying all week." Settling back into his seat on the couch, extending the beer to me, "You staying for a while?"

"I should be asking you that, considering this is my room," Swiping the beer from his hand and taking a pull. "But yeah, I think I'll stay."

I spent the rest of the day with Josh and Stella, that beer being the first of many. And then we switched to tequila.

"Let's do an Around the World Night!" Stella doesn't wait for confirmation before running to all our floor neighbors and convincing everyone to join in.

"Do you know what she's talking about?" I ask Josh, who is feverishly texting Ethan to come by given Stella's new round of invitations.

"We did one in our hall last week, every room picks a country, and has a drink based on that country. Then you go room to room, and by the time you go around the world, you're shitfaced drunk."

"I do love to travel. Now the question is, what country should we be?"

"Ethan is on his way with more tequila. You'll be Mexico."

Our neighbors were Ireland and had Irish whiskey, on the other side, Russian and they were serving up rubbing-alcohol quality vodka. And last but not least, across the hall chose to be Kentucky, *not the USA, just Kentucky*, serving bourbon.

It only took five minutes in Russia before I found myself completely inebriated, and after ten, we were standing on the coffee table, doing our best Beatles impression, belting out 'Back in the USSR.'

Around the World Night was a hit. I left Stella in Kentucky, left Josh in Ireland, and I ran back to the comfort of Mexico. Where I could unpin the smile from my cheeks. Turn off the emotional energy powered light I used to illuminate my surroundings. And I could talk to the person who always cleared my head of excess noise.

me: Wht arre yu doihng?
Reid: I think the better question is, what are YOU doing?
me: thnkin bout wht id rathder be doing ;) whaat arre u thinking??.?

That's right, add a winky face. He'll know what you mean.

Reid: I'm thinking it sounds like you had a fun night. Either that or your spelling is atrocious and I'm embarrassed I haven't realized sooner.
me: Yur tajkng to the Miami Spelking Bee Chnmpoin 1998
me: Cme over and test me for yurself
Reid: Baby, you sound like you need sleep, not a spelling test. Try to get some rest and I'll see you in the morning.

Walking back into the main room, I find my friends. Josh is sitting nursing a beer, feet kicked up on the coffee table as Stella is sprawled across the couch asleep, rather than her bed that was only ten feet away.

"Sit with me." His time with our Irish friends was effective. Clearly as drunk as I am. He's passed the point of loud bravado, instead now replaced with a sing-songy-softness and slurred speech.

He taps the arm of the chair. With far more confidence than I should, I tried to balance my butt on one side of the chair, outstretching my legs as a bridge across it to the other arm. A bridge over his lap, as he drapes his arms across my legs, the weight of them offering me a small bit of stability that I was horribly lacking.

I can *feel* myself swaying. He must see it also, or maybe I just lean too far back, when his hand quickly moves to my back to catch me from falling backwards off the chair.

His hand splays across my back quickly, with more force than I think he intended, pushing me forward, thudding me from the arm of the chair and directly on to his lap. He lets out a harsh breath from his gut as I land on top of him, as I burst into laughter. Trying desperately to get my limbs to work. To be coordinated enough to pull myself from the chair and carry myself to bed. But I was folded in half sitting on top of him.

"I've missed you," he huffs out, dropping his head to my shoulder. "But, if you want to sit on my dick, Arden, this isn't the way to go about it." As he laughs, my body shakes until I finally fumble my way off of his lap.

"Hope you enjoyed it while you could, because that's the closest I'm ever getting to your dick."

I walk off to my room and blow him a kiss. He laughs into his beer as I kick my bedroom door closed behind me.

Chapter Thirty-Five

2008

HER

The battle between my insomnia and my inebriation riled me from my sleep. My mind is fully interested in waking up, no longer comfortable being lost in a dreamlike state, while my body is still running through the effects of the Around the World Night that had me passed out in my bed like a ton of bricks just moments ago, physically exhausted.

My hands scramble in bed looking for my cell phone, trying to focus my eyes on the alarm clock on the table next to me. He could be awake, right?

Fumbling through the messages, I see our last exchange was total nonsense thanks to drunk-Arden- of-four-hours-ago. And I see the messages that came in following.

Reid: Hope you got to bed and didn't stay up trying to practice for the spelling bee
Reid: I'll swing by early before class
Reid: Love you

Three messages, each so like him. Clever. Decisive. Affectionate. He gave his love so willingly, never standing on ceremony to hide his affections. I had told him I loved him, and it felt so freeing to do it, and it had seemed like he had been waiting. Not because he didn't return the sentiment, but because he wanted me to be sure. As he did with everything.

'Love you.' It was simple, easy, and casual for him to say. We've said it hundreds of times since the first. Curled into his body. Over the phone when we were apart. In scrabble messages left on the counter. In ways that didn't use the words at all. And yet, there was never a time it didn't immediately run through me like a pulse.

I check the clock again, hoping time moved forward. He said he'd come by early, that could be anything for him, but I doubt it's now, still very much night out. But as much as I want to call him, I made the decision to stay here tonight, I quite literally made my bed, and now I must lie in it. At least until he wakes up.

So I think about that, tomorrow morning with him. I'm not sure when I closed my eyes. But my daydreams eventually carry me back into a light sleep.

It's the knock at the door that wakes me this time. The knock at the door, the crash of someone bumping into furniture, the tumble of beer bottles rolling across the floor. *Jesus, Stella must have stumbled her way to the door, and our suite must be a mess.* I check the clock. *ugh.* No wonder she's stumbling, she very well could still be drunk from last night, or at least severely hungover. *That's exactly where I am.*

My eyes try to adjust as I flip on the light and hop down from my bed, the world shifts a bit as my feet hit the floor. *Yep. severely hungover.*

My body, now absent from the cocoon of my bed, shivers in just a tee shirt and knit socks. The kind that have me slipping across my floor. And while I recognize the two muffled voices through my bedroom door, it isn't Stella, but Josh, who it sounds like is talking to Reid.

I pull open my bedroom door and find Josh leaning against the front door jamb. I wouldn't say he's blocking the entrance, but he's certainly making it so that Reid is clearly positioned on the other side. Needing to ask for entry, a move to knock his ego, I imagine. But while Reid's face looks to have some annoyance, it's more due to the inconvenience of the situation, perhaps even the surprise of the welcoming committee, rather than anything concerning his ego.

"She's in bed," Josh says flippantly. "It's really fucking early, you know."

"Maybe for some, Joshua," Reid replies and claps a hand on his shoulder to move past him.

He crosses the room, and his face changes when he sees me through the cracked door, and his smile hits me like the cup of coffee I desperately need. Landing a kiss on my forehead as I open the door and let him in. He pulls a Gatorade and a bottle of Advil from the messenger bag hanging on his shoulder and sets it on my desk.

"Thought you might need these."

I love this man. I toss back a couple of ibuprofen and chug the Gatorade for the very necessary hydration, and wrap myself around him.

"I missed you last night," I say into his chest, as his hand brushes the wild hair from my face.

"From the looks of the other room, it seems you had a good time here."

"Yeah—we really did, I didn't even realize Josh was still here." I feel his body tighten underneath me. Probably better not to mention another man when your boyfriend shows up to your dorm after a night of drinking, especially when that man clearly spent the night.

The man who always seems to say what he's thinking says nothing.

"Reid?" I look up to him from his chest. "Everything okay?" He takes a slow inhale, and my body moves with his.

"I think that's for you to tell me." As his eyes lock onto mine. He's not outright saying it, but I think he's bothered by Josh being the one to open the door this morning. And while I didn't even know he was here, *which I said,* I try to imagine myself in this situation, and I know I would be insanely jealous.

"Yeah, I just, I'm worried you're upset about something."

"No, I'm not upset. I wasn't expecting to see anyone but you this morning. I'm glad you had a great time last night, but I worry that whatever you think about your friendship, he doesn't see it the same way."

And that hit me. It wasn't the first time he'd mentioned something to that effect. But regardless, nothing was going on between Josh and I, nothing ever had, and him crashing on the couch after a night of drinking was no different than the numerous times Austin had done that at Reid's. And I said as much.

"There's nothing to worry about, Reid." He just shakes his head slightly and plants a quick kiss on my lips.

"I missed you, too." He says, responding to my original sentiment. Leaving the rest of the conversation unspoken. Categorizing it as something he doesn't want to say. *Perhaps because it's all been said.* "I missed having you in bed last night. Missed you even more in the shower this morning."

"You missed *having* me in bed?" I say, sliding his bag from his shoulder and dropping it to the floor. Wiggling my eyebrows. *Note to self. Come up with a sexier come-hither move.* I missed him last night also. In fact, as much fun as I had, at the end of the night, I just wanted him with me.

"Then it's a good thing there's a *bed* right here," I say, walking back as my hands make work of removing his clothes, tugging him forward by the waistband of his pants until I hit the edge of my slightly lofted dorm bed. His hands grab me by the waist, the smile on his lips wanting.

"Up, baby." As he lifts me up into the bed. I crawl backwards until my back hits the wooden headboard and pull my knees up to my chest, waiting for him. Stepping out of his pants and shoes, whipping off his shirt. His long limbs and the strength in his arms pull him on to the bed easily. And here we are, him kneeling on the end of the bed, me at the other end, a body length between us. I reach over to my nightstand and pull a condom out of the drawer.

His stare is heavy, and I can feel it on my skin.

"Reid?"

"Hmm?" He runs a hand through his hair, and the groan that pulls from his throat seems to emanate from the strained hardness barely contained by his black boxer briefs.

I hold up the condom between us and shake it tauntingly. He goes to move towards it, and I hold up my other hand, which freezes him in place. Narrowing his eyes at me, but not moving forward until I've said.

"You knowww..." I put the condom down to my side, flat on the sheets. "I'm on the pill, and I went back to Health Services last week." I can't help the smirk that pulls at my lips, as my core is tightening just at the sight of him. "And I got all my results, clean bill of health, nothing to report."

"Arden, be clear. Tell me."

"If you've been tested, I want you without a condom."

There is no hiding the tick in his jaw as mouth curves into a knowing, wanton smile.

"Baby, I was tested the day after we met."

He moves towards me, wrapping his hand around my ankle and yanking me towards him. My back sliding down the mattress, landing me right in front of him, he pulls down my underwear, discarding them off the bed, as I strip myself of the tee shirt I slept in.

He lowers his body over mine, trailing kisses down my neck, taking my nipple in his mouth. Dragging his teeth slowly across the skin. I bring my hands to cover my face, my makeup-from-the-night-before, hangover-face. Muttering a soft *fuck* into them, and I hear him chuckle into my breast as he drags a long finger down the split of me. Wet and waiting. Moving his kisses back up towards my neck, lifting his head, he grabs both of my hands and pins them above my head.

I'm desperate to feel him. In a way I have never felt anyone. His skin being absorbed by mine. Pulled into me. Releasing all of himself into me. Uncontained.

"Baby, there's no way I'm going to last..." He says as he thrusts a finger deep into me. I immediately tighten around him, he slips in another, and then a third.

"Just feeling you around my fingers, *fuck*," He abandons that sentence and drops his head in the curve of my neck. His fingers curled within me.

"Reid, I want to feel you, and I want *you* right fucking now." His arms come around me. Bracing one beneath my back, and one beneath my neck. Holding me tightly as he replaces his fingers with his hard cock in one swift motion, pushing us both up the bed as he thrusts. The scream that escapes me is muffled immediately by his hand.

"*Fuck*, your walls aren't as thick as mine," he whispers into my ear. His grip on me is so tight that our torsos are entirely melded, as his teeth nip at my earlobe, and he thrusts deeper.

He wasn't alone, I am not going to last long either. My fingers in his hair, pulling his face up to look at me. The only time I ever saw him without any restraint was when he was inside of me, and it undid me every time.

There is an insatiability about having him near me, even more so having him in me. It wasn't normal, the way he fucked me so completely to an inch of myself, fucked me to a point of abandoning my own understanding.

I lost myself completely. And as I tightened around him, my face buried in his shoulder leaving bite marks in his skin, he came and then came apart.

Our breathing is labored, twitching his cock inside me before pulling it out. Rolling to the side and laying next to me, his arm still under my neck, my head now resting on his bicep, as he looks down at me. Our bodies are both coated with sweat, as his cum drips from between my legs.

"I really *really* missed you," I say, as I drop a kiss to his shoulder. My lips picking up the saltiness of his skin. My eyes close as I just soak in the moment in his arms. When I feel a tingle crawl across my skin, as his fingers drag through me, swollen, and dripping of him. He runs his fingers through me like he's playing a scale. Collecting our combined wetness, as he pulls it from me, dancing his wet fingertips up my skin, drawing a heart on my lower stomach.

"Tell me, why this is the sexiest fucking thing I've ever seen. You laying here fucking glistening in a layer of sweat and cum."

It wasn't until he was dressed and standing over me, telling me he had to go, that I realized I'd drifted off to sleep in his arms.

"Come home to me tonight?" I sleepily nod, as he puts a bottle of water by my bed.

"Drink some water baby, I'll see you later." With another kiss and a quick, *'love you,'* he was out the door.

Stella is sitting on the couch in just her underwear sipping a mug of coffee when I emerge from the shower. Not that I'm any more dressed than she is, in nothing more than a towel.

She's looking a little worse for wear, probably nursing her own hangover. Given that Around the World Night was her idea, she definitely didn't skimp on having a good time. And it looks like she's paying for it now.

"You doing okay, Stells?"

"I was until I found your boy out here this morning."

"You saw Reid?" Her laugh almost feels insulting. A how-can-you-be-so-blind laugh.

"No, I *don't* mean Reid. But that explains what had Josh in such a mood."

"Oh god, not you too."

"What do you mean? Who else?"

"I mean, he and Reid had a weird moment this morning, and Reid, well, I guess he's just a little worried about it."

"Yeah, I'm sure he is, you seem to be the only one who doesn't see it. And I really don't know how."

"Because there's nothing to see! It's all talk, you know that. Just ego and peacocking. Austin is the same. It's nothing honest, he's like that with everyone. I just indulge it. It's not a big deal."

"Not a big deal? You can't be that blind. He's in love with you. He teases you, pushes you, because it's all you'll give him. Why else do you think he stormed out of here this morning, when your boyfriend showed up? He might not have said it, but it's been clear to everyone for a while. And you seem really happy, but he would shatter that happiness in a goddamn second if it meant he was the one who could put it back together. If it meant he could have you." My stomach drops, but I shake my head, and can only respond with two words.

"You're wrong."

Chapter Thirty-Six

PRESENT

HIM

Why am I nervous? I was the one that proposed dinner, it's not that different from any of the other times we've seen each other. *Except for the fact that it is.*

I thought dinner would be easier, less rushed. It's also socially acceptable to drink with dinner. Given the number of whiskeys I've had working late at my desk recently, I know I am going to need a drink with this meal.

She sent through the *'deets'* just like she said she would. Now I've spent all day in meetings, *the real reason I'm in town,* but far from present. Unable to focus on anything but this looming sense of dread. At this point, I'm not sure if it is dread or excitement.

Both. It's definitely both.

I could never dread seeing her. I saw her years ago when our schedules happened to overlap at a conference, but since then, the tectonic plates shifted beneath me. That small shift triggered a massive crack in my understanding. In everything.

I have run through it a thousand times. Pulled out every

artifact I had from our time together, from my time after. Replayed the conversations we had. All roads lead back to this one. This idea that no matter what *actually* happened, we both walked away. Neither of us saw use in clinging to each other beyond that single night. The night she thought to ask me about all these years later. Had she not, none of this would have come to light.

Now, I'm sitting in this rental car, forty five minutes early to a dinner reservation, my fingertips taking comfort in the muscle memory of playing the car dashboard. I scroll back through our messages, look back through the emails, one final time. Not sure what answers I'm even looking for, or what they would change.

I will relinquish control long enough to let this conversation happen organically. I won't force it, though I challenged her to meet me. To tell me. Face-to-face. And despite the photos I sent, or her agreeing to dinner, we hadn't gone back to talk about it. We just left it suspended in limbo.

Okay, okay, pull it together. After that mental unravelling, now I'm only–*fuck*–thirty-seven minutes early. And then I look up.

She's walking into the restaurant, her back is to me completely, so I can't be *sure* it's her. *I'm sure it's her.*

Thirty-six minutes early. *It's her.*

Wearing a black dress that hugs her form completely, while big blonde curls bounce with each step. *It's definitely her.*

She holds her phone to her ear as her hand waves in the air, holding an invisible conversation with whomever was on the other end. *I know it's her.*

She disappears through the front doors.

HER

"...Yeah, I'm really alright... I'm just getting here, but I'll fill you in later." I end the call and check the time before slipping it back into my bag.

Okay, I'm only thirty-four minutes early. That's not too bad, I'll just take a seat at the table and maybe eat some of the bread until he gets here to settle my stomach. The hostess guides me to the table, and I take the seat with the best view of the door. *You'll spot him.*

"Good evening, my name is Blake, I'll be your server tonight," he says while handing me a menu. Lucky for me, Blake must have gotten the memo about bread, because he places the basket of miscellaneous warm rolls on the table. I pluck one from the basket, tearing off a piece and tossing it into my mouth immediately. *Carbs will help.*

"I can get you started with something to drink while you take a look at the menu, and I can get this extra place setting out of your way if you'll be dining alone."

And then I hear him. Somewhere between appreciating the warm bread and listening to Blake's introduction, he cut across the room in just a few strides. Stopping directly behind the empty chair, and the smile that slowly pulled his lips warmed the space between us immediately. Just like it always had.

"She's not alone. You can leave the place setting."

I hurry to swallow the chunk of bread I shoved in my mouth, sure that I had another twenty minutes, or at least three rolls, before he was supposed to be here. *I should have known better.*

"Hi, Reid."

"Arden."

"You're early."

"What can I say, AB. Old habits."

I stand almost immediately and brush my hands to flatten the front of my dress where it had ridden up from sitting.

"It's really good to see you," I say, reaching up on my toes to wrap my arms around him as his wrap around me, with more trepidation than ever I recall over the years, but equally as warm.

I release him from my grip, but his hands move to settle and rest on my shoulders, his smokey eyes whirling over me, taking me in. It has been years since we've seen each other, and be it time or circumstance, I look a little different.

He leans down, planting a kiss on my cheek. The smile on his face broadens, nearly reaching his eyes as his hands slide down the length of my arms. Slowly removing them and slipping them into his pockets.

"You look great."

REID

It's a surreal sensation. Having her standing here. While I follow her on social media, *and yes, I checked it before walking through the restaurant doors,* that is a hidden curated view. The curation keeps private what is now visible as she stands in front of me.

I would never outright ask, but her lips pull into a slight curve that matches the one of her stomach as she delicately moves to rest her hand atop it. It's all but verbally confirmed. I'm far from an expert in matters such as this, but given the still relatively small swell of her belly, I don't think she's too far along. My only real point of reference, my sisters. Still small enough she could have hidden it with a far less form-fitting dress, but the things she hid from the world, *from me*, were always more internal.

Even still, looking at her now, she's as striking as ever. But out of nowhere, her smile dims, and concern washes over me as her face goes solemn.

"*Thanks...* Reid, you should know, the baby, it, it's yours." She says it softly with a hint of unease and a gentle touch to my bicep. Her touch is feather-light but still nearly knocks me down. My eyes widen in reply, knowing there's no physical way it's possible but there is still that momentary feeling where my brain is scrambling trying to catch up. Both because of the immediate shock of those words that I always had taken precaution to avoid, and because of the momentary *'what if'* vision that my mind thrust me into like fast forwarding to an alternate ending of my favorite movie. *That* is the scarier thought.

"Arden, that's not—" I begin, as she doubles over in hysterical laughter.

"I'm *obviously* kidding! I mean, jeez, this would be the longest gestation period in history. You can calm down." Her face is so bright and the hand that she has resting on my arm, gives it a squeeze. Bringing me out of the temporary daze.

"I thought we are already in the middle of this soap opera, might as well add in an unexpected love child as an icebreaker! Granted, I don't know the rates of conception when it's only a *'mind-fuck'* as you called it, but last I checked, it wasn't actually possible to get pregnant that way. But then again, it's always been fun just to keep you on your toes." *She's rambling. She's nervous. But at least she's smiling.*

She can barely get the words out because she's laughing so hard. I don't know fully what I expected tonight. I'm glad it's this. And there's no way not to join her in laughter.

Calling it infectious would be an offensive understatement. It would imply I don't welcome the way her joy and laughter overtake me. It's not an infection, it's sinking into a warm bath, the water completely washing over me.

Bringing her hand back to her belly, almost to settle them both down, she takes a seat. Still laughing slightly to herself and picking up her bread. She has always been beautiful in a way that wasn't common, always vibrant, as if the complexity of her mind and the richness of her heart seeped out of her skin. Now is no different, except there's an ease about her I haven't seen in years. *Maybe, ever.* Making me wonder if she's been harboring resentment all this time, at the idea I left her, broke up with her, abandoned her, *dumped* her. In some ways I suppose I did. I was furious at first, angry with her, but that anger didn't morph into any kind of action. Maybe if it had, things would have been different.

The truth though, the more I've thought about it, there might never have been the happy ending for us that she now has. The one she found not long after we broke up.

I pull my chair out and join her at the table. "And how is he?" I ask, as I always do.

"He's doing great, unbelievably excited as you'd expect. How's the future Mrs.?" she asks, as she always does.

"Doing good, she changed companies and was traveling this week like I have been," I say casually, like this is a conversation we have regularly. Like she's aware of my fiancée's career moves. *She's not.* Though it's the pleasantries we've always exchanged. This is a dance we've done numerous times before, and it's structured and choreographed, but that doesn't make it any less sincere.

We don't ask with judgment or condescension. But I do wonder if that's why we never outright say their names. The idea that it would be an insult to them or our relationships with them, to be talking points between us. Instead we keep the pleasantries high level. We ask, we acknowledge, we move on.

We ask about our partners, our careers, our pets, we cover off any good books, sometimes trading the ones we've picked up in the airport for our travels. *Still leaving her notes in them and a full review in the back cover. It still makes me smile.* These are the boundaries we've always had, and I think she's interested in preserving them now. But that's the problem with drawing lines in the sand. When you're not looking, a wave, a wind, or a petulant child can easily wash them away. And being here at this table under these conditions, the ones we established years ago, are barely visible now. I think she can read the shift in my face. Because while hers remains the same, her tone is intentionally telling.

"Annnd how *are you*, Reid?" She is calm, compassionate, and almost diagnostic.

"You don't have to say it like my therapist." I grab a multigrain roll from the basket.

We sit here as the seconds tick by, not yet sure who is going to pull the lever to direct this conversation in one way or another.

We are in our own version of the trolley problem. The most famous ethical dilemma ever crafted. *One we used to argue in bed at night.* Neither answer is wrong, but I'm not sure if either is actually *right*. Especially now.

The problem is simple: There's a runaway trolley barreling down the tracks. *The looming conversation.*

The trolley is headed straight towards five people who are tied up on the tracks. *In this case, the five people represent our lives.*

You are standing next to a lever. If you pull the lever, the trolley will switch to a different set of tracks. However, now there is only one person in danger. *Me.*

There are only two options.

Option one, do nothing at all and let the trolley kill the five people on the track. Let this conversation barrel through whatever boundaries we have preserved, let it knock down whatever pretense remains, let it potentially damage and destroy whatever is in its path.

Option two, pull the lever. Divert the trolley onto the

alternative track where it will kill only one person. *Change the topic of conversation entirely and sacrifice just my sanity in the process.*

As it relates to the actual dilemma posed by the trolley problem, I know my answer. I've taken enough ethics classes to know which choice I feel is correct.

In this case, I have no fucking idea.

This is our Trolley Dilemma. The look on her face says she knows it also.

Looking at her now, she seems more than content in her life, and I know I am more than content in mine. Rehashing all of that purely because I want answers to something that maybe I don't deserve answers to might be the unfair thing to do to her. Because as much as I want to have this conversation, I should have pushed for it the day it happened, even a week later. Not now.

The waiter takes our order, and we sit there another moment. The trolley is racing down the tracks, I leave it up to her to decide, and she does.

"I think there are some things to say."

ARDEN

He's visibly conflicted in a way I'm not sure I ever remember seeing him before. That might be because with age comes wisdom and with wisdom comes the understanding contained in his original email, that this *is* a slippery slope. And we are both standing on the ledge, looking down.

I've dated and broken up with enough people in my life to know the dangers of romanticizing the past. It's not something I do. I don't even keep anything from previous relationships. But Reid has always been different. He was different then, and he's different now. I may not have kept any of the physical mementos from our time together, but in some ways, I always kept him.

His face betrays every emotion, and what isn't translatable is then defined when he opens his mouth. Always saying what he means. Except now. When he looks like there's a lot he wants to say, but just doesn't. So, I will.

"I think there are some things to say," I begin.

When I agreed to meet, I agreed to have this conversation. And that's what I am going to do.

"Yes." He takes a slow inhale which serves to still his body, exercising control over his mind that I never could. "I think you're right."

Even though he seems ready to say something, even though I am desperate to hear what it is, I need to be the one to go first.

"I should start with an apology." He looks ready to shut me down, so I raise my hands to stop him. "Please, just wait. I've thought about it a lot, and while I don't regret the fact that we're sitting here now, I realize it wasn't fair for me to throw this on you. For you to have this all upended." I make a swirly gesture with my hand between us, as if to match the swirling in my stomach when I speak. "You said you replayed it all, that you thought through how things could have been different, about what was impacted beyond just our romantic lives, and I'm sorry about that." I take a breath to continue, and it's harder than I thought now. Sitting in front of him fills me with the memories of the feelings I had. It's familiar like a lingering scent on a pillowcase.

"Arden, the only apologies owed to either of us, are from the idiots we were all those years ago. Because that's the thing that trips me up. That I've been thinking about constantly. That's why I replayed it all. That no matter how much we loved each other, and I *know* we did, we left each other. Sure, we managed a pseudo friendship for a while, until it turned into this real one. But that doesn't change the fact that I thought you left, and I let you. I didn't chase you out the door, I didn't beg you to come back to me." His voice is clear. His thoughts are clear. Clearer than mine. I had been worried leading up to dinner, knowing some of what I had to say, but here he is, articulating like he always has exactly what he thought.

"We were young and fell in love impossibly quickly. I was all in before we even knew what it was. And then it was over before we gave ourselves the chance to figure out what it could be. And when you left, I was never going to stop you. Even if I wanted to, which I did, I couldn't. I *wouldn't*. That's not who I was.

"I didn't let you leave because I didn't care, I let you leave because I did. Because I thought that's what you wanted. Damn, it sounds so cliché to say, so stupid to hear myself say it. But that doesn't make it less true."

"I know we loved each other, looking back, I know it." I say, a repeat of his own sentiment. Not wanting him to question now, how I felt then, when we were together. Wondering if that had been a doubt, though his declaration now is both comforting and jarring.

The realization he's right. He let me go, never once extending a bridge across the rift we formed. Leaving us on different sides of the same night. Just like he had said.

Chapter Thirty-Seven

2008

ARDEN

The house is absolutely packed. It was expected, it's the annual, *infamous*, Wendell House Party, and we have been planning this night since we first heard about it back in the fall. Even Reid was familiar, having attended a few years during his own undergrad.

It's a house off the main campus on Wendell Street, which is how this infamous night got its name. The *infamous* part comes from the numerous incidents that have been written up about over the decades since its inception. Fireworks, floods, livestock, slip-n-slides. Once a year, the occupants of the Wendell house throw what has been deemed the *'ultimate rager'* celebrating the semester ending and summer being upon us.

The winter had thawed, and in many ways, so have I. Now opting for a denim jacket rather than full blown winter coat, and while I may have lost the tights, I still usually opted for a pair of boots and dress. And tonight is no different.

Stella and I agreed to come with Josh and the rest of our

friends, and Reid was going to meet me here later with Austin. We divided the night up so we could all make the most of it, the last few weeks we would all be in the same city. Even though we knew there was no hope that everyone would stay together the minute we walked through the door, the sentiment was there.

After the initial round of shots and the toasts that accompanied them, Stella and I were the first ones to run off from the group. When she found a beer pong table and challenged two of the hosts in a game that we had absolutely no way of winning.

Josh was with us. Cheering us on as he bottoms-upped his red solo cup in solidarity every time we had to empty one when the other team scored. *Which was a lot.* We absolutely didn't win. Not even close. But for everyone who surrounded the table, we were the clear winners in their hearts. *Or at least the most entertaining competitors.* We didn't wallow in our loss, in fact I think Stella only wanted to play to cause a stir.

I walk off from the table, and Josh takes up his spot by my side. Throwing his arm around me and handing me his plastic cup as a consolation prize.

Looking into it, the red punch-like drink, it has all the indicators of bad decisions and regrettable morning-afters. The bright red color, the carbonation, the candy. Whatever it is, the sugary punch masked the taste of booze but there's no doubt it's brimming with alcohol. Which tells me I need to slow down.

"Arden," Josh leans into my ear, practically screaming over the music. It's so rare he used my name, unless he was trying to prove a point. It was always *'Miami'* or even now *'AB,'* *especially* in public. Had been since day one.

His weighted arm around my neck pulls me into him for a hug. The strength of it and his lack of control, knock me into him with a force he might not have intended to use. An indicator that while *I'm* not drunk... I might be the only exception.

"You look amazing tonight." He squeezes me into his chest and my face smashes into him, inhaling the smell of licorice and pine that seemed to be threaded into his clothes. He lands a drunk kiss on the crown of my head, lingering a second longer than usual, the delay to pull himself back heavier than just alcohol. There's something different about his voice, and the compliment itself.

There is usually an overt sexual tone, a challenge or bait, the volleyball we lobbed back and forth over the net that stayed taut between us. But not this time. This time his mask slipped, and the softness that slipped from his lips was more akin to sincerity than calculation.

"You don't look too bad yourself." And he didn't, he never does. Dressed in a fitted black tee shirt and jeans, his usual uniform. He's charmingly handsome with a smirk that could drop panties; I've seen it happen from across the bar. Bewitching in so many ways. But tonight, he's far more focused on me than any of the willing and available participants that he has all but ignored since we walked through the door.

"You should know what you can do to a man's heart." His speech is slurred.

"Since when did you get a heart?" I laughed.

"Don't say that, when you're the only one who's seen it." He sounds momentarily hurt, that I would deny him something so common, something we both tried so hard to protect.

We make our way out back, and the cool night air against my skin a welcome relief. Inside was sticky and close, stepping outside was awakening. I hop up onto the wooden banister of the porch and let my legs swing as Josh leaned against it to my right.

Pulling out my phone, to see where Reid is, it's getting late, and not that I'm afraid I'll turn into a pumpkin or anything, but

I want him. I want to dance with him, drink with him, and then I want to go *home* with him. It isn't tonight I am hungry for, though it always feels like enough isn't enough.

It's tomorrow morning that I crave already.

Tomorrow morning. Maybe it would be a morning he was up before me, already in the kitchen, with a cup of coffee in hand, pulling down an empty mug for me. Maybe it would be a morning where I find him sitting up in bed reading, casually turning pages with one hand while running lazy strokes down my bare skin with the other. Maybe he would wake me up as his fingers furiously played 'Flight of the Bumblebee' from the other room. Or maybe, it would be the kind of Sunday morning where I snuck out of bed and he found me in the shower, when we would let the steam clear the sleep from our eyes together.

"Where's your Lecture-Boyfriend?"

Josh had always assigned nicknames; I think it bonded him to people. His nickname for Reid never took off. And over the last months, I think he meant it with the same intention Reid did, every time he called him Joshua. A reminder that while they both might be in my life, I am the only overlap.

"He's meeting me here in a little bit. I wanted to come with you guys, celebrate the end of our freshman year!" I swing my leg to the side to knock into him where he stands. Leaning casually against the banister. "So, what's the plan for tonight anyway?"

"I don't get it, Arden." His voice is stripped bare, and so is his face. I wonder if somehow the gummy- worm vodka bypassed the normal personalities of intoxication that I've seen him exhibit leaving only this.

"What don't you get?"

"You and him."

"There's nothing for *you* to get."

"But does he? Does he get it?"

"You know he does," I say and raise my eyebrows with a smirk.

"No–does he get *you*? At least with Ethan, everyone knew you guys were just banging each other's brains out. But we still saw you–this guy? You're never around. You jumped ahead into *his* life. You want to celebrate the end of your freshman year? What freshman year? Not the one *you* told me you wanted. You said you wanted to 'do college,' remember? But you chose to just *do him* instead."

"That's not fair."

"It's not fair, but it's not wrong, either. You want to know the plan for tonight? Let me predict it for you. You'll take shots with Ethan, dance with Stells, you'll hang out by my side because you don't want any of the future-finance-frat-bros to bother you, and then five minutes after your boyfriend shows up, you'll leave with him. You abandoned your friends and jumped into a relationship with someone who doesn't know you. A relationship you made clear from day one you didn't want. And now, you're never home, you sleep in your own bed, what, maybe once a week, and only after we *beg* you to stay? For what, someone who doesn't even show up for you? When it was us wiping sweat from your forehead and vomit from your mouth. He's got a life, and you are going to be left here with us when he leaves. But I'm not going to be your backup plan."

"You've never begged me for anything, Josh, and you're way too busy hopping between everyone else's beds to worry about whose I'm in."

"Come on, Arden. You think he's going to finish his degree and just go on to date a college sophomore? You think you'll charm his colleagues with chit chat about your classes at the corporate Christmas party? You've gotta see how this plays out. I've known you were a lot of things, but I never thought stupid was one of them."

"I think *this* is stupid," Stella chimes in and I hadn't noticed she was even here. "Let's play another round of beer pong."

"I'm not in the mood to lose again. Sorry, Stells."

"I think it's better than whatever *this* is." She waves her hand between me and Josh, doing her best to diffuse the situation.

"Stella, it's fine..." I turn my body to face him more directly. "You don't mean that," I say calmly.

"Which part? The part where you came all this way to college only to spend no fucking time on campus? Or the part where I tell you you're an idiot for thinking it's something more than your freshman fling? Or how about the fact that you have friends who know you, who love you, and you decided to shack up with the first guy to pay you any attention?"

The normal friendly tension between us is more palpable now, and far less friendly. He's heated. His tone is rough and raw. It isn't banter, it's an actual fight. One it seems like he's been stashing artillery for since the beginning. *And I fucking missed it.* I hate to admit that while I did my best to put up every shield, he lands more blows than he realizes.

I don't know how it happened, what exactly I said that seemed to push him over the edge, but for the first time I can see what Stella had warned me against. There is a possessiveness to Josh in the way he looks at me. In the way he speaks to me.

I jump down from the banister to stand in front of him. While most people would want the added inches, I want the stability of my own two feet. Stability I need as the contents of my own red solo cup began to course through me.

"The first guy to pay me any attention here was *you,* and right now it sounds like *that's* your problem. Not who's in my bed, but that I'm no longer spending nights in yours."

Josh opens his mouth to say something, but instead the words that fall out were more a reaction than a thought.

"You've got to be fucking kidding me." He laughs darkly as he tilts his cup all the way back, emptying the contents down his throat. Stella is tugging on the sleeve of my denim jacket. We're so close, barely inches apart, as I look up at him challenging his last accusation, ignoring the emotional bleeding I pray no one can see.

I turn to follow Stella's direction. *Reid, finally.*

Though had he been here ten minutes earlier, it would have saved me this whole conversation.

He's walking out the back door to join us on the porch, accompanied by Austin, who, as usual, is just dripping in charisma. The two of them, tall and poised with an air that most people here didn't have. Be it the lack of alcohol, or generally just them being exactly who they are. Reid and Austin are mid conversation when he sees me and the smile immediately falls from his face, replaced with something I can't identify.

He comes up alongside me and leans a kiss to my cheek. Austin does the same as means of hello before he turns his attention to Stella, *still very much in a relationship,* Stella.

But my eagerness to see Reid changes to annoyance that he wasn't here sooner. The arrows Josh had shot, piercing parts of me, and I need to stifle that bleeding somehow. Suddenly an entirely different conversation began to take shape. I fought with my best friend. Differently than I had before. For all the small disputes Josh and I had, this was something much more real. And it triggered real concern.

"What's going on?" *So much.*

"Nothing." *Tell him.*

"Did I miss something?" *More like I did.*

"Yeah," I'm grasping for something, anything beyond the truth, and it sounds as ridiculous as it feels when I say it, "you missed us playing beer pong!" *He'll see right through this. He knows you.*

"You wanted me to watch you play beer pong? You're terrible at beer pong." He smiles at me, but it changes as he glances over my shoulder towards Josh. He's more skeptical than I've ever seen him.

"It doesn't matter if I'm terrible at it if I love it." *None of this matters.*

"Since when do you love it?" *I don't love it. I love you and that feels out of control right now.*

"I've just been waiting for you. You asked what you missed. That's what you missed, the party's almost over now."

"What are you talking about?" He checks his watch, looks back to Austin who shakes his head confused, before Reid turns back to face me. "I told you I'd stop by, and I'm here earlier than I said I'd be. But the party clearly isn't almost over." His gaze is billowing smoke into mine. Perhaps an S.O.S. Maybe anger. Whatever it is, I can't see through it.

"Clearly," I say back to him. His hand had been dragging up and down my arm, but it stills abruptly. I think that might be how he sees me, like I am a temporary stop over. Somewhere he can just drop in like he did tonight. A party-pit stop. "The party might not be over, but my favorite *part* of the party is over, the part before everyone is too drunk to remember anything."

"Is that what's wrong, you had too much to drink?" He reaches up to tuck the hair behind my ear. It's patronizing how he looks at me. I turn my head out of reach. And his face changes as his eyebrows pinch together in question.

"No, I'm fine." I'm not drunk, not in the way he asked, but between the candy-punch and the electricity charged fight with Josh, I feel totally out of control. *And for all that Josh said, I just want Reid to prove him wrong.*

"Then why are you fighting with me about beer pong? Why are you fighting with me at all? We had plans, I'm here. I didn't realize you had a *'favorite part of the party,'* but you're acting like you're in high school right now." *Looks like Reid is going to prove him right.*

My voice is getting louder. I can pretend it's because the noise from the party is escaping making it hard to hear. Really, it's the detonation of the mental landmines I didn't even know were buried. Exploding with every step I take down this path. But I can't stop myself, not when he is painfully calm. Not willing to show me an ounce of the passion that I've seen from him in the past. Maybe it's only reserved for when he fucked me. *Maybe that's it.* Some romance he keeps locked away until the alarm on his phone goes off and he has to move on.

He shot a silver bullet. So, I shoot my own.

"I'm acting like a teenager, because I am. But you? You're acting like you don't know me at all."

His face goes instantly cold. He's nearly unreadable except for an imperceptible flinch as the words landed and he forced out his own muted reply.

"You don't mean that."

As I stand here and take him in, the same stoicism and fortitude I always held respect for, is now shielding him from me. The emotions he usually wore and gave me freely, are tucked away completely. He's more focused on containing himself, than engaging with me. Refusing to show any concern, just looking to run away from a public display.

"Great, so now I don't know what I think? I don't know my own mind? When did you become the sole arbiter of truth? Because from where I'm standing, Reid, it looks like I fit myself into your life. And now what? It was always going to be over when you graduate."

I don't realize it until it's too late just how loud I've become. Maybe I should care, but I don't.

The dead air between us is more a defense of my argument than his own. I said it, not even knowing if I meant it. I just hurled it out to see if it would stick, and maybe the scariest part is, he knows it does.

He says nothing, and the seconds drag on. It would be better to say I was drunk, that this manifested from one too many questionable solo cups of punch. But standing here now, I am extremely aware of what I've just said, and it didn't come from any vodka-soaked gummy worm. I'm filled with so much self-doubt while he looks at me dripping with self-assurance.

Finally, he takes a breath and breaks the silence. He's visibly uncomfortable. The fact is, there's no silence, and there hasn't been. Not really, there are noises coming from every direction. But still the air between us is heavy and quiet.

His voice is steady, calm and low, but it's forced. He's forcing himself to stand here. I can tell by the tension he's holding in his body that he's doing it because he feels has no alternative.

"You think I forced you into my life? No, Arden. Some things aren't that complicated."

His tone is so low, each word so thought out and delivered with such steadiness that I find it completely aggravating. He attempts to take a step closer to me, but despite the physical proximity, we've never felt farther apart.

"I was all in. I was all in while you were figuring out what you wanted. I was all in before you knew, or admitted, what this was. I told you months ago, it was your choice. I know who I am, I know what I want. I wanted you, but I told you if you didn't want a relationship, that was fine. I'm not going to compromise myself or my dignity to chase after someone who doesn't want to be with me, and right now it looks like that's what I'm doing. You seem to have made up your mind about something before you even clued me into the fucking conversation."

Josh lets out an ill-timed chuckle not more than a couple feet from where we are. Clearly reacting to the show. Reid's eyes shoot up from where they were burrowing into mine. Right over my shoulder to where Josh stands off to the side.

"You've done enough." I glance between them. Josh looks like he wants to say something, to challenge it, to deliver a targeted insult. But he's known Reid now long enough to know that type of baiting game doesn't work on him. He had tried. And Reid notes it, too. The hesitation on Josh's face, the interest in jumping into this argument as more than one of many bystanders.

I watch as they appear momentarily locked when Reid speaks again.

"Not another fucking word, *Joshua*." His face is frozen, as his words cut the air between them. Landing darts on a bullseye, one after another. He was the only one to ever call him that. And it was in moments like this, *okay—not like this,* but moments when Reid sought to reestablish that they were not friends that had earned him the casual use of the nickname, nor did he ever want it. For some reason, this time, Josh doesn't argue. He just grabs a beer from a nearby cooler and walks off. Maybe finally realizing this isn't his fight.

With Josh's departure, Reid refocuses back on me. As I remain standing in front of him like a child waiting to be reprimanded. *And again, it seems he's going to prove me right.*

"Arden, I'm done. I'm not going to argue with you." His voice to me is softer than a moment ago, but remains obligatory, almost indifferent. The smoke behind his eyes has gone out, instead right now they are steel gray. And I can't read them. He won't let me.

"Tell me, why not?" He's always the one to ask me to explain, but now it's *his* turn to be clear.

"Because I'm better than this, and I thought you were also."

"I'm not better than this, *this* is who I am."

"I'm not going to have a girlfriend that I fight with in public, so lower your voice and let's go home."

"No, that's your home, not mine."

And even though it's technically true, there's so much that made it feel like home every time I walked through the door, but most of all it's always been him. I think he might be as stunned by the statement as I am for saying it.

The difference between us is that while he says things he means, I say things I don't. I couldn't stop myself from regurgitating the things that had been thrown at me earlier. The insults I then sharpened into my own weapons.

I take a step back and the crack at our feet splinters a little bit more, but I plant my feet just like he has. Standing firm in what I said and putting distance between us that I don't really want.

"Do you realize I never sleep in my own bed anymore? That I never see my friends anymore?"

"That's how you feel? Fine, sleep at the dorm." *He's just going to send me off to bed like a child without supper.*

"How do you feel, Reid? Because right now, I can't fucking tell." I yell it, and while you can still hear the music from inside, it pulls people out of their conversations, and their focus is solely on us.

The lack of response from him is tangible, I can taste it, bitterly, as I stand here looking up to him, waiting for him to say something. I open my mouth to prompt a response, but he cuts me off with his own.

"I'm not fighting with you like this. I don't want a relationship like this. I'm going."

I feel like I've been punched straight through. But I don't move, I don't blink. *I don't understand.* I wanted him to bridge the space I put between us, not retreat from it.

"Is it, just... that easy to walk away?" I asked. My voice is suddenly soft.

"Apparently." His tone is dry. Could it be so simple for him? My throat is strangled by what he just said. The only words I could get out were a meek question to desperately try and gauge his feelings.

Could this man who I thought loved me so completely, so easily unlove me? From day one everything was so black and white. Like he could easily flip a switch. And it looks like finally he flipped it back.

At the end of the day, no matter how many coffee orders, favorite books, or most played scrabble words we know about each other, maybe we don't actually *know* each other. And now that he's gotten to this layer, a layer he doesn't like, he's done.

He takes a long slow breath, placing a hand on both of my shoulders, as I look up at him.

"I'm sorry, I can't do this, I'm leaving."

His large hands run the length of my arms, and when they reach the ends of my fingers, he lingers momentarily, as he steps forward and presses a soft kiss to my cheek for what feels like the last time.

"Okay," is all I can say. I immediately want to apologize, apologize for causing a scene, over things that barely matter, but the truth is, beneath the layers of nonsense are legitimate questions. Does he know me? Does he love me? Is this more than just a fling? *Does that even fucking matter?*

He threw the words out like they were nothing. *'I'm sorry, I can't do this, I'm leaving.'* What was the apology for, manners or actual regret? He had told me before he didn't have a lot of regret, because he said the things he meant. So how could I take his words now to mean anything but?

He nods at me once before turning back to Austin and Stella. Stella, who looks like her eyes are barely contained in her skull, as her hand covers her mouth that hangs agape. She looks like she's on the verge of tears. Why? I have no idea. *She isn't the one left standing here like a fool.*

Austin, raises his hand to me in acknowledgement, a goodbye perhaps, and follows Reid out the door.

He's gone.

The mirrored emptiness from where he just stood reflected back into me, as I'm frozen in place.

Trying to work through all the things that just happened. Trying to understand how it unfolded. I might have been thoughtless or even provoking, but I needed to see him care. But he didn't. He refused to engage with me beyond the patronizing discrediting of how I felt. He was so much more concerned with whatever self-respect he had, or worse, perceptions of those around us, than focusing on what I needed from him.

I'm frozen.

Physically.

Mentally.

Emotionally.

What the fuck just happened. Did he care *so little* that he could end it right then and there, no remorse, no second thought, and just walk out the door?

My breathing is short, but it's the only way to keep myself from crying. Because I refuse to cry over someone who just dumped me at a party.

Josh clearly hadn't gone far; he and Stella immediately approach me where I'm left standing. My lungs are working quickly, as if I can't take in enough air. Suffocated entirely by what just happened. My heart is racing. *No, my heart is breaking*. It's not speed I feel in my chest, but a shattering.

Josh extends a cold uncracked can of PBR that I open and chug, as if I can rehydrate myself, or rewind time.

"What the fuck just happened?" Stella says, asking the same question on loop in my own mind. She slips her hand into mine and squeezes for support. And I feel a body sidle up next to me, wrapping his arm around my shoulders and pulling me into a side hug. I let my head rest on his chest for a minute before taking a long slow inhale and straightening myself entirely out of his embrace.

"I think my boyfriend just dumped me."

"Then it doesn't sound like he's your boyfriend anymore, Miami."

Chapter Thirty-Eight

2008

REID

I don't know what happened. How I'm sitting here. How she isn't. Why she didn't want to leave with me. Instead, she opted to stay surrounded by arrogant sycophants and aggressively drunk college students, but that's her choice.

Sometimes I forget she's only nineteen. *Fuck. Most of the time I forget she's only nineteen.* But I'm pretty sure *she* forgets it also. But tonight, there was no doubt who she was, as she acted like I didn't know her. No, not acted, she said it. Whoever that was, it was only a fraction of herself. I've seen it for months now, who she was around me versus everyone else. And somehow, *I'm* the one who doesn't know her. *Bullshit.*

I told her I was leaving. I wasn't going to fight with my girlfriend at a house party. *I don't want to fight with my girlfriend, period.* But I'm absolutely not about to stand there and have it out in public for everyone around to watch like animals in the zoo.

While her fucking friend rattles the bars of the cage.

I had hoped she would leave with me, but when I said I was

leaving, she said *'okay,'* just like that. I wasn't going to drag her away from her friends if that's where she wanted to be, but I also have enough self-respect not to be a part of something like that.

Austin came by for a bit, had a beer, and we talked about the outright shit show we just put on. He doesn't see the big deal, he wouldn't, he loves a spectacle. Maybe she does also, but I resent them. She knows that about me. *I thought she did.*

What was all of this even about? I was on time. I stopped by the party like I said I would. Was it because she stays here more than she's at the dorm? Fine. Semester is almost over anyway. I'll cram into her twin bed if that's what she wants, and after a week, she'll remember what it's like to stretch out in mine.

What am I missing? I'm sure she'll stay at her dorm tonight, just to prove a point. Because as much as I love her, she is mind-blowingly stubborn. She might have softened with me, but the intensity she possesses when she wants to plant her feet, and build a fortress, good fucking luck. She's immovable.

It hasn't mattered how many times I've approached the topic, she refused to acknowledge that Josh clearly clings to her coattails, and she lets him. She's far from stupid in all things, but somehow in this she elects ignorance. I have no doubt in the role he played. Likely taking a bow as soon as the curtain fell on tonight's performance.

This brilliant girl has blinders on for this one thing, and it's the one thing I asked about from the very beginning. All the while, I've fallen so in love with her, and she seems to have one foot out the door.

Do I know her? I certainly thought I did. And what the fuck did she mean, this would be over when I graduate? Has she been thinking that this whole time? Did she put an expiration date on this? *I wish someone would have told me.*

I take a sip of the beer I've opened, not like it will take the edge off. But as I set it down on the counter to check my phone, *for her*, I hear the frantic buzzing of the front door. I know who it is, as I take large hurried steps to press the button to let her in.

Steadying myself for the inevitable fight that is to come. Pouring out two glasses of water and leaving them on the counter.

She was clearly aggravated when I left, voice raised, emboldened with some liquid courage and the needling of the devil on her shoulder, prodding her.

But at least she's here. Wait, did she walk here, alone? *I'm sure she did.* Warmed by whatever fire she has burning in her right now. Goddamnit though, I thought she was just going to go back to the dorm. Walking back with her friends, not braving the city by herself. *Jesus Christ. Add that to the list to talk about tomorrow.*

I pull the door open, and her breathing is heavy. I'm sure she took the stairs two by two if she didn't outright run here. It's her eyes that absolutely crush me. I can see it so clearly. A face I've never seen her wear before that tells me she's not here to settle anything. Her mind–it's already settled on something.

The rims of her eyes are red, and they have a glassiness to them that indicates she probably cried on her way here. It's dangerous the way she looks right now. The most vibrant blue I've seen reflecting like a mirror I can't look away from.

This girl never cries. I've seen it twice, both times because of the sad dog commercials, not for any actual emotion that she wanted to release. Looking at her now, I know why. As she stares up at me breathing in short spurts, blinking as if that will contain the tears, my heart absolutely splits. Because though her eyes are welled with an emotion she usually contains, she is hardened and prepared for something else entirely.

"I'm glad you're here." I don't know if that's the right thing to say, but it's true. Even though looking at her like this has my stomach bottomed out.

"Why, this is over." Her tone is colder than I've ever heard it. She's frozen. I say nothing. Maybe there *isn't* anything to talk about.

"I have books and things here. I'm going to need to take them home." I hear what she's saying, but I've never been more confused. I know what happened, but in the time from then to now, *what the fuck happened*. Where did her mind go, where did her *heart* go? Because I thought I had it, but now she's here to pick up her things? To take them home to her dorm? She never moved in, but she was here most of the time. That was a main point of contention earlier. *Which still makes no sense to me.* But somehow from then to now, she decided that this is over? Did she move up whatever timeline she alluded to earlier? I need her to say it. I need her to be clear.

"Tell me, I need to understand what you're saying."

"I'm *saying* that I'm here to pick up my stuff because I'm not your girlfriend anymore."

"Slow down, you don't have to do that, it's late." It *is* late. She needs to settle down. She's not drunk, just furious. Intoxicated only on whatever has fueled this. She needs to take a minute; I need her to take a minute. She moves around so quickly, from spot to spot, like a squirrel digging up all the nuts buried in the winter. But they aren't nuts, they are memories, things, pieces of her she left here to grow into something more, and she is here to take them back. Ripping them from the ground before they could take root.

"Well, breakups aren't always convenient, are they?" She's being clear, she's said it multiple ways since she walked through the door. *It's over. Breakup.* Two expressions meaning the exact same thing.

"And that's why you're here at 2:14 a.m.? To break up?" *God, she could have waited until tomorrow.*

"I'm pretty sure this part is just a formality, Reid."

"Well then tell me, Arden. Why are you *really* here, your

books? That's bullshit, you could have come by tomorrow. What do you want, to rub salt in the wound?" My resolve cracks, I hear what she's saying. Despite her directness in part, her reason for showing up like this is just an excuse.

"I wanted to see you; I want closure." All she wants from me is an end. Even if I'm not ready to give it to her yet, I don't think there's anything I would deny her now, but I need to see her, need her to slow down and take a breath. So I take a deep one as I grab her by the shoulders trying to steady her in one place.

"Baby, sit down, please. Stop moving for a second. If you want closure, fine, but you need to stop fucking moving and look at me." She does. She's sucked her lip into her mouth, and it's taking all the power inside my being to not pull it free. I can feel my thumb twitch in response. *Fuck*, I can feel my cock harden as if its own desperate attempt to connect her to me even if it's nothing beyond a physical reminder. The look on her face is pure fire. She blazed her way over here, and the tears that might have fallen must have been boiling.

I need to hear her say it. I need to know what to do.

"Arden, please, tell me. I need you to tell me what you want from me."

"I want you and I want to be clear that this is over. But I want us to have closure."

I don't know what kind of closure I can give her, but that's what she wants. I just need her to focus on something else, to join me in this moment, rather than the one she's decided comes after this. I can feel her turning the final page, getting ready to seal the secrets in the pages of the book between us. Our commingled ink left in the margins.

I do the only thing I can think to do. I press my lips against hers in a desperate attempt. *Thankfully she responds.* Her kiss is strong, her tongue, battling, warring me, but still wanting.

She drops her things on the ground, glass shattering at our

feet in the process, and throws her arms around me as the grip of my fingers brace the back of her neck and interlock her thick hair. Keeping her face on mine. Her eyes drift closed, though mine scan her face for any indication. But the walls of ice we spent months thawing, melting down, and evaporating away, are now refrozen.

Chapter Thirty-Nine

2008

ARDEN

The walk to *his* apartment had become second nature, which is helpful now, as I am blinded and blurred by tears welling in my eyes.

It isn't a far walk, not more than ten minutes, and I know regardless of what just happened, *maybe even because of what just happened,* he'd be mad that I'm walking around by myself this late at night. But I'm not drunk, I'm painfully sober. Any final drops of alcohol leaving my body when he left me.

He probably thinks I'll just go back to my dorm and maybe contact him about picking up my things another time. *I considered just leaving it all there.* Knowing him, he might already have it packed up in a box by the door. That seems like something he would do, it's efficient, *clear.* If anything, I'm actually going to be doing him a favor, stopping by to pick them up now. At least that's what I'll say.

I just need to see him. I just need him to pack one more *I love you* in the box with the rest of my things. Even as he walked away from me. So stoic, so calm. I hate him for it, the indifference he seemed to have as armor in that moment. Maybe it wasn't armor.

Maybe it's just how he feels. *Indifferent.*

He was always so clear, so direct. He was in this case as well. But in all the ways I ever saw our future, *together or not*, I never thought I would be dumped at a house party. Who knows what would have really happened? Despite the plans we might have begun to draw. *I didn't see this coming. It was unexpected, and I am not prepared for it.*

"I'm glad you're here." He says, though his face for once betrays nothing. He's flipped a switch and stills himself, regaining control over the emotions he so easily gave me before. Standing in the doorway, his assessment of me drips of pity as his gaze lingers on my water-lined eyes.

"Why?" I ask, taking a page from his book. Forcing myself to keep the control I lost completely on the walk over. "Why, if this is... if this is over?"

He says nothing. *What else is there to say?* He just opens the door the rest of the way and steps aside to let me in. I walk past him, neither of us offering up even the smallest touch of intimacy. Even our bodies don't graze each other in recognition. Knowing what maybe I haven't fully admitted to myself yet.

I came here because I just need to see him. I need to read him. But for the first time, looking at his face I can only read the printed text. None of his thoughts are left in the corners of the page for me. So, I say the only thing that makes even a fraction of sense, that I'm here for my stuff. *That's what he wants, right?*

"I have books and things here. I'm going to need to take them home."

"Tell me, I need to understand what you're saying."

"I'm saying that I'm here to pick up my stuff because you don't want me to be your girlfriend anymore."

"You don't have to do that *now*, it's late." It is late. But I couldn't care less about my books. I'm here because I miss him already. That doesn't stop me from moving. I walked through his apartment, first to the desk where I had a couple of textbooks. Making stops along all the main focal points picking up the pieces I've left behind over the last six months. But I wasn't going to come back tomorrow. In daylight when my shredded dignity and fractured heart would be a lot more visible.

"Well, breakups aren't always convenient, are they?" I'm gathering things in my hands. Filling them with *stuff*. Stuff that doesn't matter. When what I need to fill is this silence. What my hands need is to be on him. And when he looks at me, he's still.

"And that's why you're here at 2 a.m., to pick up your stuff because we broke up?"

"I'm pretty sure this part is just a formality, Reid." He had said it. Called it. Told me he wasn't interested in this anymore. That he wouldn't do this anymore. And I wondered how long he had felt like this. That it would be so easy to cut the tether between us. Snap the thread of love that he tugged on constantly. The thread he used to unravel me.

"Well then tell me, Arden. Why are you here, your books? That's bullshit, you could have come by tomorrow. What do you want, to rub salt in a wound?" *Well, there's some emotion, though not the regret I was hoping for.*

"To see if you really meant this is over. If this is over, then I want closure." Closure is such bullshit. I don't even know what that really means. I need just a bit more of him before I close the chapter altogether. I need to know it wasn't always this. I don't want the book to end, but if it has to, I at least want an epilogue.

And his face gives it away. It's not regret, it's sadness. The look of pity he greeted me with is now the only thing I can see when he looks at me.

"Baby, sit down, please. Stop moving for a second. If you

want closure, fine, but you need to stop fucking moving and look at me."

He grabs me by the shoulders, and takes a slow inhale, as I pull my bottom lip into my teeth, biting down, the pressure and pain preventing the tears that are no doubt gathering in the corners of my eyes.

"Arden, tell me. I need you to tell me what you want."

"I want you. I want to know for sure if this is over. And I want closure."

His hand snakes to the back of my neck, his fingers grip my hair, and he pulls me into him. I want this. I want him. In more ways than this, but I will take this.

His mouth steals any more words from mine. Accepting closure as the offer. We stand there, not far from the versions of ourselves who shared their first kiss just feet away. I can feel the memory of them in this room. But the taste of him in my mouth is different now. Not the dark chocolate that coated our lips, but the saltiness of my tears as we take what we need from each other.

He had warmed my heart so wholly my entire body temperature warmed with it, until now, when I knew I had to protect it once more. As his tongue moved against mine, he kissed me with the desperate desire of a goodbye, and I know it's only building to one thing: An ending.

Chapter Forty

2008

REID

I kissed her unlike I ever have. In the past, I might have been desperate for her, to feel her, because I wanted her. This need came from somewhere else entirely, a different type of possession, even fear, and I can't be sure. It isn't my body reacting to the sight of her, though there is something about her fury that makes her more devastatingly beautiful. *Maybe just devastating.*

The things she had held in her hands had dropped to the floor, including the one photo of us I had framed that found a home on top of the piano. It was a photo of us here, in the chair just across the room. Stella had taken it one night when she had come over; Arden was sitting in my lap, a book perched on the arm of the chair, as I pressed a kiss to her forehead.

It was just a moment like we had shared hundreds of times before, but it happened to be preserved in that second with Stella's camera. *Thank God she signed up for a photography class. Thank God she carried a film camera everywhere for months, because that single photo became one of my most favorite things.*

She printed it in the dark room on campus, and Arden gave it to me one day just out of the blue, I put it in a frame, and it sat atop the piano since then. Until now. When she took it back.

She dropped the items from her hands, and with it, the frame shattered, and glass flew across the floor. Her books crunching it as they landed on top of the shards and hardwood. As I wrapped my arms around her and pulled her into that kiss. The kiss that nearly crippled me.

She said she wanted closure. She said she'd thought about ending this before tonight. Well, fuck, I wish someone would have told me. I guess she did though, the second she walked in.

She said I didn't know her, she said *he* was right. The only part of her I didn't know was this. Whoever she was right now. But if I don't know her, how does every atom in my body recognize her? She's familiar in my arms, and her breathing synced with mine so immediately. *I know her but I don't understand her.*

I pull back from the kiss, the kiss that was melting my resolve and soldering our bodies together. I place a gentler one on her lips in pause. A hesitation, confirmation, consent of what we are doing before we get too lost in ourselves to realize.

She steps backwards from me, her boots crunch on the glass shattered around us. It surprises her, and her face changes completely, washed over in guilt. Looking down at what we've both just destroyed.

"I'm sor–" she begins as she bends at the knees and starts to pick up the shards of glass with her bare hands. The apology, the guilt, for the glass at our feet, not the mess we're standing in. I grab her by the arm and pull her back to stand, taking her hands in mine and brushing the glass back to the floor.

"It's fine, it doesn't matter, I'll deal with it when you leave."

There was no part of that sentence that sounded the way I meant it to. Yet, I have no energy to try and clarify. It *doesn't* matter. That much *is* clear.

"I can leave now, then." She straightens as if she's readied herself for battle and I have no idea why. I'm not going into war. I was frustrated with her before she walked through the door tonight. I was aggravated when I left the party, but now, after storming in here, telling me it was over, the tight grip I keep on myself has loosened.

"I'd rather you didn't, but I'll walk you back."

"No, you don't have to."

"I know. But I hate that you are already wandering around upset at this time of night. If you want to leave, okay, then at least let me make sure you're fine one last time. Or, if you came here for something else, want an ending, if you came here knowing it's over and still wanting something, then let's not worry about anything else right now."

She steps back a bit more until the back of her legs hit the couch and she collapses into it. Her elbows on her knees, she drops her face into her hands. Hiding physically what she is already working so hard to wall off emotionally. I move to take a seat in front of her. Sitting on the coffee table, our knees knocking, due to the short distance between us.

I place my hands on her legs, another way to just keep us connected a bit longer.

"Just look at me, baby, *please.*"

Her breath hitches on the word like it almost pains her. Something I've called her hundreds of times in moments of pleasure or joy, in seriousness and comfort, but right now it hits her differently. And my heart breaks a little more at her sharp intake of air.

"Just take a breath, with me. We can worry about everything else tomorrow."

"Okay. But what about right now?"

"Right now, you just have to tell me what you want." The look in her eyes is a deep blend of anger and wanton lust. But she needs to say it. I can't look at her and assume I know anything anymore. She said I didn't know her, and while I don't believe that, she seems to. If right now she wants something from me, she needs to say it. Clearly.

"... just right now?" she asks, emphasizing the *'just,'* as a reminder that this has an official expiration date. I nod because I can't bring myself to say anything more. Like opening my mouth would tear my eyes from her, and I don't want to look away afraid I'd miss something.

"Just right now, I want *you.*"

How can I take her to bed, take her, period? Like she's throwing me a pity fuck. And the most pitiful part is how desperately I want her, even now. *God how I want her.* Not *'just right now'* as she emphasized. I want her, too. Just differently than she seems to feel. *I want her longer.*

But, I won't have that. Not if she doesn't want it. This will be the end.

I move my hands sliding them up her bare thighs, and I feel her skin prickle with goosebumps. If I was a foolish man, I would say she was nervous. But there's nothing about the look in her eye that indicates it's anything more than the tickling of my fingertips against her.

She brings her hands to my face, leans in, and kisses me. Like water set to boil. It heats us slowly. Building as small bubbles gather at the bottom of the pot. The water heats until it has become raging, dangerously hot. Ready to spill over the brim. *Just like us.*

My mouth is hers. Every part of me is hers. She lets out a moan, and I am undone. My lips move to trace her neck. To remember every line.

"Reid, *please.*" She mewls into my ear. My arms reach the short gap between the couch and coffee table where we each respectively are sitting. Our mouths are the only bridge. The sound of her saying my name, begging for me, now on repeat in my mind. The only thing I can hear. Drowning out any other voice that might tell me this is not a good idea. I don't care. I will torture myself about it later. For now, maybe this is what she needs to stay.

My arms grab her by the waist and lift her into my lap. Her dress is riding up as she locks her bare legs around my back. And all I can think is *please, don't let go.*

Not realizing that I've said it out loud until she responds.

Chapter Forty-One

2008

ARDEN

"I won't." I say, tightening my legs around him and bringing myself closer as my arms wrap around his neck. There is so much strength in his arms as they brace my back. Standing with me in his hold, plastered to his front.

Suspended in the air, suspended in the moment, in the middle of this brick bubble we built. That we somehow dismantled brick by brick tonight. Still, giving us enough coverage and safety to have this moment. This final moment as our short breaths indicate we are ready to tear into each other.

I am still fully dressed, as he stands here kissing whatever exposed skin he could find. My skin being the only thing left I could expose to him. No longer able to show him the parts of my heart that were scattered amongst the glass on the floor.

His mouth moving possessively across the top of my breasts, only the silk of the dress containing them. The incredible irony that this was not that different from the dress he discarded the first night he really had me.

His hands move to grip me from underneath, sliding them

up my dress. My legs are locked around his waist as I'm pressed against his abdomen. But his palms splayed across the bare skin of my back stabilizes me so I can release my arms from his neck and shake the denim jacket off, letting it fall to the floor.

The second it's gone, he pulls his face from my breasts where he's been nipping his way across the freckles that spot my skin. Pulling the soft tissue between his teeth. His fingers dig into my skin, and I know tomorrow there will be marks left behind where each fingerprint tries to be absorbed into my flesh.

I reach for the hem of it that is bunched around my waist, my black panties exposed against his torso. As I look down, so does he, and it's the first genuine smile I've seen on him all night. A smile dripping with interest and craving. I pull the dress over my head, and as my breasts fall from the silk cups that contained them, he drops his mouth to my nipple and pulls with his teeth.

"*FUCK, Reid!*" I scream and grab a fistful of his hair, yanking his head back in the process. I'm holding myself high and tightly against him. I drop my forehead against his and listen to his breath as his chest moves up and down with me on it.

I want the marks his touch would leave behind. I want the small bites and fingerprints. Because come tomorrow, *come a few hours from now,* That would be all that was left. And I intend to leave him with the very same reminder.

I lean down closer and drag the tip of my tongue across his lip. Tauntingly slowly, his mouth opens in an attempt to pull me in. Instead, I return the favor of the bite. It's as if that was all the sign he needed, his hands moved from my back to his own hips where his drawstring sweatpants hang low. Having been slipping from the movement of my ass and thighs locked around him.

Losing the stability of him holding me in place, I have a

moment where I try to catch my breath afraid I'm about to hit the ground. But I don't.

I have my own strength. I can hold myself up. And I do.

He pushes his pants and boxer briefs down, stepping out of them, and moving away from the living room. As I rip the shirt from his body. He's completely nude. The only thing left between us, the pair of black lace underwear I'm still wearing. Though it hardly counts, as the wetness dripping from me isn't contained by them in the slightest.

He takes another few steps toward the bedroom, and I think he's about to lay me down in the bed we've shared for months. But with a groan, I feel my back hit the wall. His left hand cups the back of my head, blocking it from hitting the brick, as we are slammed against it. He looks at me then. Takes me in as I'm balanced against the wall. I can feel the imprint of the rough brick etching into my skin. Using the wall for stability, slipping his hand from beneath my head, he palms my breast with one hand and grabs my ass with the other. His forehead lands on my sternum as my breasts fall to the sides, and he drags his tongue up the center, up the base of my neck, until his mouth is positioned just above mine.

It's in that second, his fingers grip the lace of my underwear, yanking them to the side, as he slams himself so deeply into me and closes his mouth over mine with the same claiming motion. He has lost all sense of control he ever exhibited. And for everything I haven't said tonight, noises pour out of me without restraint.

I want him to have me, and if he won't keep me, then at least I want this. The passion he didn't show me earlier. This raging possession he has, because I have it too. My legs locked around him so tightly I barely understand how he's able to move. *But he is.* He's thrusting into me as my back scrapes harshly against the brick. Egging him on, begging for more. Begging for everything he will give me.

I'm building so quickly. The crescendo is so great. Threaded with all the passion and love we've had, but also the anger and sadness that we need to let go of. I can feel myself tightening, the walls of me throbbing as each thrust hits this spot he's learned so intimately.

He brings a hand to my face, his touch is rough as he brushes the hair from my eyes, though it just continues to fall. He's trying to see me.

"Baby, I–" he pleads through panting desperate breaths. I think if he had the choice between oxygen and orgasm at this moment, he would gladly never breathe again.

Maybe that's just how I feel.

"*Baby*, I need you to come. I need you to come for me. *Please*. I need to hear you." The look in his eyes, the swirls of smoke return and surround me. I can feel all of him in his stare. All of him inside of me.

I'm so close already, as he continues to thrust in a ravenous way he never has. Like this might very well be his last meal. But I need him, still. I need more. I need something unfairly, and in a fucked up way, I think he does too. Despite what happened. Despite what's changed. *I need to hear it.*

"Tell me," I say. Locking my eyes on his. Eyes I've never seen so dark and molten. He leans his mouth to my ear, "I love you." It's a whisper, one I think would have preferred to contain.

"I love you, too."

As his hand braces the wall by my head, he unleashes the final bits of himself, I come furiously, passionately, desperately, and he does with me.

We don't move immediately, but when his touch softens, our breathing slows, he gently lifts me off him, to lower me to my feet. I emotionally sobered as soon as my feet touched the ground. We haven't moved off the wall that offers us the only steadiness either of us might feel right now. Instead, his arms cage me in where I stand.

"Are you okay?" He asks, looking down on me with concern. I wonder if he has regret in this moment. I know he would have preferred a clean exit. Something not messy, not public, something clear.

"Yeah, thank you," I say, and he winces. Uncomfortable at the expression of gratitude but I don't know what else to say.

He composes himself with a slow inhale. I can feel the cum running down my leg, my back suddenly sore, and feeling slightly unstable on my own two feet. *Maybe this is what he meant when he asked if I was okay. Maybe he meant physically.*

As if he can see it, he steps backwards into the kitchen just a few feet, and grabs two glasses of water I hadn't noticed he'd poured. Handing me one, encouraging me to drink it.

I go to rest my back against the wall for support and slightly flinch at the feeling of the brick against my somewhat raw skin. Not having realized just how intense, things had gotten in the moment.

He sees it, *sees me.* He reaches for my hand to pull me away from the wall and into his naked body.

"How about a shower?"

I shake my head, terrified to prolong the inevitable. That every minute I stay it will be that much worse when he tells me it's time to leave.

"It's alright," he says softly, "you don't have to go yet, we can deal with reality when the sun comes up."

I glance over his shoulder to see just how soon that would be. Maybe about four hours if I'm lucky. I would black out every window here and barricade us in the darkness if it meant I didn't have to go.

Maybe it's his use of the word 'reality' that made me relax. It wasn't a word he used often, considering to him everything is reality. He didn't exist in things that weren't real.

Except maybe, after tomorrow, only in my memory.

I let my cheek rest against his chest, "Okay then, a shower sounds nice." He slips his free hand between my legs and catches the cum dripping down in the palm of his hand, as he runs that hand up over my thigh, smearing himself into my skin. Making the need for a shower even more necessary.

He takes his fingers and hooks them around my underwear, which he didn't bother to remove moments ago. Sticky, slightly torn, he drags them down, lowering himself in front of me, lifting my feet one at a time to take them off. Same for the heeled booties I was wearing. The ones we didn't take off in urgency and desperation. He lifts one leg, slips off the boot, then the sock, and places it back down. Only once I'm standing there in front of him totally naked, does he kiss my hip bone and make his way back up my torso until he is back to his full height.

"Okay, AB. Let's wash some of this night away." He isn't wrong, but I hate the way it sounds. He said it because of something I told him once, I know that. But now, it felt like he was using it to wash away himself.

Whenever I found myself sad, or stressed, or angry, I always took a shower and washed my hair. As if the physical act let me clean out whatever it was that felt glued to my skin. Like it was something physical or sticky I could get rid of, not just a film left on my heart.

He reaches in and turns on the water, the room already beginning to fill with steam as I stand there with my hands braced on the bathroom sink assessing myself in the mirror. One of the curses of having fair skin means that every mark appears, and appears quickly.

That while he can wash the cum from my skin, his fingerprints will be left behind for days.

That's when I see his face; he looks pained as his eyes roam over my body. The pink marks of his hands, and teeth, nothing he hasn't seen numerous times before. As he comes to stand behind me brushing my hair off my back, I'm watching him in the mirror as his feather-light fingers run across my shoulders. He shakes his head as if to himself.

"We should have known better." My throat tightens at the thought he's already full of regret, and I can't get any words out.

"Your back is scratched from the brick. You should have said something." Oh, *that's* the lesson he thought we should have learned. The one where he had fucked me against the wall before, and by the time we were done, parts of my skin were raw to the touch. But I didn't mind. I found pleasure in the pain in the most euphoric way.

And this time, this time I was lost completely. Nothing could have pulled me from him, or away from that wall. The ripping of my skin against brick, the physical pain to match what I was too terrified to say. A distraction from what was in my head.

"It's fine. It's what I wanted. It was," I pause wondering if I finish the sentence, "it was really fucking great, and the perfect last time."

"It doesn't have to be–" perhaps the smallest smile begins to pull at his lips.

"I know, sunrise, right?" I say as I raise my eyebrows. Trying to seem cool-girl relaxed, not desperate and clingy.

"Right." Nope, not a smile, at least not a real one.

We take a shower, I wash away the sadness as I wash the conditioner from my hair, and he steps out first, wrapping a towel around his waist, returning with his tee shirt, the one I had often defaulted to. Calling it my favorite, his high school academic decathlon shirt. I think I liked it because in some ways it made me feel like we would have liked each other even then. Although maybe that wouldn't have been enough, either.

He leaves it sitting on the sink and hangs a towel over the shower door. But as I step out of the bathroom, I can see him sitting there on the edge of his bed, in nothing more than the towel around his waist. He's rubbing his eyes with the heel of his hands. Likely a combination between the same emotional and physical exhaustion that even I feel.

I dry off slightly, just enough so that my hair doesn't drip across the floor, and walk across the room to him covered in nothing but the few beads of water that cling to my skin. His head turns as he hears my footsteps. And whatever exhaustion he was wiping from his eyes is gone and replaced with a churning sense of singular desire.

I stand in front of him, position myself between his legs. His hands move to my hips, and he smiles softly. I unwrap the towel at his waist and let each flap fall to the side, exposing him, exposing how hard he already is. I had felt him against me in the shower, but he refrained. But as I look down at him where he sits and begin to open my mouth to speak, he beats me to it.

"Come here." His voice is soft yet demanding while his body is hard and harsh. I straddle him, sitting up on my knees. His hands roaming my face, my neck, and this time when he pulls my lips onto his, it is mellow and unrushed. Like he didn't have to steal this moment. Like we wouldn't lose our last time. Having already claimed one.

His lips are as soft as his dick is hard, and I lower myself onto him. Still swollen and pulsing from our intense break-up-fuck less than an hour ago, but this is different. My body absorbs all of him, and I hear the groan from deep within him as I settle onto his lap, him seated fully inside of me. Neither of us move beyond that at first. Not until I squeeze around him.

He leans back onto the bed, his body half on the mattress, as I ride him until I come. Slowly letting it build. The only time his eyes move from my face, when I find myself teasingly riding the top of him, before taking him all in again completely. Watching hypnotically as he enters me. His cock glistening with our combined cum, and when he watches me come, he gently rolls me onto my back, the soft fabric of his comforter cool against my skin. And had me patiently, slowly, like breathing, he was regaining the control he lost entirely earlier.

He comes with my name falling from his lips, and I again with him.

We crawl higher into the bed, and I curl into his chest, as he throws the blanket over us, covering up what we had exposed.

I fell asleep in his arms one final time.

Chapter Forty-Two

2008

REID

To say I woke up would imply that I slept. Which I didn't, not really. I closed my eyes briefly when I realized she had, but I was too afraid that she would sneak out the second the sun came up, maybe even before that. It felt irrational, but at the same time, entirely probable.

She managed to find some peace and comfort in her dreams for a few hours. Her eyes closed almost immediately as I held her against me. Her breathing followed mine in long slow patterns. I didn't let myself think too much that it was possible to stay like this. That the comfort she seemed to have now would stay the second she opened her eyes. I tried not to imagine that we could stay like this or that we could wake up without the memory of last night, but I knew that was wrong.

I knew that when she woke up, she would be snapped back to the reality of her decision. She was a whirlwind when she walked through the door. Her mind made up, but we still talked in circles as she told me that I didn't really know her, all the other things she claimed. I'm not in the habit of begging for things, not attention, not relationships, and if she had decided that this was over beyond this *'closure'*, then so be it. I'll be fine once I'm fine. But I'm not going to chase someone who doesn't want to be chased. No one has time or energy to play games like that. She made it clear it was over. So, *it's over.*

Looking down at her though, if only she would just stay asleep a while longer.

Eventually the sun rises, and with it so does she. Not one for sleeping late on a good day, let alone one that has a deadline. She wakes in my arms, her hair covering her face as she brushes it from her eyes. Not letting her vision be clouded by anything.

In the morning, the blueness of her stare is sharp. Today more so than ever, as my mind tries to capture the marbled coloring of them, and the power behind them. She rubs the sleep from her eyes, and with it the realization that we're still here.

"Morning." The shape of the words land in my chest where her cheek remains pressed to my bare skin. She didn't bother including the prefix of 'good' to that salutation. We both know it isn't. It won't be. The only *'morning, sunshine'* is not the greeting we usually traded, but the light breaking through the blinds reminding both of us time is up.

"Morning," I want to say more, but I'm out of words. You would think, for all the reading we've done. We would be able to borrow some words from the greats before us. But I'm at a loss, and she said everything she needed to.

We stay here in silence. Then she makes the first move. Sitting up, getting out of bed, and walking into the other room. She calmly picks up her things, setting them on the counter. She gathers her clothes from the night before and carries them into the bathroom. Where she emerges only a few minutes later fully dressed. Her hair brushed back and pulled into a tight ponytail. She's not wearing any makeup, but she looks refreshed, she looks beautiful, her eyes are clear. No longer red rimmed by tears. The reflection in them shatters of ice, splinters of glass that lay on the floor of the living room.

As much as it breaks my fucking heart, looking at her like this, I think she made the right decision. The way she looks at me tells me she thinks she did. Who am I to question that? Who am I to question her? Question what she wants. I always wanted her honesty, and last night she gave it to me, even in the moments I didn't want to believe her. The biggest pain I felt was that she had hid it from me. That she hadn't seen an opportunity before the public display to tell me the truth about what she was feeling. For months, I thought she was herself with me, but as she said last night, that wasn't true. I always thought she was fragments of herself with everyone else, but that was wrong. I tried to make space in my life for her, and she felt forced. I won't force her anymore. I'd never force her again.

I get up from bed, and pull on my sweatpants, leaving the shirt on the ground. I know she doesn't want me to walk her back so I have no reason to put on anything to pretend otherwise. I head into the living room, momentarily forgetting the glass scattered across the floor, surprised I didn't step on any of it last night. I'm sure it will be the least painful thing I feel today.

Her things are stacked, waiting on the kitchen counter for her to grab when she leaves. I stand there, leaning against the counter, waiting with them.

She looks at me as she walks through the bedroom door, looks at the mess around us, looks back at me.

"Hey, AB," I say, trying to call her attention back to me. I know where this is going, and I will let it, but I'm also not ready yet. Against my better judgment, I try one more thing.

"How about hot chocolate and a game of scrabble? You can go first."

I know as she pushes her lips together in a flat line, her eyebrows pull together, and she shakes her head.

"No, it's time for me to go."

She's done.

"I'm sorry." I apologize generally. Knowing there are many things I could apologize for, but mostly just one thing that matters now. "I'm sorry this didn't work out." She seems to accept that as she steps her body into mine.

ARDEN

He's standing against the counter waiting for me to go. I step into his final embrace and raise up on my toes to reach his lips. He leans down and meets me in the middle. With a much softer kiss than the ones before. He's not taking anything from me this time. His lips don't pull secrets or thoughts from my head.

Now, he's returning them back to me.

His eyes in this moment are not smokey as they have been, but when he opened them this morning, the smoke from the smoldering melted metal had dissipated and the molten steel solidified back into place. Much like him. Cold and unbothered now. It's ironic that a man who only sees things in black and white, looks at me through gray eyes. It doesn't help this situation. As we look at each other through the gray. His feet planted in the white. Clear minded and clean. Me, standing in the black. Hidden and shadowed.

He pulls away from our last kiss, planting one more quick kiss to my lips like he always did.

Like a period at the end of the sentence.

The last sentence of our book. The final chapter was written last night.

He punctuated my lips with that final kiss.

Giving me what I asked for.

Giving me an ending.

He stands wordlessly as I walk out the door.

REID

I'm in a place far worse than anger. The emotion I possess is so much more depressing than sadness. Those two emotions or any on the spectrum between can motivate, inspire action. The pendulum swings between them, but where I stand is different.

The emotion I possess is paralyzing.

It's resignation.

I'm resigned.

There is nothing to do but understand that there is nothing to do. Knowing that, I watch her walk out the front door. The softness of her lips fading from memory as the door closes behind her.

The door closes on us.

Chapter Forty-Three

ARDEN

He runs his hand through his hair, not strained, but clearly trying to keep himself composed now that we're here, having just traded our accounts of that night, laid most of our cards on the table.

"How were we both so stupid?" He laughs, but it's forced, more of disbelief than humor.

"I've asked myself that a lot lately, and I think we both just leaned into our worst traits. I let my mind get the better of me, let myself get swept away in dangerous expectations and thoughts, and you let the hard lines you draw keep you square in a box. I don't think I had realized I had any of those fears, about us, or our future, and I let other people get into my head. I was in denial. I spent a long time in denial. Ignoring what was right in front of me."

"I know." He says it as if he accepted this a long time ago.

And yet, somehow, even as I marched my way to his front door that night, I wanted to look him in the eyes and be so sure he meant it. I figured once I got there, once I acted through the motions of gathering my things, he would snap out of it, realize there was more left for us. But that's not what happened. I know I blazed through the door. A whirlwind wanting to tear through the little apartment that I had grown so comfortable in. Wanting to leave a void where I had been, even though he seemed to easily accept that, not accept, *want. He seemed to want that.* At least that's what I had thought.

That's what I had thought as he stood there watching me collect my things while I repeated over and over to him what he had said to me, '*this is over.*' My body was practically vibrating with the words, with the manifestation of goosebumps running across my skin as a literal representation of what I was trying to contain. I can't help but wonder what would have happened if I just said those things. *But I didn't.* I said things that were worse. Calculated. Things that weren't true, things that I said purely to try and elicit some reaction so he could feel some of the pain I was feeling in that moment. Now I understand, *he did.*

I needed to be sure that I hadn't made up those few months. But I can still remember the look on his face as we stood on the back porch with the music thumping from inside, our friends around us. As he looked at me like a stranger, like someone he didn't know, like someone he didn't *want* to know. I remember his face when he opened the door after I frantically buzzed up to his apartment, uncomfortable. And yet, what happened next could only be described as desperate.

"Not that it matters now, but I never meant that *we* were over. That fight was over, the drama was over, the *party* was over. I wanted us to leave, to have a conversation without onlookers and participants, I wasn't going to stand there and argue with you. That wasn't the type of the relationship I was interested in. I was done being there. *Done fighting with you.* But fuck, I should have just seen what was happening. I was too caught up in my own pride to acknowledge that you needed something from me." He presses his knuckles to his lips, and shakes his head just the smallest amount, as he closes his eyes and takes a slow inhale. Filling his lungs with the air he needs to continue. "I always thought that there was nothing I wouldn't have given you if you asked, and when you showed up later, what you asked for was closure. I should have paid attention, that you standing in front of me, yelling at me, that *was* you asking. You were asking, *telling me*, literally screaming at me, and I let you down. I let you go. Worse, I let you think *I* wanted you to go. Turns out I could have given you anything you wanted except the things I didn't know how to give."

I'm losing myself now, in hearing so much of this from him. Things I wished I had heard then. I don't even realize that I've put my face into my hands. Overcome with more emotion than I could have predicted. But he's steady as he continues. His tone is even, and kind. The warmth of him crossing the table.

"Maybe if I had said something, maybe if I had done something, things would have been different. But, Arden," *He takes the breath I haven't been able to.*

"Please, look at me..." I release the smallest shake of my head. Unable to speak, feeling transported back in time.

"Baby, look at me." The term unintentionally falls from his lips as his resolve cracks and I pull my hands from my face and look up at him.

"They wouldn't have been better, do you understand me?" He reaches across the table and slips his right hand into my left.

"Not better than this," He gestures with his free hand between us, the acknowledgement of our friendship.

"And not better than this." His thumb rubbing across the back of my knuckles, catching on my wedding rings. His approval and gratitude for my happiness.

"I didn't realize until recently just how much of a lesson that was for me. Not to let things walk away, that you have to be willing to fight for the things you can't risk losing. And because of that, because of that fear, that loss I felt, I've never made that mistake again and I have a full life. So do you... You're happy, *right?* Truly?" His eyes burrow into mine in a way I haven't seen in more than a decade, searching for honesty in my answer. I nod.

"Then we can't sit here and feel anything but gratitude."

Maybe these were all the things he had wanted to say before, maybe the things he refrained from saying in email. Instead waiting to have me in front of him, to gauge truly how we had ended up here. Always the one to be clear in his thoughts, except clearly, one notable exception. One that damned us both to hell. But right now, his gratitude is overwhelming and sincere. I feel my nineteen year old heart fracturing all over again, but this time the pieces won't fall at our feet. It's protected now by its thirty-three year old shell. One that has been built up and reinforced overtime.

I had already pieced together the parts of the breakup, where I felt we miscommunicated. *Damn miscommunication trope strikes again.* The worst part is, I saw it immediately, and now he's confirmed it. We both should have known it, given that we knew each other, but that night, we focused on the worst parts of ourselves instead.

"It's not like I helped clear anything up." I shrug and offer him a smile, which he accepts gracefully returning one of his own. "I felt like my heart was being broken in slow-motion, and I needed you to feel that too, I just said and did whatever I thought might help. I didn't know if there was a chance to get you to change your mind, so I did what I thought could at least level the playing field."

"You leveled it alright. Whatever we were standing on fell out beneath our feet. The ground opened and we were swallowed by it."

He was right. We fell in. We fell in, stayed there long enough to desperately claim each other one more time in the dark underground beneath the cracked foundation of our relationship. And when we crawled out the hole the next morning, we ended up on different sides where the earth had been cleaved in two. Neither one of us was willing to try and bridge it.

"Arden, I need to know, the one thing I never understood," he pauses, and his face changes to one of curiosity. The wheels visibly turning behind his eyes, thinking through the same problem he's clearly tried to solve more than once in the last weeks, maybe in all the years. "Why didn't you leave it closed? If you thought I didn't want to be with you, if you thought I *dumped* you, why did you reach out before leaving that summer?"

That is the question, and I've worried the answer might do more harm than good. The answer only a handful of people, *and a couple of therapists*, really know.

"Alright Reid, but maybe we should get you another drink first." He doesn't even try to hide his concern as I order him another whiskey, *this one a double,* and myself another basket of bread. Fuel for us each to make it to the other side of this conversation.

Chapter Forty-Four

2008

ARDEN

I think I ran back. Not figuratively. I literally ran back. Through the streets of the city square that we walked so many times. He didn't ask to walk me back this time. He did last night, he would have insisted due to manners and expectation, but now in the light of day, he looked relieved he didn't have to. Not even getting dressed for either of us to pretend, and do the obligatory dance.

I clutched books to my chest as my feet landed on some of the old stones of the campus. The weight of what I was carrying was so much heavier than I realized.

It's still early; the campus is coming to life slowly as it does on the weekend. I cried on my way to him last night. The tears streaming down my face, so hot with rage I felt them burn my cheek as they trailed my skin. But I won't cry in public now. When I got dressed, I stood at his bathroom sink and pulled my hair back into the kind of tight high ponytail meant to keep my forehead and eyelids taut. Preventing tears. So, I left his apartment without shedding any. And I haven't since arriving in his doorway last night.

But now, as I get closer to my own dorm, my own bed, I am beginning to lose that strength. The stitches holding it together coming apart at the seams.

I land in the quad and enter the main building, it's quiet, even for a Sunday morning. *Maybe that's just me.* Drowning out all the noise and commotion from people who don't matter, the sounds around me are muffled by the blood pumping in my ears. I take the elevator to the basement, to the tunnels. Knowing how desperately I don't want to be alone, I follow them to the only place I know.

I try to open the door, but I'm locked out. So I knock with one hand and ferociously jiggle the handle with the other. As if it will magically open at my touch. Despite the very clear fact it is locked. *No one is here. Why would they be? Everyone had a life without me these last few months, and they told me time and time again. They kept busy without me.*

I used up all my strength to get here. I used it all holding myself together and containing the collapse that now felt inevitable. My hand slips from the handle in acceptance that it won't open and I just sink down onto the floor in front of their door. I squeeze my eyes closed impossibly tight. Wishing I could be anywhere but here, knowing that to make that happen, all I have to do is stand up and move. But I can't. I can't move. So I sit. In the hallway outside a dorm that isn't mine. Wearing clothes from the night before. And cry.

What a fucking cliché.

I'll give myself one more minute.

Just 55 more seconds and then I can stand up.

Only 43 more seconds and then I will be okay.

In 28 more seconds, I will go.

And then the door opens.

"Not interested in whatever you're selling—what *the fuck?!*"

Josh drops down to the floor next to me, quickly abandoning whatever traveling salesman joke he had queued up for whomever he thought was at the door. Whatever he was expecting, it wasn't me, and it wasn't me like this.

The tears are streaming down my face now in a way I can't control. And I think it's stupid I ever tried. *Never the cool-girl. I've always only been this.*

"He doesn't w-want to be with me. It didn't matter. He doesn't want to be my boyfriend anymore." I'm choking out the words through such hysterics I'm not even sure they're understandable. The thoughts aren't. *But he understands.*

"He's a fucking idiot."

My mind is overwhelmed by every word we exchanged in the last twenty-four hours, even worse by the ones we didn't, trying to put them together like a puzzle without the box as a guide. No idea what the picture will be when it's finally complete, just struggling to line up edges to match. To make sense of it.

"You were right." I say and drop my head completely as I pull my knees to my chest. My concern for modesty is out the window, unbothered by the fact that my lace covered ass is completely exposed to anyone who walks by. Much more interested in shielding my face and everything written on it.

I feel his hand on my back, offering a gentle stroke to steady my breathing.

"Come inside." I can feel him trying to help me up but I've planted myself in this spot. This is the spot where I will let myself cry. This is the only one. The second I move I bring the tears with me and I refuse.

So here I stay. Outside the door of my best friend and my ex-whatever-Ethan-was. *That makes sense.*

"I can't move."

"You can, Arden, come on."

Whether it be the tears that have overtaken me, or the time

362

I let lapse. I feel Josh's arms come around me. One underneath my back, and the other underneath my knees. And for the second time in twenty-four hours a man has lifted me into his arms. And the two sensations couldn't have been more different.

Josh hoists me into his hold, pushes open his door, and my hope of containing my tears to one location vanishes as I cry into his shoulder. Walking into the main room, my eyes are so welled with tears I can't see anything in front of me. My head is so loud, I can barely process the noises around me. When I hear the exchange of words, I have no idea if they are directed to me. I hear my name, and I can feel the vibration of Josh's chest as he speaks, but I don't know, and don't care, if anyone is talking to me, or just about me.

Josh takes a seat on the couch with me in his arms. And hugs me tightly as I cry into him. He takes the books and items clutched to my chest and tosses them on the table as his hand holds my head in place, meant to comfort me as I lose more and more of myself.

The tears are not the controlled single drops running down my face in rage. The ones that were present when I walked to Reid's apartment last night. The ones that escaped the containers of my eyes and spilled over the rims in a combination of fury and fear. These are the tears that had been building. These tears are wild and unpredictable. The kind you see when someone doesn't cry often enough to know how to do it well.

I lost time as I sat there curled up in him. I tried to pretend I was back in the brick bubble. Held in Reid's arms, in pleasure not tragic comfort. But every breath I took, it was licorice and pine, not cinnamon and cedar. Every inhale was wrong. My cheek rested against skin that wasn't his. The grip around me is tight without the same tenderness. I can't pretend.

I don't know how long I've been here. It isn't until I feel

another set of hands brushing hair from my face, wiping tears from my cheek, that Stella's voice cuts through and has me open my eyes.

"Ethan texted me," she says to Josh. I wasn't sure if she was responding to something specific or proactively answering something he had yet to ask. Either way, he shifts and moves from beneath me, placing me gently down into the corner of the couch. Dropping a kiss to the crown of my head as he stands and walks into his bedroom.

Stella tries to get my attention, but I left it behind in his apartment. All I have to give her is the shell of myself I cracked open outside Josh's front door.

"Are you okay, what happened, AB, what's going on?" AB, the nickname he had given me that had taken hold. Now fucking stings to hear. Josh comes back with a blanket, tucking it around me, perching himself on the arm of the couch. I'm bookended by these two people, the two of them there for the first act of the show last night, but even still I can think of nothing to say. Clearly they know the ending.

"You were there, Stells. He dumped her, and her throwing herself at him like the lovesick teenager he claimed she was, didn't fucking matter. She showed up here this morning... like this."

That's what had happened. Last night after he left, I stood there with my friends trying to replay how it went so wrong so quickly. And while they weren't exactly in the right state of mind to help me, they both heard him say he was done and saw him walk away. But I hadn't been done, I wanted to hear it from him. I was convinced, *somewhat by Stella,* that I just needed to talk to him, or better yet not *talk.* And when presented with the opportunity to have me, he would rethink what he said.

She was wrong. We were all wrong. I went over there with the intention of testing the waters. The deep end I floated away in. Never realizing how easy it was to drown in him. I repeated back what he had said to me, and then said I wanted him. And he gave me just that. Him. For one more night.

Josh was right. I had thrown myself at him, and it wasn't enough. Somewhere along the way Reid decided I was both too much and never going to be enough, all at once.

I feel like I've swallowed barbed wire, and my mouth is full of sand. The combination makes it impossible to speak. Which is fine because for once, I have nothing to say.

"How about we head back to our room, you can get into bed, I'll sit with you! We can talk about what happened." I take a slow deep breath. One I've watched Reid take time and time again. Whenever he looked like he needed to steady himself. And that's what I need to do.

I know that swallowing down the emotions in this moment would only mean they might resurface later. I blame him. Not just for the fact that he dumped me, ditched me, and then fucked me. *Okay, that last part is really on me.* I begged him for one last time and he obliged as he always did. I don't blame him for the end of our relationship like I should, I blame him for the beginning. The parts of it that made me fall so quickly, that positioned him as the sun, only lending me his warmth, thawing out the frozen parts of me. Layer by layer melting it away in his natural glow. I blame him for that. The part that left me completely exposed now.

"No, Stells, I'm too tired to move," I rasp out as she tucks the blanket more tightly around me.

"You don't have to." Josh directs the words more to Stella than me.

I didn't move. Not when Ethan took Stella's place on the couch and asked how I was. Not when Lindsey came by. Not when Stella brought lunch. I didn't move for dinner. It was only when it was just Josh and I on the couch, that the sand in my mouth dissolved, and I felt like I had enough words to speak.

My relationship with Josh required effort more than most. But when I needed him, really, he had been there. Even last night, the main point of contention between us was ultimately that he missed me, that the things I had told him I wanted, I had abandoned. My friends, my freshman year. I compromised them to play girlfriend to someone who ultimately could walk away without a look back. Because he didn't look back. Not when he left the party, and not when he left my life. He doesn't have regrets.

"You *were* right," I say, but as I do, my brain wars with my heart at the idea. Regardless, last night I used a lot of what he said. Some of Josh's greatest-hits. *'You aren't spending time with your friends'* and *'how well can he really know you'* and of course *'this was never going to last'*, and I loaded those poison dipped arrows and fired them directly at Reid in a moment of desperation about fourteen hours ago. In a bitter hope that he would refute some of it. *Any of it.*

Which he didn't.

"I know," he says, "I'm not happy about it."

"You seem fine." He smiles a little at this. Maybe pleased that I am stepping on to the verbal volleyball court. He looked like he was readying a soft serve over the net to be sure.

"Better than you at least."

"You should enjoy the feeling while you can."

"Oh, I will, Miami. Don't you worry about me." His tone is playful. Similar to the one he used with me regularly. Teasingly, and threaded with innuendo. And it's in this second, Stella's warning chimes through. She'd said I was blind to his emotions, but I'm not sure that's true. Although, I'm also not *not* sure that it's true. I just know that right now, he is here.

"I'll be fine, you know..." I say to him, using my foot to nudge him on the couch next to me.

"I'd be disappointed if you weren't." He says grabbing my

feet still wrapped in the blanked and extending them over his lap so I can stretch out.

"Can I stay here tonight? I'm not ready to go back to my own room yet."

"Of course you can, I was never the one who kicked you out of *my* bed, Arden." I didn't bother changing, instead just stayed curled on the couch in the same silk dress I'd worn for the last twenty-four hours.

I woke up the next morning to the sounds of a Monday. People in the halls, the coffee machine running, Ethan's alarm clock being ignored, muffled behind his bedroom door. I rubbed my eyes, trying to wipe the memories of the last day, of the last six months, that wanted to pull me back into a spiral.

I pop my head into Josh's bedroom before I leave, he's sleeping in just his boxers, sheets kicked around his feet. I scribble a note and leave it pinned to his corkboard, just next to the polaroid of us from the newlywed game.

I grab my books, bag, and the miscellaneous items I'd taken from Reid's. On top of the stack, the picture that Stella had taken. Still some tiny splinters of glass stuck to the glossy black and white photo. I look at it intently, hoping to see something in it I hadn't months ago. Hoping this might be the image of the puzzle my mind is trying to piece together. But I know it's not, and I toss it in the garbage and I walk out the front door.

Chapter Forty-Five

2008

ARDEN

When I left Josh's this morning, I stood on the street corner knowing that if I turned right, I could head back to my dorm. If I turned left, I could retrace my steps and walk back into Reid's arms. *Except that I can't.*

I looked across the street, and saw the Coffee Haus on the corner, positioned equidistant between the two of us. *Our* table in the window, occupied, not by us, but looking through the glass, their faces are blurred by the reflection, and for just one more moment, I can pretend.

I am pretending. Have been pretending.

Pretending it's us in the window as he reaches across the table to pop a kiss on my lips.

Pretending to be playing house with Reid, waking up on *my side* of the bed.

Pretending there might be a future, one I couldn't predict, but still could exist.

Pretending that he knew me, in all the ways that matter.

Pretending that he loved me, in all the ways he showed.

Pretending I'm okay to know that he doesn't, in all the ways he said.

Pretending that I'm okay, at all.

And that's why I turn right, and head back to my dorm.

———

Standing in the shower, the water beading and rolling down my skin. This is a better place to cry. *The only place to cry.* Where the tears can be lost in the crowd of water droplets.

A knock on the bathroom door pulls me out of my own mind. The one that was filling with water. The door cracks open as Stella pops her head in, not waiting for my invitation.

"Heyyyy." She says slowly. As slowly as she eased the door open. Nudity never mattered to her. Not her own, and certainly not mine. The only reason she wasn't just naked around the dorm always was because we had people coming and going so regularly. Especially when Reid started spending more time here. She compromised and spent most of her time in a bra and underwear. It also meant that she would regularly walk in on me in the shower.

I think she joins me in the bathroom because she knows I'm trapped. My body is soapy and my hair is wet. Buying her just enough time to have whatever conversation she feels I need to be captive for. Meanwhile, I just want to hide in here.

Hoping I can scrub away the parts of the last two days that left me feeling so much.

The shower door is fogged up, likely only allowing Stella to see the outline of my body, and as usual, she's completely unfazed. *And so am I.* She just takes her normal seat on the floor with her legs outstretched on the closed toilet. She rests her head on the wall and her fingers tap against the coffee mug in her hands.

This is a scene that has played out on many occasions, but

in this instance, it feels like she's intentionally using her body as a barricade on the ground.

"You didn't come home last night." Not a question. Not an accusation. But a fact. She knew where I was, but she clearly has something to say on the topic now.

"I know." Not sure what else she's looking for in response.

"How come?"

"I told you, I couldn't move. Not yet."

She takes a sip of her coffee, trying to think of what best to say. Maybe it's the steam that lets me feel like my words might evaporate into nothing, that lets me feel like I might say what I need to, that finally motivates me to say more.

"I felt like a slug."

She outright laughs at that. "A SLUG?! No one in their right mind would think of you as a slug."

"I'm being serious, Stells. I *am* a slug. I trailed my emotional goo all the way to Josh's front door, and it just piled up, and it was going to follow me anywhere I went. I wasn't ready for it to follow me here. The sticky sluggy trail all the way back to *our* door. We still have to live here... I, I couldn't bring that here. I couldn't *be* that here. I don't want to feel that here," *I don't want to feel anything here,* "it's going to be hard enough. I haven't even gone into my room yet because I know what's in there. Polaroids of us when we were together, the sheets we slept on when we were together, and all the physical reminders that we *aren't* together. And the last thing I needed was my emotional goo to follow me here. So I couldn't come home."

"Does that mean you're taking up the bathroom as your new residence?"

"No, I'm just... washing off the emotional goo. And this way, when I get out, I'll be myself again. The version I was without Reid. The one that you guys know, not whoever I was pretending to be."

"I never thought you were pretending, and I don't think he did either."

"It doesn't matter what he thinks anymore. He ended it, and Josh was right, I went and threw myself at him like the lovesick teenager he thought I was, and it didn't matter. He still didn't want me. I wasn't here with you guys; I was off with someone who barely knew me."

"Josh wasn't right. Who said you needed to be here with me? I didn't. And what gives Josh the right to say anyone does or doesn't know you. He might think he's the one who is the keeper of your secrets, and I know you guys care about each other in a complicated way that I don't try to understand, but I'm worried he might get the wrong idea."

"There's no 'idea' to get. He just–"

"No, Arden, he's just nothing! Unless the end of that sentence is 'he just–has been waiting for this' or 'he just–has been in love with me since the beginning' then nothing. Let me ask you something, and you need to think about it... do you love Josh? Fuck, I don't even care about love, do you want to be with Josh?"

I step under the shower, letting the water pour down my face. Thinking about what she's asked me. And no, the truth is that while I might have love for Josh, feel connected to him, I've never felt more. I knew that immediately. That who we could be for each other was not meant to be more than whatever this is. And save one dramatic newlywed-orchestrated kiss, which was filled with showmanship, not affection or passion, we'd never crossed that line. He has been my friend. Picked me up off of the bathroom floor when I was sick, and the hallway floor when I was devastated.

Maybe I hadn't been a friend to the same degree, but we've spent months where I served as his wing woman, his cheerleader, his tutor, and confidant. I don't want more than that. Not with him, not with anyone, and especially not right now.

Whatever sexual tension we had between us had always been crafted verbally. Banter. A challenge. Nothing more tangible than that. There wasn't a touch that had ever been shared in the nights we slept next to each other that was more than the comfort of a warm body. And while I had begun to see flickers of what Stella meant, he had still never expressed anything more to me than the same things I felt.

I slide open the shower door and pop my head out so she can see me. She's sitting there on the floor looking back up at me with a raised eyebrow waiting for my answer. The one I think she already knows.

"No, Stells. I don't."

"Then just be careful, because I don't think your friendship will survive the rejection."

"That's fine, because we won't find ourselves in a position where I need to reject him."

She seems to accept that answer and smiles up at me. My head still dripping wet, I shake it out over her like a wet dog.

"Good, because he's in the other room." As she gets to her feet, I nab the coffee cup from her hands.

"Well then, I'll need this."

"That's why I made it for you."

When I open the bathroom door, Josh is sitting on the couch.

"You snuck out," he says, as his eyes seem to linger on my skin, though I'm covered by the towel wrapped around my torso, it feels like he's trying to refrain from saying something more.

"I don't think you can call it sneaking if I left you a note and just came home."

"I think the note is exactly what makes it sneaking

considering that in order to leave the note, you were already in my room."

"So, you came by to make sure I made it home safely?"

His face pulls into that Cheshire Cat smile, one I have seen frequently enough to know there was always something hidden behind it.

"I came by to make sure you're okay." *But this doesn't feel hidden.*

"I'm okay... I have to get dressed though if you want to wait, we can head to class."

"Haven't I always waited for you?"

I wonder if it's my responsibility now, to reaffirm the boundaries of our friendship. I hadn't done anything differently, hadn't changed. Why should he feel like I was now available to him just because I was no longer with someone else?

His voice sounds different as he says it. Like it was a moment of honesty. He had waited for me. But that's *his* perception of honesty, not mine.

So I reply, disregarding the depth of his remark, or at least how I understood it, and instead respond with the literal interpretation.

"That's not true, Josh, because I'm never late."

Chapter Forty-Six

2008

REID

What should have been a quick sweep yesterday turned into a compulsive cleaning of my entire apartment the second she left. By the time the sun set, I had tricked myself into thinking that I had cleaned her out of this space. She had taken her things with her, anything *of her* included. That photo wasn't hers to take, but it didn't stop her.

Nothing stopped her.

She wasn't mine to stop.

Being in my space that I had worked for years to make conducive to work and success, eventually love, now felt wasteful. The memories of her here are all I can see, even though I lived here longer than we were together. She could do that, change something completely.

I run my hand through my hair and lean my head against the back of the couch. The same place it rested when she told me she loved me. My eyes were closed like this and I think about pretending that she's here now, but that's not who I am.

I won't wrap myself in the comfort of illusions. No. I am not the person who dilutes themselves into a false reality. The reality is, she left.

The reality is, my apartment is spotless.

The reality is, I miss her already.

That reality doesn't matter.

My eyes are closed as my thumb rubs against the leather arm rest of the couch. I don't have to open my eyes to know what it is that feels like morse code beneath it. I guess she couldn't take all parts of her when she left. She couldn't take the bite mark she left in the leather, and she certainly couldn't take the memory from me.

She just took everything else.

She isn't going to text.

She isn't going to call.

She isn't going to show up.

I need to get a fucking grip.

The sound is like an electric shock. I jump to my feet at the buzzer, crossing the room in three steps to press the intercom and buzz her up...

"Hello!" I say it with a combination of excitement and relief. Holding down the button waiting to hear her tell me she needs to talk. To apologize. To anything. It will need to be a conversation, a fight, but we can get to the other side of this if we are clear.

"Buzz me up, bro." Not her. *Austin*.

This, I remind myself, is why I don't pretend.

I haven't seen him since Saturday night when we walked back to my apartment and he filled the entire distance with his voice. He tried to distract me from the embarrassing public display. He was unsuccessful. His views on the matter are so different from mine. That was *before* she showed up. We sat on the couch, had a couple of beers, and he told me to sleep on it.

Most of his advice had to do with sleeping it off or getting off. I tried both, neither worked. One matter of factly sealed the deal on the end of our relationship when I fucked her goodbye. When she walked out the door, I texted him to let him know. His only response, the hundred bucks he bet me that we'd get back together.

I open the door, and he just holds up a hand with a six pack as if that's all that's needed. *It's the thought that counts.* Then he lifts the other hand with the bottle of whiskey. *This thought is better.*

He drops the alcohol on the counter, *a counter I can barely fucking look at,* and wraps me in a hug. Slapping his hand across my back a couple times and then tightening his arms around me before releasing with a sigh.

He cups my face with my hands, like this is the fucking Godfather. We've known each other since undergrad and roomed together a few of those years. Even though we couldn't be more different, he's a good guy. Evidenced by the way he is holding my face like he's trying to get the truth out of me. I shake him off narrowly avoiding the Fredo style kiss he looks ready to deliver. *Austin fucking Becks. Always the showboat.*

"How fucked up are you over this?"

"Whatever the scale, max it out."

He claps his hand on my shoulder and grabs a couple of glasses from the kitchen. I throw myself back onto the couch. Choosing the seat where I can still feel the imprint of her as opposed to the one that time had previously molded to my body. Austin hands me a glass as he joins me, and by the time he's hit the cushion the warm liquid has slipped down my throat. He just swaps my empty glass with his full one. Watching me down that just as quickly.

"I fucking love this apartment." He says as his feet land on the coffee table in front of us. Looking around the room, no doubt his own memories flooding his mind. We've had good times here.

"The lease is coming up, you should take it over." The words come out of my mouth faster than my mind can process them, a decision I didn't know I had made.

"Don't be ridiculous. You're not leaving. I hear they are making you an official offer next week." He switches topics, covering off the big thing I have looming. My career plans once I complete my MBA, something that will be official as soon as I file the paperwork this week. Austin and I have been working for the same consulting firm, him having the leg up as an actual employee while I fulfill the work requirements of my degree, which means he actually hears some of the gossip. Like when they are making me an official offer. One I've expected, wanted, but now, who the fuck knows.

"I'm not being ridiculous. I have options that I worked hard for, and there are several outside of this city. I'm not going to settle for one just because I have a good apartment."

"Settle? You're really gonna pretend you didn't have your mind made up already?"

I'm not pretending. I don't pretend.

"I have two weeks to make a decision about the job. Either way, I'm not living here next year."

"Fine by me. But don't insult my intelligence by pretending this isn't about her. You're making decisions based on something that will snap back into place the second you pick up the phone."

I'm not 'pretending', if I was, I wouldn't be so fucking miserable that's for sure. I had always planned to move, maybe now, I am able to do that without any regret. *Regret, really? This is who I've become? Fuck.*

"You didn't see her. She's done. I'm not lowering myself to chase after her now."

"If you don't, I promise you someone else fucking will..."

Then his tone shifts, and under his breath the words come out in a calculated whisper I know he intended for me to hear. "...and they already have."

Those four words whip my head in his direction.

"What does that mean?" I'm asking for clarity I don't know I want. That in this case will be the nail in the coffin. *That's one way not to have regrets.*

"You don't need me to confirm what you already know. That she's not alone, or won't be for long. It should be you, but you're going to let this bullshit morality bar of yours keep you here rather than being the one to call her. You'll be back together by fall regardless, but it would be easier for everyone involved if you just fucking got on with it and stopped torturing yourselves."

He's dancing around the topic. The one he wants me to hear. Thinking it might motivate me in some way. He always liked her, and this might be his attempt to push a reconciliation. *It's not mine to fucking push.*

"Tell me, Austin, what do you mean *they already have?*" He shakes his head slightly, no sign of the megawatt smile he normally possesses.

"I spoke to Josh. I called him to see what kind of damage control was needed. That's when I upgraded to the good bottle."

"And... what exactly made you upgrade?" It's the question I don't want the answer to, except that if I have it, maybe I'll also be able to claim the closure she sought out when she showed up here.

I have no intention of chasing after her, not when she was clear. *It's going to have to be her.* If I end up losing the hundred bucks Austin wants to bet on our rekindling, it will be the best money ever spent. *But it will have to be her.*

"She spent the night there. She was with him." *Of course*

she was. Just as he fucking intended. I never trusted their dynamic, but I trusted her.

I'm a fucking fool.

"You might as well pay up now, Austin. Doesn't look like there's much hope on that front."

"Only if you don't want there to be."

Chapter Forty-Seven

2008

ARDEN

One week of classes. My final freshman classes. One week of meals. Or pushing food around while pretending. One week of sleeps. Or sleepless nights.

The first couple of days, I replayed it all over and over. I sobbed in the shower and thought about what was said, how he felt, and then, I began to convince myself I was okay.

It was surprising how quickly I could fit back into my life; after just a few days, I realized it was because I never really left it. Despite what I had said to Reid. I still very much was present; I hadn't given up my life to be a part of his. The parts of me that were shared with him weren't present here. I didn't have them here.

Whether it be breakfast with Stella, or walking to class with Josh, or all of us, the whole gang, going out to The Commons for game nights, karaoke nights, or whatever other theme was on, everything seemed to just be as it was. It was like it had been PR as they dubbed it. *Pre Reid.*

Everything was as it was PR. Except for me. I had

convinced everyone I was okay, tried to convince myself I was okay. But that's the problem, I don't want to be okay, because that means it's really over.

———

Stella is sitting on my bed while I'm at my desk with my makeup sprawled out in front of me, picking through it piece by piece. The mirror I have in front of me magnifies my face, illuminating every freckle with more detail than I want to see. But it's all superficial.

Even with classes and finals, we've managed to go out every night this week. On some level, I think everyone knows it's a distraction. Josh and I remained as we were, keeping the status quo. Our normal games and boundaries remained intact, but I didn't let my guard down any more than that. Knowing better than to actually let him sleep in my bed, knowing *that* part of our friendship was over. *Finding it far easier to sleep during the day now than I do at night.*

"You should go for red lips tonight, it's such a badass look!" Stella says, leaning over and grabbing the lipstick from the pile in front of me, dangling it in my face for me to take it.

"Well badass *is* the look I am going for. Plus, red lips mean no kiss. It's the rule."

The Red-Lips-No-Kiss rule was less of a rule, more of a reminder that most boys aren't worth smearing your lipstick. Especially when that lipstick is a powerful red. Red-Lips-No-Kiss means that you'd be making a mess of your night, *and* your face, and would likely end up looking like a clown all for a boy who wasn't worth the cost of the cherry red lipstick you applied.

I walked the line. Not sure if I wanted to throw myself in someone else's bed for a night or keep a distance from anyone who might remind me what it was like to be held. And though it had only been a week, the fact that we'd gone out regularly meant that I surely could have found companionship if I wanted it. But I didn't. Not yet. Instead, I came back to my own bed and cried alone every night.

Which means the Red-Lips-No-Kiss rule is perfect for tonight. I purse my lips in the mirror, coating them in the smooth cherry red, smacking them together to get it evenly spread before leaning back and assessing myself. This will do.

We finish getting ready, I let my hair down from where I had it pulled back from my face. I preferred it down and a little wild right now, and the big curls I had started to wear more frequently in the last months, a part of myself I used to polish, now I let them out, too. Not only is it freeing, but they covered my shoulders and fell in my face, making it easier for me to hide behind them if I wanted.

Walking into The Commons, the scene is typical. It's packed, but given the proximity to campus, it was always easy to immediately spot someone we know. And we did. There they were, much like the first day I met them. Josh, Ethan, Lucas, Marlie and Jack, all gathered in a booth.

The noise in the bar is what I needed, and the chatter from my friends even more so. Approaching the table there are already shots lined up. *Tequila.* Good. But I wouldn't have turned down anything at this point.

I pick one up, I tilt it towards the group as if to toast them, not really thinking of anything meaningful to say. So I don't. Not toasts. No show. I just shoot it back, no salt, no lime. Just the liquor down my throat. When Josh hands me another.

"Red-Lips-No-Kiss night, huh?" Josh asks, as I scoot into the booth next to him.

"YEP!" I say with emphasis as he laughs a little to himself. He never understood the idea of the Red- Lips-No-Kiss rule when Stella and I explained it, none of the men did. 'Why can't you just wipe it off?' they had asked. We tried to explain the principle of it. The girl power behind it. He might not have understood the rule, but he remembered it and knew what it meant.

I might not know what time it is, but I know it's Saturday, so I don't have to worry about anything other than purging my mind of the events of exactly one week ago. I want to scream. And this was how I can do it. The noise may not have escaped my lips, but as I dance and drink, it's a release of energy that I've held on to so tightly for the last seven days.

I'm sitting at the bar, swinging my legs on the stool. Sipping on water for the first time all night. Okay, not *just* water. But there was a splash of water in Josh's whiskey. So as far as I'm concerned, that counts.

"I want to know what you're celebrating." I hear a voice say. I spin around on the barstool and lean forward falling into this stranger. He's young, my age, maybe a little older. He has a beer in hand, not that it matters, between fake ids and friends, underage drinking isn't exactly hard to do. Or maybe he was twenty-one. *I don't care.*

He catches my wrist as both my palms land on his chest, not roughly but strong. Letting go as I sit back, but I'm not removing my hands from him.

"I'm not celebrating anything... I'm *mourning* it." The words sound slurred even coming from my mouth. At least I think so. Like they are being spoken in cursive.

"How about some company and another drink?"

We have another round; he tells me his name, tells me about how he's pre-law. I can tell even in my current state that just means his dad is a lawyer and as long as he does the bare minimum he will step into a cushy job after law school. Not possessing any real passion or apparent intelligence, everything he's said so far is just general nonsense. I mean, is he seriously talking about his PlayStation? *Does any of this fucking matter?*

He's a perfect example of the Red-Lips-No-Kiss rule. But at

the same time, the attention he's giving me is something more dangerous than the alcohol I've been consuming all night. And it's making me just as drunk.

"I need to pee," I say, and I hop from the bar stool and stumble towards the back near the bathrooms. I *do* have to pee, maybe even vomit, but I also needed to get away from him knowing he's not really what I want. My head is absolutely spinning, and I know I am in for a mountain of regret tomorrow. The alcohol running through me right now might be clouding my senses as I need it to, but I'm sure in the morning, when the headache takes hold, I'm chugging Pedialyte, and the memories of last week flood my mind once more, I will regret thinking that tonight could have been a reprieve.

Maybe it doesn't have to be.

Maybe I can apologize.

Maybe I just need him.

I can barely think, barely see as I take out my phone and open the text thread. Glancing at the last one he sent. It was exactly a week ago when he told me he was on his way. '*See you soon.*' Simple. Before everything got so complicated.

I haven't spoken to him since I walked out the door. Neither of us tried to communicate. Bridge anything. He said what he needed to, made the decision, and once I was there, standing in it, I set fire to any chance of salvaging the framework of our relationship.

I look at my phone but my vision is blurred, not able to see the keys. I don't even know what I want to say, but I wish he was here, wish he was with me. Wish I could talk to him. I have so many regrets, starting with the number of tequila shots I've had tonight and backing straight into the moment we were standing on the back porch of Wendell House. As I threw words at my boyfriend in anger rather than just throwing my arms around him. I can have regret, but I can also make it right. I can text him. Tell him. I can't undo what I said, I can't undo the tequila, but in this swirled, blurred, state, I know that I need to see him. To tell him, and this time I don't think we'd find ourselves on different sides. I'll cross the bridge to him if he'll let me.

I make it to the back wall of the bar, the line for the bathroom a few people deep so I take my place using the wall to steady me as I fumble over my own feet. My phone in hand, I type it out.

"Looks like your red lips rule is fucking bullshit." My attention snaps up, I shake my head to disagree, but I'm overcome with dizziness as the room around me spins. I reach my hands out, as Josh takes them in support, must have noticed that I was losing my balance.

"It's not bullshit, there's been no kissing." The string of words tumble from my mouth.

"Coulda had me fooled. Your new boyfriend was also pretty upset when I had to tell him you weren't leaving with him."

"I wasn't leaving with him!" *Wait, was I leaving with him?*

"I know. I made fucking sure of that." He doesn't let the glass in his right hand prevent him from gripping my arms, holding me in place. It's cold against my skin. Still, I swayed.

"I'm just... waiting... I have to pee..." *Maybe vomit. I have to vomit.*

His remaining grip of my arm tightens as he removes the other hand with his whiskey and lifts the glass to his lips. Drinking down nearly all the remaining liquor. He extends it to me, in offering. I take it. Drink it. Hoping this will be the sip that pushes me into amnesia. Hoping this will be the sip that wipes the missing memories of Reid from where they remained. *Nope. Still here.*

"Who are you calling?" He slips the phone from my hand, not that I have a good grip on it anyway, and laughs when he looks at the screen. Sliding it into his back pocket with a shake of his head.

"Come on, Arden—it's time to go."

————

I don't remember the walk back, but my senses tell me this is his dorm, not mine.

I know that it's his arm wrapped around me, as I lean into him. *As I have always leaned on him.*

For all of Stella's warnings, she had to also admit that when I needed him, he was there.

And right now, he is here.

At least that's what I think as I rest my cloudy head against his chest.

He is here.

And he is kissing me.

I can taste the whiskey on his lips. Or maybe that's mine. I can't be sure. I can't feel anything. Not my lips.

Not my heart.

Nothing.

He pulls me to his chest, and I fall into it. His arms around me are the only thing keeping me on my feet. But it's when his tongue slips into my mouth that I put my hands to his arms, applying enough pressure to separate us as I scramble to unknot what's tied up in my brain. Taking a step back until I hit his bedroom door. The back of my head taking the brunt of it. I bring my hand to my forehead trying to rub the pain from it. Throbbing. Cloudy. My vision. My mind.

He steps forward, with his hand to my cheek, and kisses me again. Much like our first kiss. The one on stage for the newlywed game, it's all pressure. The force of his lips pressed against mine. I had thought that was because neither of us wanted anything more, but now I wonder if this is just how it feels to kiss him.

But I'm not kissing him. *He is kissing me.*

I take my hand pressed gently to his chest.

"Josh," I say in low warning as I turn my mouth from his and have him step back. He does, with more irritation than I've seen from him before. I blink repeatedly trying to sober myself. But it's not working. The darkness at the corner of my vision is not clearing. The darkness all around me, not clearing.

He turns from me quickly, his back is to me, with his hands linked behind his neck as he cracks it from side to side. Trying to release whatever tension he's holding. He lets out a dark devious laugh and I can hear it deep within me, unsettling me in a way that I can't quite explain.

I've heard him laugh so many times in the past. Different ones.

Playful ones.

Victorious ones.

Sarcastic ones.

And this one, possessing a blend of aggravation and disbelief. A challenge he's put to me before, one I have met time and time again. But there's something different now.

I don't like it one bit.

"What the fuck, Arden." This isn't banter, this is actual frustration, anger.

"What the fuck *what*, Josh?"

"You *aren't* that stupid, you can pretend you just want to fuck around, to not take people seriously, but you *know* what this is. What this *could* be. And yet for some reason you decided that I'm the one that's not good enough."

The mask he's held in place all these months finally falling from his face completely. The fear and insecurity pouring out of him in this moment of rage. I'm in no place right now to manage what's happening. No place to leave.

Too drunk to make it much farther than the other side of the door, but still, it might be the best move, as I reach for the doorknob blindly. Before anything more happens that we will regret.

"Don't say that...you've been my best fuck–" My hand hung on the doorknob, as the other splayed open against the wooden door. I feel like I could sink to the ground forever if I lose even the smallest amount of focus.

"Your best fucking friend. *I know.* Don't you think I fucking know? This whole year I just figured you were wasting your time. I watched you fuck these losers, these idiots, *that* fucking idiot." He gestures to the wall, and I know he means Ethan whose currently empty bedroom is just on the other side.

"I watched as that pretentious douche bag made you someone you aren't. I watched as he took you from us, from me. Because day fucking one you decided we could only be friends. Fine, if we were only going to be friends, then we would be the *Best. Fucking. Friends.* But now what? Huh?"

His voice isn't friendly. It isn't calm. It's elevated. Yelling.

He's yelling at me.

His words are like physical blows, no idea how I am still standing, yet in all their effort to knock me down, they have just steadied me in place. Merging with the grains of wood in the door I am pressed against.

"What are you talking about?" I finally say. Not say. *Scream.* I scream back at him across the room. I can see his chest is heaving. Something's burning within him. Within me as well. But I don't think it's the same thing.

"You were the same. I watched you fuck whoever you were able to convince to let you into their bed. And you know what, I don't have to apologize for not being one of them. I am not going to apologize. Not to you. Not for whatever I've done. Not for *whoever* I've done." I make the same gesture to the same wall he shares with Ethan. "You're not going to stand there and make me feel like a slut, because you know what, it doesn't fucking matter."

I said it, and as much as I wanted to mean it, my heart broke a little more at that moment. Knowing that it wasn't my friendship he valued, but the idea of me. As something he could have. As something he could collect. He was right, how could I be so *stupid*.

He laughs at that, before stepping close to me again. Huffing out a breath of air so close I can feel it hit my skin, and my stomach tightens. My body stiffens against the door, as he cages me in against it.

His voice is lower, more gruff. It's not calm but it is slow.

"Do you want to hear a joke?" I shake my head, *no,* but it doesn't seem to register. I shake my head and my brain rattles from side to side. I say it clearly. Mustering whatever sobriety I can find. *Which isn't much.* My grip slipped more and more with each small use of energy in response and with every passing moment.

"No," I say it. *I think I say it.* I definitely say it.

"Come on, Arden," he says as he tucks a strand of hair behind my ear. "You'll think it's funny."

"Doubt it, this isn't funny." Using the door to brace my strength, I look at him as I say it. But I can tell from the smirk on his lips he's made up his mind.

"What's the difference between a slut and a bitch?"

I refuse to answer. I don't have an answer.

"A slut has sex with everyone. A bitch has sex with everyone but you."

"What's your fucking point, Josh?" I bite out the words and blink desperately to try and see what's happening, but for every word I say, it costs more energy than I have.

"I've never called you a slut, Arden." It's like a stake through the heart, one I didn't even know was still intact. But it pierced straight through me and pinned me to the door.

He leans in and kisses my cheek. *Just move.* Kisses my neck. *Just move.*

Kisses my collar bone. *I can't move.*

His hand comes up my ribs, keeping me in place.

I'm not sure if he thinks he needs to hold me here. His hand seems to feel he does. The truth is I'm frozen. My body totally fails me. My hand is on the doorknob. But I can't feel my fingertips. I'm losing my grip. *On it, on this, on everything.*

My eyes are blurry. I'm blinking rapidly to clear them. It doesn't clear the haze, just releases the silent tears that had been building. That had been balanced on the edge of my lash line. I blinked them free.

His hands are holding my face, looking at me intently. Wiping the lone tears that created wet paths down each cheek.

"You're fine, Arden. I'm here, you're alright."

"Josh, *please...*" I say, struggling to keep a hold, struggling to stay clear, to stay on my own feet. The alcohol is coursing through me, but he seems surprisingly sober. Maybe just in comparison.

"You don't have to beg me, not for *this.*" His mouth moves across to my cheek, tasting the salty sadness that lingers there, as he presses his lips to my skin. As he moves his kisses slowly down the curve of my neck. Down my chest. While his hands move to explore my body in a way like they've finally been allowed entry. He moves his lips to mine, and his hands to the straps of my dress, pulling them and the bra straps down over my shoulders, pushing it down around my waist.

"I think, I'm too..." I manage to get the words out, but they falter. *Say it, say you're too drunk. Say you're too sad. Say you want someone else. Say anything.*

"It's okay, I know you. I have you. I'll take care of you."

My hand falls from the doorknob. A sign of surrender to this moment.

My palm had been pressed against his chest, the arm's

length I used to keep his body from mine, finally bending at the elbow. As I bend in this moment. At the release of pressure, he steps closer to me. Bringing my bare breasts against his clothed chest. Wrapping his arms around me as he pulls me close, I let him kiss me then. My arms around his neck are the only grip I have on anything.

Before I lose my grip on everything.

He's here.

He's kissing me.

Maybe I am kissing him.

Taking the path of least resistance doesn't mean the road itself is an easier one. But the sobering thoughts I'm desperate to cling to, the ones I hope will pull me from this moment, they slip away. Instead, I am lost to the cloudiness of intoxication. Stealing my thoughts and comprehension of reality. This isn't my reality. But here I am.

It's the next morning, and my mouth is dry and the headache is immediate. As is the familiar ache of my body. Sore, tender, touched. I rub my eyes hoping they adjust to the darkness of the room, small streaks of sunlight seeping through the break in the blinds.

I drag my body out from under the weight of him. Heavier than anything I've felt. He's unbothered. Comfortable in a deep slumber.

As I get quickly dressed and sneak across the room, I don't think he would wake up even if I did make noise. He's content in his dreams.

I slip out of his bedroom, look back at Ethan's door that's been left open. Either he wasn't here or already left. Probably for the best. I wouldn't even know how to explain what happened if I was asked.

Because of what I do remember, I'm heartbroken, and what I don't, I never want to.

Chapter Forty-Eight

2008

ARDEN

The physical hangover that overwhelmed me was nothing compared to the emotional one.

My liver was busy filtering through the alcohol I had consumed but my heart and my head, they couldn't filter out the rest.

Last night was a blur.

It was blurred.

I know where I woke up, how I woke up. I had flashes of what he said as he kissed me with the illusion of tenderness and affection, with pent frustrated passion and entitled desire.

All of the buildup over the last nine months, coming to a head.

Stella had been right. *Reid* had been right. Both seeing something I had refused to acknowledge. I had leaned on him as my friend, as my best fucking friend. Maybe the banter or the games we played might have given him a different idea. Something I refused to accept, to admit, no matter who warned me. Instead I opted to remain in a place of denial.

I am an idiot.

Sunday mornings were some of my favorites. Not today. The irony that this time last week I showed up collapsed on Josh's front door. This morning I ran from it.

Now I walk through my own door, directly into bed, pulling the blankets over my head, looking for darkness and quiet to subdue what's warring in my mind.

My consciousness tries to find the thread to pull. The one that would unravel the memory. But I can't find the right one. Maybe I don't want to.

————

I wake up and know I've slept most of the day away.

I don't need to check my alarm clock to see the day is almost entirely gone. But it's what's next to my alarm clock that has me more alert. Sitting up in bed and reaching for my cell phone. Completely unsure of the last time I had it, only recalling the briefest of memories where I was going to text Reid. *Maybe I did text Reid?* I'm trying to sift through the memories of what happened last night, but the only parts I remember, I wish I didn't.

I hop down from bed and get changed, pull my hair into a big bun on top of my head, and find Stella on the couch in our main room. I land myself down on the cushion next to her with my phone in my hand. The screen remains black. *Dead.* Probably blacked out the same time I did last night.

"Oh, good! You got your phone! Josh stopped by with it, so I left it on your nightstand, he said you forgot it there last night."

"Yeah, that's right," I say.

"I thought you were going to be careful with all that."

"Me too, but it doesn't really matter now."

"What do you mean? What happened?"

"Exactly what you thought would happen, I had just been too busy clinging to our friendship to see what he really wanted from me, that he really wanted me, so I gave up and let him have it."

Her face is frozen, and I'm not sure exactly what she thought. For the first time since I've known her, not offering it up either.

I had let him have me. I just hadn't realized how much of me he wanted. What parts of me he wanted. As he kissed me and pulled me into his arms. Telling me he cared about me, would take care of me. He meant that in a way that broke my already broken heart. That he felt he had earned some piece of me, all because he had been my friend.

He thought that the place in my life Reid left empty was now his to fill, but it isn't. It isn't anyone's to fill, anyone but myself. I hate that I ran to him. Right into his arms. Right to him seeking comfort that I knew he would give. I just didn't realize the cost. *Or maybe I didn't want to admit it.*

Stella doesn't say anything; I think she reads my face as regret. *Which it is.* I regret that I put myself in a position where I allowed myself to lose such control.

"Can we just have a lazy morning?" I ask, leaning my head onto her shoulder.

"The absolute laziest." She flicks on the tv and curls her feet up onto the couch, throwing a blanket over both of us. Resting her head atop mine.

I chuck my phone on the coffee table, not worried about what I missed. The only thing I *knew* I missed last night was Reid, desperately. And of all the things the alcohol blurred, how I felt about him wasn't one of them. I loved him. *Love him.* And somewhere along the way, mental landmines had been buried in a game of psychological warfare when I let my guard down enough not to realize I was playing.

And one by one, I stepped on them.

One by one, they exploded.

The idea that Reid didn't know me.

The idea that I was missing out on college. The idea that Reid didn't want to be with me. *Well, maybe that one was true.*

Josh wanted me, and he would take that in anyway he could. When posed with the choice, Josh chose me, in sad broken form. The one he helped shatter. All so he could be the one to put me back together. I ran to him, the voice in my head, who time and time again acted as though he was the only one who loved me, the only one who knew me. The only constant. And maybe in his mind, that was true.

He knew the version of me I let him know, the shiny parts he collected like a crow. But all of that was on him. That was what he thought, not me.

He was my friend.

My best fucking friend.

I set the boundaries immediately. But I'm not responsible for his expectations. For what he thought I owed him. I was responsible for my thoughts, my *actions*. And right now, even those felt out of my control. It isn't anger. It's resignation. Acceptance.

And I needed to regain a semblance of the control that I lost.

No, I didn't lose it. It was taken.

In a night I don't remember. With a broken heart and shattered resolve.

And the way to regain that control? Relive last night. With consciousness and conviction that can't be taken from me.

Let him wake up the next morning with the understanding of loss. And it would be easy because he still wants me. His anger wasn't at me, *at least not as he saw it,* it was everyone else who got me. And that's why I would tear myself from his life. I would tear myself from his life after I showed him exactly how much he wanted me in it.

"Actually, Stells, I think I need to raincheck lazy morning. I need to do something. Can I borrow your phone?"

"Whatever you need, AB." That nickname is perhaps the only remaining part of my relationship with Reid. While it still makes me flinch slightly, a shock of the memory hearing it for the first time, maybe this is the one thing I don't have to let go.

Stella hands me her phone and the answer is immediate.

"What's up, Stells?"

"It's Arden, my phone is dead, are you home?"

"That explains the unanswered text. Yeah, I'm home." Josh's tone is eager, but even through the phone I could detect a hint of nerves he never really let anyone see.

"Alone?" I ask, my tone is calm. *Exhausted*. But I can feel Stella's prod, clearly curious.

"Yeah–"

"I'm coming over."

"Great, I'll be waiting."

———

I open the unlocked door, and when he sees me, the smile on his face is shocking. Genuinely excited to see me. Like he'd been waiting for me, just like he said he'd been.

He jumps from the couch, where he was sitting in just a tee shirt and sweatpants, dropping his phone on the cushion before making his way to me. Wrapping his arms around me in a hug so tightly it feels like he's trying to say something. Pressing a kiss to the crown of my head as he holds me against him. Only releasing me to say whatever it is his embrace couldn't.

"We need to talk." His hand comes to my lower back and walks me further into the room.

"That's a good idea." I take a seat in the chair, thinking he will sit opposite me on the couch, but instead he paces, anxious. *He's nervous.*

"I owe you an apology." He does one more lap across the room, and finally takes a seat to continue. "I said some really fucked up things." I don't dignify his apology with a response. Don't acknowledge the severely deficient nature of it. He's not known for apologies, only ever offering one when he needs to in exchange for something else. As he was with any action.

He takes my hand into his, with his eyes locked on mine in a way I refuse to break. If he's nervous, let him be.

"I'm sorry, Arden. I didn't mean anything I said.

I was upset, I was so upset."

"Why?" I think my response softens him a bit. Comforts him in knowing I am open to the conversation.

I asked him why, but his answer was focused solely on what he had said. Not understanding that I am still so confused, so hurt by the rest of what I knew happened between us, even with no real memory of it.

"Why?" He brought his clasped hands to his forehead, holding mine between them. As if there can be some transference of thought. He brings my knuckles to his lips to press a gentle kiss, before again repeating my single word question. '*Why.*' This time, not sounding like a question at all.

"You were so heartbroken over some guy who never deserved you. You said you didn't want a relationship and I settled for your friendship, and then I watched you fall in love with *him*. I watched you fall in love with him while I fell in love with you. All for what? For him to kick you to the curb the first moment you show him who you are? For you to land right on my doorstep, come right to me? And it made sense then. When you showed up at my door. When you cried on my shoulder. In my lap. I held you. I'd been fucking holding on to you. You had spent so much time ignoring your feelings, that finally when you let them out, he rejected them, you came to me because you knew, like I've known, that this thing, this magnetism between us, these fucking games we played were all so much more than that."

He takes a breath and then looks at me. Waiting for a response. "Go on..."

"I couldn't watch you end up in the arms of another asshole. Not now that you were finally back here, and in just a week you were back to being yourself, we were going out, having fun, just fucking living, ya know? But I couldn't watch you fumble out of there with some stranger. Not again. Not when you were barely standing on your own two feet. I was upset, upset that no matter what I did, you didn't see how much I fucking love you. I said a bunch of shit, cruel shit, just to get you to react, just to get you to admit that you feel *something*."

I can't explain what I feel at this moment. But in some ways, it's the most honest he has ever been.

"You love me?"

"I love you."

"And you want me?"

"I want you."

I am numb. But it is different from last night. I am numb of emotion, but I am clear.

I stand from the chair, my hand still in his and I step between his legs where he's sitting on the couch. I look down at him now. As he drops his forehead against my stomach and places his hands on my hips. I bring my hands to his hair and run them through the dark locks. Freshly showered and still a little damp.

But I use my grip on his head, my grip on this moment.

I tilt his head back and kiss him.

My eyes open completely.

They are open enough to see his close.

To see him find comfort in me, as I take control back from him.

I reach for the hem of his shirt and pull it over his head.

He looks up at me as I lean over him and his hands find purchase on my waist. Reaching for the straps of my dress as he had before, but I shake my head at him. This time he halts his movements completely.

"No, you first," I say. Nodding towards his pants.

He stands up quickly to oblige my request. No hesitation. Eager. Like a child told he can open his brother's birthday gifts. It might not make sense, but he isn't going to question it. Not when it's something he so clearly wants.

The way he looks at me doesn't feel like love. *Not how I remember it from just a week ago.* This is different, it feels like victory.

He can't hide his excitement, not emotionally, and not physically. While he stands there completely naked and leans in, kissing the line of my jaw.

He was the last person I was with; his lips on my skin feel familiar in a way I don't like. In a way that the memory couldn't fully form in my mind. My body didn't unlock for him, the way it could, the way it had for others. But it accepted him. Recalling the action of doing so before.

I wondered if this was what he was like with me last night.

I know we had fought terribly. The things he said are hanging in my mind. What wasn't clear, was the rest of it. The moment I decided it was easier to let him have what he wanted from me. When I decided I didn't have the strength or clarity to resist what felt inevitable.

Standing here with him now, stripping him of his clothes, down to *his* vulnerability, allows me to make this choice this time. It will reset the status quo. His fingers run up my thighs, finally catching on the hem of my dress, as I raise my arms letting him pull it over my head, and he takes this as a sign that his apology has been accepted.

Has it? I didn't come here thinking that he would apologize. But what did he say to me, that he said some fucked up shit?

Some cruel shit? That was true. But what about the rest of it? He didn't apologize for the rest of it. For the part where I woke up in his bed unlike I ever had. *Did that happen? Could I have been confused?* I came here so clear. Feeling confident that while I couldn't define the memory, that I knew it existed. His hands roam my skin with a familiarity to it I can't place. *I don't know.*

I came here to replace the empty memory with a new one. *One I consent to making.* That's what I'm going to do.

"Condom?"

"Bedroom." He pulls me towards him as he walks backwards, keeping me in his sights. Only releasing me from his grip when he's standing in his room.

For a quick moment, I think about all the times I've been here. The parties, the movies, the moments of friendship and laughter. I catch a glimpse of the polaroids pinned to his cork board. And I throw them all into the mental bonfire of our relationship. Burning the memories as fuel for this moment.

I ask the question I've been afraid to. That I didn't have any evidence of. Knowing that in asking it I get two pieces of information I need.

"You used a condom last night, right?" You used a condom? I asked. Needing to know if I needed to schedule an appointment with Health Services. You used a condom? Because I don't remember. Maybe he'll be confused by my question, maybe he'll show concern at the idea that I don't know. 'You don't remember,' he'll ask. Maybe...

"Fuck, of course I did." *Maybe not.*

He's reaching into his drawer to grab one now, making quick work to slide it onto him. I don't look, not away from his eyes, that betray the insecurity he's flashed from time to time, never intentionally, and I don't think he means to now, either.

"I've been thinking about this, about you. You snuck out this morning, so I dropped off your phone and you seemed to be nursing a bad hangover, but I wanted you back. Back here, like this."

I'm standing in my underwear, I left the rest of my clothes in the main room. He's seen me this undressed before, I cringe internally when I realize he's seen me in less, but it doesn't stop the way he drinks me in. Absorbing every inch of my skin like it's the first time I'm allowing him to see me. In many ways, it is.

I reach my hand behind my back and unclasp my bra, letting it fall to the ground. His gaze is heavy. Like I can feel his eyes crawl across my skin, setting the path for his hands to follow when I'm in reach. I take a step forward, his eyes sharpen.

I hook my fingers and pull down my underwear. Dropping them around my feet as I step out of them.

And take another step forward. Each step I take detonating whatever remaining landmines that remain. Refusing to leave them buried in my mind. Knowing when this is done, there will be none left he can explode.

I'm laying here, leaning back on my elbows, as he moves closer, climbing onto the bed positioning himself on top of me.

"This is what you want, Josh?" His hand runs up my side, until he can grab my breast. I haven't touched him; I am waiting for him to say it.

"Yes." It's almost a choked sound.

"I'm telling you, you can have me." The words and the shift of my body, the permission he didn't ask for. Allowing him to push into me.

What I feel in my core is something beyond the lust I see on his face. What's building within me isn't an orgasm like it is for him. When he loses himself, he loses what I came here for.

Control.

There's no lingering affection here, but I don't move yet, just taking in this moment. And how I feel.

His lips never landed on mine as he pumped himself into

me. I wonder if this is what it was like last time. But now, his face is boyish. The sharpness he always wore around me is gone.

"I always knew it would be like this."

"Like what?"

"The fucking best." His weighty arm wraps around my waist, but I slip from his grip and my feet hit the ground.

"Where are you going? Stay." He sits up in bed as I pull up my underwear and put on my bra.

I make my way towards his bedroom door, and I can imagine the feeling of wood grain against my fingers. Maybe even spotting the crescent moon shapes of where my nails might have been.

"I'm not staying, not now and never again."

"What? Why?" he asks, the edge to his voice sharpens, and so does the look on his face. I don't say anything, and it's the realization that washes over him. That this isn't the start to some great delusional romance he's made up. That his apologetic profession of love means nothing to me. It's why his voice gets louder and less coherent as he continues.

"Why did you come over, Arden? You just wanted this?" He gestures frantically, I think perhaps towards the bed, but he's aggravated, hurt even, and his hands gesticulate without actual sense. "You wanted to fuck me? To use me and leave?"

"No, Josh." I let out a sigh with a great steady calmness. Channeling someone else entirely. "I didn't *want* to fuck you. I *never wanted* to fuck you."

"Then what do you call that?!"

"A power shift." My voice is steady. I feel it in this moment, as I stand here barely dressed, watching him emotionally unravel, that there *has* been a power shift. The game of tug-of-war that tied us together is over. I've won. The verbal volleyball won't be lobbed across the net anymore. And if it is, I won't pick it up.

I replaced the empty memory with this one. This one, where I decide who has access to me. Confidence and cockiness are not consent. We might have been magnets. We both saw it. But no matter how strong the magnetism, no one just gets to stick to you. And much like magnets, they can have the strongest pull. Snapping together when set on opposite sides. But when they are the same, they repel.

"A fucking power shift? I tell you I love you, that I want to be with you, and this is your fucking

response? Who the fuck are you?"

He says he loves me. He might believe that. I don't. Not in any way that matters.

"I'm glad you finally care enough to ask, because it never really mattered to you, did it? You just liked the idea of knowing me, not actually anything more. Well... I guess you wanted *this* also. You don't love me, you don't want to be with me, you just *want* me, that's not the same."

His hands are tightly interlocked behind his neck as he paces the room. I stand there in just my underwear, not hiding my body, not hiding myself. I have nothing to hide from him anymore.

"YOU FUCKING USED ME!"

"You think I used you? No. I asked you, and then I gave you what you wanted. What you told me you wanted. I gave you what you took. *I* gave you me. And now, I'm taking it back. You think I used you? I was on fire, and instead of putting it out, you poured on the gasoline to keep it burning, to keep *yourself* warm. You think you love me? You don't. You wanted me because other people did. I was the person you thought you earned just by being my friend. But you didn't. You were jealous. I thought you were my friend, but you were just biding your time. *Waiting for me*."

"I WAS your friend. I was your BEST FUCKING FRIEND!!!" *My best fucking friend*. The same term was used the first night we shared a bed and is used now as I left his for the last time. As if including the amplification of *fucking* made our friendship stronger. *I was your best fucking friend.* He yelled as I turned the knob and pulled the door open.

"Josh, you weren't even close to my *best fucking lay.*"

"You are a fucking bitch, you know that?"

"Ha! I'm pretty sure now that *this* is done," I say gesturing between us, "by *your* rules, I'm just a slut." I force a laugh. Though there's nothing even remotely humorous hanging in the air. Referencing the joke he made, the one that no amount of alcohol could shield me from remembering.

"But I'd rather wake up every day as the bitch you think I am, than wake up one more day as the idiot who thinks you actually care about me. Maybe one day, you will realize why this was never going to be possible, but that's not today, and that's not my problem."

Chapter Forty-Nine

REID

I thought my heart had broken before. *What an excruciating mistake.* This is a different kind of wreckage. I just listened to her, not saying a thing, not reaching for her, just watching her as my mind took in everything she said.

How she was too drunk, how she said she just *'let it happen,'* how she didn't even remember it well enough to know what really happened. How she dealt with it, with that confusion, with that missing memory. By going back to him on her own terms. *FUCK.* It's almost too much to process. And what a selfish thought that is. How *I* would process it.

I feel unrecognizable. Surely it must be readable on my face. The devastation. She's not. She's composed. Unfazed. Like this was something she resolved within herself a long time ago, never planning on bringing it up. All while I was doing what? Being her friend?

Some friend I was.

For months, there was not a day that went by following our breakup that I didn't think about her. Months where I battled my own boundaries at the idea of calling her. Even with what I'd heard through the grapevine, the thing that kept me from reaching out to her was never *him,* it was me.

That's the detail I can't overlook now, that maybe if I had. If I hadn't stood on ceremony, *on my fucking pride,* we could have figured it out.

She could have been safe.

With me.

Instead, she left me, *left my apartment,* and went right to him. *'Why didn't you leave it closed?'* Is what I had asked. It's why she went back and told me the parts of the story I didn't know, except for one detail that I am hung up on. She reached out to me a week after we split, hoping to meet for coffee, and I ran. Thinking it might be a reconciliation, but when I saw her, it wasn't. Just a friendship she was trying to build. One I had offered her months prior, one she finally decided to claim.

Now, I think she needed more.

Now, I think this is why.

Now, I need to know for sure.

I have never exhibited as much control as I have right now. I'm not sure what I want to do, but when I go to speak, it takes every fiber of my being to steady my voice in a way that isn't threatening. One hand gripping the whiskey glass, the other I moved under the table to hide the flexing of my fingers. Stretching them out before pulling them back into a tightened fist for a punch I will never be able to throw. All I can muster when I look at her, is one word.

"When."

"There was a night I texted you. It was a few days before we met up, before I left for the summer."

She saves me the trouble of asking exactly what I wanted to know. Lining up the timeline with my own. With that, reality bottoms out. "I... I'm sorry, I'm really *fucking* sorry."

ARDEN

He looks upset in a way I wasn't expecting. I tried to explain what happened almost clinically. It's not a story I tell, and one that took years for me to come to terms with completely, not easily understanding or accepting it for what it was when it happened, and even longer reconciling my actions following it.

The words Josh and I exchanged that day never repeated. I never wanted to talk about it to my friends, or acknowledge it beyond a mistake. And Josh was too embarrassed; his ego took the biggest hit that day, not his heart.

I had considered not sharing this part of the story with Reid. Or just sharing it in part. But there's nothing I get from abridging it now. I wasn't sure if it would do any good or if it would really matter as part of his understanding of what happened between us, what happened with me, as despite best efforts afterwards, and some miscellaneous emails that summer, when I got back to campus the following year, he had turned down the offer he'd been planning to take, and instead moved to New York City.

There was a gap in our friendship that spanned nearly eight months that year. Only eventually did we begin to trade emails casually enough that it evolved into this version of friendship we had preserved now for more than a decade.

"You don't have anything to apologize for," I say. I mean it, but the look on his face tells me he doesn't agree.

"I do. A lot more than I ever realized." He pinches the bridge of his nose and closes his eyes to take a steadying breath, before releasing it, and looking back at me. He genuinely thinks that. That he can take some responsibility for what happened. Something that happened so long ago it feels like it was lived by a different person. In many ways, it was.

His eyes darken, full of regret and remorse. And it's hard to watch.

"Reid, you have to know that there's no part of this you're responsible for, you weren't there."

"I should have been. You were a mile from me. While I was stubborn, missing you. You were only a mile from me. I let my arrogance fill that distance. I let my pride keep me from calling you. I knew you and I wasn't going to crawl after you when you so willingly left. After I heard you were with him..."

"I didn't *leave*." My voice is quick and strong, jumping in at the idea I left. Which *technically* I walked out the door, but that's not what he meant. But I was caught on the second part of what he said. "Wait, what do you mean *with* him?"

"Austin spoke to him after you–after we–well, after the breakup. He told him you were fine, you were there, he told him," he pauses, turning over what he wants to say next, and see the moment he elects not to, "none of that matters now."

I scoff at that. It feels like it all matters now, but I know better, and know he is right.

"I always hated that you ran right to him, but God, what an arrogant asshole I've been. Because it didn't matter what rumor I heard, what he said. He's not the reason I never called you, *I am*. You can't blame anyone but me. Who I was, *who we both were*? It didn't matter if I wanted to be with you. I wasn't going to beg you for something I understood you didn't want even after you texted about meeting up. It had to be you to tell me you wanted me. Because I thought I had already done that when we were together, and if there was any chance, I knew I needed you to be clear about what you wanted. But it just became clear, that wasn't me. Maybe I thought it was him, but as time went on, slowly I convinced myself you weren't who I wanted to be with either."

He was always composed and contained, each sentence premeditated. Except for right now when the words began to race from his lips directly to the finish line seated across the table from him. *Directly to me.*

"When you texted me, regardless of what I had been feeling, or how mad I had been... When I saw you, it was the first time I felt like I wasn't underwater since you walked out the door. I can still see you sitting there, stoic as ever. It reminded me so much of the day we met, as you just took me in, watching me, and I pretended I didn't notice. Even though this time you were back to being guarded, and I thought it was me." He stifles a laugh that doesn't display any form of humor. "Of course you were guarded. It *was* me. And yet, you were making such an effort. I was so proud of you, with school, with all the things you had decided to do. You just went on and on, clinging to any topic you could. And I was trying not to cling to you. Then when you said you wanted to be friends. When you asked me if the offer was still good, I wasn't sure what to do. Wasn't sure I could do it, that I *could* be your friend. You deserved one better than me. Someone who *knew you*." He let out a sigh that was weighted with a version of grief, and I felt it, the words he used. The ones I had said to him when I pushed him into thinking he didn't know me.

"Better than you, Reid? That's really what you think? There *was* no one better than you." I feel strangled as I say the words. Choked by my own hand as I recalled all the things I said to him that night. That would have made him think that. When I told him he didn't know me, he was the only person who had really tried without motive beyond my happiness. "When I texted you, when I needed you, even without you knowing that I did, you were there. That's because there was no one better. You were the best person I knew. And maybe I don't know you the same way anymore. Maybe we only know each other through Instagram posts, and a random coffee every few years, but '*who you were*,' who you were for me," I say, repeating back the phrase he used with intentional emphasis. "You were the best."

I can see him absorbing what I've said, or at least trying to.

And that's why I can see when his eyebrows pull together, his lips press into a flat smile, and the infinitesimally small shake of his head, he rejects it.

"I have a lot to be sorry for, Arden. More than I realized. More than you blame me for, but it's true. I'll take responsibility for it now. For the breakup," I see his jaw tighten, before continuing with a voice so flat I know he must be exercising a great deal of control to keep it steady. "For what happened after. I apologize for the fact that even sitting here, despite what I said, about us being better off, about being happy as we are, I feel like I'm fucking twenty-two all over again, ready to pull you into my arms, to throw you over my shoulder. I can still see the future that we could have had if I stayed. The one you currently have." His eyes drop from mine to my belly but quickly recover. "The only reason it's not on the table even now, isn't because I'm a good man, but because I'm a bad one."

"You can't mean that."

"I do. Every word. Because there should have been no room for miscommunication. It should have been clear that in whatever I said, you wouldn't be able to think it meant anything but I love you, because I really did love you. There should have been no reality where you looked at me and doubted that. Where you looked at me and thought I didn't know you, didn't try to know you. Where you were in my bed one night and running from it the next. Where I was clouded by my pride. A good man would have chased you, fought for you. *God, I should have fucking protected you.* Instead, what did I do? Absolutely nothing. I pushed you away from me and into his arms.

"You said I didn't know you, and I accepted that, even knowing it wasn't true. You felt it, and I wasn't going to try and prove it to you. But I should have; I should have proved it all. Because you had let me know you, before you knew it, before you ever accepted it, you let me see you, and I fell in love with you for it."

His hand reaches into his jacket pocket, pulling from it a folded piece of paper. His grip on it tightens as if he's afraid to let it go as his thumb runs across it in memory. He reaches across, extending it to me, and I accept, as our fingers brush just slightly before retreating back to their respective sides of the table.

His handwriting will always be recognizable to me, so much of our relationship spent leaving notes for each other in the margins of books. My eyes don't need to run down past the top of the paper to know what this is. My initials next to his, a line down the center. At the time, I thought he was keeping score. Never did I realize he kept the actual scorecard. Nor did I know that when he told me he didn't care about points, just how honest that was.

The first few rounds are here. Where I was calculating the scores and telling him to write them down, but beneath it, words. Notes. Answers.

Every turn I played was written here. *Only mine.* My favorite movie, my coffee order, all the small things I answered. And all the things he saw beyond that. Next to *'violin,'* he wrote *'precise.'* Next to the word *'political,'* he wrote *'caring.'* Next to the word *'student,'* he wrote *'brilliant.'* Next to the word *'interested,'* he wrote, *'me too.'* Circled and underlined thrice.

There are dozens of words here, the ones I shared, the ones he saw beyond them, even just within the first hours of meeting me he was focused on knowing me.

He lets me take it in. The gravity of this artifact of our relationship. This fossil of us when we were together. My eyes scan the page again before I look back at him, his eyes waiting for mine to reconnect to his before he continues.

"I'm sorry, AB. You can't tell me I shouldn't be. That's that truth. I've lived without you long enough, if you don't think I have reason enough to apologize, then you're making me live without your forgiveness as well. Even if I don't think I deserve it, even if you don't think I need it, I don't know what else I can say or do to express how incredibly, tragically, devastatingly, sorry I am."

"And you think you need my forgiveness so you can finally have closure?"

"Closure?" The sound that punctuates that question isn't a laugh. "Haven't you realized by now... you and me? There's no closure for us, for this. There wasn't then, and there isn't now. We can only choose to accept it. Everything that happened between us, after us. All the time that's passed, I didn't know what I was missing. It was you. It was all of this.

"I came here because I needed to see you. Fuck that, selfishly I *wanted* to see you. Not knowing what it would be like now, knowing how colossally we fucked up back then. And I'll be honest, it's not easy." His elbows are rested on the table, and his hands interlocked as thumbs alternating run the path of his lifelines. His eyes following their track, maybe dangerously thinking, like I am, about the lines our lives could have taken. But he halts the motion, releasing the thought, and settling his hands back to where they had been resting.

I want to say something, but he doesn't look finished. Maybe he's been holding on to some of this as long as I have, mushrooms in a dark damp corner that overtook his mind in the last weeks. But just because you don't want to hold on to something anymore, doesn't mean letting it go is easier. Knowing once you do, you can never put it back where it was before. I note the decision in his eyes before he opens his mouth to speak.

"It's not about us being together now, but I'm here because I needed you to understand, without a shadow of a doubt, how I felt about you *when we were.*

I need you to understand how I felt. How I still feel, in many ways. So, Arden, while there might never be closure for us, finally, there can be understanding."

His tone isn't soft. The waterline of his eyes seems to be the edge of the reflecting pools of silver. Thank goodness our plates have been cleared; otherwise, there would be no room for what Reid set down on the table between us. The harshest of truths. Some of which I had never really considered. But listening to him now, I can't say I completely disagree.

It's a lot to take in, more than I ever was expecting from this conversation.

REID

She looks painfully beautiful, or maybe pained and beautiful. I don't know. She might not want to believe what I'm saying, but there is inarguable truth in it. Her face now is a clear indication she agrees on some level, even if she doesn't want to.

She moves her hand to rest gently against her stomach underneath the table. I don't think she's intentionally calling attention to her pregnancy, but instead, it's her way of tying herself back to her current reality.

Grounding herself. I get it. I wish I could do it.

I think about my home, my career, my *fiancée*, my terrible cat, these things should ground me. It's not that they don't. But sitting here across from her, it's easy to see how this could have been our life.

We're just sitting here silently for a moment, maybe three, as we let all the words and emotions wash over us.

"You want me to understand how you felt? How you still feel? Well, I'm here. So, tell me, Reid..." Her words aren't bitter at all, if anything she's eager to understand.

I'm hit with the realization that the slippery slope I aimed to avoid, I am now perched right above. I'm precariously balanced, one step will wipe me out completely. I don't know what good this will do, but for all the control I've ever held, this is not one of the times I choose to exercise it.

Though everything within me is screaming to step back. I don't. She doesn't want me to. It's our time to be honest in all the ways I never have before.

"I've missed you. You were the love of my life, and I will always care about you more than circumstance allows."

She takes a short breath, like she's inhaling the words I shouldn't have shared. But I needed her to know. I needed her to know that despite everything. She was the love of my life, the love of *that* life. The one that existed in my small apartment and the streets of Cambridge, Massachusetts. The young love that made me feel bold, and terrified, that left me ripped in two when she left. And when she did leave, when I *made* her leave, when we ended up with this twisted painful understanding refusing to meet in the middle, I forced myself to close that book and start a new one. But even forcing it closed didn't wholly erase the story from memory.

Her eyes rim with tears. No. Those are mine. Maybe you're a fool, sitting here like this professing emotions from a lifetime ago. I don't know who could look at her like this and feel anything but the resurgence of that love. I've lied to myself long enough that it hasn't always been here. Perhaps just the smallest ember of those fires we set within each remained, but we never stoked it, never tended it, it never grew. Instead, it just flickered as a memory. Until now.

"I've missed you," she says, and my eyes snap up from where they had landed on her stomach, imagining the alternate paths of our lives. Her voice is small. Something she's not. This woman is wildly fierce, and roars, she doesn't eke out small whispers. Which tells me she's almost afraid of what she's admitted.

"Reid, you can miss me now, the way I miss you. The way I

think I'll always miss you. But I learned a long time ago that you can miss something without wanting it back. Knowing that what you miss is just the memory. The version we preserve to protect the imprint of something, or someone, important."

Whatever hesitancy, if that's what it was, is gone now and her tone strengthened with each word.

"But memories aren't always honest, ours clearly weren't. They are filtered and viewed through whatever lens we need them to be. And you don't make decisions on that. You can't build a life on the blueprints of memories alone."

Chapter Fifty

2008

REID

I refuse to be the man who gets dumped by his girlfriend and wallows. I know that the reality of the situation is that nothing lasts when you're twenty-two, or more so, when you're nineteen, but I have written on these very pages that I had thought the opposite was coming true. I watched her leave and it was of no difficulty as she did it. Didn't turn around, no final look back. No final I love you except the one I gave her as I fucked her against the wall. What a foolish man I was, to think that I could have gotten her to focus on us rather than run away. Yet, what fuels my anger most is that I know who will comfort her. I know who is comforting her. Not comfort, she is fine. Austin spoke to that asshole and fuck if that didn't confirm everything. She ran right to him. I can't keep rehashing this in these pages. The story does not change. My feelings are the pendulum between loss and anger, regardless when it stops swinging, I stay in this position of acceptance. I am not the man to follow Alice down the rabbit hole. Even still, it's been an effort not to text her this week. Not to call her. Not to just knock on her door. The thing that prevents it, sheer will power. That and the fact that I don't know what the fuck I would say. 'Hey, it's me, how's your week been, mine was shit.' or maybe 'I'm moving soon, there's your closure.' how about 'Pretty sure you've moved on already, tell your boyfriend I say hello.' That isn't really a viable option, but I can't stop myself from the thought that he swooped in as he tried to throughout our whole fucking relationship. Driving the wedge further between us, until he was the devil on her shoulder, taunting her, pushing her, until she snapped, deciding whatever the fuck it was she decided. No. I might fucking hate Joshua, and I should have trusted my instincts, but for as much as I hated him, I fucking loved her. How stupid. How misplaced. It's messy. It's so fucking messy and goddamned unclear. To make matters worse, she texted me Saturday night. Late. 'Hey' was all she said. 'Hi' was what I said back while I waited like a fucking teenager, waiting for the follow up 'I miss you' or even 'Can you come over' that the timestamp would have indicated. Surely alcohol fueled, but at least it was an opportunity to open this conversation again. To see her. And then she just never fucking responds. Ultimately whatever it was she thought she might want from me, another pity fuck perhaps, wasn't going to be worth it. Or maybe she *retreated to him. While I don't usually respond to drunk 2 a.m. messages, for her, I did. Probably for the best, things were finally clearing up, and I can focus on next steps rather than getting tangled in this mess. Austin will take over my lease, I can't be here anymore. I swear if I have to look at that fucking piano much longer, I'll take an axe to it. Leave it here as firewood. I have choices, a lot of them. I worked hard to have them, and I was going to ignore all of that and just stay here. I have interviews this week to confirm what's next. But maybe it's time to close this chapter and the NYC consulting gig looks like a top contender. Austin will be pissed if I don't stick around but I think I'll be pissed if I do, after all it's not like—*

The buzzing in my pocket hasn't stopped. I drop the pen in the spine of the notebook to retrieve my phone, distracting me from the final thoughts of this entry, abandoning mid-sentence to see what's so urgent.

This can't be real.

AB: Didn't mean to leave you hanging

Understatement of the fucking century.

AB: My phone died this weekend after I texted and I've been kinda busy since

Don't I know it, baby. How kind of you to remind me.

AB: Want to grab a coffee?

When We Were

What. The. Fuck.

How unlike her to just leave herself disconnected all weekend. I can't quiet the thought that it might be a lie. A follow up, as the regret she had from sending the drunk text, and maybe the only way to save face now. If that's the case, why ask to meet? What does she even want, besides coffee apparently? She got her closure. Her farewell fuck. *This girl.*

I never fully understood her, though I tried desperately. Is this an olive branch, could it be a reconciliation? I'm not obligated to see her, I don't owe her anything.

I gave her anything she asked.

I tried to, or, I would have, *eventually.*

Her interest in coffee now, doesn't interest me.

Stop lying to yourself, of course it does.

Even with the Joshua update. Austin claims to know that it's only a matter of time before she comes back. I hadn't believed him, but now? I don't know. I check my wallet. *Yep, I've got a hundred ready to pay up for the best bet I ever lost.*

It's with that thought that I pick up my phone to text her back.

The truth is, no matter how much I'd prefer to preserve my dignity and not go running back to my ex-girlfriend after she dumped me, fucked me goodbye, and hasn't spoken to me in a week, there is no way I could stop myself. I can't beg her to come back to our relationship, but I can meet her for coffee. We can talk it out and when she says she misses me, we can figure out what's next. But it has to be her that says it.

me: Coffee sounds good, when?
AB: Tomorrow?

Tomorrow? That's urgent. Maybe this is a good sign. Fuck, that doesn't work for me. This whole week is nuts.

419

me: Can't tomorrow, not available until Friday.

I don't *want* to wait. What I want now is to cancel every meeting I have scheduled just so I can see her. *That might be what I want, but I know better.* I am taking the train to New York City tomorrow for interviews and won't be back for a few days, and without knowing what she wants, Friday is the soonest I'm available.

AB: Can't wait! See you Friday

She didn't confirm the time or place, but she must know like I do that it will be the standard coffee date we had for weeks when we first started dating. The coffee date we still shared when we had to squeeze in time before classes. Now, it will be the coffee date where she tells me she didn't want it to be over.

Friday, 8 a.m., Coffee Haus.

I picked up the pen I had dropped between the pages of my moleskin journal, the sentence I left now hanging on the line of the page unfinished. I scratch it out, unable to recall what I was originally going to say. It doesn't matter anymore. Replacing it with a new thought.

Maybe this chapter isn't over.

ARDEN

I'm ready to leave this school, ready to get out of this city for the summer, but not before seeing him. The last two weeks have felt like they moved in slow-motion, and I am ready to live my life in real time again. I just know I can't do that here, not right now.

I have a meeting with my advisor later today, one more

paper to drop off by the end of the week, and an airline ticket to leave a few days from now. Going home for a bit before heading across the pond with my mom. Six weeks, uninterrupted in Europe. Starting in London, ending in Amsterdam.

My feet are dangling from my lofted bed, my phone held between my cheek and my shoulder, and I scroll through the university facebook group on my laptop, seeing everyone's statuses about farewell parties and tough finals.

"Hi sweetheart, how's packing going?" My mom answers the phone and jumps right in. As she does with most things.

"Bittersweet, but I'm excited to come home… Actually, before I leave campus, I have to talk to advisement. But I wanted to talk to you and dad about it first, can you put him on the phone?" She calls out to my father, and switches the phone to speaker. I can tell by their silence, they are both likely terrified about whatever shoe I'm about to drop. *Maybe they should be.*

"Alright sweetheart, we're both here."

Okay. Do it. Rip the bandaid off. It will be better just to get it over with.

"I'm meeting with my advisor to review my courses for next year, but I've decided I want to focus on business courses, not science. I was thinking, maybe eventually an MBA rather than MD. Maybe neither… but I just want more options than being a doctor." *Stop rambling. Stop rambling. Stop rambling. But stay strong.* There is just silence on the other end of the line. I'm not sure what I'm waiting for, maybe a lecture from my dad about why this isn't a good decision, maybe my mom's disappointment that I won't be following in their footsteps. But what I get is something else. It's none of that.

"That's it, kid?" *Okay, not the follow up question I expected from my father.*

"Yeah, I guess that's it," I say with caution. Unsure what parallel universe I've landed myself in.

"Sounds good," he says.

"That sounds exciting! Can't wait for you to fill us in when we see you," my mom says, and she *does* sound excited.

"You guys aren't disappointed?" I move to lay back in my bed, so confused by their lack of response. Having spent so much of my life talking about a career like theirs, following in their footsteps, and now they seem incredibly unaffected.

"Only if you are, sweetheart. You talked about being a doctor from the time you were little."

"I know, but I guess I just thought it was what was expected."

"It was only our expectation of you because we thought it's what you wanted. We want you to be successful, we want you to be happy. Our lives took this path, and if that's one you want to follow, we would be immensely proud of you, we can even help you in many ways, but if it's not what you want, that's not a disappointment, sweetheart. You've never been a disappointment to anyone but yourself, and I doubt you ever could." *Well, recent events prove otherwise.*

I wrap up the phone call with my parents and lay in my empty room. Stripped of so many of the memories we made here this year. Stella and I packed up all the boxes we could, just leaving out the necessities. We could technically remain on campus for another four weeks before the dorms closed, but we both are done and ready to go. She misses her boyfriend and *so do* I.

Most of these boxes will be unpacked at some point. Some when I get home, some I'll leave stored until next fall when I return to a different dorm, where I can then unpack and begin again. But there are some things I have no intention of ever unpacking. I boxed them up, shelved them away. Sealing them with my own actions.

Josh called me a cunt from behind his bedroom door as I got dressed and walked out. Our friendship, our—*whatever it was,* began so quickly, and as I learned after it blew up in smoke, all of our friends, *no,* all of *my* friends, seemed to be unsurprised when I told them what happened.

What happened in the version I reduced for my own comfort, the parts I could be sure of. What I shared with my friends when they asked, was simple.

'Something happened between us, it won't happen again, we aren't friends anymore because of it.'

―――――

I still wake up at night, my insomnia worsening, and I look forward to not being in this bed, in this room, in this city. And when I let myself sleep, the walls I worked so hard to reinforce during the day came down. The mental patrols I had guarding them vanished. And the fortress I used to protect my conscious sanity becomes wholly exposed in a way I can't control. Making the restlessness of sleep worse than the alternative of an exhausted awakeness.

It wasn't until I found myself sitting on the bench of the ice rink some time after two in the morning that the exhaustion and emotion came completely to a head.

The ice had melted in spring though the benches and frame of the rink remained in place. I sat there on the bench staring at the empty space where the ice had been. Now just the frame of the rink, a reminder to the nights I spent here laughing with *him*. Now I sit here, crying a*lone,* similarly just a shell in comparison to what I was then.

Reid had told me that this rink had a season. At the end of fall, when the first frosts came, they would freeze the rink and leave it here until the weather began to warm in spring.

For me, I thawed in winter. Warmed in ways I hadn't expected. Layers of ice melting, evaporating overtime. Only to refreeze when everyone else shed their coats.

Chapter Fifty-One

2008

ARDEN

We are meeting at 8 a.m., which means we will both likely be there well before to claim *our* table. It's still our table, right? The two-person, cafe style, small table in the window. That was our table, and for everything I've given up so far in the short amount of time since I left his apartment, I'm not giving up *our table*.

With most of my clothes packed away, save a few miscellaneous tee shirts, I pull on one of my favorites, and always a conversation starter. *Sometimes an argument starter, depending on the person's ideology.* But Reid laughed the first time he saw it, and I thought he might laugh now.

A white cotton shirt with three words printed—*Hot Piece Of*—and a picture of a cartoon donkey below it. Underneath the donkey, more text that reads *No One's Heard of a Hot Piece of Elephant.*

Is it political? Yes. Is it also punny? Yes. Two things I love. I'm wearing jeans and converse, even though I had freshly shaved legs. *Just in case.* I told myself.

I had thought about texting him en route to confirm we were still on but decided against it. We had agreed to meet, there was nothing else to say. That's not true, there is *so much to say*.

I pull open the door to the coffee shop, 7:02 a.m., right on time. Or, early-on time, and I look immediately to the table we shared when we shared ourselves. He isn't there. Someone else is. With their laptop propped open and a coffee cup to the side of it, clearly that person has hunkered down and isn't moving. *Maybe I can ask. That's acceptable right? 'Hi, how are you, please move because the love of my life is meeting me and my plan will go to shit if we can't sit here.'*

In the times we met for coffee, he was always here first, and that fills me with different nerves than the ones that have been brewing. Becoming deeply unsettled at the idea that despite what I want to hope for, this moment, this meeting, *isn't* like the others. I can't expect him to be here early, waiting with my coffee. Waiting with a smile that would knock me down. I can't expect anything.

I scan the small coffee shop, and find an empty table. It's on the other side of the room, not in front of the window, but against the wall.

Our table was drenched in light. The brightness from the sun shining through the window meant that even on the coldest mornings, I could still feel the warmth. *Maybe it was never the sun, maybe that was just him.* It was never clearer than now. This table is different. It's illuminated by the artificial light overhead. No matter how much I want to sit across from him and pour myself into the space between us. To tell him what's happened, how badly I want to watch him calculate the triple word score before jotting down the points. I want so much in this moment, but all of those things are trapped in a place that can't be said.

So I will prepare myself for the things I can say, hoping that he will recognize in some way that there's more. I'll give him the thread and he can pull it until I am unspooled completely and he can weave it into something beautiful like he did before.

I hurried to order our coffees and take the available *not-our-table* table. Even though the chair is identical to the one across the room, it's uncomfortable. I squirm, waiting for him, unable to get situated. *I don't think it's the chair, in fact, I know it's not.*

I check my watch and note the time. Thirty-four past the hour. Maybe I shouldn't have ordered his coffee yet. While I'm sitting here, counting the minutes that I've been waiting.

Though, I don't think it can be considered *waiting* until the agreed upon time has passed. Then I see it out of the corner of my eye. The laptop invader who had taken our table, stands and leaves! It's not that I'm superstitious but it almost feels like a bad omen to be sitting anywhere else.

Before I can make a move to switch seats, the door opens, and I watch as his eyes land directly on our empty table. It's almost as if he senses my presence behind him, he turns to look around the room, immediately making note of me and the *not-our-table* table.

His smile is different, maybe forced, and I wonder if that's how he feels. *Forced* to be here. And my stomach sinks at the thought. He takes a few steps towards me, and in his seat before I can stand to give him a hug.

"Hi, Reid."

"Hey, AB, sorry I'm late."

"You're not late, I'm just early."

"Old habits."

He takes a seat as I push his coffee towards him. "Thanks," he says as he takes a sip of his dry cappuccino. "Nice table."

I don't know if he means it sincerely, but I know it isn't worth explaining. There was something about him that I haven't seen before or maybe it was that he isn't letting me see it now, and that's what's different. Normally, his expression is transparent. Right now, it's distant.

It makes sense. He had put distance between us, and I pulled him to this table. And without the physical space remaining, he could only do what I have done for so long, keep the emotional space.

But he is still here. Less than two weeks after everything happened. He still showed up.

"I heard you've been well," he says. I think he's gauging the water. Trying to decide if I'll be emotional or volatile like I was when I ran through the mental minefield, exploding them all in my wake.

"I've been busy." He's the person I've been most looking forward to sharing this with. "I've had some meetings with my advisors. I officially declared a major."

"Isn't it a little early?"

"Usually, yes, but apparently, because of my extra courses, I am already classified as a sophomore.

So, I was able to declare a major and at this rate I'll even graduate early."

"I'm happy for you." He really seems it. The reservation he has is likely out of concern for whatever reason he thinks I asked him here. The clingy college girlfriend who is desperate for him to take her back. As much as I would like that to be me, to tell him that I miss him, that I'm sorry, that so much happened... I won't put him in that position.

"I should thank you."

"Why is that?"

"I declared as a business major." He smiles more sincerely now, and I take it as a sign to keep talking. "I'll also have enough credits for a minor in literature if I want it, maybe even *Russian* literature, or I could pick something like a focus on computer science or economics..." I keep going. Keep talking. I fill the space between us with words. *Not the ones I want to say, but ones that he seems willing to accept.*

The more we discuss anything besides *us*, he seems okay, he seems to be loosening up. His nodding along became responding, which became interest, and we just flowed back into each other casually.

"How did your parents take the news that there won't be another Dr. Bancroft?"

"Apparently, they never cared beyond my happiness, and I just never gave them the benefit of the doubt to think that they might." He nods, understandingly.

"Why business?"

"I thought a lot about it, and I just think it will give me the chance to be so many different things, rather than just the one thing that everyone wanted me to be, or what I thought they wanted me to be."

"You've never been just one thing, Arden. You're incredible and will be incredible in whatever you choose."

We talked like that for some time. He told me how he had taken interviews in New York, that's what he had been up to this week, that he also has an offer for the company he's been interning at all year, but he's far more interested now in some of the other offers he has on the table.

I told him about the plans I made with my mom to travel, just her and me doing a tour of museums in Europe. He told me how he was going back to Michigan in a few weeks after he packs up the apartment to spend some time with his family.

And we just chatted, casually, as if we could both just avoid the third rail topic. The topic that neither of us tried to broach. Recalling the night two weeks ago we stood on either side of it too afraid to get electrocuted by reaching across the middle.

Maybe there will be a time for us to try again, but I can tell it's not now. I didn't have a lot of faith that I would be able to tell him all the things I wanted to. They were frozen in blocks of ice, and I couldn't melt them down fast enough if I tried.

I sit here, listening to the modulation of his voice as he tells me about his latest read. Pulling it from the messenger bag that hangs from the chair and setting it on the table between us.

"I've just finished this, you might like it."

Might like it. In the last months, we traded dozens of books and, in doing so, essentially ended up reading everything twice given that we experienced it for a second time when the other finally began. In all those months we were able to recommend books with far more confidence than this moment delivers. I follow his gesture, having also just finished the novel I was reading, and offer it to him in friendly exchange.

"Here, I liked it." He smiles as he slides the book towards him, flipping the pages through quickly, I can see he's scanning for ink.

"My notes are in there," I say, attempting to answer the question his actions asked.

"I'm glad, they're always my favorite part." He sets it down, takes a breath, and breaks eye contact with the novel and looks at me.

"Arden, can I ask you something?" His voice is passive. Softened by the exchange, more so the significance than the actual books themselves.

"Ye-yeah, of course." I sputter out, my mind unable to think through all the ways this could go before. He had expressed no romantic inclination while sitting here, he expressed no interest in me beyond pleasantries. And while there are things I hope he'll ask me, threads I offered for him to pull, his face tells me that's not what's coming.

"I'm glad to hear about school and your travel plans. But tell me, why did you text? What is it you want?" It isn't insensitive or impatient, it is genuine curiosity.

He had once asked me what I wanted. In fact, he asked it regularly.

In the most general of ways. What do you want for dinner? That answer changed frequently.

In the most intimate of ways. What do you want me to do to you? That answer always lit him on fire.

In ways that made this conversation even more difficult now. What do you want in the future? That answer was always the same, *'more of this.'*

He always asked me to tell him, never wanting to assume.

And when he asked me what I wanted out of our relationship, before I had called it a relationship, he offered me an alternative. He had offered me his friendship, and it felt sincere. In this moment, when I know I don't have him, that there was no other part of him he wanted to give, I would take that, not in consolation, but knowing that his friendship, independent of anything else, was worth more than any other I had.

I folded my hands in my lap, squeezing them tightly together. The only way I can control physically what's pulsing through me, nerves, sadness, want. I want him. Maybe soon I won't, but two weeks? But I know what *he* wants. Or rather what he doesn't. I remember what he said that night. *'I don't want to be in a relationship like this.'*

"I want us to be friends."

"Okay, AB. Let's be friends."

Maybe we *have* found a middle. Somewhere we can exist right now. Maybe if the rest of the story is over, we can stay in the margins for just a bit longer like this. *This can be it. We can be friends like this.*

He reaches his hand across the table, extending it to me. Across the middle. More softly than a handshake, as his palm slightly upturned, open. *A sign of submission, I read once in an anthropology course.* And I slipped my hand into his. Not my right, not the one that would make it more transactional. Make it an agreement. But my left. I thought he might pull his away, but instead he stroked his thumb against the back of my hand, and we both just sit here, wordlessly in the moment. Sitting with the resignation that when we walked away from this table, we would be walking away from the moments that had been like this.

These are our final chapters.

No sooner did I have the thought, than I hear the familiar alarm buzzing from his pocket. His hand jerks, he blinks himself to a moment of clarity, and silences it.

He takes a long slow breath and presses his lips together.

"I have to go, I'm sorry I can't stay longer."

"No, it's fine, of course. I'm glad I got to see you before I left. I'm glad we can be friends."

"We've always been friends, Arden. We can always *be* friends." As we both stand, grabbing our newly exchanged books from the table, I take a step forward, as he steps to the side. I'm not sure if it was intentional, as he blocked my path out, but his arms came around me, in the hug we didn't exchange in greeting.

It's incredible how quickly our bodies line up. Our breath, our heartbeats. But we step back, his hands lingering on my arms, as they often did when he wasn't ready to let go.

We will be friends. He's right, we had been friends, even when we were more.

He looks down at me and something breaks free, not sure if he had tried to contain it, but a smile spread slowly across his face, and he lets out a small, huffed laugh in a way that inspired one of my own. Without even understanding the cause.

"Did you know this is one of my favorite tee shirts?" He nods down at the political commentary and colorfully worded shirt that hugged every curve of my body.

"I do now."

We stand here on the corner as we have so many times before. Knowing the significance that we had to go our separate ways. Not just in this moment, but in all the ones that follow. I wrapped my arms around him once more, quickly, before he can react.

"Thanks for meeting me."

"I can't imagine my life if I hadn't." He smiles with resignation, and looks so handsome standing here, the sun climbing in the sky, as his full lips and perfect teeth charmed me just as they did the first time he smiled at me. That look had me pull my lip under my teeth. Sucking it in to control the urge to jump into his arms. Knowing it would be undoing the agreement of friendship we had just made. And there would be nothing I would do to risk that.

His face gives it away, the flash of lust, and I know why. This habit I have. This nervous tick, not done to provoke him, but the Pavlov's dog nature that built each time he saw it, made my mouth yearn for the reward of the kiss I always got when he pulled my lip free.

He shoved his hands into his pockets and cleared his throat.

"Would you do me a favor?" he asks instead.

"Yeah?" I can't imagine what he could possibly want from me.

"Email me or something, I'll want to hear all about your travels this summer." And that was it. He leaned down to kiss my cheek, and we both walked our separate ways.

Chapter Fifty-Two

2008

REID

I can't describe the feeling of walking into that coffee shop and thinking she didn't show. But that is what I thought when I opened the door and stared at our empty table in the window.

Normally, I would have thought nothing of it, but as I was already late, or later than she likely expected me to be, the fact that she wasn't already seated at our table floored me.

Maybe it was an unfair expectation. Maybe I should not expect anything from her now, she set that standard the night she broke up with me. But I did expect things from her. That's partially how I ended up here. Both in this moment, and in this situation.

I expected her to match me, to meet the standards of my life. That might sound like a pretentious thing to say, but it wasn't unrealistic.

I hate being the guy to stand on principle, but what else do I have? I'm not going to chase after her when she made it clear that's not what she wants. This isn't a romcom where I show up at the train station with flowers or make some sweeping proclamation of love and apology under the glow of a streetlight.

I convinced myself she drew a clear line in the sand, and I will stay on my side of it. After all, how many people find the love of their life at twenty-two anyways.

Then she went and texted me. While saying no felt like the smarter choice, worried that I would only reset my desire for her as she sat in front of me, I said yes. Because I knew I would handle that if it came to it. It would be the worthwhile cost of seeing her.

Then I walked into the coffee shop, and our table was empty. We weren't those people anymore. When we were them, we would have been at that table for hours. But as I took a seat at the poorly lit table against the opposite wall, I knew we weren't them. She did too, that's why she chose a different seat.

I wondered what would have happened, if I hadn't been delayed by a few minutes this morning. My pre-interview call regarding the meeting I had this afternoon, it should have been five minutes, but turned into twenty. Those twenty minutes cost me *our* table.

We'd left the Coffee Haus and the symbolism that we needed to walk in different directions isn't lost on either of us. When she throws her arms around me, I want to pull her more deeply into me. To walk with her in my chest, back to the place it all began, and this time not let her call it closure.

"Thanks for meeting me," she says, as if it was that simple. I know what she meant; I know how she meant it. She meant for coffee. It would have been kinder to respond as simply as that. I let it slip though, the truth of how I feel right now.

"I can't imagine my life if I hadn't." I smile at her resigned to the fact that while we might not have a future, I loved her. That's something I am grateful for, even if it isn't permanent, it can't be undone.

Then she does it. The thing that tests every ounce of my

control. I watched her pull her plump bottom lip under her teeth and my body jumps to respond with muscle memory. I don't know that I can hide the look on my face, and I figure she must see it, but if she does, she doesn't give it away. Knowing it would give me false hope. She might not want to be with me, but despite what I may have said, to myself, my journal, and *fuck,* even my friends, she isn't cruel.

I shove my hands into my pockets, and clear my throat. I want her friendship, and I'll ask for it as she did, I'll make sure she knows.

"Would you do me a favor?"

"Yeah?" Her caution is palpable.

"Email me or something, I'll want to hear all about your travels this summer." That's it. I lean down one last time and plant a quick kiss on her cheek, knowing I could move a fraction of an inch and catch the corner of her lips. But if I want her friendship, which she is offering, this is how it has to be.

The feeling of her skin on my lips is gone faster than I can commit it to memory. I smile and turn to walk away.

I put in my earphones and walk to the music playing. I should be better, not dwell right now, but I'm going to give myself the distance, and then, no more. I pull up the first song that reminds me of her, knowing that when I get to my front door, it's over.

'Short Skirt/Long Jacket' by Cake comes through and drowns out the noise in my head. All I can see is her standing there looking at me. In that ridiculous donkey shirt.

It's a lot like her. It's bold, challenging, *political,* but clever. Damn, it's downright funny. And while the idea of her in one of her more go-to dresses and boots was always the way I imagined her, the way I first had her when we were just learning each other. When we were just falling in. It was the way I still imagined her, *the way I've been imagining her,* as I

435

stood hand pressed against the tile shower as I fucked my own fist. The way I imagined her in the future, underneath her cap and gown, in all the other memories and photos we would capture. But right now, I don't think there's any image I'll enjoy more than this one. In that fucking tee shirt.

It wasn't easy to take the step back, to walk away. To turn around and leave, taking with me only that image of her. Because she had taken the one from my apartment after it shattered on the floor, and she had already wiped any memory of us from social media.

She looked at me, and as I turned, her eyes captured the light, and I swear they looked on fire. That impossibly hot blue gas flame that darkens around the edge.

The music continues to play and I accept it all one more time.

Then, it's over.

We won't be who we were when we were them. Who we were when we were happy in the blissful ignorance of 'young love' or whatever it is people say to be cliché. Whatever it is, people call it to make you feel like you're under a common spell and prepare you for the idea that it isn't permanent in any way that matters. And you aren't unique for experiencing it.

We won't be who we were.

But we will both be who we should.

Chapter Fifty-Three

PRESENT

ARDEN

There was space between us, both physically and emotionally, but perhaps sitting at this table, for the first time in all these years we finally had closed the distance we had put there to protect our hearts, that we clung to out of self-preservation and eventually out of respect.

As time went on, the time we spent apart became longer than the time we had spent together. Further solidifying our friendship as just that.

You can love a memory without loving the person. And as I look at him, I know that the love we have for each other in this moment is that.

We had just both shared the last piece. Something I wouldn't have dared say under normal circumstances, but something about having every thought on the table was freeing. All the things we had been too stubborn to ever say before.

"I don't really know where to go from here."

He had said initially he never wanted to go down a path

that could result in anything that would disrupt the lives we have. And he has been truthful, respectful, and so considerate.

"I don't know." he says, taking a sip of his drink before continuing.

"There was a time I hoped you were lonely and miserable. It's a shitty thing to say, but it's the truth. I was mad at you for so long, mad at myself because of you. Even after I saw you. When you asked to be friends, I had hoped you regretted what you did. *What I thought you did,*" he corrected himself. "I had hoped you would look back and know that what we had wasn't common. It wasn't just young love meant to burn hot and burn out. Then I watched you move on; I took another step back. We couldn't be close friends, but we could be acquaintances. Knowing that it would be easier for me that way. Eventually, I didn't hate you anymore. I just hated myself for ever wanting anything for you but happiness. I don't want you to be miserable and lonely, I want your happiness, which you have, Arden.

"So it doesn't matter how we choose to remember what happened between us. I know two things..." He looks deep in my eyes, preparing himself for something that seems difficult to admit.

"One." He holds up a finger, and lets the soft smile pull on his lips. "I loved you."

"Two." He extends a second finger, and the smile falls flat. "Not enough."

His eyes looked away from mine, ashamed, perhaps with regret I never thought he would have. There is a momentary silence hanging between us as we consider what to say next. Until his phone rings and breaks our concentration.

"Did you set an alarm?" I ask, partially in humor, but I can't help but wonder as he reaches into his pocket and pulls out his phone.

"Not this time," he looks at the screen, "but it is a wakeup call." He answers the call and smiles at me with apology. For what, I'm not yet sure.

"Hey baby," he says, and as he does his face pinches, as if realizing the word had fallen from his lips earlier tonight in a different manner. I've practically zoned out, taking a sip of my iced tea. Trying not to eavesdrop, but proximity makes it difficult. His call wraps up quickly, bookended with an '*I love you too*,' and he slips it away as his eyes meet mine again.

"Reid, I think you're right. That was a wakeup call. One we both clearly needed. We should probably get the bill."

REID

When I saw her name across the screen, it was like a punch in the gut, and the look on Arden's face as I used the same term of endearment she'd heard from me hundreds of times, and once without intention earlier tonight, was like a full-blown knockout. I don't know if she even realized that there was a discomfort that washed over her in that moment. She certainly wouldn't have wanted me to see it.

Traveling for work right now, the time difference has made connecting difficult the last few days, which meant that her call, which hadn't been entirely unexpected, was necessary to answer. It was necessary to answer for so many reasons. Arden sat there, sipping her tea, with her wedding ring adorned hand resting softly on the slight curve of her belly, but it grounded her. I can tell. It pulls her back into her reality where I have been a kite with too much string. Picked up by the wind pulled into the clouds. Had we continued with this much longer, it would have been very possible for the string to snap all together and I would just float away. *Until my phone rang.*

"Do you want dessert? Coffee? Hot chocolate?"

"No, thank you, I think we should probably go home."

With that, she pulls the lever once more and puts us back on track. This time, separately. Two trolleys that are coming up to the same potential fork, each one ready to split off and follow the individual track to the appropriate destination.

It's surreal how much this mirrored that day in Cambridge. Where she told me she wanted to be friends. In all ways but the important one. She doesn't say that this time. Maybe knowing, like I do, that it might be too hard for us to go back to that. We knew too much now, about how we felt, what had happened. Things I haven't even fully been able to consider the impact of.

When we step outside of the restaurant, standing here at an impasse. Under the glow of the streetlight, her hair is golden and her skin is porcelain. Freckles spotted across her nose make her look young as she looks up at me, and all I can see is her *then*.

Standing on the corner outside the coffee shop, in that silly political tee shirt.

She stole my breath away. But I would never be the thief of her happiness.

We both know we have embers left in the ashes.

We can either stoke them, feed them the oxygen they need to grow into flames again, knowing that that fire would burn down the lives we've made, *or* we could suffocate them. Instead, taking the deep breaths *we* need to fill our own lungs with air and allow ourselves to breathe.

There isn't enough oxygen for both.

She steps into my embrace; one I had opened to her without decision. As she lifts onto her toes and places a kiss on my check. The corners of our mouths so narrowly missing it feels like I'm holding two magnets separate from each other that are desperate to snap together. But I don't let them go. Neither does she. She doesn't pull away instantly, but eventually settles back onto her feet.

"You were the love of my life also."

"Arden." I offer her the reprieve, the idea that she doesn't owe me anything, and doesn't need to return any of the sentiment I shared. But she doesn't take it. She looks up at me, focused, clear. Her hand resting on my arm, a conduit for the emotion she shares.

"I used to think that maybe you were just the right person but at the wrong time. You know? Like maybe there would be a time for us. That there would be other chapters, but you would eventually be my epilogue. But I was wrong. I think you were the right person, at the right time, and we can blame the miscommunication trope all we want, but like you said, none of it was enough. So you were right, Reid. While things might have been different between us, they *wouldn't* have been better. You loved someone else, someone I used to be, and maybe I'm still her, and maybe in some ways you're still him, but it was never going to be enough, and we won't be them again, at least not together."

I pull her back in for one more hug, because in some ways this feels like the ending we never got. The closure she said she wanted then when we were tearing each other apart. This time, it was putting us back together in ways we had not known were needed. I never thought closure was possible. Just because you close the back cover on your favorite book doesn't mean it doesn't stay with you. But if I've learned anything in these last weeks. These past years. Maybe I'm wrong.

My chin rests on top of her head, and I feel her breathing sync up with mine, as if no time had passed, I wrap my arms around her tightly as she relaxes into me. Those embers between us glowing in recognition, but when we pull away, they will be extinguished once and for all. So we stand here. Absorbing the moment we didn't let ourselves have before.

It's when I feel her hands begin to drop from my back

where she had them holding tightly around me, I realize it's over. Knowing that when I let go, we let go.

We choose to breathe.

The ember is out.

It's now just ash.

Chapter Fifty-Four

ARDEN

When I stepped away from him, there was a completeness I hadn't felt before and I hadn't expected to have now.

This all started by chance.

When I texted him so out of the blue, emboldened by history and friendship we built on top of our almost great love story.

When he and I threw the same words at each other in a moment of frustration and anger. More focused on holding our ground than understanding that it was just a gross misunderstanding

When he loved me, kiss by kiss. Laying them down over time like scrabble tiles to reveal the words that made up our story.

When he sat next to me, and let me watch him without interruption, letting me soak him in, absorb him.

All of those moments bring us to this one.

As I got in my car to go home, my eyes welled with the tears that I had held back since I was nineteen. The admissions I never wanted to share. The emotions I never wanted to experience. But the only way to get through to the place of contentment and closure that I had pretended to have these years, was to experience them.

It's not until I get to my own front door. Sliding my key into the lock and pushing it open. The embrace I'm wrapped in is that of my own life. The one I have built. The smells aren't memories of cinnamon and cedar. It's my reality of warm amber musk and freshly washed laundry. It's brightly patterned wallpaper, and Elton John playing through the speakers. It's the dogs barking at the sound of the door.

It's my husband, who's on his feet making his way to me as soon as he hears the door open.

"Hello, darling." His voice so smooth it wraps around me and pulls me into him as his well-kept beard brushes across my chin as he kisses me hello. "How are my girls?" he asks with a smile, his hand on my cheek as he looks at me, trying to assess how I am. The other dropped to my stomach. Hoping he can feel her, or she him.

"I'm okay, actually." And I am. It's a weight I didn't admit to having carried all this time, only noticing now that it's gone.

"I'll make some tea, and if you want, you can tell me how it went."

"You're the love of my life, you know that?" I say, looking up to him. My hands holding his face as my fingers run through the scruff of his facial hair.

"I'd certainly hope so, but it's nice to know." He laughs a little bit, and I don't know if he had been worried when I told him that I needed to see Reid to clear the air, but he understood why. Never asking me not to, instead encouraging me to get the clarity I needed. He walks off to the kitchen as I walk down the hallway into our bedroom to change. The hallway lined with the photos of our life. Chronologically building through all the memories we collected with space still on the wall for the ones that remain.

For the first time in a long time, I follow the timeline of our life. Looking at the photos that document it, recalling not just the smiles for the camera, but the moments leading up to it.

———

I sit here waiting for Amanda in our coffee shop, at our table. I'd brought a book with me to sit and read while she continued her writing. She had told me she was incredibly close to finishing it but wasn't entirely done with the ending yet. She needed to think about what was left, and how they might end up together.

She'd been writing a book based on her own love story, so I thought it was funny for her to have to wonder through some of the alternative endings, but who am I to question her, when she's had so much success writing love stories. Maybe sometimes even if there is a happily ever after, the alternate ending is the one worth reading. I wondered what it would be like, to look at my own life, to wonder about my own love story, and no matter how happily ever after I am, the last weeks made it dangerously easy to romanticize an alternative.

The Sunday after I had dinner with Reid, Amanda and I sat at this table for six hours. I told her the rest of the story, what happened with Josh, and how Reid and I had laid ourselves bare over the course of one meal. Naked to each other in a way I don't think we ever truly had been and then how we went our separate ways, just as we have done for years. Though, I think this time with more understanding and admiration for one and other. More finality that we didn't know was missing.

Reid had apologized, deeply, and sincerely, for things I never knowingly held him accountable for. Though, perhaps in some ways I always had. If not, the likelihood would have been that I *didn't* keep him at arm's length. But I did. And because of that, our lives ended up in very different places. We ended up telling different sides of the same story that night, figuring out where we misunderstood each other, but it was the epilogues we both wrote where we had happily ever afters. It just wasn't singular; we didn't share one. We had happily ever afters, apart.

I spot Amanda making her way across the coffee shop and she's practically skipping to me.

"Before you start," Amanda says, "I have something to give you." She takes her weekly seat and reaches into her large tote bag.

"If it's the baby books, I told you, Will already bought out the store."

"No, it's a different book."

"You finished it? That's incredible! Where have I been, why didn't you tell me it was done?" She pulls out the bound pages, her manuscript, and lays it down in front of me. The stack of easily three hundred pages thuds against the table. It's always one of my favorite sounds, because what happens next is I get to dive into my best friend's brain. Experience the world through the eyes of a romance novelist, and it's beautiful here.

I flip open the opaque plastic cover, and run my hand across the crisp white title sheet.

DUMPED: An Almost Lost Love Story
By: Amanda Bentley

My face pinches together in confusion, but as I flip open to the dedication it comes much more into focus.

**To my best friend, who never let losing a great love,
prevent her from loving greatly.**

It only took the first paragraph to know what this is, but I can't stop.

"You wrote about Reid?"

"How could I not? There's so much there, so much I don't even think you realize. And I'm so happy you're happy, this isn't about changing any of that, you guys, you and Will, are this epic love," she says, sounding slightly concerned that I may not receive this well. A love story, not centered on my husband, and father of this growing child. She's not wrong though, William Sterling and I do have that epic love. And regardless of all the alternative paths I could have taken, there is no path I walked in this life that I wouldn't want to lead me to him. To the life we have now, and especially to the one that will arrive in another few months.

"But there's more to your story, and I think there's a lesson to be learned for people here. And I think Arden and Reid, or um... Abby Barnett and Ben Jenkins," she taps the page to highlight the characters' names, "I think they can have a Happily Ever After, I think they actually deserve one."

"Okay, but who besides us would even want to read it?"

"According to my editor, a lot of people..."

When I went home that day, I curled up on the sofa, with the manuscript in hand, and read through the pages that detailed my first great love, my first great love story. The one that she managed to pull me back into, that I pulled him back into, all because she needed to write about breakup sex.

When I texted Reid, asking about our breakup, he had made a joke, asking for a dedication, an acknowledgment, finally agreeing to accept a signed copy. At the time, just thinking there would be a small reference to something unique about our circumstance. Nothing like this. Not a novel. Not a love story. Not one that potentially could give them the *'ending they deserved'* as Amanda had described it. When he and I were catapulted into this surreal experience, over dinner dissecting every word we exchanged, culminating in a final goodbye, we agreed to not fall too far down the slippery slope. To keep our strolls down memory lane on the well-lit portion of the street so as to not get lost. We haven't spoken since, while it was never uncommon for us to go months without exchanging a text or email, I think we both felt this time was different.

Names are changed, details changed, and the ending, well that is obviously most different, but this book, this is our love story. Our love lost, story. Our alternate ending.

I sit with my feet curled under me, reading through all the memories I'd shared. Every so often glancing up from the pages and looking around my home, my life cataloged on the walls, the smell of my husband lingers in the air, a combination of his shampoo and cologne, our dogs next to me, our child growing within me. I've always been able to get lost in a book. Hold my tears for the characters I fall in love with, a controlled way to express emotion I otherwise keep reserved. But this time, they aren't strangers.

I know them, and I feel them intimately.

I get to the final sections, as she has divided it up into parts, the third and final part, the previously unwritten part.

The future.

DUMPED?

An Almost Lost Love Story: The Future

7 YEARS LATER

Their little life came together as quickly as they first fell in love. It has been almost seven years now since they sat across from each other at dinner. That night laying out all the cards on the table they had never been too proud to play. Where after closing out the restaurant, and walking to their cars, they accepted there was no way to walk away again.

"I have loved you for more than half of my life, Abby. I know we can't go back; we can't change any of what has happened. Of course, there are things I would change, but right now, all I care about, all I want to change is the future. I want us to have a shot. The one we were too naive to give ourselves before. Because I was so in love with you then, and we might have pretended to move on, we might not be who we were, but the only person I could ever love more than you then, is you now."

Ben stood in front of the restaurant and didn't hold back a single thought as he leaned down and kissed her. The kiss that was filled with all the ones they had missed. All the ones they hadn't allowed themselves to lean into over the last years as they kept themselves distanced as friends. Never crossing the boundaries set by time, space, geography, and the different relationships they had found themselves frequently in and out of. And it was a surprise to Ben that night when they had exchanged pleasantries, to learn that for the first time in their adult lives, they were both romantically unattached.

Perhaps it might have been different if Abby had told him she was seeing someone, though, he couldn't be sure. As he often replayed it, there was never an ending to the evening that didn't result in his mouth taking hers. There was no ending where he could let her leave without saying the things he didn't previously. And that's why, this time, there was no ending for them. At least not one that wasn't together.

"I think we deserve that shot, Ben." Abby said as he held her to his chest. And they did. They had remained tied to each other all this time, and maybe this was why. The misunderstanding that split them apart was the same thing that tied them back together in the end.

It wasn't instant love. It was the roots of their old love that had remained deeply intertwined. And Ben was right, he loved her more now. This version of her she'd grown into. And Abby felt the same.

For a man who had always been so black and white, had thrown himself into the gray. He welcomed it, and their lives melded in the middle.

When he relocated for work to be nearer to her. When the late-night runs were no longer ice skating but ice cream cravings. When they welcomed their first daughter into the world, followed quickly by their second. And six months after that, with their daughters in tow, they got married just the four of them at the courthouse.

They crafted their life for them. Which meant they could have lazy mornings like this. As Ben stood in the kitchen, fixing himself a cup of coffee, pulling down a second mug from the cabinet he felt the slender arms of his wife wrap around his waist.

"Good morning," she cooed into his back. His arm captured hers as she went to pull away. Turning around so he could face her.

"Morning, Sunshine," he responded, "it's surprisingly quiet..."

Abby shook her head, "Don't jinx it. They are looking for the cat."

"Oh god, I'm not sure who it will be the worse for when they find her." Ben laughed to himself, thinking of their geriatric feline, who never was especially known for liking people, now had two humans of her own who never gave her a moment of peace. She'd taken to living under one of the beds.

And just like that, the charging sound of little feet came rushing down the hallway and into the kitchen. As she barrels into the room, her soft strawberry blonde curls bouncing so reminiscent of her mother.

"What's going on?" Abby asked the little one, who came to a halt in front of her parents. Out of breath from the mad dash down the hallway, her little chest heaved under the cotton of her dinosaur print pajamas.

"Where's your sister?" Ben asked. His two girls, born a year and a half apart, were inseparable, mostly because Sammy dragged her sister around since the moment they brought her home from the hospital.

Little Samantha was born two years to the day after that fateful text message. Two years after Abby asked Ben about their college break up. A date now celebrated as both an anniversary and birthday in Barnett-Jenkins home.

"Sh-sh-she's STUCK! Under the bed!" Ben's focus snapped back to reality, eyes focusing on the frantic little girl in front of him, just shy of five years old.

"Told you not to jinx it," Abby said as she cut a glance to Ben.

"Here, there should be fresh almond milk in the fridge," he said, as he handed Abby his coffee cup. It was still steaming, which means he had just poured it, not yet even having taken a sip from it. "I'll take care of this."

Ben picked up his daughter, who reached for him urgently. As they began to walk away, Abby heard him…

"What is she doing under the bed?"

"She's not doinggg anything daddy, she's STUCK!" Abby laughed to herself imagining the scene that played out. Little Sammy sliding her sister under the bed to try and lure out the cat.

"Well, let's go get her unstuck then."

Abby could hear his chuckle as he continued to walk further down the hall, she loved moments like these. The ones she never quite imagined they would share. She took a sip of her coffee and began to make her way towards the bedroom where she thought her daughter might be stuck under the bed, though the five-year-old wasn't exactly forthcoming with detail. But when she heard something familiar fill the house, she knew the rescue mission had been a success and which room her little family had ended up in.

The sounds of the piano danced down the hall, the upbeat tempo of the 'Good Morning song' and Abby could hear the little voices singing along with what had become a frequent request. Especially first thing in the morning.

Abby walked into the living room, to find her husband sitting at their piano, the top lined with picture frames from the last years, and some, from the many years before.

Ben sat there, Maddie bouncing on his leg as he played with Sammy next to him, having been tasked with one key for her to play in tempo. Her little focus was intense, and it always made Ben smile knowing exactly where that intensity came from.

Abby took a seat next to him as Maddie reached for her, where Sammy's hair had more strawberry, Maddie was more dirty blonde, where Sammy's eyes were blue, Maddie's were smokey and gray. Just like her father's.

"Again!" Maddie cheered, clapping as Ben removed his hands from the keys. Positioning them over Sammy's to show her something.

"Maybe your mother can take over for the next round?" Ben replied to his daughter lovingly. The smile was not only visible on his face, as it was anytime he looked at his family, but you could hear it in every word.

"Alright, alright... just one." Abby kissed the crown of Maddie's head and began to play 'Under the Sea.' The same song her husband played when she sat next to him nearly twenty years ago for the first time.

When the song was finished, they stood, everyone still clad in their pajamas. "How about some hot chocolate?" Ben asks.

This book, the one they wrote together, each day had new pages, but they had stopped writing their notes in the margins. Stopped leaving ink in the empty places hoping the other could figure out whatever it was they meant.

Instead, now, there were no thoughts ever left unsaid. No questions not asked. The only notes they left each other were I love yous. Leaving no room for miscommunication.

Chapter Fifty-Five

ARDEN

Back in our seats at our coffee shop, I've had to push the table away so I can fit in my normal seat against the wall. Just weeks from welcoming this little babe into the world, I still meet Amanda every Sunday for our coffee date. And this Sunday is dripping with excitement as she pulls it from her bag and lays it on the table in front of me.

The cover is in tones of gray and brown. Different than her usual, but this isn't her story, just the story for her to tell. The cover is a combined image, collaged of torn book pages with handwritten notes in the margin, the word DUMPED spelled out in scrabble tiles on top of it.

When Amanda told me about the book, she said they deserved an ending. I hadn't realized how true that was until I read it. She had written the story mostly as we lived it. And now, here it is in front of me. She pulls out another copy, placing it on top of the one already in front of me.

"For you to send to him, I even signed it, per your deal."

She winks, acknowledging how he had asked for a copy. The idea of that though, unsettles what had become a complacent sadness. One that has been dissipating slowly. Finally breaking up after all this time. I haven't spoken to Reid since we parted ways at dinner. And there's no indication we will have anything to exchange between us in the future. Walking away, realizing that we had somehow preserved something that neither of us understood, but that it was time to let that go.

I throw my arms around her and pull her into me.

"I don't think I've thanked you. For all of this." I lean back in my seat and open the cover. The familiar dedication now printed on the cream page, I start again from the beginning, eager to get to the front door of the house we never built. This story is different from the real one, and then it's not. Nuanced changes, but the biggest ones come near the end.

I told her I didn't want to undo my life and wipe it away just for a happily ever after. And she told me this wasn't that, it's more about the lives they could have had if things had been different. It didn't give us back the middle of our relationship. She didn't wrap up the story in the standard boy-meets-girl, boy-loses-girl, boy-gets-girl-back-at-the-end kind of way. Instead, she told the story with the gap between. It was the second chance romance we had joked about for weeks.

It takes a lot to get to the happily of ever afters, that's what this is.

All of these things, these memories, these moments, the ones I chose and the ones I didn't, are all just different houses on the same street. And as I start my stroll down Memory Lane, each house is different, filled with different memories.

Each inhabited by different people. People who raised me. Who challenged me. Who loved me.

Stored with different things. Packed, and smelling of time periods when I occupied them. Of sunshine, cinnamon and cedar, of licorice and pine, smells of libraries and Cambridge, trips around the world, the smells I collected over time. Some houses I'll never return to. I walk past them and don't wonder what's inside. The street lights don't illuminate the path to the front door. Other houses I frequent.

As I sit here in this coffee shop, dreaming of all the houses I've built on this street. I see it, two houses all the way at the end. One I know immediately. Not a new house, but the newest addition to this block. Tucked away perfectly nestled sweetly in the cul-de-sac.

It's the house that smells of amber musk and clean laundry, with the brightly painted front door, and through the window, the figure of a man I could recognize intimately from the back of his head and movements alone. He hangs a framed photo on the already lined hallway wall as two dogs bark at his feet. I know this house, I live here. We built it together over time and have plans to expand it.

Next door is a house I've never seen, yet it is familiar in a way I can't explain. I've never been here before, but as I step closer, it begins to take shape and I start to recall the blueprints we drew up those late nights in Cambridge. With the scrabble tile notes and midnight skates. But those plans were hidden away in a drawer somewhere. Folded scraps of paper tucked between pages of a journal.

Until now.

This house we never built, and now it only exists here in the pages of this book.

We sit here in silence as I read it. No longer a manuscript, but the first copies that have already received raving reviews. As I reach the end of this story, for the second time, I can feel my eyes well with tears.

And it's not in mourning, but acknowledgement that some houses, no matter how beautiful, only have blueprints.

They remain unfinished wood frames, the empty foundation on a plot of land. While visiting might be a gift, one I've been given, it's not home.

The End.

Author's Note

When We Were is a story about relationships, sexual and romantic, friendships, relationships with ourselves, and the expectations set in all of those.

While the setting of this novel is identified at Cambridge, Massachusetts, the university remained intentionally unnamed throughout. You can postulate or you can ignore it, because the experience isn't about the walls and classrooms that make up the college, but the people and experiences who fill them. It is the people who are the true setting of this story, while Cambridge herself is more of a supporting character.

Sexual assault does not wear one face. It is not always violent and aggressive in a way that makes it obvious to name, even at times, to those who experience it. Over time and generationally, we have gotten better at calling it what it is, but statistics show that it still remains dramatically under-reported and highly experienced by vast numbers of women, and other intersectional groups. For more resources on sexual assault, and understanding consent, please visit https://www.rainn.org/.

Acknowledgments

Writing acknowledgments for a book you never intended to write is kind of a bizarre thing to do. I have always wondered how at award shows, winners could stand up on stage after receiving the award only to say "I never expected this" or "I don't have anything prepared" but here I am. With time enough to prepare something, but still so shocked that there is no amount of time that would be enough.

There are so many people to acknowledge, and more than just acknowledge, but genuinely thank. Much like Arden's story, the writing of When We Were did begin with a question.

Amanda, this book just wouldn't exist if it weren't for you and your interest in my sex life. (Or rather, my breakup sex life.) But beyond that it wouldn't exist without your support and friendship. You encouraged me to write and publish a version of a romance that doesn't have the same version of a happily ever after people are used to. But that doesn't make it any less valid. And I'm so grateful for all of your encouragement.

Madeleine, you put the A+ in Alpha. You're a cheerleader. And anytime I doubted if this was something worth doing, you reminded me how important sharing emotions can be.

Sophia, thank you for working with me to create this incredibly special cover illustration. When I decided to republish with a new cover, I wanted something that would represent not just their love story, but the entire story, you delivered that and more.

Kaitlyn, thank you for creating the beta support group. I never imagined I would tell a story that would have such an impact. And to know this book came into your life at a time that it could mean so much, and stick with you, is the highest praise I can imagine. You started out as a beta reader, transitioned to editor, and have become my friend. Thank you.

Jordan M., thank you for turning one heart-felt review into a lesson on how to use a semicolon. Thank you for all of your help, and what became even more special to me, your unfiltered reactions left in the comment section of a google doc.

To the most engaged group of Beta/ARC readers, who felt so connected to these characters they formed friendships to support each other through the ending. Doing far more than just providing feedback, you provided me a place to tell Arden's story. You shared it, cried about it, posted about it, and you made it better. Jordy, knowing this helped you confront your own history makes me feel nothing but gratitude for the opportunity, though perhaps I should apologize for any holes in your walls from throwing things in response to it. Cassie, crushing your soul has been an honor, and I don't know that I will ever hear that phrase again without thinking about your reaction and I hope to have the honor to crush your soul again in the future. Jordan V., your response to WWW was one of the first submitted that made me think this novel might be something, your feedback and questions helped me make it so. Isabella, I am grateful for your tear stained kindle and if you are reading this now, tear stained pages. Feel free to send me your Kleenex bill. Manwa, thank you for your deep love of all romance and including Arden's story in that. I also hope you appreciate the acknowledgement of Mr. Darcy. That's because of you.

Alyssa, Maine, Liz, Marissa, Meg, Hanna, Baby G. Tori, Naomi, Molly, Alex, Lesly, Leslie, Julia, Xia, Mads, Kenadié, Sabrina, Lex, Maya, Dana, and so many more, for the content, the feedback, the emotion you were willing to share is incredible in a way I never imagined.

To the Unhinged Book Club, there has never been a group chat that escalated faster, or gave more unhinged support.

Dora, thank you for giving so much of yourself in how you read, *and* how you live. Pouring your emotions into my inbox changed my life. And Ava, thank you for being an "I've got a passport and bail money" kind of friend, and encouraging me to do all the bookish things that give me crippling anxiety.

Cecily, thank you for being the reason I never use the term "folds" in describing womanhood. (I won't be using term womanhood either.)

The friendships you have all offered in addition to your feedback is beyond meaningful.

Tara, thank you for the nights you chose to 'bad-mom-it' and spend your time hiding in the other room reading from your cell phone while your kids ran wild, all so you could encourage me to actually publish this book.

Natalie, Scarlet, Taylor, and Maudie, thank you for keeping my secret and not telling the family I wrote a book.

To my mother, who spent some of her own formative years in Cambridge, Massachusetts. Who inspires me in ways of strength words can't begin to express. Who taught me to read, and who showed me that falling in love with reading is one of the greatest joys we get to experience in our lives.

To my husband, Sam, who has loved me since I was twenty years old. Who has shown me how that love can change over an adult lifetime. And love without the dedication to show up and work hard, isn't enough. Thank you for not once asking me why I wanted to write a love story that wasn't ours. Thank you for supporting me in all the ways that matter, and being my biggest fan, and while I am grateful for your dedication to the marketing of this book, perhaps we can stop chasing people down the aisles of book stores now.

To the readers, those who loved it, those who didn't. Those that fall somewhere in the middle. Giving me your time is something you can never get back. There's no greater gift you can give to someone than the one you've given me. For all the words I wrote in When We Were, there will never be enough to express the gratitude and appreciation I have for all of you.

Finally, to Diana Elliot Graham. Thank you, whoever you are, for letting me use your name. When I decided to actually publish this novel, I knew for a multitude of reasons I didn't want to use my name. So I chose one that meant something to me. Names chosen to honor my grandparents. My grandmother, who was the first person I ever knew to read smut and did so, anywhere, without a discreet cover, and with zero shame. And my grandfather who has spent my entire life as a storyteller, documenting and sharing all the events of his life, even if we'd heard them before.

To the people who inspired this novel, and will never read it. And to the people who inspire me, that will. I'm grateful in a way you'll never be able to comprehend.

Made in the USA
Coppell, TX
09 September 2023